HARLEM MOON
BROADWAY

ALSO BY NORMA L. JARRETT

Sunday Brunch

Sweet Magnolia

A NOVEL

• • •

Norma L. Jarrett

HARLEM MOON / BROADWAY BOOKS
NEW YORK

PUBLISHED BY HARLEM MOON

Published in the United States by Harlem Moon, an imprint of The Doubleday Broadway Publishing Group, a division of Random House, Inc., New York.
www.harlemmoon.com

All biblical quotations are taken from the King James and NIV versions of the Bible.

Book design by Jennifer Ann Daddio

LIBRARY OF CONGRESS CATALOGING-IN-PUBLICATION DATA
Jarrett, Norma L.
Sweet magnolia : a novel / by Norma L. Jarrett.—1st ed.
p. cm.
1. African American women—Fiction. 2. Sisters—Fiction.
3. Sibling rivalry—Fiction.
I. Title.

PS3610.A77S94 2006
813'.6—dc22
2005046774

ISBN-13: 978-0-7679-2142-8
ISBN-10: 0-7679-2142-9

PRINTED IN THE UNITED STATES OF AMERICA

10 9 8 7 6 5 4 3 2 1

First Edition

Dedicated to

MY MOM, THE LATE ETHEL JARRETT

You are the air that I breathe and the wind beneath my wings

and

NORMAN SR. AND CARRIE JARRETT

JAMES JARRETT

JESSE AND FRED LEE JARRETT

JOHN HENRY AND REESY PAGE

SAM AND ANNIE PAGE

HAROLD CRUTCHFIELD

FRANCIS MARIE SMITH

And many others who have gone before me.

I hope I make you proud.

SPECIAL DEDICATION

New Orleans

You taught me how to laugh, live, love, and sing; You encouraged me to be free. Your spirit has touched mine and I am ***forever*** *grateful.*

Two years ago I began this book. I had no idea what the story was going to be. In obedience to God, I just began to write. Soon I learned that this would be a novel about family, tradition, healing, redemption, and restoration. I wanted the novel set in a city rich with character, full of history and soul, one that perhaps had its own stories to tell. God soon gave me New Orleans. I'd been there before, but when the book was near completion, I decided to visit New Orleans again. A few weeks later, after I'd returned to Houston, Hurricane Katrina hit. When it was over, I grieved as many others did. If you have ever grieved over anything, you know it hurts at first, but then you're able to remember the good. Later, as I'd reflect on that last

New Orleans visit, I felt grateful for that trip. I ate, danced, laughed, smiled, and yes, fell in love.

I fell in love with the city's music, people, energy, and charm. I walked through the French Quarter, ate beignets at Café Du Monde and po' boys at Mother's. I walked the pier along the Mississippi River and met an old friend. He offered to play me a song on his sax . . . just because.

I rode through the Garden District, admiring the architecture of the stately mansions, and walked through above-ground cemeteries, finding myself amid century-old tombs. I went to the neoclassically inspired City Park and walked across the peristyle, where dances were held in the early 1900s. I was inspired. To the people of New Orleans, I can't say I know exactly how you feel, but I know about the loss of love, material possessions, hopes, and dreams. I've asked why, how, and what do I do now?

I've also learned in the journey of life that no one is spared from trials and tragedy. But what I can say is, after enduring my own trials, I've been restored: financially, mentally, and spiritually. It wasn't instant, although it can happen this way. It was and still is a journey . . . life is just that, a journey. As we continue to walk, let us put our hands in God's. For He promises in Joel 2:25 to restore the years that the locusts have eaten. Regardless of what you felt has been lost or stolen, God has the power to give us back that and more if we trust Him!

I believe the heart of New Orleans was not its landmarks or structures, but in the undeniable spirit of the people. I thank God in advance, for the complete healing and restoration of its people *and* the city of New Orleans and for the many testimonies to come. This book is my gift to you.

God Bless . . .
Norma

Acknowledgments

First, to my Lord and Savior Jesus Christ, I will never figure you out, so I'm just going to go along for the ride. I know you look at me sometimes and say, "What am I gonna do with my child?" But you've always shrugged your shoulders and said, "Just love her." So that's my challenge, to love myself and others. Thank you for this gift of writing. It is so much more than putting words on paper, book sales, earning an advance (although I have to make a living—and I know you are *so* okay with that!), but it's about the message. Father, I pray that my vision is never cloudy, that at the end of the day, you are pleased with what I'm doing.

Lord, thank you for my family. Family is a gift and I love them all. To my father, Norman Jarrett (AKA "Stormin' Norm"), you are still my rock and my best friend. I'm forever a "daddy's girl." You know how much I love you. Your support is priceless and I am so pleased you are lovin' the Lord. To my sister, Paulette Jones, and brother, Stephen Jarrett, I love you more than words can say. You know you're in my heart and prayers *always*. Your support has been undeniable and a major blessing to me. I haven't forgotten the books you carried, the events you supported and all you have done! Paulette, I am so proud of the mother and wife that you are; you and Al have given me such a gift in my nieces and nephews. Stephen, keep your head up; you'll always have a special place in my heart and I'm always proud of you. You both mean the world to me—believe that. To my brother-in-law Al Jones, you are like a real brother to me. You have a big heart and we have come a long way since our A & T days (smile). I am proud of the father and husband you have become. To my nieces and nephews, you may think you are grown, but you are still my babies and I'm still the "cool aunt" (smile). Seriously, I am so proud of you. You're all blessed, smart, positive, and destined to do remarkable things. Quiana, you have grown up to be such a beautiful and classy young lady. I'll never forget your help at my last book release. I could not have done it without you! Ashley (the fashionista-diva-princess), I look forward to your bright and blessed future; I'm proud of the way you carry yourself. Continue to keep God first! Al the II (because we can't call you little Al anymore), I'm glad you are following your dreams; you are such a sweetheart and very talented. Remember, we can still hang out! Ariel, my sweet and sensitive niece, you have such a heart for God and I am proud of your commitment to Him; stay beautiful. To little Stephen, can we say "genius"? How'd you get so smart—oh yeah, it's in the genes. You are a blessing and make sure you take care of grandpa! I love you to pieces.

To my prayer mother: Mary Upshaw, you stepped in and answered God's call to minister to me. I know I have been a project. What a selfless, loving person you are. Words cannot express your dedication to my life. I love you. To my *other* mothers: Arlene Jarrett, Bessie Crutchfield, and Quinne Ewing, I appreciate you. Also, to Leroy, Alfred and Tish Page and the rest of the Jarrett, Page, and Jones family, I love you.

I'm always amazed by the friendships and support God always blesses me with. For everyone mentioned, you know the journey. Thank you old friends: Denise Williams (very first best friend), Sherri Davidson, Leon Richardson, Kim Thomas, Mildred Britt, and Sabrina Eastland. I will never forget our good times and your support. To Soror Alicia Lacy Castille, I will never forget your friendship, love, and midnight prayers. I know you still have my back and I have yours. To Michelle Austin ("Thrifty"—smile), were we separated at birth? Girl, you have had my back in so many ways I can't even explain it. I don't even have to tell you. Thank you for the special gift in my godson Nile. Thank you for trusting me and teaching me along with you. I'm proud of you, mama! To Soror Tracy Hines, can we say lifelong friends? You have walked with me when no one else has. You know the tests and trials on a spiritual level. You are such a beautiful, loving person. I'm so proud of you, girl! Let your light shine.

To my beautiful sorors of Alpha Kappa Alpha Sorority, Inc., especially Fall '86, you're still fine and holding it down! (Audra Foree, Andrea Walbrook, April Hinson-Mack, Michelle Baker, Sheila Cash, and the rest of Alpha Phi . . . big ups!!!). Shout-outs to North Carolina A & T (Aggie Pride) and Thurgood Marshall School of Law.

To others who have shown up along the way to walk with me in this journey: Carol Guess, Esq., Evangeline Mitchell, Esq., Patrice Carrington, Esq., Victoria Christopher Murray, ConSandra

Jones, Evangeline Mitchell, Esq., soror ReShonda Tate Billingsley, Tosha Terry, and others—thanks for your friendship, prayers, and words of encouragement.

To unexpected blessings along the way: Nicole Bent, Alzaada Aikens, Ahmad K. Wright, Quinella Minix, Tonya Adkism, Soror Shatika McGraw, Melvin Banks, and J. Brown (of New Orleans)—I think of you often. You all know why you're listed.

To my sources of inspiration: Jesus Christ, Joel Osteen, Bishop T.D. Jakes, Ce Ce Winans, Oprah Winfrey, Monique Greenwood, Patrik Bass, and many others.

To my literary "squad": Clarence Haynes, Janet Hill, and Victoria Sanders, thanks for the guidance, support, and contributions to my current and future success! To Dr. Melody-Moore Richardson (consultant) and to book clubs, bookstores, and my unofficial "street team"—thanks for your support. To all the readers who sent e-mails to encourage me, thank you! To all my author friends named and unnamed—it is a journey, not a destination. You have stories to tell and people to bless. God Speed!

"The best is yet to come . . ." (Frank Sinatra)

Norma

Sweet Magnolia

La Famille

Summer felt the bumps of ancient tree roots beneath her thin flip-flops as she balanced the containers holding the French king cake and chocolate pecan pie through the maze of trees. On her way to the picnic table, she passed the Hens, her father's twin sisters, Evelyn and Rose, joined by her Aunt Joy, her mother's sister. There they were, perched on their thrones, fluttering church fans, near the murky bayou. She was tempted to tell all three of them to get off their royalties and help unload some of the other bags out of the car. But she was raised to be a lady, a Southern lady, no less, and to always respect her elders.

She couldn't help but think they were quite beautiful in this setting, each one in her own pastel linen sundress and oversize round sunglasses. Rose and Joy wore opulent straw hats, but not Aunt Evelyn. She refused to cover the latest selection from her extravagant wig collection, no matter how beautiful, ornate, or regal a hat could be. This piece was her "one of a kind" Lola Folana look. So instead of donning a crown, she held a bright yellow parasol, shielding herself from the vibrant sun.

"Summer, get those lazy teenagers to tote the rest of those bags. I don't understand these young people, Generation Next or whatever y'all call them." Her Aunt Evelyn hiked the bottom of her ruffled dress to the top of her slightly parted knees, unashamed of the white bloomers peeking beneath. Her flabby arm swung like a shutter in the wind as she cooled herself with a faded church fan. Rose and Joy engaged in their "catching up" as they would call it, because Ledouxs and Rousseaus *never* gossiped, of course. Rousseau was Hannah's maiden name, and she'd always managed to keep both sides of the family in check.

In an instant, eight little feet scurried by Summer with Frisbees, a hula hoop, wiffle balls, and other games in tow. Her Grandmother Hannah, or Grandmere as they often called her, had banned all electronic games and gadgets at family reunions. "Those games will zap your creativity, fry your brain, or give you cancer," she'd say. Hannah thought *everything* could give you cancer. The family still kept Hannah's rules despite her passing several years ago. Summer's cousin Reese had four adorable "crumb snatchers" despite her constant proclamations that she was "about to leave her husband, Efrem Joseph LaSalle, *M.D.*, any day now." That day had stretched to seven years. Summer eyed the next generation, wanting to drop her bags and run away with them.

As the wave of youthful energy encircled Summer, one of the children bumped into her knee. Before she could yell he sped past her, leaving only a trace of giggles as she resumed her mission to get her treasured desserts to a safe resting place. "Finally," she huffed. As she reached the closest picnic table, it became a challenge to find a home for her prized possession among the spread of potato salad, grilled shrimp, barbecue chicken, briskets, coleslaw, catfish, baked beans, sock-it-to-me and red velvet cake, banana pudding, and a host of other desserts and dishes. Adjacent to the picnic table were her uncles and several other men engaging in their barbecue sauce preparation, a Ledoux family ritual.

"I told you, you will never, *ever* get the family recipe. I'll take it to the grave," she heard her Uncle Sunny say as the dripping sauce sizzled when it hit the coals. He dipped a spoon into his concoction and savored his own masterpiece.

"Already know it," Uncle Friday taunted as he lifted the bottle of cream soda to his puckered lips. They called him Uncle Friday because every payday Friday he used to go to the gambling boat. Now he was saved, sanctified, and delivered, so supposedly his gambling days were over.

Summer watched Uncle Friday's Adam's apple bob with each gulp of soda. He slammed the bottle on the table and rubbed his protruding belly, outlined in suspenders. "Too bad they stopped making the glass bottles . . . soda just don't taste the same in plastic."

"For true, for true," her other uncles chorused.

Summer suppressed her laugh but could not help but release a chuckle as she studied Uncle Friday's outfit. *Hmmm, dress shoes, ankle socks, and shorts . . . and he wears it with such confidence*, she thought.

Taking in the atmosphere made her realize how things change yet seem to stay the same. When she was a little girl the same scenarios played out, but she'd never paid attention to details. All she remembered was playing with her cousins, laughing until it hurt, swimming in water she'd never even touch now, and almost losing her virginity.

Well, it was just a kiss. Luckily I discovered he was my distant, distant cousin . . . no Jerry Springer action here.

Each year the voices around her got louder and clearer. "So-and-so's daughter got her period the other day . . . My Nathan got a scholarship . . . So-and-so bought a house, pledged, got a bra, got a divorce . . ." Lower voices. "You know Julius is stepping out on her, and she's just flaunting around here like she was Queen Esther . . . But you did not hear that from me, because you know Ledouxs and Rousseaus don't gossip . . ."

When Hannah Ledoux would come within earshot of the "catching up," everyone would hush. The only sound would be lip smacking from eating Uncle Sunny's barbecue or her Aunt Joy's homemade pecan pralines. Hannah would just cut her eyes and point her precut ceremonial butt-whipping switch (because somebody's child always made it necessary) and say, "If folks will gossip *to* you, they will gossip *about* you! Now quit all that messiness and whip out the cards. I need to beat somebody down with some spades." A wave of laughter would break out, and in two seconds there'd be a heated card competition going on. In the backdrop would be dominoes slamming the table and a bunch of trash-talking that to this day Summer never understood. Zydeco music blaring in the background charged the open air with a festiveness that followed everyone back home.

As the years went on, young and old folks died. The most painful loss for Summer had been her mother, then Hannah a few years later. They were the most prominent women in her life. Nevertheless, the family cycle continued, both in and out of wedlock.

"That mess started after Hannah passed," Aunt Rose would say.

"Hannah never tolerated 'children out of wedlock'; the same thing's goin' on at Mt. Calvary. Can't just be saved anymore—you got to be saved, sanctified, and delivered!" she would declare, and then turn her nose up to the heavens.

When Summer was old enough to better comprehend what was going on, she'd hear bits and pieces of Ledoux business leaking out. Broken conversations and whispers would drop hints about threats to the beloved Ledoux name. Hannah had been very protective of the family name, and now so was Summer.

"Summer, no family is perfect. Trust me," her sister, Misa, had said one year. When Misa had turned thirteen and Summer was eight, Misa quickly grew tired of the simple children's family reunion games. Suddenly Misa became a stranger to Summer. She spent hours at the mirror, putting on makeup just to go to the park to see her cousins. "You never know who will be there," Misa'd say, tossing her glossy jet-black ringlets away from her mahogany face. Summer would just stare at her sister with her arms folded. She'd look down at her baggy shorts and tennis shoes and eye her sister's halter top and neon mini. She would shrug her shoulders, vowing never to be so "girly."

That same year, Summer had caught Misa in the woods with a neighborhood boy. Although they were fully clothed, he was on top of her. *Misa probably lost her virginity that year,* Summer thought.

"Summer. Summer! Didn't you hear me?"

She blinked as her father's voice snapped her back to reality.

"I said I'm about to whip up on your Aunt Joy in some horseshoes. You want to come play?" Her eyes shot up to her father. She took in his tall frame. Each year the gray at the edge of his neatly trimmed sideburns crept up higher. She still thought he was the most handsome man on earth, setting a high standard for any suitor who crossed her path.

"I'm sorry, Daddy, I was just thinking."

"Well, get your butt over here."

Summer happily agreed because that was her favorite game and her favorite memory (outside of watching her Uncle Groovy, who she later discovered was not her real uncle, try to do the latest dances). It was the one thing she would always play with her mother and father. That was *their* game. The only image more familiar was seeing her mother and father smooching like teenagers and walking through the woods on their private excursions. Summer promised herself to always remember her mother in that way. She blocked out everything else . . . even the questionable tragic end.

The Big Easy

Summer pressed her body against the metal rail, lukewarm to the touch, as her eyes studied the paddle wheeler creeping toward the pier. She found comfort gazing at the floating mass. Inching near, it greeted her like an old friend. *Louisiana is still a good place*. She gazed out on the "Mighty Mississippi," inviting the old mystique of New Orleans to dance in her soul. Each time she returned to the Big Easy, her love of its history, music, food, and flavorful people grew even more.

Above all, she savored the music. At any part of the day, somewhere music was playing in the birthplace of jazz. From Bourbon Street's oozing blues and Preservation Hall's brassy, rustic jazz to the homeless man horn-blowing for change, music *was* the air. She inhaled deeply, drawing in melodic elixirs to soothe her spirit. But the hunger pains dancing inside her stomach then took over. A craving kicked in for homemade pecan pralines from Aunt Sallie's, the famous storefront in the French Quarter. She swallowed, pressing her mouth together, then bent down to scoop up several pieces of gravel. She tossed them one by one into the water, watching each stone's quick disappearance into the dark liquid abyss. Staring at the river always gave her a peace, the peace that had often eluded her in the past. The quiet state of mind others took for granted became hers at such a price.

She walked away from the water toward a nearby bench and sat down, smoothing the white linen fabric of her sundress over her thighs. Despite the light, airy material, she felt a small layer of sweat accumulating on her back. She tucked her hair behind her ears, leaned back, and crossed her ankles. Summer relaxed, discreetly eyeing the parade of sightseers through her shades. She could see how people came from all over to the "City Without a Care," a place she'd come to love.

Shortly after she'd settled on the bench, last night's vision crept into her mind. She recalled images of her mother balled up in a corner, weeping, crying, and rocking back and forth. People kept walking by her, staring, pointing, and telling her to get up. Yet no one would bend down and help her. *Not the way I remember her. Only the good, remember only the good.*

Early in life, Summer had quickly realized the ways to deal with mental illness, both her mother's and her own. Counseling, medication and prayer . . . she'd been a witness to her mother's treatments and tried counseling and medication herself. However, her relationship with God and *many* hours of prayer had finally released her from pain and prescription drugs.

Her mother hadn't been so fortunate. After years of suffering, she'd lost the battle. Eventually, Elizabeth Ledoux had succumbed to an accidental overdose, with some question as to whether it was truly an accident. Although Summer knew her mother was finally at peace, her premature death still haunted her.

The kind of depression that hit the Ledoux women wasn't your everyday blues or the once-a-month PMS. It was a deep, life-altering darkness. When getting out of the bed is an achievement. It's a life in which happiness is abnormal and sadness is effortless. It's the type of depression in which laughter breeds guilt and smiling is painful. It prompts outsiders who don't understand to ask, "Why can't he or she just get it together?" The darkness was so thick, and the glass was neither empty nor full. *There was no glass.* Every event, day, idea, hope, or person was shrouded in negativity.

Since her mother's death, Summer's hunger to understand this disease had become an obsession. *What was this dark spirit that destroyed my mother's chance for a normal, healthy life?* she questioned. It was a deep-rooted desire that gnawed at her insides. When she reached her early twenties, the disease began to threaten her own life. But she fought and fought until she finally overcame.

She inhaled deeply and released her breath. Exhaling, Summer wondered what could have triggered her most recent nightmare. *Maybe the old black-and-white photos Aunt Joy showed me yesterday,* she thought, staring blankly at the sky. The pictures stirred up emotions she hadn't felt in a while. Sensing the negative energy, she immediately propelled her thoughts to a positive place. She became excited, thinking of all the joyful events the weekend had in store.

Summer extended her legs, offering them further to the generous light. She definitely didn't need a tan, but basking in the amber beams felt good on her skin. Again, she took deep meditative breaths to calm her spirit. Thoughts of the big weekend slightly overwhelmed her. Summer's muscles tightened, moodiness and fatigue taunting her serenity. The sight of freshly manicured nails deterred her usual nail biting.

Ledoux family reunions always seemed bittersweet; this one was no different. Summer figured having a wedding during this time was logical. *Why not kill two birds with one stone?* she'd thought. Although she loved her extended family, they could be a handful. *What could I have been thinking?* She sighed, wiping a bit of moisture off her forehead.

"Excuse me, miss, I don't want to interrupt. I couldn't help but notice you. Do you mind if I join you?"

She paused, eyeing from head to toe the clean-cut man holding a box of kettle corn. "Well . . . normally I wouldn't entertain such an invitation." She sat up taller. "*How-ev-er,*" she enunciated as she slid her shades down with her index finger, "you seem like such a gentleman. I guess it couldn't hurt. Please, have a seat. I have to warn you, though, my fiancé will be back any minute. I can't be responsible for what he might do," she said coyly, inching over.

He sat down and handed her the box of popcorn. "*Uh-huh.* I see how dedicated you are. I'm gonna have to keep my eye on you." He gently caressed her face with his right hand, then slowly eased toward her face. He licked his baby-soft lips. As always, he bypassed her mouth, planting a gentle kiss on her soft earlobe. Before inching away, he closed his eyes, inhaling her familiar floral scent. He leaned back, grabbing her bare legs to place them across his lap, cradling her, almost like a baby.

"Are you trying to show my goods to *everyone* in New Orleans?" she protested as she tugged on her sundress.

"Are you crazy? This is *all* mine," he said, playfully slapping her thigh, "especially after waiting all *this* time."

Summer couldn't help but smile as she recalled the night she and her fiancé, Evan, had met. She couldn't believe it had all started with a trip to the grocery store. Ironically, she had looked her absolute worst. Summer never wore much makeup, but she was bare-faced from her earlier workout. She'd been too lazy to shower and had kept on her same funky exercise gear.

Evan kept showing up in the same aisle she was in. She knew he was watching her. They finally met up at the vegetable table, and he started making conversation. As the talk continued, they realized they'd been standing in the produce section for about twenty minutes. He later invited her out, and they'd been on one continuous date ever since.

After dating awhile, she grew anxious. She worried whether her family issues and bouts with depression would change their relationship. *How much should I tell him? Will this change the way he sees me? Can he handle this?* were thoughts that nagged her spirit. She eventually took a chance and opened up. It wasn't easy, because she was used to keeping things inside. But therapy was helping her change that. A few months later, Evan proposed. Finally she was accepted for her true, authentic self, and she couldn't have been happier.

Summer snuggled under Evan's shoulder in response to her thoughts. They watched the Canal Street Ferry as it ushered others in to the Crescent City. She then closed her eyes, relaxing with the man she knew was her soul mate. They surrendered to the moment, realizing that the next day their lives would never be the same.

Jack and Jill

Summer inspected her black patent leather shoes, twisting each foot from side to side as she sat on the edge of her white wooden bed. She grabbed a handful of Lucky Charms cereal and stuffed her mouth.

"What are you doing?" Misa asked as she ran her fingers through her curls and adjusted the white headband that swept her hair from her face.

"What do you mean?" Summer said as she turned her attention to the black-and-white portable television, featuring the cartoon dog Huckleberry Hound and his usual antics.

"You better not get crumbs on that dress, or I'm going to tell Daddy on you. We probably won't go anyway," Misa said as she plopped down next to Summer on the pink lace bedspread and folded her arms.

"Why do you say that? Mother likes plays. We've been planning this for a while. This is the only time we may get to see Black people in a play. I woke her up this morning and she promised she would go. She promised!"

Summer put her cereal box down and a few crumbs spilled onto the carpet. She jumped from the bed, got on the floor, and began rearranging the furniture in the Barbie Dream House.

"I know, but you know how she gets sometimes. I just wish she was normal like all the other mothers in Jack and Jill."

Summer continued to eat and tried tuning Misa out. She is normal, she thought as she forced caramel Ken and Barbie to kiss.

Misa shot up and went to their mother's room and saw that her bed was empty. She walked toward the bathroom and peeked through the cracked door. Her mother was on her knees, bent over the toilet, gagging. The back of her long white nightgown was moist from sweat. Misa knew her mother was not alright. It's happening again, she thought. She put her head down and walked slowly back to her own bedroom. She walked straight to the window and looked across the street. Misa loved everything about their home in the Garden District, except their neighbor. She watched as Mrs. Souchon pointed her white-gloved finger at her two children, Phillip and Lila, to get in the car. Misa felt angry and jealous at the same time. Mrs. Souchon was the president of the local Jack and Jill chapter. Misa didn't like her because she'd overheard her talking about her mother on more than one occasion.

"It's a shame Elizabeth can't keep herself together enough for those children. The only reason we let Elizabeth in Jack and Jill was because of Alfred. He's such a sweet, respected man. He has so much to deal with. I think the woman is just out of her mind . . ."

Misa would never forget that. How could a woman always dressed in such pretty pastel colors be so mean? Misa vowed to never smile at that woman again. She took a deep breath and smoothed her white and *yellow dress. Sure enough, her suspicions were right. Alma Souchon was sashaying her tight powder blue skirt over to their door.*

"Shoot!" Misa said.

The doorbell rang. She heard her father's voice: "Oh, that would be nice. Yes, Elizabeth is under the weather . . . No, we wouldn't want the girls to miss the play. Thank you again, Alma, for understanding and being so helpful."

Misa by this time had come to the top of the stairs to eavesdrop. She also noticed how much Mrs. Souchon was smiling and touching her daddy. Misa frowned even more. Mrs. Souchon seemed to think everything Daddy said was extra funny. She'd throw her head back and laugh out loud with her orange-colored lips and shift her hips, which was a feat with such little room in a skirt. Her daddy never seemed to notice, but Misa knew something was not right about Mrs. Souchon.

"Misa, Summer . . . Mrs. Souchon is here. She's going to take you to the Jack and Jill event."

"Shoot!" Misa said aloud.

"Misa, did I hear you say something?"

"No, sir," she yelled down the steps.

"Well, stop your yelling, go get your white sweater, and tell your sister to come downstairs."

Misa stomped down the hall, but on the way to her bedroom she stopped in to check on her mother. She was asleep, and Misa touched her forehead with the back of her hand like she had seen her father do. It was damp with sweat. She kissed her on the forehead and whispered, "Don't worry, Mother, you can't help it. I'm gonna make sure I keep an eye on that Mrs. Souchon too." Then she quietly crept out of the room to get her sister.

Magnolia Lane

Summer felt a familiar heavy presence as she struggled between her conscious and subconscious. The weight of the presence was thick, like someone had climbed on her back. She knew morning was near, as the warmth of the sun's rays bathed her body. Still, she refused to open her eyes. She imagined daylight invading an indigo sky she'd kissed good night. She wrestled, refusing to allow the dark spirit to extinguish the light of her soul.

"Darkness cannot dwell with light. I take captive every thought and make it obedient to Christ," she uttered slowly in a raspy whisper.

A momentary cloak of fear paralyzed her body. She continued to cinch her eyes shut, despite her knowledge that daylight had arrived.

She wrapped her arms tightly around her, shielding herself from invisible forces, repeating those words.

Summer knew this struggle too well. It used to happen often. Like clockwork, at around two or three a.m., the invasion of her sleep began. She'd spent hours praying through the night . . . weeping and begging God for rest. If only she knew then what she knew now. She would've destroyed those demons much sooner and could've saved her mother's life.

"I don't have the spirit of fear, but of love, power, and of sound mind. Greater is He who is in me, than He who is in the world . . . I am a new creation . . . Old things are passed away and all things become new," she whispered, slightly twisting her uncovered body.

Slowly, gently, she was released from captivity. She opened her eyes, relieved that she was okay. She had exercised God's power once more. She faintly smiled as a tear trickled down the side of her cherubic face. The day she'd been praying for had finally come. These were tears of gratefulness and joy. God had been so good to her. It wasn't just about the special weekend but about all the promises He'd *finally* delivered.

Her life had been a spiritual metamorphosis, a transformation. Tragedy had been to Summer's doorstep on more than one occasion, making her see life as a gift. She clutched the soft fabric of her satin nightgown, pressing her legs together as she thought about that night. The night of the incident. She should have died, yet she was still here. God had removed most of the details of that night from her memory. She rarely opened that door of her mind; only when *she* wanted to.

Summer stared at the sheer fabric of the swag draping from the canopy. Her body made a quick jerking motion in response to the air conditioner's chill. She reached down toward the foot of the bed and yanked an old tattered quilt close to her chest. She loved that quilt.

It was made of mismatched fabric squares, stitched with love by her great-grandmother, Camila Rousseau. She was so engulfed in the comfort of the generous rice bed, she didn't want to get up.

Finally, she eased into a sitting position and threw her hands up to stretch. As she twisted her torso, her eyes shifted to the antique Victorian chaise nearby. The mahogany wood framed the faded floral pattern of her favorite piece of furniture. She was often found there, reading, daydreaming, or napping, when she was little. The chaise, strategically placed under the window, had been her only companion for the night.

Summer rubbed her eyes, then abruptly focused on a long white dress that commanded her attention. Its dainty, regal presence dismissed the possibility that this was her imagination. The dress had a soft whisper of grace and elegance that quietly beckoned, *Summer, get up . . . It's your wedding day!*

"Wow!" she uttered. The dryness at the back of her throat made it hard to swallow. The excitement rising in her belly propelled her out of the bed. She placed her perfectly pedicured feet on the stained wood floor, feeling the coolness on her soles as she shuffled toward the window. She kneeled on the chaise and rested her arms on the crackled paint of the windowpane.

She focused on the trees dressed in Spanish moss, transforming the backyard into a small forest. Some were bent over with age, weeping. Others lifted their arms, shouting to heaven. Others huddled in clusters, whispering a generation of secrets. Summer smiled, recalling childhood memories of running through those trees and cooking in Hannah's large kitchen when they came to visit. She could almost smell the homemade biscuits and taste the raspberry lemonade quenching her morning thirst.

Although she was grown and living in Houston, this was still home too. Her grandmother's house held so many memories. The

Ledoux mansion was always painted a soft pink, symbolic of money by New Orleans standards.

Summer surveyed the garden, remembering the many weekends and visits with Hannah. She had also stayed here when her mother would go to the hospital. The times she and Hannah had spent in the garden—one of Hannah's prized possessions—were special. Summer would watch her pruning, praying, plotting, and singing in "nature's sanctuary." They both wore special hats just for gardening.

Then after such tender care came roses in all shades, azaleas, and, yes, the magnolias. *Ummm . . . the magnolias*, Summer thought. *My favorites*. Without even opening the window, she knew their sweet aroma. Summer waited each year for their grand debut. Until she was old enough to understand, she grieved as the blossoms turned brown and fell to the ground. She'd gather some of the dry remains and keep them indoors to smell their sweetness despite their fading beauty. Magnolias were Hannah's favorite too.

"Why do you love magnolias so much?" she'd asked Hannah.

"Because every last one is different, no two are alike. God hand made each one. Each one's special, just like you."

Hannah would get so lost in her gardening, she'd ignore any warning of coming showers. She'd just keep humming, planting, singing, and trimming. Summer couldn't believe the number of times they'd gotten soaked before Hannah finally moved. On rare occasions Hannah would hike up her dress, grab Summer's hand, and dance as the heavens' showers drenched them both. The best times at the Pink Mansion had little to do with expensive toys or lavish affairs, but instead were about just good old-fashioned, no-frills fun.

The plantation home on Magnolia Lane had been the family gathering place for several generations. The big white columns and massive entryway boldly invited guests to a rich tradition, a mansion full of antiques that represented all the old charm of New Orleans. "There's a difference between a house and a home," Hannah would say. For Summer, the stately structure was definitely a home, worn and welcome in all the right places.

However, with passing years, it became clear that everything wasn't always so sweet on Magnolia Lane.

Summer's father had sold their own house and moved back to the mansion to care for Hannah until she died. Summer always knew this would be where she'd have her wedding. To her it was a very spiritual and memorable place. It represented all she knew that was happy and safe.

The corners of her mouth curled into a grin as she surveyed the transformed backyard. The gazebo was adorned with gardenias and lots of tulle. Chairs decorated with bows and flowers were lined up for guests. The tent had already been assembled, with a dance floor in place for the reception. She was glad that she and Evan opted for a simple wedding with family and a few friends as their guests.

Summer's ears perked up when she heard noise and muffled voices outside her room. She resisted the temptation to go downstairs to the kitchen. She was certain her father was in there cooking up a storm. She could just feel it. There was no better warmth than the warmth of cooking. She pictured the Hens and her Aunt Joy around the table, fussing, gossiping, and eating. She opted to spend a few minutes in solitude with her first true love . . . *God*. She needed to dedicate part of her morning to meditate on the Word. She wanted to thank and praise Him. She wanted the Lord to serenade her before the wedding and soothe her soul. She needed to pray.

Summer wondered what her fiancé was doing. He was very settled and a lot more serious than the men she'd dated before. It felt like a long road, but definitely well worth the wait, and in the evening they could finally have each other.

Summer laughed as she recalled the times when they couldn't even sit too closely together on her couch. She and Evan were both on fire! Then there were the jokes. *Poor Evan.* Although his friends knew how strong his faith was, they rarely missed a chance to joke with him about "not getting any." This certainly didn't help their situation. Just thinking about it forced her to squeeze her legs together tightly. Nevertheless, after tonight she could scream the words like an old Negro spiritual: *FREEDOM—OOOH, FREEDOM!* She felt a sudden urge to do a one-woman wave.

She jumped in response to the ring of her cell phone. She knew it had to be Evan. They hadn't talked since the rehearsal dinner last night. She almost tripped over a footstool as she raced toward her purse to answer it. When she grabbed it, her heart deflated when she realized it wasn't him.

"Hello?"

"Hello, sweetie!" a familiar, enthusiastic voice yelled. Summer strained to hear the voice that was almost drowned by lots of noise in the background.

"Hello? Misa?"

"Well, how is the little bride-to-be? I am just bubbling over with excitement for you!"

Summer paused, recalling instantly the words of her always diplomatic friend Paige. *Give your sister the benefit of the doubt, and don't let anything spoil your day.* Summer struggled, because she was still very mad at her. She felt Misa, her *only* sister, was *supposed* to be there on her wedding day.

Couldn't get out of the fashion show my a—

"What is all that noise in the background?" Summer's forehead wrinkled and her lips tightened. Her mood had been instantly busted.

"Fashion show madness, *dar-ling*. Wait, wait just one moment . . . Will you please stop pulling my hair so tight? Never mind. Just wait till I get off the phone. Can someone please get me some water? I am dehydrated! Okay, sorry about that, sweetie. So are you ready?"

"Yeah, sort of. I was just looking out the window. The backyard looks beautiful, and . . ."

"Oh, that's marvelous—again, I apologize I couldn't be in the wedding, but I promise, I will be there in time for the reception," Misa assured her.

"Well, I'll just be happy to see . . ."

"I can't believe this. I didn't ask for juice. I *said* water . . . does anyone understand me? I'm sorry. Now what, Summer? What did you say? Summer, honey, I have got to go. I just wanted to call you this morning and wish you the best. Tell Daddy I said hello and that I'll be there soon. I can't wait to meet my handsome brother-in-law. Bye, love."

Summer's hand went a little limp as she held the phone. She took a deep breath and tried not to let the hurt consume her. It was hard enough that neither her mother nor any grandparents would be there, and then her sister couldn't be in the wedding. *Why couldn't she do this one thing for me?*

The frustration she felt was familiar, the push and pull, the getting closer yet not *too* close. *Will our relationship ever heal?* she thought.

Growing up a Ledoux was never easy, but Summer still enjoyed her childhood in Louisiana surrounded by family. Her father had been a dean and physics professor at Dillard University.

Summer shared her father's love of education. She'd follow him to class and watch him inspire students. Eventually she became quite the scholar. Misa, on the other hand, was more interested in the social aspects of Dillard. Looking older than she was, she'd show up on campus and sneak into parties. College men relentlessly pursued her, but some backed off when they discovered Dr. Ledoux was her father.

At seventeen, Misa's life would change forever. A modeling agent approached her at a restaurant in the French Quarter. Against her parents' wishes, she left for New York two months later to start her career.

Her mother particularly had a hard time letting Misa go. Summer hurt too. For the longest time she'd looked up to her big sister. Misa had been her protector, and despite their battles she loved her. Summer understood her need to leave but still resented the pain the whole issue caused.

Her sister had done and seen it all, Summer supposed. She remembered the postcards Misa had sent her from places such as Brazil, Greece, and Africa, which Summer would then hang all over her bedroom wall. She dated rap industry moguls and modeled everything from Gucci to barely there underwear. Misa seemed very happy.

Summer was nervous about Misa's visit. There was always a chance for negativity and strife when they got together. Like any other family, they had their dysfunction. They were just better at hiding theirs. At that moment she resolved that no one, and she meant *no one*, would ruin her day. "I'm about to put every single member of this family on the altar this morning," she said aloud. "Before I put on an ounce of eyeliner, a pair of drawers, or anybody's garter, I'm going to have a talk with the Lord. If anybody can control this family, He can."

These Are the Good Ole Days

Alfred Ledoux was bent at the waist, searching the bottom cabinet for his mother's iron skillet. The clanging of pots sounded his frustration. He had a thing for cast iron skillets and could accept no substitute. For him it made the food taste that much better. He prided himself on the culinary skills Hannah, or "the Queen" as she was known, had passed down to him.

After several minutes of clanging metal, he shouted, "A-ha!" as he pulled the heavy skillet from the back of the cabinet. He kissed the large pan on the handle and placed it on top of the stove. He ignored the three women who were sitting at the table behind him, engrossed in conversation. Soon his breakfast spread would be complete . . . pecan-crusted bacon, sweet potato and chicken breakfast hash, Cajun cheddar biscuits, and, finally, his favorite—Creole eggs en croustade. His kitchen was his domain, and anyone else who stepped into it was just a fixture.

The butter began to crackle and Alfred whisked eggs, tarragon, green onions and milk in a bowl with passion. The women at the table kept talking. The saxophone music from the old radio enticed his hips to sway slightly from side to side. He was tempted to go and grab his own saxophone, but he realized Summer was probably still resting.

Alfred's mind drifted to the family restaurant. After retiring from Dillard University, he had taken over the management of Queen Hannah's. The restaurant had earned its place right alongside some of New Orleans' best: Brennan's, Dookie Chase, Dunbar's, and Mother's. It was a must-visit on every tourist's list.

Alfred always admired his mother's wisdom. She believed that the success of the family was determined by working together (though Alfred believed that the biggest reason she let his father's band play at Queen Hannah's was to keep an eye on him). Smiling at his memories, he refocused on his chore, pouring the eggs into the heated pan. Once finished, he swiveled around and grabbed one of the women's hands to dance.

"Alfred, what in the world are you doing? Leave me alone. I'm not tryin' to fool with you now," his sister Rose protested as she pushed him away.

"Woman, stop fussin'. C'mon, that's the problem. All you all want to do is sit at the table and gossip."

"Catching up," she said indignantly, still fighting off his attempts to pull her out of her chair. "Alfred, go somewhere."

He finally gave up on her. "Have some fun for a change. It keeps you young. You don't have any problem dancing in that church. That's what's wrong with ya. You turned into an old nun."

"I happen to like working in the church. What should I be doing at this age, hanging down at the clubs or the red-light district?"

"All I know is, spending all your extra hours in the church isn't healthy. You need a little more balance. You just wait till I finish these eggs. Somebody at this table is gonna dance," he said as he picked up his spatula and turned back to the stove.

"Umm-huh," they all said in unison, then resumed their conversation.

He chuckled as he stood over the sizzling pan, becoming lost in his own world. Despite his laughter, he felt a bit sad. The wedding brought him joy, yet the chatter of the Hens and cooking the big meal were reminders of the missing parts of his life.

When Hannah was living, there had always been plenty of family gatherings at the Pink Mansion. There were holiday feasts, dances, Sunday gatherings, birthday celebrations, and other festive occasions. Yet as years passed the events became fewer and far between. Although he considered himself blessed, the loss of his wife and mother had left a big void in his life.

Queen Hannah had been every bit the family matriarch. Her restaurant, Queen Hannah's, was named appropriately, after the diva who ruled the kitchen with the mastery of Creole Cajun cuisine. *God bless good food and good music* were simple words that defined and warmed the hearts of several generations.

Hannah also had everyone under control, from her children—Alfred, his brothers, Friday and Sunny, and his sisters, Evelyn and Rose, aka "the Hens"—right down to every last grandchild. Thoughts of Misa invaded Alfred's memory and ushered in feelings of regret. If he could have raised his firstborn differently, he would have. *No one ever gives you a manual on how to be a good parent*, he thought as he opened the door to the oven. The warmth from the bread rushed to his face as he peeked in on the biscuits. He closed the door and stood back up, holding his side for a moment. *I did my best with my girls. How much longer will Misa make me pay for my mistakes?* Even the comfort of the familiar aroma could not suppress the ache in his heart.

Despite the pain of his loss, he found different ways to honor the memory of two of the most important women in his life. In honor of his mother, he cooked her famous recipes to perfection. For his wife, he vowed not to marry another woman. This was a challenge, since everyone tried to fix him up. He was quite the catch—the handsome, young-spirited, educated entrepreneur that he was. Still, he was content to be alone.

"Alfred, do you hear us? We're *talkin'* about *you,*" Evelyn said, tugging on her stocking cap.

"Uh-uh, leave me out of this," Joy said.

"Oh, I'm sorry. What were you saying?" Alfred replied.

"We were just talkin' about that woman you went with to that old school concert."

"I thought you were going to let that die. We beat that to death at the *last* family reunion. She had the tickets, and you know how much I love the Manhattans and the O'Jays. I never forgave Joe for that. He fixed us up." He started humming along with the music to deter further conversation on the subject.

"We know you enjoyed *every* minute of that night. She had to be half your age!" Rose added.

"No, she was forty to be exact. I'm only sixty-one," he said.

"She was forty going on twenty. We heard that dress was so loud and tight, if she had moved another inch there was gonna be another *free* show goin' on. Then we heard she was just *performin'*, runnin' up to the stage and everythang. Hmpf, tryin' to look like a broke Lil' Kim," Evelyn said as she poured cream into her coffee.

"And where did you hear this?"

"Professor Morgan. He was there. He gave us more juicy details."

"Oh, *brother*. Well, that was the first *and* the last time I went out with her. She wasn't my speed."

"Sure, *uh-huh*. Did you take that floozy home right after the concert? Inquiring minds want to know." Evelyn leaned back in her seat and crossed her arms, waiting for an answer.

"You all leave Alfred alone," Joy said.

"I'm a grown man. I refuse to dignify that question with an answer. That's exactly why I'm stayin' single. People all up in my business," he said, keeping his back to them.

"I'm sure Elizabeth wouldn't mind if you dated. Would she, sister?" Evelyn said as she hit Rose in the side. "It gets lonely. You're a good-lookin' man. You still have lots of years to live." She took another sip of coffee. "Harold hadn't been dead a week, God rest his soul, before Stanley showed up at my door with the mail."

"Well, I'm not *you*. I like my life, and I don't have any stress. My hair may be a little gray, but I still have a full head of it," he said, running his hand from the top to the back of his hair.

"Don't let us get started on that either. Remember when you and Sunny decided you were going to try some of that comb-in hair dye for men? Just what did you think you were doin'? Your hair turned green. That's what you get for listening to Sunny. He'll have you doing all kinds of crazy stuff. I think your hair looks good gray," Evelyn said.

"Amen," Joy added.

"There's nothing wrong with a little hair dye. I keep my appointment every week," Rose interjected.

"We know," everyone chimed in.

"Well, ever since *Sex in the City*, they say forty is the new thirty," Rose replied.

"Well, how long has it been since you could claim that age? And since when do *you* watch *Sex in the City?*" Evelyn said as she raised her eyebrows.

"There's nothing wrong with that show," Joy said.

"Sister, I *said* I *heard* it. You know I don't even have cable," Rose said. "Anyway, we Ledoux women age well *naturally*. It's the New Orleans weather. Mother used to always say the humidity was nature's moisturizer," she added as she patted her face.

"I still think a little liposuction or Botox doesn't hurt," Evelyn interjected.

"Sister, that's not the way God intended for us to age!" Rose shot back. "I swear, ever since Hannah passed, you have just lost your mind."

"God made the man that invented the Botox. Besides, He helps those who help themselves . . . and Rose, you know we all loved Mother, but I realized after she died, I felt, well, quite liberated."

"Do *not* disrespect Hannah like that! She taught us well. We're responsible for carrying on her legacy, for training the next generation. We practically built this city, and I'm going to make sure our name maintains its respect throughout the parish."

"Rose, get a grip. How did we go from lipo to somebody's legacy? Can you please take it down a notch! All I'm saying is, Hannah meant well, but she was a little overbearing. You know I would never disrespect our mother. Loosen up a bit."

"I'm not *that* uptight. I've taken yoga classes. I volunteer at the shelter. I teach salsa classes at the church." Rose rolled her eyes and sighed.

"Oh, brother," Evelyn said. "I'll be sure to look for you on *Girls Gone Wild*. Rose, now let's be honest. You can be a bit of a hypocrite. I *do* remember you spent all that money to go to that spa in

Arizona for miracle youth mud imported from some island in South America. Honey, that dirt was probably from somebody's backyard right here in New Orleans—"

"It was a *religious* retreat," Rose insisted as she refilled her coffee cup. "Refreshing and renewal. We had Bible study . . . there was nothing artificial about anything we did! We bonded with nature and had a spiritual cleansing. Unlike you with all those wigs you wear. Every time someone comes out with a new collection, there you go off to buy another one. I bet if you cleaned out that wig collection, every cancer patient in New Orleans would have a head of hair."

"Can you two tone it down a bit?" Joy interjected.

"As far as my wigs are concerned, that's *my* business. They're the top of the line, sweetheart. There's nothing wrong with a little versatility. Stanley likes sleeping with a new woman every week," Evelyn said, feeling the skin under her chin.

"Sister, you can spare us the details of what happens with you and Stanley at night. I can't believe you even sleep in a wig. Besides, can't be too much action goin' on. Stanley can't even stay awake past nine o'clock," Rose quipped.

"Don't be a hater, Rose, don't be a hater . . ." Evelyn said as she reached for a beignet.

"Okay, *you've* been watching way too much cable," Rose said.

Joy kept her words to herself, but she couldn't contain her laughter.

"*Anyway*, we were talking about our brother. All I'm saying, Alfred, is that you have this beautiful home all to yourself. You need someone here with you," Rose said.

"Can we drop it? I'm just looking forward to seeing my baby walk down the aisle," he said, still facing the stove.

"Sister, leave Alfred alone. It could be worse. He could be partying and trying to digress. Remember Beverly Turner's husband? Girl, he's had all kinds of women up in that house since she passed away. Last week they had the disco lights all in front," Evelyn said.

"Disco lights?!?" Joy asked.

"You know, the cops. Anyway, I got one word to say about Mr. Turner . . . *Viagra*. Folks just losin' their mind over the stuff," Evelyn added.

"You think everything somebody does is related to either crack or Viagra. Let's just change the subject. I will say, Summer made a good choice with that Evan. I'm so proud of that girl. He's smart, handsome, and had he been in the next income bracket, he'd be perfect. At least he's a good money manager. Mother always said, 'If you can't marry up, marry a good money manager,' " Rose said.

"How do you know he's a good money manager? I suppose you've checked his credit report too. Besides, he looks *alright*, but he ain't no Harry Belafonte or Denzel Washington. I've got to have somebody that makes my toes curl." Evelyn rolled her eyes as she leaned back slightly.

"I guess that's Stanley," Rose mumbled to Joy.

"I heard that."

"Anyway, I can spot a good money manager a mile away. God gave me special discernment in that area."

"Yeah, Rose, I'm sure God anointed you *especially* for that," Evelyn said as she looked sideways, "but I *still* have doubts about this celibacy thing. I think those two have cut the rug already. I can just tell. What do you think, Alfred?" she said, sipping her coffee.

"Evelyn, please . . . that's between them and God," Joy said.

"I agree, Joy," Rose said. "However, I do wonder . . ."

"You know I've never had any problems speakin' my mind. We're all over fifty here," Evelyn defended.

"I'm not gonna even answer that," Alfred said. "Just 'cause you obviously couldn't hold out before your first or second marriage doesn't mean it's impossible. That's the mistake we often make. We hold people to our own standards. I'm proud of them both."

Evelyn paused and cleared her throat. "I beg your pardon. I had to hold out for my first husband, Harold. You know Hannah would've killed me. Anyway, so when's Naomi Campbell rolling in? I need to make sure I have my best wig on for the paparazzi."

"*Misa* will be here around seven p.m., just in time for the reception. I'm about to charge you for breakfast or put you out!" Alfred said, placing the bowl of eggs on the table.

"You can't put me out of this house. It's still our house too. You're just living here. Anyway, I know she is going to have to make her grand appearance."

"*Evelyn,*" Joy said slowly.

"Okay, I'm just having fun. I'll behave." She paused briefly. "I just think it's a shame how that child rarely came back to see Elizabeth. It broke her heart."

"Evelyn, please. We don't want to talk about *any* of that. You weren't here, so you don't know everything. We're here to have a good time without mess. Elizabeth is gone now. Let my sister rest in peace," Joy said softly. "I'm going upstairs to check on Summer. She's probably up by now."

"Okay, but there's one last thing I have to say and then I promise I'll be quiet."

"What, Evelyn?" Rose commanded.

"I still don't see why we couldn't have had just *one* stripper last night."

"I don't know about you, but I'm on the usher board at St. Peter AME. Things have a way of gettin' back."

"Rose, nobody cares about your old dusty behind."

"Now see, that's what I'm talking about. In case you didn't

know, there's a difference between being saved and living a *consecrated* life. Evelyn, you may squeak into heaven, but you can't have the best of both worlds. You've been sittin' on the fence servin' two masters for way too long," Rose remarked.

"Been havin' a good time too," Evelyn said as she grabbed a toothpick.

"On that note, I'm heading upstairs to check on my favorite niece," Joy said. She'd had enough of the Hens.

"I'll fix a plate for you and put it to the side until you get back," Alfred said as he winked at his sister-in-law.

"*Um-hum*," the Hens said in unison.

Alfred just rolled his eyes and refocused on stirring the bubbling grits in the pan.

Summer heard a knock at the door then a sugary sweet voice. "Summer, it's your Aunt Joy. Can I come in?"

"Oh yeah, it's open." Her aunt's voice sounded exactly like her mother's, and they looked so much alike.

"Mornin', Aunt Joy!" she said as she walked over and grabbed her for a hug.

"Wow, you've never been that happy to see me," Joy said as she brushed a silky gray strand of hair away from her face.

Summer observed how wonderful her aunt looked for her age. Her smooth honey skin was vibrant as it glowed against her tangerine-colored sheath dress. Her silver hair was glossy, and its tapered style framed her face perfectly. The dress hugged her slightly curvy size-twelve frame. Summer loved her aunt's style. She managed to combine grace, elegance, and a little sass. Whenever Summer saw a picture of Nancy Wilson or heard her sing, she immediately pictured her Aunt Joy. She was growing older gracefully, and still had it going on.

"So how are you feeling?" she said as she walked over to inspect Summer's wedding dress.

"I'm doing fine. I just talked to Misa."

"Oh," Joy said, lifting the hem of the dress. "Well, what did she say?"

"She's still going to be here for the reception." Summer slid her knees to her chest.

"Umm-hum," her aunt said, still focused on the hem.

Silence.

"This is going to be such a beautiful day. Girl, your father made a wonderful breakfast. I had to get away from your other aunts. You know how messy they can be," she said as she sat on the bed next to Summer.

"Uh-huh. I know."

"The Hens asked your father if he really thought you and Evan hadn't had sex yet," her aunt said lightly, tapping Summer's knee for emphasis.

"Auntie, I can't even go there right now."

"Well, I know one thing for sure," Joy said after a pause. "Elizabeth would have been so proud of you."

"Yeah, I still wish Misa was here right now. I just don't understand."

"*None* of us understands your sister, but sometimes it's like that with siblings. Look at all your aunts. We're *all* different, but we're still family. Rose is a snob, Evelyn is cuckoo for Cocoa Puffs; I'm the only aunt on your mom's side, and I represent the sane folks! Let's not get started on your uncles." She started to crack herself up laughing. "You must learn to respect and love the differences of your family members. Everything else has to be left up to God."

Summer burst out laughing in a delayed reaction. " 'Cuckoo for Cocoa Puffs'? Aunt Joy, you're a *real* trip."

"At least I got you to laugh. We're going to focus on the good today. Snap out of it, girl. You have so much love around you! Trust me, whatever you and Misa are struggling with, God's gonna work it out. Just let it go."

"I'm trying. It's just that I've been praying over our relationship for years," Summer added with a sigh. "When is God gonna do something?"

"He is always doing something, even when you can't feel it. Everything has its own timing. You have 'cast your bread upon the waters,' and remember, 'to everything there is a season.' For now, this is the season to party and celebrate. You are about to get you some!"

"Auntie, no you didn't!"

"I'm still a woman."

Summer watched as her aunt walked across the room to look out the window. A few moments of silence passed.

"Aunt Joy," Summer said with hesitation, "I just wish I could bring her back."

"I know. I miss her too. Sometimes I think that I could've done more. She was sick for so long. Not everyone understood her, but I did." Joy walked back over and sat next to Summer on the bed.

"I know you did. It took me a while to understand what she was going through too. I hated seeing her come in and out of those hospitals. One day she was fine, the next she was miserable . . ." Summer said, her voice trailing off.

"One thing I know for sure. Elizabeth would've never killed herself. Your mother was strong in her own way, a fighter. Hey . . .

beautiful girl, this is supposed to be a *joyful* morning. We need to talk about this lovely dress or Evan . . . Don't you want to talk about something else?"

"I'm not sad. You're just one of the few people I can talk to about Mom who *really* understands. I wouldn't have been thinking about this at all, but I had this dream the night before last."

"What kind of dream?"

"About Mom. Just forget it. You're right. Let's talk about something else."

"Summer, you can't change the past. Besides, you still have your dad, and your sister. Oh, and don't forget the Hens," she said, trying to get a laugh out of her again.

"Yeah," Summer said as she smiled. "I just don't know. Misa was the one who struggled with Mom's sickness the most. Why couldn't she realize that Mom couldn't give what she didn't have?"

"Summer, don't blame her. You don't know what Misa's feeling. She probably has more hurt on the inside than you could imagine. She's dealt with your mom's death in her own way. You see things through your spiritual eyes. Maybe Misa just doesn't have that capability yet." She placed two fingers on Summer's chin, lifting her head to inspect her eyes.

Summer gently pulled away and slid back to the headboard, folding her arms. "Well, I just don't want her to suffer alone. I know deep down she's facing some battles. The last time I went to visit her in New York, I found prescription bottles. I'm scared, Aunt Joy. It's that same generational curse that stole mom's life."

Joy grabbed Summer's hands. "I know you're scared, but, Summer, you've broken that family curse. What happened with your mother is not going to happen to Misa. Sometimes people have to come to terms with their issues in their own way. You can't fight her battle. I know how much you want to fix every problem. You've always been that way. Through God's grace you've borne the family cross in many ways, but you have to know when to let go. Trust me, I understand. I was like that with your mother. It hurts, but it won't be like this forever. Just step back and let God have His way with Misa."

Summer was about to say something else, but the phone rang. She looked at the caller ID. "It's Paige!" she shrieked.

"That crazy girlfriend of yours? That's my cue; I'm headed downstairs before the Hens eat up all the food." Joy sprang off the bed and walked out.

Hot Grits and Al Green

Summer stood tall and erect, gazing into the full-length mirror with a childlike excitement on her face. *You really look goofy, girl,* she thought to herself. She could honestly say she had the bride's glow, despite a little crust in the corner of her right eye. She couldn't figure out if she was happier about getting married or about the intimacy that would follow.

She leaned in closer to the mirror. She felt a sexy rush as the strap of her apple green satin nightgown slid down, slightly caressing her left shoulder. Amusing herself, she struck several sultry poses like she was in a photo shoot. Then she imagined Evan standing behind her. Her body trembled slightly and tingled in several places as she thought of their potential wedding night. Her smile quickly turned to a frown, then sheer *panic* . . .

Whoa, God, You wouldn't do that, would you? He has to be good. I've waited too long to be disappointed . . . What am I thinking? I'm talking to God about my sex life! Well, didn't He invent all of this love and relationship stuff? Trust Him, Trust Him . . . At least I didn't get my period . . . that would have been a nightmare. She cut off her thoughts and refocused on the purpose of her solitude: prayer and meditation.

She pulled out her Bible, then sat on the bed. As she fanned the pages, she stopped on the page her mother's picture marked. So far she hadn't allowed any tears, but she felt water forming in her eyes. Instantly she was assured that her mother was right there in the room. If she could believe in God, she could believe that she was with her.

Just then a brisk wind came through the room. She heard a very soft sound, like church bells or tiny chimes ringing, but the window was closed and the television wasn't on. *I'm trippin'*, she thought. Her wedding dress fluttered slightly. The picture of her mother resting in the Bible gently floated to the floor. She rubbed her forehead and then reached down to pick it up. She opened the Bible again and began to place the photo between its pages. Before she did, her eyes focused on a previously marked scripture.

He that findeth a wife findeth a good thing.

She smiled, looked up, and said, "Yes, Mom, I *am* a good thing." She remembered the old piece of paper stuck in the back of her Bible where her daily confessions were written. One by one, she was able to cross off her prayer requests. There were a few more requests regarding her sister. But reviewing the paper assured her that

God had and would continue to answer her prayers. At that moment, she closed her eyes, knelt down, and became very still.

God, You are so wonderful, thanks for loving me. Please forgive me of my sins. If I've said or done anything to offend anyone, or if I have walked in my own willful way, I'm sorry. Lord, before now, I really wasn't ready for Evan. You knew the perfect time and the perfect way for everything.

In the midst of it all, You've healed and delivered me, and I'm complete. Although Evan and I aren't perfect, we're perfect for each other. I'm thankful he's a man of God and accepts me just the way I am.

I realize that a wedding is not a marriage, but let it be the blessing and spiritual experience You intended. Lord, please let everyone arrive safely. And finally, I pray a special prayer for Misa. Please, Lord, I want her to know You as her personal savior. Let every good and perfect gift You have for her manifest. I love You, in Jesus' name, A-men.

Okay, enough quiet time and meditation, she thought as she bolted from the floor and turned on the radio. *I need a major lift!* She immediately livened up when she recognized Al Green belting out one of his anthems on the old-school station, crooning one of his classic jams. Al Green was as much a part of her life as the cornbread and seafood gumbo her mother used to make.

A few minutes later, a knock on the door interrupted her private concert.

"Hey, baby, can I come in?" her father asked through the door.

"Yeah, Dad, just a minute." Summer turned the music down a little, grabbed her robe, and walked toward the door.

"Come on in," she said as she opened the door.

"Are you hungry? Your Aunt Joy probably told you I made a big breakfast. Everybody's up," he said as he stepped in.

"You know I am. I've been up for a while. Paige is on her way over," she said, rubbing her stomach.

"I made your favorites, and if you hurry up there may be some hot beignets left." Summer grabbed her father and hugged him as she inhaled a mix of woodsy cologne and culinary delights. She pressed her cheek against the soft fabric of his yellow golf shirt, feeling the warmth of his chest. They rocked subtly as if dancing to the music. She felt safe wrapped in her father's frame. As they separated, she briefly studied his face. His skin reminded her of supple brown leather. When he smiled, she noticed the tiny wrinkles around the corners of his eyes that looked like a permanent wink. She could see why all the women at the university used to flirt with him.

He grabbed her hand and started twirling her around.

"My baby is going to be beautiful," he exclaimed.

"*Whatever, dude*," Summer mused, trying to lighten the mood.

"I know this is hard—"

"Dad, let's not talk about it. I'm happy. I'm looking forward to seeing Misa."

"Well, your mom would have . . ." His words trailed off as he sat on the bed and placed his head in his hands. She sat next to him and just rested her head on her father's shoulder. "Summer, I've done the best that I could. I know most of the time you tried to be strong for me. I'm so proud of you."

"Dad, I have no complaints. So no more sad stuff, okay? We have a big day," she said as she jumped off the bed. She turned up the volume, shuffled back to her father, and pulled him off the bed. Al Green continued to belt out one of her mother's favorite songs, compliments of the radio station's miniconcert.

"Let's stay together . . . Loving you whether . . . Times are good or bad . . ."

She stood back a minute, noticing his bow-legged stance. They began to two-step as Al Green crooned.

Paige knocked on the open door, announcing her arrival. "Hey, all right now," she said, walking in and moving her round hips to the beat. They all began laughing.

"Paige, what do *you* know about Al Green?" Her father's conservative demeanor had shifted to soulful Southern comfort with ease.

"Please, Mr. Ledoux, I *love* me some Al Green. I'm the old-school queen."

"And what do you know about the *real* old school? I'm not talking about the Sugar Hill Gang."

"I'm not sure you want to go there, Mr. Ledoux," Paige said with her hand on her hip and her head slightly tilted to the side.

"Hey, I like the Sugar Hill Gang," Summer yelled. "That's when they rapped about 'soggy macaroni' and 'chicken that taste like wood' instead of sex and shootin' people."

"Anyway, that's my cue. I'm going back downstairs to see if any food is left. It's bad enough your aunts got a free place to stay; they get complimentary breakfast too. What is this, the Hilton? It's a doggone shame. Nobody in this family can cook except me."

"Daddy, you know that's not true. You should be ashamed of *yourself*. Besides, you said you loved my cooking," Summer interjected.

"Baby, it's time for the truth." He patted her on the shoulder. "You know I love you and everything, but I was just trying to build your confidence up. Baby, you can't cook. I guess we're still going to have to pray about this issue. Now your mama, she could make a meal out of anything. All she needed was a skillet and some Crisco. I don't know what happened to you and your sister."

His daughter punched him softly on the side of his arm. "Daddy, I'm not even tryin' to mess with you this morning."

"I'll see you downstairs," he said, chuckling on his way out the door.

"Girl, your daddy is *so* funny."

"Yeah, he is."

"And fine too . . ."

"Girl, stop trying to push up on my dad! By the way, your hair looks really good."

"Are you just now noticing? I just got it done right for the wedding," she said as she sat on the vanity bench and inspected her style in the mirror. "You know, it's rare that I spend some money to get a perm. I need to get some oil sheen before the wedding."

"It's not that I'm ignoring you. It's just so much is going on," Summer said, touching her own satin scarf wrapped around freshly relaxed hair. "I appreciate the effort, Paige. I know it has to be serious for you to sit in a salon chair for several hours."

"Well, this is my Halle number five look. You know whatever Halle does I *must* do."

"Paige, you are *seriously* ill."

"Girl, for real, I think Halle and I are related. We must be distant cousins or something. I just sense her in my spirit. She's an icon, a trailblazer, just like me. You know I'm just a few sit-ups away from getting the abs."

Paige was very serious about the Halle thing. Whatever Halle Berry did with her hair, she did. Today it was styled with the shorter flipped and layered look. Summer had to admit, she did have the haircut down, but that was about as close to Halle as Paige was gonna get.

Paige Lenoir was far from the glamorized world of Hollywood. Her daily drama played out in the classroom. She taught junior high students at an alternative school. Her pupils were young adults and often had more life experiences than Paige. They'd talk about abusive relationships, incarcerated relatives, drug abuse—things truly foreign to her own life. Yet she realized she was supposed to be there. "It's my calling," Paige would say, "until God tells me any different."

Summer took a deep breath and smiled, once again thankful that Paige was there with her.

"Summer, I know in my spirit that your life *has* changed. So much labor in prayer, but it was worth it; no more depression, broken relationships . . . all that garbage is gone. That fight is over, girl."

They grew quiet as Summer's eyes fell down. She smiled faintly, thinking how grateful she was for Paige's love and friendship. "My prayer partner . . . Girl, I don't know where I would be without you," Summer said as she hugged her. She recalled how often they prayed, working through her deliverance together. No one understood Summer's challenges better.

Paige grabbed her friend's shoulders excitedly. "Well, you finally got it right! Lord knows we have seen enough of Mr. Right Now, Mr. Imposter, and Mr. All Wrong."

"Yeah, it was rough. If something didn't happen soon, I don't know how much longer we could have lasted," Summer said, waving her hands to fan herself.

"Well, you're an inspiration. But I'm not sure if I ever want to get married. Marriage, kids—I'm just not feelin' it. I never have. Maybe something's wrong with me. Personally, I enjoy being by myself. Besides, I've always had a thing for older men. The man of my dreams is Sidney Poitier."

"Are you *serious?* I can see back in the day. He was so charming and sophisticated. But now, girl . . . Well, to each his own. You learn something new every day about your friends."

"He's *still* fine. I just admire the way he carried himself." Paige sighed as she looked up in a daze.

"Yeah, okay. I didn't know it was like that. Anyway, I don't think anything's wrong with you because you're not feelin' the marriage thing. Who knows what the Lord has in store for you?"

"Look, let's just get you through this day. We'll worry about my situation later. I know you want to call your man, with his nerdy self. I'm going downstairs where the grub is."

"Some things will never change, Paige," Summer said, watching her friend sprint out the door.

Jumpin' the Broom!

"Are you doing okay?" she heard Paige and Eva Broussard, her future mother-in-law, say from outside the bedroom.

"Yes, but I may need some help getting into the dress. You can come in."

Summer crossed her arms in front of her. She felt a little embarrassed about her bustier and thong. The fact that Sisqó could write a song and revolutionize the whole underwear industry still amazed her.

Paige took the dress from its hanging position. "Let me know when you're ready to step into it."

Summer took a few deep breaths to calm her spirit. "Okay, I'm ready."

After she was fully dressed, she looked in the

mirror and couldn't believe what she saw. She tried not to fill up inside, but couldn't help it. Today she felt *beautiful* inside and out.

Summer remembered longing for Misa's looks and confidence. Gaining self-esteem had been a process for her, a gradual transformation. At family gatherings her relatives would innocently remark, "Oh, Summer, you turned out to be so pretty." *What was I before, a dog?*

Misa had always been a stunning, exotic beauty. Her slanted eyes made people question if she had East Asian heritage. Her cinnamon brown skin remained flawless despite the ton of makeup she wore for fashion shoots. Her sumptuous lips seduced and charmed anyone she encountered. Misa's thick dark hair had large waves that cascaded past her shoulders. Well, it did until she recently straightened and dyed it almost blond.

Summer shared Misa's skin tone, but that was about it. Her style was quite understated, and she wore her hair in loose shoulder-length curls or a ponytail. A little lip gloss or blush was the most makeup she'd wear. Despite her own comfort with her style, Misa was always trying to "update" Summer's look. All that aside, she was now happy that God had created her just the way she was, B cup and all. *Now, that is something to celebrate*, she thought as she spun around. She was finally high off life . . . nothing else.

"I love you like a daughter," Mrs. Broussard said. "And I know Evan really loves you. You are good for him."

I'm good for him. I'm good for him, Summer thought to herself. *Just me, without anything extra. Just me with or without makeup. Just me, on good days or bad . . . I was good for him and finally good enough . . . because God said so.*

• • •

Once the soloist began singing Ave Maria, Summer took the first step and her father followed after a pause. Seeing Evan waiting for her gave her a sense of peace. Most of the ceremony was a blur until the pastor read from Summer's favorite scripture. She listened to every word. "Love is patient, love is kind . . . love keeps no record of wrongs . . ." Summer had read I Corinthians 13 over and over again, and now it was becoming a reality. Then finally she heard the words she'd been longing for ring in her spirit so profoundly:

"I now pronounce you husband and wife. You may salute your bride."

Summer closed her eyes. She felt very serene, so special . . . so loved by God and her new husband. She'd never felt a kiss like that before. *Nothing like my first kiss with Nathanial Burgess.* As she opened her eyes, she felt the Holy Spirit give her one last embrace before she could even hear the cheers of her guests. She took a deep breath as Evan placed his hand in hers. She imagined Jesus standing at the end of the aisle with eyes of adoration and arms open wide to receive them. With that, they proceeded down the aisle with a peace that surpassed all understanding and a love supreme.

Summer couldn't help but get agitated. She'd asked Evan for the time. It was eight-fifteen p.m. and she hadn't seen her sister yet. The best man was about to make a toast. He cleared his throat, raised his glass, and then out of nowhere there was a dog bark.

No, she didn't, Summer thought. Her suspicion stood confirmed at the entrance of the tent. Misa, her mutt in tow, made her fashionably late entrance. She blew a kiss to Summer and waved her gloved hand as if to tell the best man to go on with the toast.

Summer continued to smile and remain calm, even though she couldn't believe she'd brought the dog with her. Her sister always had a way of getting attention, and this time was no exception. For what seemed like a frozen moment, all eyes were on Misa. She did look beautiful—colorful, but beautiful. Her one-shouldered red dress trimmed with a red and fuchsia chiffon ruffle around the bottom fit her perfectly. She accented the festive attire with a large red hat and gloved hands.

Summer wondered how Misa was able to maintain perfect posture in her red stiletto pumps. Summer thought the ensemble was a bit over the top. Misa looked like she was about to go salsa dancing immediately after the reception. Summer smiled, as she knew only Misa could get away with an outfit like that. *At least her hair is conservative*, she thought, as she noticed Misa's hair had been slicked back in a ponytail that dangled behind her back. From what Summer could tell, it was dyed back to its original dark color. Before the toast was over, her sister glided across the dance floor.

"Hello, princess," she said as she came behind the head table after the toast.

Summer cringed then reached to hug her. Misa gave her a kiss on each side of her face. Summer hated that modeling industry gesture. It was so fake, but she played along with it anyway.

"I'm glad you finally made it," Summer said. "I've missed you. Dad had everything videotaped and took lots of pictures."

Misa stared at her sister. "Look at you . . . you've come a long way, Summer," she said with a Southern accent she seemed to turn on and off like a light switch.

"Misa, *please*."

"Okay, I promised I wasn't going to embarrass you," she said as she placed her hands on Summer's cheeks.

You already have.

"Now, this handsome gentleman *has* to be my new brother-in-law," Misa remarked as she embraced Evan.

Summer noticed her husband blushing. He'd seen pictures of Misa, but he seemed surprised at how beautiful and vibrant she was in person. Summer felt invisible all over again as Misa appeared in 3-D, grabbing and hugging him.

"We are so glad you made it," he said as he slid his hand around Summer's waist and pulled her close to him.

"I wouldn't have missed it for the world. I had to see the man who swept my baby sister off her feet. Oh, I forgot. She's not a baby anymore. Well, Evan, we must get a dance in before the night is over," she said, lightly poking him in the chest.

"Misa! You look wonderful," her father said rushing over. He grabbed both her hands, then hugged her.

"Hello, Daddy. You look good too," she said, adjusting her smile and the tone of her voice.

"This makes me very happy. Both my beautiful daughters at home."

"How was your flight? Of course you're staying at the house, aren't you?" Summer asked.

"Sweetie, you don't need to be concerned about where I'm staying, especially tonight," her sister said. She started looking around at the people.

"You *have* to stay here. Daddy has planned a big brunch tomorrow. Afterward we're going to hang out in the French Quarter, ride the ferry boat, and maybe go listen to some zydeco."

"Honey, that's for visitors. I just want to relax. I'll be right at the Ritz on Canal. I didn't think there'd be any room to breathe at the house. You know how your aunts are; they take over every damn thing. Oh, excuse my French, Daddy. Even with all those bedrooms, having them there makes the place seem so crowded.

But Diva will be staying the night. Won't you, poochie?" she said as she gave her Yorkie a pretend kiss.

Summer wasn't surprised. She knew Misa would limit the time she'd have to spend with the family. Misa's reluctance to stay at the house clearly indicated something was still unresolved.

Summer could only speculate on Misa's thoughts. Her sister rarely expressed herself. They *never* discussed their mother. Misa never appeared to grieve. The only thing Summer heard from Misa was how "Summer had everything handed to her on a silver platter." How everyone was so much harder on Misa. *If only she knew,* Summer thought. *She'd never be able to handle the truth.*

Summer blinked to stop water from filling her eyes. The Lord had made this day, and she was determined to rejoice in it. She watched as her sister made her way around in her usual social fashion. Misa obnoxiously kissed everyone on both cheeks like she had just flown in from Paris instead of New York. Of course, the men didn't mind.

The reception was finally winding down. The DJ played music from every decade, from the sixties on to the present. "Can't Hurry Love," "My Girl," "Ain't Nothing Like the Real Thing," "Papa Was a Rolling Stone," "Disco Nights," "Ain't No Stopping Us Now," "Best of My Love," "Aqua Boogie," "Beat It," "Thriller," "Rapper's Delight," "Planet Rock," "Kiss," "It Takes Two"—and the list went on and on. The DJ had something for everybody.

I didn't think my family was going to sit down, Summer thought as she recalled the antics of the rowdy and festive bunch. Uncle Groovy was in a chair snoring, worn out from doing the Electric Slide by himself. Summer smiled as she watched her Aunt Evelyn and Uncle Stanley slow dragging to Al Green's "For the Good Times." Her uncle was helping himself to a heaping of her aunt's robust rear end. Summer was truly ready to call it a night after this sight.

"Y'all don't need to go home, but . . ." Evan said to a few of the lingering guests.

"Go handle your business, partner," Quinton, the best man, said, waving him off. Misa looked quite comfortable resting on Quinton's lap. Summer suspected they had been drinking more than punch, especially since people kept making trips to Quinton's trunk. She cut her eyes at them since her father was only a few feet away. Her father knew what she and her husband were about to do, but she didn't want to remind him about it.

She walked over to her father. "Good night, Daddy," she said as their lips smacked.

Her father hugged Evan and gave Summer a lingering look. "Good night, baby," he said softly as she forced a smile and his eyes fell to the ground.

She felt like a little girl, but she was someone's wife now. They headed across the lawn. Halfway to the guesthouse, Evan picked her up in his arms. Slowly the music and the noise from the guests started to fade.

They'd barely made it through the doorway before Evan wrapped his arms around her. He gave her a tight squeeze, then kissed her softly on her lips. They paused for a moment to notice that their friends had decorated the place with floating candles and magnolias. Tulle was draped everywhere. Bowls of truffles and chocolate strawberries were placed on the tables.

"I'm going upstairs to the bedroom," Summer said, picturing

the lingerie waiting for her upstairs. "Got a special sumtin-sumtin for you."

"Summer, I want the package. I don't care about what it's wrapped in!"

She ignored him and climbed the stairs, which were littered with white rose petals. He stood at the bottom, rubbing his forehead. He finally followed. By the time he reached the top stair, she was already in the bathroom.

She looked in the mirror and said, "Well, married lady, you are about to finally *get some!*" She carefully removed the tiara and headpiece, then heard Evan knocking. She really felt sorry for him, so she reluctantly opened the door. "I hope you know you're ruining the whole mood," she said. He had already stripped to his silk boxers.

"That's *impossible*," he said with a grin. "You look really beautiful." He held her face in the palms of his hands and planted several tender kisses on her face.

"I love you," Summer whispered between his kisses.

The kisses became more intense. He turned her back to him and softly grazed her neck with his lips, then planted tiny kisses on her earlobes. He then began to unzip the back of her gown, kissing her back ever so softly. She held the front of the gown to her chest, eventually allowing it to loosen and slip down. The cost and care of the dress was no longer an issue.

He grabbed her hand and led her to the bedroom. Evan sat on the end of the bed and wrapped his hand around her waist. He placed his head close to her stomach and began to sob quietly. "You're my baby. I'm gonna take care of you," he said several times. Summer didn't know what to do. She just stood there silently while softly stroking his hair with her fingers.

When he lifted his head, she wiped his tears and kissed him

softly on the lips. He stood and they embraced again. He finally picked her up and gently laid her back down. Within seconds, he covered her like a blanket. Right before their bodies connected, she heard the subtle patter of God's tears against the window. She smiled, then gave full attention to her lover. Their bodies created, arranged, and danced against the background of lyrical storms. She felt the warmth of his body as they consumed one another. She was speechless as their bodies harmonized and completely surrendered. She sensed every part of him—all of his spirit, his entire mind, every inch of his body. Somewhere in the night, she was quietly, and completely assured:

He was the one.

Homecoming

Summer couldn't wait to get to the football game. Every year, the family would attend the homecoming of Southern University, Alfred's alma mater. She loved seeing the step shows, parades, and the halftime battle of the bands. On the years her mother came, it was extra special. This year her mother was in the hospital, but she was to come home Sunday, the next day. It was just Summer and her dad, but she didn't mind.

She watched her father shake hand after hand, shout at the football game, and offer every treat she could eat—hot dogs, peanuts, soda, and candy. Summer stood when the crowd stood and cheered when they did, because she didn't really understand the game.

She danced as the marching band played their rendition of the latest contemporary music. She watched as the "foxy dancers" shook their thang and the Ebony King and Queen circled the stadium with their royal wave. "That's going to be me one day," she announced to her father. He smiled and planted a kiss on her forehead.

Summer noticed that during the game her father rubbed his brow and got really silent despite the roaring crowd, brass instruments blaring, and heckling fans. She supposed he was thinking about her mother.

"Mommy will be home tomorrow," he said, as if to confirm her suspicions. "Good as new."

"Good as new," she'd say right back, holding his hand. She searched the crowds for Misa, her neck stretching. Misa, now fifteen, wanted to hang with her friends and not her ten-year-old sister. The last thing she'd heard her say was "We'll meet you guys at the Greek show."

Summer couldn't wait to get to the step show. That was her favorite part. She didn't understand all the clapping, stomping, dancing, and taunts of the sororities and fraternities; she just knew she liked it! Her daddy would escort her on to his fraternity plot as if they had some sort of special privilege. All the men wore the same colors and did some sort of special handshake. When she asked her daddy what it was, he said, "It's a secret." She just left it at that.

Hours after the game, they finally caught up with Misa. She chose to ride with friends. Summer and her father headed to Queen Hannah's for the big homecoming dinner they prepared every year. When Summer walked into the restaurant, she was instantly scooped up by her Uncle Sunny. She smiled.

"Uncle Sunny, I'm getting too big for you to pick me up!" she insisted. After watching all the pretty college girls in their tight jeans and makeup, she had made up her mind that she was no longer a baby and would trade in her corduroys for a pair of designer jeans.

"Enjoy it while you can, baby. Before you know it, you'll be off to college, getting a job, and paying bills!"

"That doesn't sound like any fun," Summer said as the aroma of spicy red beans and rice danced under her nose. He set her down and she ran toward the back. She wasn't even looking when she ran right into Hannah.

"Look where you're going! You could get hurt back here in the kitchen!"

"Sorry, Grandmere," she said as she stopped instantly in her tracks.

"Where's your sister?"

"I dunno," Summer said as she shrugged her shoulders, eyeing a tray of salmon cakes as it passed by.

"Pardonner?"

"I mean, I'm not sure, Grandmere."

"That's more like it." Hannah looked at her watch and then removed her apron.

Summer knew, when there was a restaurant full of people and Hannah removed her apron, there was going to be trouble.

"Tell your daddy I'll be right back, sugar."

She smoothed her silver-crowned hair back, grabbed her purse, and headed out the door, almost knocking over one of the Hens.

Misa liked the way he grabbed the back of her hair and then raked her curls with his fingers. She liked the way he was pressed against her. She felt warmth and tingling all over her body. She felt free and easy.

"Will you trust me?" he asked in a voice mixed with deep breaths and sighs.

He started pulling at her pants. She shielded her zipper as a reflex reaction.

"Don't do that," he said as he gently removed her grip from her zipper. "You're beautiful, more beautiful than any woman on campus."

Each word coaxed. Misa not only moved her hands away from her zipper, but also took her sweater off.

He stood up and unbuckled his pants. Not bothering to even remove his shirt, he climbed on top of Misa. "C'mere. Damn, you look good . . . ahhh."

"Mmmm . . ." she said as she wrapped her arms around his neck.

"Would you mind getting your hot and bothered behind off my granddaughter?"

Too startled to speak, Misa jumped up so quick, she stumbled to the floor.

"Now, you got two choices. You can either take your horny behind to your car, or go to jail for messing with a minor. We're going to act like this never happened," Hannah said as she stood at the edge of the bed in her own guesthouse.

"Yes, ma'am. I didn't know. She said she was in college . . . I, I didn't know." He was hopping and zipping at the same time.

Misa just stood there, dumbfounded. She waited until he left before she even attempted to explain. Before Misa spoke, whatever words were about to spill out were slapped out of her mouth by Hannah's backhand. There it was, without warning, the "Ledoux slap," meant to slap all taste out of one's mouth, leaving an imprint, dependent on one's pigmentation, or an everlasting impression.

"What in the hell do you think you were doing? Look, just because your mother is losing it does not mean you can just do whatever you want!"

"Don't you talk about her that way! Don't you dare talk about her!" Misa said, wiping away tears and the sting from her grandmother's hand.

"Sit your hot behind on this bed. Now, I love Elizabeth, God knows I do, but we all know she's struggling with some issues. In the meantime, I'm the one who has to step in and raise you girls. I don't mind, because I love you, but you don't have to make it so hard. Just don't say another word."

Misa sat trembling. She pressed her lips together and kept her eyes on the floor. She knew better. Hannah was one person she didn't cross.

"Look, child, you have to know by now, you can get pregnant, since you have your period. Did your mother have a talk with you?"

"Yeah. I mean yes . . . she did."

"Obviously she forgot a few things. Misa, you're a beautiful girl. Don't let some Negro, educated or not, talk your draws off for nothing. Damn, did Elizabeth teach you anything? Starting next week, you'll work in the restaurant in your spare time. You hear me?"

Misa didn't say a word. The last thing she wanted to do was spend time cooking, sweating, and serving in a restaurant. She had her mind set on bigger things.

"I said, did you hear me?"

"Yes, Grandmere."

"Go in there and wash your face so we can go back to the restaurant. I'm going to act like none of this has happened. Next week we're going to the doctors to get you on the pill. I may just take you to a church counselor right outside the city. I'll be damned if we bring any children out of wedlock to this family. Ledouxs marry, then *have children. Once you let the door open to sin, it's hard to close it! I better not ever catch you acting like common street trash again. There's a whole other side of town for that. All that money I've spent at finishing school, piano lessons, and ballet . . . and everything else, is not going to go to waste. The Girlfriends Debutante Ball is coming soon. We're just not going to tolerate this type of behavior, you hear me?" Hannah said as she gripped Misa's face with her fingers.*

Once Hannah and Misa arrived back at the restaurant, she was true to her word. Hannah went on carousing, laughing and smiling, but she cut her eyes at Misa every now and then. Despite the raging storm in Misa's spirit, she maintained perfect demeanor, as any Ledoux would.

First Sunday

The day after the wedding, everyone had agreed to meet in the morning at St. Peter's AME Church for service. There was an intimate brunch scheduled afterward for family and close friends at the house. They'd open some of the wedding gifts there, and then Summer and Evan would take off for their honeymoon during the week.

Summer loved the Lord, but she was really struggling with making it to church the next morning. Evan had been up and showered. She was still lingering in the bed.

"See, that's when I know I've done my job," he said with his chest puffed out.

"I beg your pardon?"

"Look atcha. Just can't move."

"Evan, I'm not thinkin' about you. I'm just

tired. This is the first time I've settled down since we got to New Orleans."

"Well, you need to go on and get up. I let you sleep as long as you could before we would be too late."

Summer noticed how sexy her husband looked in that towel. Although she was tired, she wished they had time for one more round of passion.

"Alright, I'm getting up," she said as she sat up and swiveled her hips, then planted her feet on the floor. She stepped into the bathroom behind her husband and kissed him on the cheek while he was brushing his teeth. "Hurry up. I've got to use the bathroom."

"Go ahead. I think I saw it all last night."

"Whatever, just move."

He rinsed his mouth quickly with his wife hugging his waist. He smacked her bottom, then left the bathroom. In the midst of basking in this couple's dance, she noticed the toilet seat was up. *Okay, God, I got it; he's still just a man.*

Summer was embarrassed at their tardy arrival. They couldn't get out of going to service because the church was going to announce and congratulate the couple on their nuptials. As she walked closer, she noticed the letters on the sign near the entryway were turning brown. Nevetheless, she loved the stained glass, moss-laden brick, and other quaint features of one of the oldest landmarks in the city.

Upon their entry into the church, they were quickly ushered to the front, although the service had already begun. Their lateness prompted murmuring from the elders, which she ignored while politely smiling and walking briskly.

She steadied herself as she listened to the sermon. It was contrary to the more contemporary, fiery services of her church in Houston. They sang hymns from the old tattered hymnals, the monotone sermons went on forever, and everyone was very serious. It was more about rituals, and the spirit wasn't allowed to move freely. Everything seemed so controlled. She was glad when they announced their marriage, because it was close to the service's end. Eventually they were able to make their way through the crowd after countless handshakes, smiles, and congratulatory wishes. As they stepped outside, Summer's eyes grew wide at the sight of Misa. She shoved Evan in his side.

"Ouch, what's wrong with you?" Evan whispered. Summer nudged him again, directing his attention to Misa and Quinton walking arm in arm. Summer kept from making assumptions since the two had just met the night before.

"Misa!" she called.

"Hey, you two. I almost didn't make it. I had a slight hangover," she said under her breath. The two men greeted each other with a handshake.

"I'm surprised to see you here," Summer said.

"Yep, I know you thought I was a big heathen. See, just when you think you have me figured out." She waved her finger as her other arm remained looped through Quinton's.

"You never cease to amaze me, Misa. Well, let's head back to the house for brunch," Summer said.

"I hope this won't be an all-day affair," Misa said. "I have plans later on."

"What kind of plans?"

"Summer, now that you finally got some business, you need to mind it."

She refused to respond.

. . .

Summer couldn't wait to make her plate. She was starving.

"Oh, no, honey, you need to make your husband's plate first."

"Aunt Rose, how do you know this *isn't* his plate?"

"Because I know *you*. Look at that skimpy thing. No man can live off that," her Aunt Rose said as she grabbed the serving tongs from Summer's hand.

"Well, Summer isn't the most domestic person," Misa added.

"How do you know? You don't know what I can and can't do." She took a deep breath. "Never mind."

"I don't know. Evan looks like he could stand to gain a few pounds. I know my baby sister only has about three meals she can cook well."

"My wife is taking good care of me," Evan said as he walked over. He grabbed Summer from behind and kissed her cheek.

She smiled and relaxed in his embrace. *I'm definitely going to make his plate first.*

After most people in their party had finished eating, the couple decided it was time to open some of their gifts. Although they had plans to go downtown late in the afternoon, Summer could already see folks getting lazy. The men had started playing dominoes and cards. She looked around and noticed that Paige hadn't gotten there yet. She didn't want to start opening gifts without her, yet she knew if she waited any longer, everyone else would be too engrossed in activities. She was relieved when she saw Paige walking across the lawn, looking quite cute in her floral slip dress and sandals.

"What took you so long?"

"I overslept. How was service today?"

"It was . . . well, it was okay. Misa came," Summer said while cinching her lips and smiling. Before Paige could respond, Summer started motioning for everybody else to come over.

"Hello, Paige. Don't you look precious," Misa said.

"Misa," she responded with a forced smile, "you look gorgeous as always. Hey, Quinton."

"Hey, Paige, what's up?" he said without even looking her way.

Paige couldn't help but be amazed. She was used to Quinton not paying her any attention, but she thought she was going to have to pull a tissue out of her purse to clean up all the drooling he was doing over Misa.

"Alright, everybody. Evan, come over here. We're about to open some of the gifts," Summer yelled.

"Summer, must you *yell*?" her Aunt Rose said with raised eyebrows.

Summer sighed, then went and sat in a chair near Evan. As she opened all the pastel-colored packages and carefully removed the beautiful ribbons, she was amazed at the generosity of her family with monetary and other much-needed gifts.

"Can I get a loan?" her Uncle Friday yelled out. "Just kidding," he said right after everyone cut their eyes at him. Just before they opened the last of the packages, her sister interrupted.

"Summer, in addition to the beautiful china I gave you . . . I have another gift. Something you've been wanting for a while now."

Summer did not respond, but waited patiently for Misa to continue.

"I have decided to move to Houston!" she said, loud enough for everyone to hear her.

"What?"

"Yes. Aren't you excited? You *have* been trying to get me to come back to the South for years."

"I, I am, but I thought you were just talking. What made you decide?"

"I don't know. I need a change, I guess, from the crowded streets of New York. Besides, I had someone convince me that Houston was a great place to live."

"Quinton?" Summer said as her forehead crinkled.

"Yes, darling, Quinton. He's going to start looking for some lofts right away. He said there are some great ones downtown," she said as she hung on to his shoulder.

"Well, I'm happy. I'm sure this will be a good move for you," Summer said.

"You don't seem too excited."

"I am. I guess I'm just thrown off."

"You know me . . . unpredictable."

Summer looked at Evan and he just shrugged his shoulders.

Summer began cleaning up the gift wrapping as she tried to cool her anger. "Can you believe her? I have been asking her for years to move closer and she never would. All of a sudden she meets some guy for the first time, hooks up with him, and decides to come to Houston. *Unbelievable*," Summer said as she stuffed paper into a plastic trash bag.

"Babe, she's a grown woman. It's been a great weekend. Just let it go," Evan said.

"I'm not going to trip. She kills me. She just does the exact opposite of what other people want. She hasn't said more than ten words to Daddy."

"Didn't you say you weren't going to let anything spoil this time for us? Just let it go."

"So far it's been cool. But I guarantee you, something's going to hit the fan before we leave. Did Quinton tell you anything?"

"Like what?"

"You know, did they hook up . . . sleep together?"

"He didn't say anything to me. Then again, he wouldn't. He knows I would tell you. But he did kind of give me the look," Evan said as he cut a piece of apple pie.

"What look?"

"It's a man thing, babe. Look, just forget about it. Before you know it, we'll be in the sky on our way to crystal blue beaches. I can't be worried about other grown folks. We have to savor every minute of this. The next thing you know, we'll both be back at the corporate grind. Didn't you say you were going to give this issue over to God?"

"Yeah, I did say that, didn't I?" Summer said as she bit her lip. "I'll try my best to let it go." She brushed the front of her dress as though brushing away the stress building on the inside.

Summer gave Paige the key to the guesthouse so she could start moving some of the gifts over there after brunch. Before Paige opened the front door to the house, she heard voices, then several bumping sounds. She thought that maybe some kids were playing a little too rough and decided to make sure they weren't getting into something they had no business getting into. She eyed a nearby tree in case she had to grab a switch.

She put the box she was carrying down in front of the door and walked around toward the back. Without warning, she turned the corner and saw Quinton and Misa up against the wall, groping each other in the heat of passion. She couldn't believe it. Misa's skirt was hiked a mile high, showing all her goods. Between moans, groans, and roaming hands, they failed to even notice her. Paige covered her mouth with her hand and bolted back to the front of the guesthouse. She decided she wouldn't tell Summer about this little show until she got back from the honeymoon. "Scandalous," she mumbled to herself. "In broad daylight." Part of her was horrified, the other slightly jealous. She didn't like what she was feeling.

Later on, during the early part of the evening, Summer was in the guesthouse attempting to finish packing for the trip. Paige was lounging on the bed. Her father and Evan had taken some of his relatives down to the House of Blues to listen to some jazz. She hadn't made much progress. They were doing more laughing and talking than anything else.

"Okay, Paige, you know if Evan comes back and I haven't finished, he's gonna fuss. You aren't any help either. You need to get off the bed. You're just in the way."

"Okay, fine," she said as she started looking at all the old photos on the vanity. "Your grandmother was so pretty back in the day."

"Yeah, girl, she was something else too. Hey, did you hear a knock at the door?"

"Let me go see," Paige said.

Before she could get halfway down the steps, she saw Misa coming up.

"Hey, I thought I heard a party going on," she said.

"I don't know about a party, but we're just hanging out. Summer's trying to finish packing," Paige said as Misa headed up the steps.

"You're not finished packing yet?" her sister barked, standing in the doorway with her hands on her hips.

"I have a couple more days. Besides, I just needed to relax and laugh a little."

"Well, don't stop the fun on my account." Misa strolled around the bedroom, picking up and putting down small objects along the way.

Summer noticed her sister had changed into an aqua blue crochet halter top and low-rise jeans. She was glad she'd joined them, but it felt a little awkward. There was now an edge replacing the carefree laughter and banter of moments before.

"Girl, let me see what you're taking. I know you are not wearing this one-piece thing," she said as she held up the swimsuit and threw it on the bed. "You need a bikini."

"Misa, some of us are not as comfortable running around half-naked."

"Everybody wears bikinis. And you have a cute figure. I should've picked out some clothes for you. Anyway, I'm staying out of it. This will be a great trip. Mexico is a festive and fun place," she said as she flopped on the bed.

"Yeah, the water is mesmerizing," Paige added.

"Oh, you've been too?" Misa asked.

"Yes, I took a cruise," Paige said, trying to forget what she had seen of Misa and Quinton earlier.

"Oh, was it one of those single Christian cruises? Anyway, I have to tell you, Mexico doesn't have anything on Brazil," Misa said.

"Well, all of us haven't had the chance to travel the world like you," Summer replied.

"This is true. So, Paige, how's everything going in your little world? What do you do again?" Misa said, inspecting her nails.

"I teach."

"That's definitely a labor of love."

"Well, I love what I do," Paige sang.

"Unfortunately, all of us can't do what we love and get paid lots of money for it."

No retaliation. This is a happy occasion. Think of Summer, Paige thought.

"Boy, we had some good memories in this house," Misa said, looking around.

"Yeah. I loved the tea parties I used to have with my friends," Summer said as she folded a T-shirt.

"Yeah," Misa said. "Parties. Remember our neighbor Randy Covington?" She sat up taller as her voice became excited.

"No!"

"Yes, girl. I used to sneak him in here all the time."

"I don't want to know any more. That boy was way older than you."

Misa waved her hand in dismissal. "Oh, Summer, stop trying to act like you're so naive and innocent."

"Don't start. Anyway, what are you doing tomorrow?" Summer asked as she paused from folding.

"Dad wants to go to lunch and have a Cosby father-daughter bonding moment. You know I'm *really* looking forward to that. At some point I'm going to the French Quarter. I haven't had a tarot card reading in a while. What's on your agenda?"

"Tarot card? You know Hannah taught us not to mess with that stuff," Summer said.

"What? Oh, the tarot card thing. Please, Summer, please don't bust out the holy water. It's just innocent fun. Besides, Hannah is no longer here to regulate everything."

"It's not that simple. It's messing with evil. Never mind. I know you're going to do what you want to." Summer paused. "I was going to go to the cemetery tomorrow. Wanna come?" Summer's eyes locked with Misa's.

"Umm, I'm going to go over there, but I don't know exactly when," Misa said.

"So where are you going to lunch?"

"If I go? I'm not sure. I think he mentioned Olivier's. But I'd be down for a po'boy from Mother's or something from Copland's."

"Misa, what's the big deal? Why don't you try enjoying your time with Dad? Being difficult requires so much more energy."

"Summer, everything is so simple in your little world, isn't it? You just don't understand."

Summer folded her arms. "I guess I don't. Explain it to me then. He's reaching out to you, Misa. You shoot him down at every opportunity."

"Okay, do you want me to be really honest?"

"Yes."

Paige sat like a referee ready to blow her whistle at any time.

"Part of the problem is that whenever we get together all I hear about is you . . . *Summer this* and *Summer that*," she mocked. "Hey, I may not have gone to college, but I've done well. I'm not Tyra Banks, but I've made a name for myself. I have a beautiful apartment in New York, I've traveled the world, and have men falling at my feet. I'm not some scrub. Besides, Mom and Dad were so much harder on me."

"Oh, so I guess you did *everything* right? You didn't deserve to be punished for anything? Besides, you were their first child. Parents are always harder on the first one, but did Mom and Dad do *anything* right?"

"Whatever."

"Misa, Mom and Dad were *very* proud of you. He brags about you all the time. He was always showing your magazine pictures around. Mom missed you more than you could ever know."

"Well, she certainly didn't act like it. She always jumped on his side." Misa paused. "Did he really brag on my magazine pictures?"

"Yes, Dad did."

"The fact is, he's never told me I did a good job to my face. Mom barely spoke to me, even when I sent her things. She never forgave me for leaving. Summer, just leave it alone; it's bigger than you realize. You weren't there the night . . . Never mind, some things you just don't know," Misa said as she waved her hand.

"Well, all I'm saying is that you broke Mom's heart. Besides, there's things you don't know either."

They both eyed each other curiously.

Paige at this point was moving her head back and forth as if she were at a tennis match, and she'd had enough. "Okay, all righty then," Paige said. "I'm gonna go get some more of that wedding cake. Yes, wedding cake—that's what I'm gonna do," she sang. She jumped off the bed and headed for the door.

"Paige, my dear, let me remind you. You can never take my place in this family. No matter what, blood will *always* be thicker than water."

Paige stopped in her tracks and placed both hands on the door frame. She quickly turned around. "You know what, Misa? You don't realize you're really missing a great relationship with your sister *and* your father. Yeah, she loves you, but I'd question whether or not she actually likes you."

Silence.

"Well, this has been real. I enjoyed all this female bonding, but I'm going to have to go for a ride." Misa rushed by Paige and purposely avoided eye contact with Summer.

Summer wanted to grab her sister's arm and tell her not to go. But this time she was not going to. It hurt, but Summer knew God was doing something. It was He Who was holding her back from going after her. She heard the door slam downstairs.

"Sorry for that. I didn't mean to let that fly out of my mouth.

Phew, girl, she is a piece of work," Paige said, still staring at the doorway.

"Yeah, but she is *still* my sister."

Summer put off her trip to the cemetery for several hours before she finally headed there. She thought her sister was going to come. It was just getting too late, so she decided she'd go on her own.

Summer used to be afraid of cemeteries, but Hannah got her out of that. They took countless trips to the City of the Dead, placing flowers and mementos on family tombs. It seemed as though she was always going to somebody's funeral with Hannah. She often wondered as she got older whether Hannah even knew half the people that had died. She couldn't understand why Hannah actually read the obituaries every week in anticipation of a funeral, as if it were a social event. She clearly pictured Hannah holding some dish in one hand and Summer's hand in the other.

The cemeteries eventually became Summer's place of solace; she'd wander for hours through the aisles of the aboveground tombs. She'd read the dates, marvel at the ornate and extravagant marble structures, and examine the simplicity of the more modest tombs. It made her feel connected; she could sense the peace and restful spirit of this sacred ground.

Her favorite was the Metairie Cemetery. Upon her first visit, a captivating sight stirred her soul. There she discovered a hauntingly beautiful statue: a woman draped over a podium, shielded by oversize wings spanning the length of her body. The angelic figure evoked a weary yet peaceful presence. She saw her mother's likeness in the woman's image and knew for certain that she too was at rest.

When she made her way to the family tomb, she sat on the steps of the chapel-shaped structure for a moment. She'd brought a small plant and set it aside. Unfortunately there was very little shade blocking the New Orleans sun. *This will be a short visit*, she thought as she opened an umbrella to deflect some of the heat.

There were times that she'd visit and say nothing. Other times she'd have full conversations with her relatives, especially her mother. Today she was there to tell her about the wedding, although she knew her mother had been there. Summer was certain she would have liked Evan. The cemetery was pretty empty, so she could talk without strange looks or pitiful stares.

Summer slid back and rested her head against the door of the tomb, which housed several family members. She stayed in this position for at least five minutes.

"Hey," she heard a soft voice say a few minutes later.

Summer looked up. It was her sister, coming from behind the corner of the mass of stone.

"Hi. I'm surprised to see you here," Summer said as she immediately lifted her head.

"Yeah. You know, I've only been here once since Mom passed away."

"I . . . I didn't know that. You lied to me?" Summer looked in her eyes.

"Yeah, I guess I did. You used to ask me if I'd been and I was too ashamed to tell you the truth," Misa said as she focused on the ground.

"Well, I'm happy to see you here now."

Silence.

"Look . . . umm . . . Summer, I may not show you in the way you would like, but I do love you," Misa said, her hands in the back pockets of her khaki capri pants.

That was the first time in years that Summer had heard those three words come from her sister's mouth. She believed they were sincere. Still, she wished she could see Misa's eyes, hidden behind her sunglasses.

"I, uh, I love you too." She felt the words spill out quickly.

"I mean, I'm not good at expressing things. I don't know why. We're just wired differently, I guess," Misa said as she nervously clasped her hands together.

"I understand. I'm not so great at it either, but I'm getting better. What I do know is, the more I let God in, the more love I can give out."

"Maybe that's part of the problem. I'm just not into Him like you," Misa said, shifting her weight from one hip to the other. She grabbed her silver engraved necklace and fumbled with it nervously. She finally sat down next to her sister.

"He loves you just as much as He loves me. You just need to open your heart up a little."

"It's not that easy. Some things have happened that have changed the way I look at God."

"Like what?"

"I don't want to get into it, Summer. Anyway, I'm just more private." She paused for a minute. "You know, Summer, it wasn't easy to leave home, but I have no regrets." Her eyes fell down. "Well, only one," she said. She looked at the gravel.

"Yeah?"

"I never had a chance to say goodbye," Misa said.

"Well, say it now."

"I can't."

"Misa, you have to start somewhere."

Misa paused, took a deep breath, then looked at the tomb. "I will. But this is between Mom and me. I have to do this alone."

"Misa, I can't just sit by and watch you being weighed down by this stuff. You won't be able to move forward until you get rid of some of that junk. What's holding you back?" Summer's eyes begged for an answer.

"It's not about you. Summer, you have your way of coping and I have mine. You grew up in this idealistic bubble. You don't know anything about the real world. I had to put all this mess that happened back here away somewhere to make it. I had an agenda. I didn't have time to be weak. I couldn't come back home a failure." She stood up and turned her back to Summer.

"So now what? You don't have anything else to prove. Misa, what do you think I was doing while you were gone, twiddling my thumbs? I had my own battles. Mom got worse; this was hard on all of us. Why do you insist that my world was perfect?" She threw up her hands.

"Summer, just calm down. I don't want to upset you again—let's just stop. I didn't mean to make you angry," Misa said as she turned back around.

Summer took a deep breath.

"Look, I came out here because . . ."

"What, Misa? Please just say it. Is it that hard? I'm not your enemy. I'm your sister." Summer's voiced trembled.

"It's hard for me to trust, even you. What I'm really trying to say is I *want* to be a better person. I have all these things jumbled up on the inside. Things are slowing down and now I'm forced to face some truths. I just don't know where or how to begin." Summer saw Misa's chest rise and fall through her ribbed tank top as her words gained momentum with every sentence.

"Well, this is a start. Misa, I just know the damage that has been done with Hannah trying to make this family perfect. I've even struggled with that." She grabbed Misa's hands. "I'll be patient. Just promise that if you need to talk you'll let me know."

"Yeah, I—I can do that."

"In the meantime, can I ask for just one favor?"

Misa sighed. "Go ahead."

"Can we pray?" Summer gently squeezed her sister's hands.

"Pray? In public . . . here?" Misa looked around to see if anyone was near.

"Yes, here, now."

She shrugged her shoulders. "I guess. What are we going to pray about?"

"We'll just let God lead us."

Summer felt her sister's sweaty palms shaking. They turned toward each other. She paused for a few moments and began to speak softly.

"*Dear Jesus, I'm so thankful I have my sister here with me. Please, Father, forgive us of our sins. Lord, I know you can turn any circumstance around. Father, You know my sister better than me, so only You know what she needs. God, I pray You look into her heart and remove any bitterness, fear, or confusion. Please, Father, continue to work on me too. Help us both let go of the past. We're new creations in Christ. Old things are passed away and our lives are new. Lord, whatever things that have been done, whatever mistakes or failures have been made, please resolve them so we may all move on. I trust with all of my heart, You'll meet every emotional, mental, spiritual, and physical need we have. In Jesus' name, Amen.*"

Misa sat in complete silence, motionless. She placed her head in her hands and allowed her tears to flow. Summer grabbed Misa and held her tight. She rubbed her head and ponytail until her sister's tears stopped. Finally, God had broken through. For the first time in years, she hugged her sister and her sister hugged her back.

The Laying on of Hands

"Grandmere, the doctor said I'm bipolar, not possessed. Just let me take the medication," Misa begged. "It's summer vacation—I want to be with my friends."

"We're just going to have the church counselor lay hands on you first. I don't want you ending up like . . . Never mind. There's nothing that the power of God and a little anointing oil can't handle. I'm not gonna have any mess clogging up the next generations," she said. Hannah thought the "laying on of hands" could cure anything. For two months straight, Hannah would drop Misa off on Tuesday evenings and return about an hour and a half later to pick her up, until one particular Tuesday. What happened that evening would change the way Misa looked at church and any man of God forever.

"So, Misa, how are you feeling today?" Reverend Baptiste asked. She looked at him with his receding hairline and handlebar mustache. He was a tall, scrawny man with piercing eyes. Misa couldn't put her finger on it, but it seemed as though there was another life lingering behind his gaze.

"Fine." Misa didn't answer with sentences—only one or two words at a time. Doesn't he get it? I have nothing to say to him. He doesn't understand what's wrong with me. How could Hannah ever believe I could relate to this man? Misa thought as she sat with her arms folded.

"Let's pray." He opened every counseling session with a prayer, but this time it was different. He got up and shut the door. It had started raining. The thunder was so loud, it was like God was stomping around in the sky. Misa should have known this was a warning. Reverend Baptiste walked over to her, held his hands out, and pulled Misa up. She rolled her eyes and reluctantly placed her hands in his. For her, this was just part of the routine.

"Dear Father . . ." He took deep breaths. She thought he was about to hyperventilate. Misa stood silently and swallowed, waiting for him to finish so she could remove her hands from his sweaty palms. Before he could utter another word, a loud burst of thunder shook the building. Misa jumped, and then the lights went out. In an instant he'd pulled her close to him. His hands went around her waist and quickly traveled up to her chest. He moaned, then tried to place his mouth over hers. Misa was horrified. She couldn't speak. After a struggle, she broke free and ran out the door. She made her way to the church receptionist. Without asking, she grabbed the phone and frantically dialed her father's number.

"Hello."

"Please, Daddy, come get me please."

"Misa, baby, what's wrong?"

"It's cold, and the rain . . . please, Daddy, just come get me. I'll explain when you get here."

"Isn't your grandmother coming back to get you?"

"Daddy, please just come get me."

He knew by the tremble of her voice that something had happened. He hung up the phone and was immediately on the way. He arrived in record time. If nothing else, Alfred Ledoux made sure his daughters knew they could call home anytime, from any place, for any reason and he'd be there. No questions asked.

When he arrived, he found Misa sitting on the front steps of the church, soaking wet, her arms shielding her from the weather as she gently rocked back and forth. She was fine until she saw him drive up. He jumped out of the car and ran to her. She stood and fell into his arms and the tears exploded forth.

"What's wrong? What happened? Did someone hurt you?" He pulled away from her and searched her eyes.

She finally composed herself and all she could get out was "Rev . . . Rev . . . Bap . . . Bap . . . touch . . ."

Before she could get a sentence out, he bolted through the church door. The church secretary jumped up and put her hands up as if to block him, and he pushed her out of the way. Reverend Baptiste was nowhere to be found. He scoured the entire church, and when he finally made it to the back, he noticed a door leading outside was ajar.

He stopped and put his hand over his heart, as if to slow the pace of its rapid beating. Before he walked back out, he stopped and looked at the secretary.

"You tell Mr. Baptiste, because I'm not even going to dignify him by calling him Reverend, if I ever even see him looking sideways, front-ways, or even thinking about coming near my family, I will kill the bastard. Do you understand me?"

The woman adjusted her glasses with her trembling hands and moved her head up and down slowly as she moved back behind her desk. After he slammed the door behind him, the church secretary ran to the back and told Mr. Baptiste that he could come out from hiding in the baptismal pool.

Hen Sandwich

Misa was glad all the wedding drama was finally coming to an end. Considering she'd had several anxiety attacks over the thought of spending time with her family, she'd survived so far. She had to admit, this trip was different. She was noticing some changes in her family and herself.

She thought she'd finally have a quiet moment in the garden. She walked by Hannah's prized azalea bushes. She stopped at a bench near the meticulously landscaped lawn and marveled at the topiaries. She stretched her legs out and crossed her ankles, refreshed by the waterfall sounds and scent of the fresh-cut lawn. She reached into her pocket and pulled out a pack of cigarettes. She lit one up and inhaled deeply. *Oh, this is so good.* She took another drag.

She made a mental reminder to scroll through her Blackberry and call her agency. She kept trying to block out the trip to the cemetery but could not help recalling Summer's prayer. She remembered the quiver in her stomach and the burning feelings in her hands. She'd tried desperately to block out thoughts of Reverend Baptiste, her last true spiritual encounter.

"There you are. Sister and I were just talking about you."

Great, the Hens.

"We haven't had any time to catch up with you," Rose said as she sat on one side and Evelyn on the other.

"Oh, well, nothing to really catch up on. Everything is everything," Misa said as she puffed then blew smoke in the air.

"What does that mean?"

"What it means is, *everything* is *everything*. Jeez, Rose, you really need to keep up," Evelyn said as she slapped Rose on the thigh. Rose paused, then rolled her eyes at her.

"*Anyway*, sweetie, let's put out this cancer stick, shall we?" Rose said as she grabbed and stomped out what was left of the cigarette. "I don't think anyone in our family has ever smoked. Can you recall anyone, sister?"

"So, Misa, what's going on in the wonderful world of high fashion?" Evelyn said, ignoring her sister's question.

I know where this is going, Misa thought. "It's going well, Aunt Evelyn," she said, wishing the cigarette on the ground was back in her mouth. She folded her arms and stared at the house in the distance.

"So have you had a thought as to what you are going to do after modeling? I mean, you are a beautiful girl, but you *are* getting up there. You can't run around in clubs and wear Baby Phat forever. Maybe you could come back here and help run Queen Hannah's. There are some nice young men around here. We can find you one, if you like."

Not in a million years. Misa just nodded and closed her eyes for a minute, bracing herself for the ridiculous conversation she knew was to come. Where could she go? She was in a "Hen sandwich," and that was the worst place to be.

"You know, Misa, if you haven't snagged one of those rappers by now, you probably won't get one. Besides, who wants to sign up to be a groupie or a baby momma," Evelyn said. "So *are* you seeing anyone?"

"No, Aunt Evelyn. With all this travel, I don't really have the time. Besides, I like my life. I love what I'm doing and I've saved enough money so I could start a business for myself if I want. Besides, there's the money Grandmere left me."

Silence.

"Well, you could spend some time every now and then with your cousins, especially Reese. She could use the break. All she does is run those children all over town," Rose said.

I'd rather pull my hair out one strand at a time than spend time with those four brats of hers. "Oh, I'm going to have to do that."

"Maybe she can introduce you to one of Efrem's doctor friends."

"Aunt Rose, did it ever occur to you that not everyone wants to marry a doctor? Hell, I'm sure Reese didn't even want to marry Efrem. Just like Uncle Wendell, God rest his soul, probably wasn't your first choice . . ."

"*Misa!* I can't believe you would even say that. That's so inappropriate. I loved my husband. He was a good husband, and a good provider."

"Rose, now, let's be honest," Evelyn said. "You have to admit, you *grew* to love him. And you can't even talk about Reese, because she's just like you. She grew to love Efrem too. That M.D. behind his name didn't hurt either."

"I thought this was about you, Misa. Anyway, Reese is *fine*. Her marriage is *fine*," Rose said as she stood up. "This family has never believed in divorce, and we won't start. Besides, what would you know about children anyway, Evelyn, since you can't even have any?"

Evelyn had been pierced. Her shoulders dropped and her spirit deflated. Her face was still and her eyes somber. It was the one issue Rose knew could hurt her, and it was rare that she spoke about it. Even Misa felt her aunt's pain.

"Rose, you didn't have to say that. I'm just trying to get you to understand that times have changed and there are some things in this family that we've accepted just because of Hannah. You know, the only reason Reese hasn't divorced Efrem is because she's trying to please you. I just want you to start being a little more realistic."

"Like I said, divorce is not an option. You just have to endure things. We're not going to start any generational cycles in this family. Hmmpf, Hannah would roll over in her grave!" Rose got up and marched off.

Misa tilted her head and watched her aunt stomp through the garden, the brim of her large hat bouncing with every step. Finally, after a long pause, she pulled out another cigarette and lit it. She took a drag and finally broke the silence: "You know, one day I'm going to give her a serious makeover."

"Just let me know. I got the perfect wig for the occasion." Evelyn straightened out the bangs on her bob. She turned to Misa and they both burst into laughter.

Red Velvet

Summer grabbed the locket hanging from her neck and ran her fingers over the engraved heart. She smiled and closed her eyes, trying to remember all the wonderful things that had happened that day. She asked her mother for weeks if she could try on the matching red velvet outfits she and her sister would wear. "Not until Christmas Day," her mother had said. "You tried them on once when we bought them, so I know they fit."

Still, Summer would go in her closet late at night and try on the dress. She loved the lace-trimmed socks and shoes with the red bow at the back. Then Christmas Day at the Pink Mansion arrived. Her favorite memory of the day was taking the portrait with her mother and sister. They were all in red. They sat on the velvet antique settee, as she and her sister leaned on their mother's shoulder. The picture was going to go in their living room at home. She touched the red satin ribbon that decorated her freshly pressed and curled ponytails. She almost didn't want to go to sleep and mess up her new hairdo. She was excited that her mother loved all her gifts and was laughing and enjoying herself. Among tons of other gifts, Summer finally got her Easy-Bake Oven with a specially made apron and a whole set of cooking utensils. How can I be a good housewife if I don't practice? *she thought.*

Later that evening, she sat atop the stairwell, high enough so Hannah wouldn't see, low enough so she could peek at all the dancing and laughing going on.

As she stared downstairs, she noticed her Uncle Groovy making his rounds, trying to get a dance partner. Her Aunt Rose and Uncle Wendell were sitting and watching everyone else. They never seemed to join the party. Hannah was laughing so hard at something, her face was turning red. Her mother and father were dancing as her grandfather's band played. Misa was in the bedroom, talking with her cousins.

As the night went on, the band stopped playing. Summer went to change into her pajamas and then came back to the top of the stairs. Everyone had cleared out of the living room, and she watched her mother and father dancing close. She couldn't quite make out the music, but it didn't have any words to it. They'd turned the volume down low. The lights were dim and a few candles were lit. Seeing them together was all she needed. "Thank you, Santa," she whispered. She could cross off the very last item on her Christmas list, for her mommy and daddy to hug, kiss, and make the groaning noises like they used to in the bedroom.

The best Christmas ever, *she thought as she yawned, then rubbed her eyes. She finally got up and tiptoed to the bedroom she was sharing with her cousins.*

"You smell so good," Alfred said as he kissed Elizabeth on her earlobe.

"Mmmm . . . you feel good. I love you," she said as she held him tighter.

"Are you sure about that?" he said as he massaged her back.

She rested her head on his shoulder. "Alfred, I know this has been hard."

"Shhh, I just want to listen to the music and wrap my arms around my beautiful wife," he said as they moved slowly around the living room floor. The party had cleared and it was just the two of them.

After a few minutes, he kissed her slowly. Once on her cheek, then on the back of her ear while his hand traveled to her exposed back as she moved to the soft music that sprinkled melodic rhythms around the room. His hand moved down to her hips, then around her waist, then to her bottom.

"I love this dress. Damn, woman, you are still fine as the day I met you."

She chuckled.

He loosened her hair and let it fall to her shoulders. He ran his fingers through the thickness of her tresses. He drew near to her face as he tried to smell her, then touched her cheek as if to make sure she was real. He kissed her once again.

This time he reached around to her back zipper and began to unzip her dress. She grabbed his hand, interrupting his attempt. "The children . . ."

"They're all in bed. We can go upstairs. Please, Elizabeth, please. It's been a while. I need you." Unashamed of the begging, he said it again. He got on his knees and grabbed her waist. "I need you so much," he said as he kissed her stomach. Despite her attempt to pull away, he grabbed her with enough strength to keep her from moving.

"Alfred! Alfred, no!" Finally she broke completely away. "I—I'm sorry. I'm just not ready. I want to. Alfred, I really do. I just don't feel

good. Please, I don't mean to take you through this." She touched his face with her hands. "I love you. Maybe it's the medication. You know . . . I just don't have those desires. I mean, I need to go slow."

"Don't say anything else, Elizabeth. I've heard it before." He walked over to the doorway, grabbed his jacket, and headed out the door.

She walked slowly up the stairs. With every step of the steep stairwell, another tear was shed. Once she got to the bedroom, she looked out the window and saw her husband walking toward the garden.

"What is wrong with me, God?" She fell on the bed and cried herself to sleep.

Alfred sat staring into the darkness. He heard footsteps. He turned and saw Joy, his sister-in-law, walking toward him. Despite the lateness of the hour, she was fully dressed, looking relaxed in slacks and a pink cashmere sweater. On first glance his heart jumped because he thought it was his wife, until she spoke.

"Thought I was the only one who couldn't sleep. Mind if I sit?"

He was almost relieved. He welcomed the interruption. "Not at all," he said. He didn't make immediate conversation, just stared at the sky.

"This was such a nice day," she said, looking up at the sky too.

"Yeah. Yes it was . . . a good day. Everyone was laughing, no fights, the food was good. I guess we should be grateful," Alfred said softly.

"Alfred, there's something I need to say."

"Huh?" he said as he snapped out of his daze.

"I've watched you with Elizabeth. I know you love her. She's getting better. Still, I'm not so sure if these doctors help or make the situation worse, you know? It's like they've created a dependency for her."

"Joy, I don't know what to do. I don't have a lot of experience with *this. It seems like for the first five years of our marriage she was fine, just a few headaches. All I know is, I love my wife. I want her healed right now. This is getting too hard, for all of us."*

Joy twisted the pearl ring on her finger, debating whether or not to tell him.

"Alfred, I know you're doing the best you can. I'm not sure if Elizabeth ever told you about her past, but she's never really talked about it with me."

"What, Joy? C'mon, just say it." His watery eyes looked directly into hers.

She looked down then back up to meet his gaze. "Well, you know our mother died young and both of us went into foster care. At least that's what they always told us. Thank God, Elizabeth and I stayed together. Well, for a brief period, Elizabeth was institutionalized as a child. When she came out, she was never really the same. She never told me what happened. Alfred, all I know is, she came back different. That's when I started seeing little changes in her. When she turned seventeen, she started having anxiety attacks and her nerves would get bad. Then when she met you, she was fine. I just don't know what triggered all this.

"I'd sort of put that whole time out of my mind. It was so long ago. I just recently started thinking again about when we were kids. Trying to search for anything that could make sense of all this. Alfred, this isn't your fault. It's bigger than you. I'm not so sure these doctors know what they're doing, but I guess we have no choice but to trust them. I don't like how they keep changing her prescriptions either."

He sat there quietly for a moment, and then spoke. "I just want it to be over." He closed his eyes. "I wonder what happened in that place? Dammit, all I know is that I love her. I said for better or worse, in sickness and in health, and I meant it."

She took a deep breath and let the air release from her lungs. She looked down to the earth. "Like I said, it was so long ago, Alfred. Who knows what happened in there? Things weren't so legitimate back then. She was a kid, a Black child at that. I don't want to even think about it."

He wanted to say something but didn't. He felt scared, tired, and empty. His heart was aching. His eyes began to well up and he blinked to keep any tears from falling.

Joy looked straight ahead because she sensed his pain. She finally turned toward him and grabbed his hand. She held it for a few minutes, and he lifted her hand and gently kissed it. "Thank you, Joy. Thank you for being the person you are. Thank you for loving her, for being good to my children."

When he kissed her hand, a rush went through her body. She pulled it back and placed it on her lap and began to rub her hand up and down her slacks out of nervousness. She lowered her head slightly. He reached over and placed his finger under her chin, forcing her eyes to meet his.

"You look so much like her." His facial expression relaxed. He removed his finger, then placed his hand on her thigh.

She wanted to move. But she was paralyzed. Before she knew it, he'd placed his other hand against her face and softly caressed it. She moved in closer toward him. Their eyes locked, and then an embrace.

At a distant veranda, she squinted to make out the figures in the garden, then crouched down, staring intensely. Finally she returned to bed, hurt, confused, and tired.

Newlyweds

Summer was just about to sip her coffee and indulge in her morning bagel when she sensed someone behind her. She'd heard the dark liquid speaking to her from the cup. *Java! Java! Java!* Oh, the anticipation of the taste of the warm bagel and a swallow of piping hot flavored coffee. But then she noticed the reflection of a short bald man in her computer screen. Her insides tightened with irritation.

"Good morning, Summer. How was the honeymoon? Where'd you guys go again?"

"Playa del Carmen, Mexico," she said without turning around.

"Yeah, that's right. Great place, great place. I took the wife and kids there last year. Just one quick thing. Do you have the report from the focus group?"

"It's ready, Bill. I will e-mail the final report to you today," she replied, deciding to finally turn halfway to face him.

"Good deal. Thanks," he said. He smiled and walked away from her cubicle.

Summer was especially touchy since it was only five days since she'd been back from her honeymoon. Summer loved being a computer engineer but hated the corporate world.

Lord, please help my attitude today.

After her second bite, the telephone rang. She quickly tried to chew and swallow the piece of bagel in her mouth before she picked up the receiver.

"Engineering. This is Summer."

"Girl, stop playing that role. It's Paige."

"What do you want? You know I can't talk long. I'm behind," she said while checking her e-mail for any urgent messages.

"I tried not to call you until the end of the week so you and your hubby could get settled in."

"Paige, you called as soon as I got back."

"Yeah, well . . ."

"You called Wednesday night too."

"I was just reminding you that the Image Awards were coming on."

"Paige, is it something important you want?"

"Hold on for a minute, girl . . . SETH, KEEP YOUR EYES ON YOUR OWN PAPER!"

"Where are you?"

"In class on my cell phone."

"Lord."

"Anyway, I was just calling to see if we can get together for breakfast tomorrow. I know it's going to be a busy day because you're going to have to do some unpacking and cleaning, but you can spare an hour for breakfast, right?"

"Evan's going to play basketball during the early part of the day. He's not even thinking about unpacking. I know you want the full scoop on the honeymoon. Where do you want to go?"

"Mama's Cafe. I'm craving some cinnamon coffee. When's your sister coming?"

"Girl, you can go to the grocery store and just buy some cinnamon. It's not that serious. Misa said she'd be coming back in about three weeks. She has 'her people' looking for a place."

"It must be nice," Paige remarked. "And for your information, I tried the cinnamon coffee at home. It just isn't the same."

"Whatever. You know when my sister gets here, the Galleria Mall will never be the same," Summer added.

"Houston will never be the same," Paige said with a chuckle.

"You are so crazy. Girl, I have to go. You're gonna get me fired. You know they're already talking about layoffs."

"I'll see you tomorrow."

Paige folded her hands and raised her eyebrows. "Excuse me; we've been waiting here longer," she reminded the hostess, who was about to seat another couple. It was Saturday morning and the entryway to the restaurant was crowded with young urban professionals. Most were couples outfitted in yuppie uniforms from J Crew or American Eagle Outfitters or Texas A&M paraphernalia.

"Oh, I apologize," the girl said and looked down at the list.

"Paige, calm down."

"I'm not normally a complainer, but I'm really hungry this morning. If it wasn't for the cinnamon coffee . . ."

"And the Texas-size breakfast burritos, and the hot fried apples . . ."

". . . all for under six bucks," they said in unison and clasped pinkies.

"Okay, alright, we aren't going anywhere."

"Give her the benefit of the doubt. This place is always packed at this time."

"I guess I need to be a little empathetic."

They soon slid into the cushioned seats of a booth. After perusing the menus briefly, they placed their orders.

"So, I want you to start from the beginning and go to the end—tell me *everything*. Don't leave out any details. But before you start, just let me tell you this one thing."

"Why do you always do that? Ask me to start talking and then cut me off!"

Paige waved her hand. "I'm gonna work on that. But girl, I've been having these dreams lately. It's like the more time I've been spending in prayer, the more of these serious dreams I'm having. I had one about a student of mine. The Lord had put it on my heart to pray for him a long time ago, because I thought he was involved in some kind of gang activity. Well, in my dream, I saw his face and all I could see was a spray of bullets. I prayed for God to protect him. The next week in school he came to me after class and told me he had just missed getting caught up in some gang violence. One of his friends had gotten shot. He said it could have been him, but for some reason he'd changed his mind and stayed in that night."

"Wow. That's deep."

"Yeah, that's not all. I've been having this other recurring dream. So far all I've been able to make out is glass and rain. Each time the dream is a little longer."

"Hmmm . . . so now you're Miss Cleo," Summer said as she leaned back and smiled.

"Oh, so you got jokes! This is serious. Alright, then, if I have a dream about you, see if I tell your behind."

"Okay, I'm sorry, girl. Seriously, maybe your dreams have some kind of spiritual meaning. I've never heard you talk about them before," Summer said as she picked up the menu.

"Like I said, I only have them when I've been praying hard." Paige shrugged. "I don't know, maybe it's nothing. Anyway, so where are the pictures?"

"Girl, I forgot them. So that means you need to come to the house."

"I can't believe you. Anything to get me to visit. I'm still thinking about how beautiful the wedding was. I think everyone had a great time," Paige said.

"Yeah, I couldn't believe how great everything turned out. My sister even behaved. Well, sort of. I've seen worse."

Paige's mouth twisted a bit.

"What's that look for?"

"Oh, nothing. Speaking of your sister, what's up with her and Quinton?"

"I really don't know. I'm staying out of it. But there is something that happened between Misa and me in New Orleans that I didn't mention."

"What?" Paige said as she leaned forward.

"Well, my sister sort of apologized about that night in the guesthouse."

"What do you mean, 'sort of apologized'?"

"When I went to visit the cemetery, she showed up there. We started to talk. For the first time, she opened up. She said she loved me."

"For real? That's definitely a breakthrough. I'm glad that y'all talked. It's about time."

"You have to understand, Paige, you and I have taken time out to deal with our hurts and pain. Some people aren't delivered from their past because they are in denial. It wasn't until Mother passed away that I realized I had some serious baggage. Remember? This is a start. At least she's beginning to change a bit is some ways."

"Yeah, in *some* ways."

"What do you mean by that?"

Should I or shouldn't I? Then her words poured out like water from a hydrant. "Summer, this is just killing me . . . I have to tell you. Sunday after the brunch, when I was taking some of the gifts to the guesthouse . . . I . . ."

"What? Whatever it is, Paige, I can handle it. Just say it!"

"Well, umm, Misa and Quinton got busy behind the guesthouse after the brunch. I mean for real—R. Kelly–style bump and grind, girl." She let out a huge breath of air.

"What?"

"Yes. They were workin' it out," Paige said, snapping her finger and moving her arm in a zigzag motion.

"Okay, Paige, I got the picture." She paused and closed her eyes for a second. "In broad daylight?"

"Yep."

"Misa's had these episodes since she was a teenager. They say bipolar disorder sometimes affects a person's sexual behavior. I don't know. At the gravesite I saw this other side of her. She was so mellow, even vulnerable. We prayed together," Summer said as her eyes looked away from Paige's face.

"Well, I guess you can be vulnerable and freaky at the same time. It doesn't mean she wasn't sincere."

"Paige . . . please. I have to admit, it is a bit embarrassing to the family. We'll just believe and ask God to move in *every* area of her life, before she catches something," Summer said before sipping her coffee.

"Yeah, Misa is a pain, but I can still lift a sister up in prayer . . ."

"Gee thanks, Paige. You certainly have a way with words."

Contrary to what Summer promised, she decided she was going to start unpacking and fixing things up before Evan made it home. She still wasn't going to let him off the hook. Boxes were everywhere. She was still waiting on some items shipped from New Orleans, but she had more than enough to keep her busy. She looked at the room that reflected months of the painstaking house-building project. She was definitely satisfied with the color schemes, carpet, and house design and felt glad that the whole process was over.

Summer had changed into her T-shirt, shorts, and baseball cap and was ready to go. She turned on some music to get her juices flowing. The lyrics of Kierra Sheard's song were blasting: "You don't know . . . what the Lord has done for me." The beat sounded more like an R&B cut rather than gospel. The bass pounded her new floors, filling the air of the half-empty house. She moved her hips as she sprayed the polish and dusted a bookcase shelf.

She started thinking about her sister and realized that she was getting more excited that she was moving to Houston. She knew God had a hand in this. It would be their first time living in the same city in fourteen years.

Summer felt at one time that God wasn't hearing any of her prayers. It was like she was standing at the wall of Jericho, yelling, beating, screaming at it to fall down flat. Now she could see God's hand moving. All these changes were happening at once.

About two years ago she gave up trying to make things happen. Before, fasting to the point of dehydration and getting up in the middle of the night to pray had become regular activities. Finally she decided that if "change was gonna come," God was going to have to do it without her help. "Maybe He wanted it that way all along," she mumbled to herself. "But he could have told a sister sooner." She sucked her teeth, feeling a bit confused. On one hand, she knew she was supposed to pray consistently, but at the same time, "Let go and let God." *What's the difference between letting go and giving up? Lord, please show me*, she thought.

She made her way around to unpacking a few pictures. She traced the frame of her mother's photo with a white cloth as she thought about the few weeks before her death. It was right before the start of her sophomore year in college. She was supposed to have left for school a week earlier but had stayed longer because her mother wasn't feeling well.

At the time, they stayed near Dillard University. Summer loved that house too. It had plenty of trees. For her, the simple things meant a lot.

She and her mother had spent many days just sitting out on the porch or in the triangle park across the street. On some evenings, they'd watch the people go by while eating big bowls of ice cream.

She didn't realize at the time how special and sacred those moments were. They'd laugh, talk, and play jokes on each other. She loved to do her mother's hair, experimenting with different makeup and styles. As pretty as her mother was, her self-esteem had never seemed to be where it was supposed to be. Like two girlfriends, they'd often fall asleep watching television.

They'd talk about things they hadn't shared before. Her mother talked about her dreams to own a hair salon, making sure to add that she had no regret staying home and raising her children.

The talks would be sad at times. Somehow they'd always go back to her mother's childhood. That time with her mother was a special gift. Summer thought she was a great mom, despite her flaws. If somebody had told her she'd lose her soon after, Summer would've never believed it.

She tried to stop her mind from racing to that day, one of the most significant events of her life. It was the week of her parents' anniversary. Summer wanted to help her father pick out an extra-nice gift. Her mother was looking forward to the special day, but she hadn't been feeling her best. The medicine she was on was taking her in and out of moods.

Summer wanted to surprise her with a pair of diamond earrings. She and her dad went to the mall to pick them up. Before she left, she checked in on her mother.

"Mom, are you alright? We're just going to go to the mall for a little while. Do you need anything?" Summer asked.

"No, I'm just a little tired. I've been trying to take a nap but I can't seem to go to sleep. If I could just get to sleep, I'll be fine," she said, her voicing straining.

"Okay—do you want some water or something?"

"Yeah, that would be good. Just bring me a tall glass of water."

Summer returned with a large glass of water and checked the bed linen. She kissed her mom on the cheek. "I love you, Mom." She ran her fingers through her mother's hair, then walked out the door.

"I love you too, baby," Elizabeth said, her face turned away from Summer.

Once at the mall, Summer and her dad became separated for some reason. She finally found him over in the peanut section of a drugstore. She had picked up the gift, and soon they were en route back home. When they got to the house, she sprinted to the top of the steps with excitement.

"Mom?" she called. "Mom? Are you up?" She crept down the hall and cracked open the door to her mom and dad's bedroom. "Mom . . ." Summer felt a chill in her body as her voice trailed off. The next thing her father heard was a scream.

"Dad, Dad, please, come quick. Something's wrong," she said as she walked over to the bed.

"What, what's wrong?" her father said as he reached the doorway.

"It's Mom. She's not moving," Summer said as she touched her mother's face. *Cold. Very cold.*

Her father picked up the telephone immediately and called 911. In Summer's heart, she knew she was already gone. Her mother's eyes were open, and her body, well, just felt different. Still, she kept calling her mother's name. She tried to perform CPR, to no avail.

The paramedics came with all their equipment. Summer moved to the corner to watch what she felt was a scene from a movie. She watched them take her, lifeless, still hooked up as if there were hope. Her father left with them. He insisted Summer stay, thinking it would shield her from the unpredictable outcome. He commanded her to call Hannah and her aunts so she wouldn't be there alone. She just waited and prayed. He returned home with no words, holding his wife's things in a clear plastic bag. Summer relieved him of the burden of speaking as she turned and walked away.

The hardest part was telling Misa. "They said accidental overdose . . ."

Summer cringed at the memory. She snapped into reality as a

vase she'd removed from a box crashed and splattered into tiny pieces of broken glass across the floor.

"Honey, are you alright?" Evan said. He was walking through the doorway.

She just stood there staring at the glass. "I shouldn't have been gone so long. We could have saved her. She was cold and alone . . ." Summer said, staring at the tiny glass pieces.

He stopped in his tracks. "Baby, what are you talking about?"

"Mom . . . I . . ."

He walked over slowly, recognizing the time and place she was in. He grabbed her arm, carefully guiding her around the broken glass. It had been a while since she'd been like this. She apologized to him in the voice of a repentant child. He embraced her. She felt weak, like she'd let him down. Instinctively, with a gentle touch and tender kisses, he assured her that everything would be okay.

University Blues

"Not this again," she said. It was late afternoon when Paige walked into the dorm room. She went to the window and yanked the shade up, letting the sun cut through the darkness.

"Summer. Summer!" She dropped her backpack on the floor and sat on Summer's bed. She poked at her roommate's body through the covers, finally getting a response.

"What? Leave me alone," Summer's muffled voice said through the blanket.

Paige took a deep breath. "Did you go to class today?"

"None of your business."

Paige pulled the covers back and yanked at Summer's arm until she sat up.

"Paige, would you leave me alone! I'm fine. I'm just tired."

"Tired from what? Summer, this has got to stop. All you do is come in and get in the bed after you go to class. Excuse me, that's when you go to class. One thing I can say, you are not doing fine! Summer look at me."

"Yes, I'm paying attention," she said with a yawn.

"I understand you had a big loss this year. I've heard the tears almost every night. I can't even begin to understand how you feel, but I think you need some help. I asked you if you should have taken some time off and you insisted you should just come back to school after your mom died. But . . . maybe you should take some time off to get yourself together."

"Paige, I made a commitment to finish school. My grades are not suffering. Just because I don't want to go to every Kappa party doesn't mean that I'm having problems. This is just my way of dealing with losing her," she said quietly. She looked around her room plastered with Southern University regalia, Greek party flyers, and pictures of relatives on her bulletin board. "My dad tried to get me to take time off too, but I probably would have gone crazy, Paige. This was the best thing for me."

"Think so? Summer, you have no social life. I have all kinds of guys asking about you. We were supposed to be Kappa Sweethearts together. You missed the bomb homecoming, and all you do is study and sleep! I'm really worried about you."

"Paige, I know you care." Summer felt hunger pangs in her stomach. "I have to admit, I'm still grieving in a big way." The tears started to fall again. "I lost a major part of me, and it doesn't seem like anything makes me feel any better. I feel okay for a while, then I seem to slip back into this place of darkness, and I'm losing so much weight." She paused and rubbed her hands together. "Seriously, Paige, I'm worried about me too. I'm scared."

Paige grabbed her hand and sat quietly for a minute. "Have you been to the church counselor?"

"Yeah, but Paige, I think it's a little deeper than that," Summer said as she brushed the hair back from her face; her tossing and turning had loosened it from her fabric band.

"Well, I don't want to make you feel worse, but you know depression runs in your family . . . sort of like a generational curse."

"Now you sound like Hannah. She's been a one-woman crusade against anything she even thinks would have a negative effect on the family."

"Yeah, what's up with that? But it is a spiritual thing. Whatever you want to call it, I guess we're all threatened in a way by things that have been passed down through the bloodline. She may go to the extreme, but she means well."

"I hear you." Summer got off the bed and walked to the small kitchen. She reached in the cabinet and grabbed a package of instant noodles. "On second thought . . ." she said as she imagined a New Orleans po'boy melting in her mouth. "I think I'm gonna take a trip home." She put the plastic package back into the cabinet.

"It's Friday. You're gonna miss the Omega party. You're going to force me to hang out with Rachael McCoy. You know she thinks it's all about her, and whenever we go to a party together she's always blocking. Don't let me mention how messy she is. Oh, and there's a rumor of a panty raid going down tonight."

"Paige, please. I don't know any woman who has ever been a threat to you, much less Rachael McCoy with her overarched eyebrows. Besides, if you hit every frat party, you can kiss pledging goodbye."

"I'll be alright, but back to you, miss. I can't be praying for your behind anymore. I got my own prayer requests I need to work on. So I need you to promise me one thing."

Summer had moved toward her closet and pulled out her overnight bag. She looked at Paige and paused before dropping her clothes into the bag.

"I want you to see the campus psychiatrist," Paige said and braced herself for the response.

Summer hesitated before looking Paige in the eye. "A psychiatrist?"

"Just hear me out," Paige said, and raised her hands to halt further objection. "Summer, here's a news flash: you're not doing such a good job on your own. Nobody has to know you're going to a shrink . . . I mean, psychiatrist. Just go one time, and if you don't feel like it will help, don't go back again. Her name is Dr. Crawford. I heard she was a really together sister . . . a Southern alum." She reached into her pocket and handed Summer a bent-up business card.

"Hmmm." Summer took the card and studied it. "You've had this for a while, huh?"

Paige shrugged.

"I'll think about it while I'm home."

"You sure I can't talk you into staying?" Paige grabbed her shoulders.

"Somehow the thought of having my underwear drawer raided doesn't compare to my grandmother's seafood bisque, some boudin, and homemade cheesecake."

Paige grabbed Summer and hugged her. "I love you, girl."

"I love you too."

The Miseducation of Misa

Misa loved the ultramodern plush loft her Realtor found. It was located near the Rice Village area, not too far from her favorite boutiques and the Galleria Mall. She was amazed at how much Houston had changed. It had become so much trendier, and she loved how they'd built up downtown.

For the most part, she was settled in. But she still had to call and arrange a regular visit from a maid service. Misa vowed not to do her own cleaning ever since she had had to participate in Hannah's "house blessings." Regardless of age, the entire family would participate in this housecleaning ritual, which was truly a "cleansing of the spirits." Everything was stripped, washed, disinfected, prayed over, and anointed.

"When I have my own place, I swear I will have a maid," she'd say to her cousins. As soon as she was able, she'd kept her word.

She had a couple friends who were in the business from the area and a few bookings through late fall. Her modeling assignments were dwindling, and she was contemplating her next career move. She was thinking about opening a restaurant or starting a fashion line. And one of her friends had a possible hookup for a fashion correspondent spot at a network. Yet she was in no rush. She had a decent supply of money and could be comfortable for a while.

She decided to host a small party in a couple of weeks for her own birthday. It would be a sort of housewarming event too. She would ask Quinton to invite some of his friends. The rest would be model industry people, some people she met at an upscale Houston club one night, and a couple of her friends from New York who would fly in. She expected her sister to come, but she knew she wouldn't be there long. She and Evan definitely weren't party animals. Neither one of them drank alcohol. Plus, she wanted to celebrate in grand Misa style without being judged.

She did respect and admire Evan and Summer's relationship. Her sister seemed so safe and at ease with Evan. Misa saw so many relationships that were the opposite. People were shacking up, having babies, committing adultery—but her sister's marriage was different, in a positive way. She believed they were definitely a minority.

Misa couldn't understand why she got bored with men so easily. It was hard for her to determine who liked her for the real Misa. Most people were caught up in Misa the model. Sometimes they'd hang out with her because of her car or her perceived monetary status. How would she ever know who was legitimate? She wanted people to see just plain old Misa.

The doorbell rang. She asked who it was and she heard Quinton's voice through the intercom. He was sweet but starting to get on her nerves. She hadn't been in Houston long. She wanted to meet other potential men in the city.

"Hey, baby, what do you have planned today?" he said. His heavy footsteps caused her floor to vibrate as he walked in.

"Well, I was going to go shopping . . . *alone*."

"Why are you being so cold?" he said as he reached for her waist.

She freed herself from his grip. "I'm just kidding. I'm trying to plan a get-together for my birthday."

"Oh, I made plans to take you somewhere," he said, and sat on her couch.

"Well, that was nice, but did you ask me if I had any birthday plans?"

"No, I just assumed."

"Please don't assume. You know what they say happens when you assume, right?"

"Okay, don't trip. You need help planning?"

"Maybe just a little. I need to know where the best party supply stores are. I need a bartender, you know, stuff like that."

"Gotcha. Anyway, baby, you can make anything look good. I don't get a kiss today?" he said as he scanned her body. He eyed the wife-beater that she'd knotted to expose her flat stomach. He pulled her toward him by the waist of her Seven jeans as he licked his lips.

"Flattery will get you everywhere." She positioned herself on his lap and kissed him. She still couldn't resist his boyish smile and manly chest. His sheriff's uniform didn't hurt either.

"Mmm! You make me so weak. You know that, don't you?" he

said, rubbing her thigh with his large hand. His other hand rested on her smooth stomach.

Her eyes narrowed and focused on his. "Yeah, I know," she said in a self-assured whisper.

"Are you almost ready?" Summer yelled as she stepped inside Paige's townhouse.

"I'm ready. You know it doesn't take me long."

She thought Paige looked good in her black slacks and satin camisole. Summer decided she wanted to be comfortable in capri pants and kimono-style silk top. They walked out to where Evan was waiting in the car.

"So, who's coming to this party? Your sister hasn't been in town that long. It's only been two and a half months," Paige said as she climbed into the backseat.

"Well, we all know Misa is not an ordinary person. It didn't take her long to hook up with 'the beautiful people.' "

"*Please*, Evan," Summer said.

"So I heard she and Quinton have been kickin' it pretty strong," Paige added, fishing for details.

"Yeah, they've been hanging pretty tight. I told my boy to be careful. But I think he's sprung in the worst way."

When they reached the top of Misa's street they saw a line of luxury cars. Summer already knew they weren't going to stay very long. Besides, they had to go to the early service tomorrow.

They heard noise before they even got to the door. All three huddled on the porch as Evan pressed the buzzer. Misa herself answered.

"Hey! Everybody! This is my baby sister and her husband,

Evan. Oh, and this is Paige," she yelled as they came through the door.

Summer could tell she had already started the party. Her sister looked gorgeous as always in a white halter top and matching skirt that hung slightly below her waist. The outfit exposed her taut stomach, and accented her curves. Her tousled hair was parted in the middle and hung past her shoulders with a large yellow flower on one side. It looked as though a professional had applied her makeup. She finished the look with bronze high-heeled sandals. She planted her glossy lips on Summer's cheeks and hugged Evan. She even gave Paige a hug. Summer knew she had to be feeling good.

That's ridiculous. Not an ounce of fat. Paige suddenly remembered the body shaper she'd slipped on to get a little "contour" for her outfit. *Life is just unfair.*

"Sweetie, I got something just for you," Misa said while moving her hips to the music.

"What?" Summer replied, scanning the colorful characters in the room.

"A batch of nonalcoholic margaritas. There's the machine over there."

"Thanks."

The three of them navigated the crowd, an eclectic mix of people, to an open space near the metal staircase. Evan wandered off and caught up with Quinton. The girls had decided they were going to keep each other company.

"Where's the food?" Paige asked.

"I knew it was coming."

"You know that's the only reason I'm here, especially since it's catered. I'm going to leave here and watch *Drumline*."

"Paige, how many times have you seen that movie? It's either that or *Sparkle*. I really worry about you sometimes."

"I can't help it if I know how to entertain myself."

"Hey, what's up, y'all?"

"Hey, Quinton," Paige said in a monotone voice.

"Well, I was about to tell you that you looked nice. But with that foul attitude, forget it."

"I love you too, Quinton."

After sitting and chatting for about a minute, Summer and Paige decided they were going to circulate. People weren't really dancing. It wasn't that kind of party. But folks were loud and sociable. It was a strange mixture of people. Some looked very sophisticated, others artsy. There were also a few pro athletes, and some that looked like hip-hop artists.

"Girl, you look good. You need to back that thang up."

"Excuse me?" Paige said as she whipped her head around.

The guy smiled at her, exposing two very bright gold teeth.

Paige gritted her teeth in return and walked off.

"Don't say a word, Summer," she warned as she lifted her finger.

"Well, you know you are the platinum tooth magnet."

"Let's just keep moving to the food."

The longer Summer stayed, the more disgusted she got. The people grew louder, looser, and stranger. Paige was content for the moment, sampling the buffet. Evan seemed like he was having a good time cutting up with his boys. *Is he really comfortable in all this?* she thought.

Summer finally caught Evan on his way to the restroom.

"How much longer are we going to be here?" Summer asked.

"You're not having a good time? I know this isn't your crowd, but I thought you wanted to spend time with your sister."

She placed her hand on her hip and frowned. "This isn't exactly what I had in mind."

"Oh, well . . . just let me know when you're ready. It's eleven now."

"How about eleven-thirty? We have to get up early, remember?"

"Will you be right here?" Evan asked.

"Probably. Don't worry. I'll hunt you down in exactly thirty minutes."

Summer thought how this crowd looked like the one she'd been in the night of the incident. She was getting very anxious. She should have told Evan she was ready to go then. Misa probably didn't know half these people. It was like an open house. She saw Quinton walk by and grabbed his arm.

"Hey, Summer, what's up? Are you having a good time?"

"Yeah, great. Anyway, we are going to be leaving soon, so can you just keep an eye out for my sister? I don't know many of these people. I think you know what I'm saying."

"Your sister can handle anything, but I feel you. I'll be here until it shuts down. Besides, we have security in here. It's *all* good. Summer, just loosen up a little."

"Thanks, but this is about as 'loose' as I'm gonna get," she said with her arms folded, looking around.

She decided to go upstairs to the restroom before she left. In the midst of her trek, she took a brief detour to the patio to get some air. There were fewer people up there. She walked to the rail and heard some people around the corner. She saw that they were in the hot tub, just having a ball. She couldn't tell if they had swimsuits on or not because there wasn't a strap in sight. *Oh, that is so nasty*. Summer turned around and bolted downstairs.

"Hey, sis, are you ready to go already?"

"Do you know there are people in your hot tub, maybe even naked? It is getting out of control in here!" Summer waved her hands, then let them fall to her sides in exaggeration.

"Slow down, girl—it's a party. This is how we do it on the East Coast. Just relax, get the stick out your—"

"I'm sorry, it's just time for me to go. Happy Birthday, sis. I know you'll enjoy the rest of your night," Summer uttered, cutting her off. She then pecked her sister on the cheek and bolted toward the kitchen. Her stomach turned as the whole scenario reminded her of that night in New York.

"Wait," Misa said as some man Summer never saw before grabbed Misa's waist.

"Evan, let's go." She snatched Paige from the buffet table.

"Wait, I'm going to just wrap this plate up with some foil. I can have this for lunch tomorrow."

"Just meet us out in the car."

"Okay, I'll be there in just a second."

Paige finally made her way to her car. "Girl, where do you put all that food? I swear, the way you eat, you should be at least two sizes bigger than you are," Summer said.

Paige ignored her and continued snacking on her chicken fingers. She resolved to tell Summer about herself tomorrow, but reverently, since it would be Sunday, after all. The three of them remained in silence for the rest of the ride home.

The Velvet Rope

Summer sat on Misa's bed, watching her get ready. She couldn't believe she was finally able to visit. Her parents said when she turned eighteen she could fly to New York and stay with her sister for a weekend. She watched as Misa and her roommate, Bella, another model, bounced around the room, trying on outfits, waving the flatiron, and applying layers of makeup.

This was her second day in the city. So far it was a bit of a letdown—too crowded, busy, expensive, and noisy. Yet Summer couldn't help feeling some excitement rising in her belly. She hadn't had a chance to do all she wanted, but they'd managed a trip to the Statue of Liberty and the Empire State Building, as well as lunch at Tavern on the Green.

Misa had done most of the shopping and made sure Summer had an outfit and makeup for her first nightclub experience.

She was waiting her turn to get her makeup done since all she generally used was lip gloss and a little blush. In the meantime, Summer got up and wandered around the multicolored loft filled with African art, brown leather upholstery, coffee-table books, and posters from around the world. Summer still couldn't understand why Misa needed a roommate with all the money she was making. She walked toward the window, taking in the amber and red lights from all the buildings.

"Summer, come on so I can do your makeup." She walked back to the bedroom and sat in her sister's vanity chair. She could barely recognize Misa with her hair wild and her face sparkling from bronzing powder. Her embellished jeans sat way below her waist, and on her feet were three-inch Manolos that Misa had debated wearing for at least an hour.

"Are you sure I'm going to be able to get in? I don't look twenty-one and I don't have an ID," Summer said as she felt the sponge spreading liquid makeup over her face.

"Summer, keep still and try not to talk. I told you, we won't have a problem. I know the owner of the club. You're going to have your first VIP experience. I promise you'll be fine."

Summer still felt a little nervous, not knowing what to expect. "As long as you don't leave me, I'll be okay."

In the cab ride to the club, Summer almost gagged at the amount of perfume they all had on. She was quiet as Misa and Bella went on about modeling assignments, their outfits, and what celebrities would be at the club. Summer was still trying to get used to the makeup and hair, which had been flatironed bone straight. She had on a ton of eyeshadow, Mac lipstick and gloss, and an outfit—a very tight top and miniskirt—she wouldn't be seen dead in at home. Her other concern was *figuring out how to balance herself on the metallic heels Misa had made her wear.*

They jumped out of the cab and a large man greeted and hugged Misa and Bella in his massive arms. He was drenched in jewelry and had a bald head.

"Benjy!" they both yelled. Summer already felt like an outcast.

"Oh, this is my sister, Summer. She's visiting with me for the weekend."

Summer stood still and tried not to look directly into his eyes.

"Cute," he said. He leaned over and whispered something in Misa's ear.

He led them to the front of the line, through the mass of people, and into the VIP area. Summer almost lost them twice and stumbled a bit before they got there. All she wanted to do was sit down. They finally reached an area with a curtain. They sat in white leather chairs, and soon drinks arrived at the table. Summer noticed Misa and Bella were laughing and enjoying themselves, but she felt completely out of her element. Before she knew it, some green concoction in a glass was put in front of her. Everyone else had a glass and started sipping. She hesitantly lifted the drink as she looked at Misa. Misa nodded her head, then went back to talking and laughing. "Why not?" Summer said as she tasted the sour apple drink. "Not as bad as I thought." By the time she finished it, she actually liked it much better.

For the next hour, all kinds of people in shimmer and shades came and went. She thought that they'd go out and join the rest of the people or dance, but none of that happened. Then a tall White man came into the club with a suit and Misa jumped up. Before Summer could speak, she and Bella were leaving the area.

"Benjy, keep an eye on Summer. We'll be right back."

Summer's eyes begged for her not to leave, but she didn't want to spoil Misa's fun by saying anything. She sat there quietly and flashed a fake smile to Benjy. In a few minutes, Misa returned. As Summer watched her talk, she noticed that Misa was constantly rubbing her nose and sniffing. Finally another guy joined the party. Summer was about to tell Misa she was ready to go, but the guy pulled Summer up to go dance. He seemed nice. And he put his arm around Summer. He was a thin guy who looked just a little older than she was, and, wearing all black, he was dressed a bit more conservatively than the rest of the crew.

They danced as well as they could considering how crowded the floor was. Summer thought this actually worked to her advantage since she wasn't sure what the latest dance was. After about three songs she was feeling a little dizzy and wanted to sit down. She looked around and neither Misa nor Bella was to be found. Instead of the VIP area, the man then led her to another curtained section. By this time the drink was kicking in and all she wanted to do was lie down. This area had a white leather couch, and the young man seemed to know the staff there well. He waved his hand then mouthed something as they walked in.

"Are you okay?" he said.

Summer put her hand over her forehead. "Yeah, I think so. I just need to sit down." She felt her forehead was moist with sweat.

As she sat on the couch, the man's eyes moved from her face down to her chest, which was poking out from beneath her low-cut top. Her body shifted and she crossed her arms over her chest.

"It's okay," he said as he removed her arms. "You can relax." He started fidgeting. Then he brushed her hair with his finger and moved in to kiss her.

"What are you doing? Where's my sister?" she said as she put her hands up.

She could still hear a little of the music, and she wished she were back on the dance floor.

"It's going to be okay—she trusts me. I told her I would look out for you. It's okay. It's okay."

Before Summer could respond, he kissed her. Despite her struggles he forced her down on the couch. When she tried to move, he placed his hand over her neck and pulled her top down, exposing her chest. She tried to scream but nothing came out. The panic in her eyes soon turned to a daze. She gasped for air then tried to kick him. His once-friendly eyes soon were filled with rage. Before she knew it, his pants were halfway down and her skirt above her waist. He closed his eyes, releasing sounds amid the faint beat of the music. "Shh, shhh . . ." he said as he held one hand over her mouth. She fixed her eyes on the ceiling, silently wondering what had happened to Misa . . . and God.

My Sister's Keeper

Summer sat in her cushioned seat, waiting for the choir to get started. To her, church was starting to feel like a routine. She didn't know what it was, but lately she'd felt disconnected. The scriptures didn't come to life for her, and she was tired of the fashion show.

She couldn't put her finger on it, but something had changed. *Maybe I'm the one that's changing*, she thought. Before they'd gotten married, she and Evan had decided that this would be their church home. But she was starting to feel as if God was moving her on to another church. She inched closer to Evan and he grabbed her hand.

As the pastor was speaking, all she could think of was Misa. Part of her felt like a failure.

She was a born-again, committed Christian who couldn't get a breakthrough for her own sister. She imagined Misa at home with a hangover. She tried not to get angry, but she felt her sister needed to settle down a little. To her life was just one big party. Perhaps that was fine for the twenties, but Misa was in her thirties.

She refocused on the sermon. "If any man be in Christ, he is a new creation. Old things are passed away, and all things become new. We have to forget the former things and move on," her pastor said poetically as he adjusted his glasses.

Lord, why do You always make things sound so simple? He acts like we can just wake up and be instantly restored. Sometimes it's a painstaking process. Her mind drifted to what her sister might be doing now. She probably was still in bed. Summer decided she'd stop by after church. *On second thought, I'd better call,* she decided, not knowing what to expect if she went by there.

She sighed in response to her disappointment at the speed with which God was repairing their relationship. Perhaps she was expecting a little too much too soon. She just had to be patient, an area she still needed to work on. *God is going to finish what He started.* Yet from the looks of things, opposite forces were working just as hard as God was.

Later, she called Misa and let the telephone ring several times. Summer hung up and called again about ten minutes later. *She's got to be up by now—it's three o'clock.* She knew her sister wasn't thinking about church on this particular day. Besides, Misa had been to church only once since she came to Houston. The first time her sister came, everyone had just stared at her. It was very distracting. Her face was somewhat familiar. She wasn't so famous that people would automatically recognize her, but she'd been in enough national ad campaigns that people would know they'd seen her somewhere.

Somehow, a note was sent to the pastor, letting him know that she was a famous model. He gave her a special recognition during the visitors' welcome. Afterward, people approached Misa and soon a small huddle was around her. It was weird. They didn't even know her. They just wanted to be near someone they thought was beautiful and rich. It didn't matter that her spirit was barren.

Summer dialed her sister's number once more.

"Hello?"

Finally, an answer. But it's a man's voice. "Can I speak to Misa?"

Summer heard a bunch of noise, voices, and then a click. She looked at the phone and sighed. She dialed again.

"Yeah?"

"Can I speak to Misa?" she huffed.

"Okay, alright. Who is this?"

"This is Summer, her sister. *Who is this?*"

"This is Van. I'll get her for you." At least one minute went by. *Who in the heck is Van?*

"Hello?" a raspy voice said on the other end of the telephone.

"Misa, this is Summer."

"I know who this is. Girl, you missed a good party. It didn't end until eleven o'clock this morning."

"Who *is* Van?" Summer questioned.

"Some guy that came with one of Quinton's friends."

"Where's Quinton?"

"He's around here somewhere. What is this? Twenty questions? You need to ease up. Even your husband knows how to relax a little. He enjoyed himself last night. Unlike you, the *holy patrol*."

"Well, my husband just gets along with anyone. He's polite and tries to enjoy whatever he does within reason. I'm sorry if life to me isn't just one big party after the next!"

"What are you trying to say? I don't take things seriously?"

"Well if the shoe fits, put that mug on and lace it up," Summer quipped.

"Summer, I have a major headache. Were you calling to wish me happy birthday, or say something positive? Otherwise, I don't need to hear this whining and complaining BS this morning."

"It's not morning."

"I'll holler at you later," Misa said and hung up.

"The holy patrol. Now *that* was a good one! I can't believe her," Summer said as she slammed the phone down. She'd laugh if she weren't so pissed off.

A Man's Man

Misa was glad they'd finally reached cruising altitude. She pushed her button to recline her seat so she could just relax. The male flight attendant had been extra attentive. She couldn't figure out if he recognized her or was just trying to pick her up. For now, she wished he'd just do his job.

She was glad Van was going to meet her at the airport with Diva. St. Lucia was beautiful, but hard to enjoy alone. Her friends used to really envy her. They thought she had the greatest job in the world. She couldn't complain too much: she traveled all over the world, partied with the best, made and spent lots of money. Yet it was all getting old.

Although she'd meet lots of men and other

models on these trips, it was still hard to build solid relationships. She simply moved around too much. Her temper and controlling ways would ruin her chances for healthy relationships anyway. She wasn't sure she even wanted one, but she did want some type of stability in her life.

She leaned back, resting in the comfort of her accomplishments and proud that she had been able to escape any major trouble. She'd had plenty of close calls. She experimented with drugs a little, had several one-night stands and more than her share of island heartthrobs. Fortunately she never became addicted or contracted any diseases, despite having unprotected sex. *Somebody had to be praying for me.*

Currently her fix was a dose of Prozac every now and then to mellow her out. She'd been taking these for the past few months. She'd tried the praying for peace thing, like Summer said, but grew impatient waiting for God to put her to sleep. She figured that, for now, her manufactured peace was just as good.

Misa was glad she remembered to bring her Pashmina shawl, because it was getting very cool on the plane. Normally she wouldn't dress up for the plane ride. She'd wear her favorite blue jeans, a T-shirt, and a baseball cap. But since Van was coming to the airport, she'd figured she'd make an effort to look good, so she wore a black sleeveless dress. It fit every curve and had a deep plunging neckline, à la Jennifer Lopez. She added a bronze cuff bracelet and let her hair hang loose. It felt good against her back. She wore high sandals with straps that wrapped around her ankles. She fingered her gold pendant and adjusted her dress.

She thought she could hang with Van. They'd instantly hit it off at the party and had a good time ever since. He was full of life and such a manly man. Not like Quinton, who was cool but starting to turn soft on her. He was definitely getting too clingy. She had to let him go. She was particularly turned off when he called her up crying like a woman, asking, "How could you treat me this way?" Van was confident and knew how to take control. She liked that.

Misa was glad Van had a get-up-and-go attitude. Since he was self-employed, his schedule was flexible. They'd run up to Louisiana to the gambling boat on a moment's notice. They'd been to several clubs around town where he was well known. They were planning a trip to Vegas, then a ski trip after that. She knew things were moving fast, but that was her nature. She lived for the day.

She could hear her sister's sermon now. But she thought Summer planned too much. She was just too routine for her. Misa liked to have her fun. She was spontaneous. She worried about consequences later. She knew Summer didn't care for Van, because she never said much around him. Summer always got quiet around people she didn't like.

Her sister was going to have to get used to him. Misa liked him, and if she had her way, he would be around awhile. She was going to ask Van to move in soon. When he was there she didn't have to take the pills. She slept so peacefully. She felt protected, like he was her bodyguard.

Was Summer always wrong? No. Misa just thought she was a bit too self-righteous. *Everyone* sinned *every day*. She lived in an unrealistic world. She'd learn one day. One day her bubble was going to burst when she realized everyone, especially her own family, had skeletons.

Thanksgiving Present

"I can't believe you have me in this supermarket two days before Thanksgiving. Don't you know this is lethal?" Paige said as she grabbed a free sample of turkey a woman held in front of her.

Summer paused before dropping another onion in her plastic bag and placed her hand on her hip. "Look, this is my first time cooking Thanksgiving dinner. Give me a break . . . so I forgot a few things. Besides, you said you would help me," she whined.

"A few things? If you haven't noticed, Summer, your cart is full, *hon*. Look at this madhouse! These people are out of control. I just saw two women fighting over a can of cranberry sauce. I thought I was gonna have to go Jackie Chan on somebody."

"Paige, I am not going to move this basket until you repent for your lyin' tongue. You know you didn't see two women fighting over a can of cranberry sauce. Besides, you couldn't have anything more than a white belt. You quit karate lessons after a few weeks, remember?"

"Alright, I am exaggerating *just a little* about the cranberry sauce." She squeezed her thumb and forefinger together and squinted one eye. "However, for *your* information, I have a *special* white belt. It's *advanced*. Anyway, you have to admit, we've been in here just a little too long. It's after nine o'clock."

"Paige, in order to conserve my energy, I'll let you believe there is such a thing as an advanced white belt. There's no sense in complaining about how late it is. You're stuck here now. Let me see . . . go get me some raisins," Summer said while studying her shopping list.

Paige stopped in her tracks and raised her hand in front of Summer's face. "Hold up. What in the *world* are you putting raisins in?"

"The stuffing. I thought I'd try something different. Got this recipe out of a cookbook."

"Okay, you are my girl. You know that, right? I cannot, in good faith, allow you to put raisins in the stuffing. Cancel the raisins and just leave the stuffing up to me."

Summer lifted her finger toward Paige's face. "What was my *one* rule for this dinner?"

"I know, no criticism . . . but girl, if you cook some stuffing with raisins, your family will truly clown on you. Trust me on this one. Do you ever recall Hannah having raisins in her stuffing? *Ooh*, Italian sausage," Paige said as her eyes landed on another sample tray.

"Will you stop with the samples? I guess you have a point about the stuffing."

"I have to eat something. I told you I was hungry."

"Paige, with all those samples, you should have had a meal by now. Anyway, what are you planning to bring for the dinner?"

"What do you mean, 'bring'? My plan was to just grace you with my presence. Do you think Halle Berry brings a dish to people's houses for dinner? No, she just shows up looking all beautiful."

"Get a grip. I'm sure she can do something else besides look good. Anyway, I don't even know why I responded to that comment. Paige, I know your mama raised you better than that. You don't come empty-handed to anybody's house for Thanksgiving dinner. You need to bring more than yourself and those tired movies we've seen a hundred times before."

"I've updated my movie collection, thank you very much."

"Regardless, you need to bring something or take your *tired* butt over to your relatives'."

"You know I'm just playing. I'm bringin' some sweet potato pies and don't forget I'm gonna hook your stuffing up. Anyway, I couldn't miss your first Thanksgiving dinner. When's your dad getting in?"

"He'll be in tomorrow. Evan's going to get him in the afternoon. I'm so excited—this is the first time he'll get to see the house."

Paige continued pushing the cart through the mass of people as Summer studied her list. "So is Misa bringing Van?"

"Yeah," Summer mumbled under her breath.

"Don't sound so enthusiastic."

"I'm sure it's still going to be a nice time. I made up my mind. I'm gonna be nice to Van, despite what my spirit is telling me about him."

"You don't even know the man."

"I know enough. I know he's been spending a lot of time with

Misa. I know he says he's some type of sports/entertainment agent but no one seems to know who he represents. Something in my spirit is just telling me he isn't right. I usually have pretty good discernment."

"Summer, what do you think your sister did before she moved down here? You are doing it again. You get so absorbed in your family's issues you can't even think straight. Sometimes you just have to let things go. If you start talking to your sister about the 'Holy Spirit' this and the 'spirit' that, she's not going to respond. She won't have a clue as to what you are talking about. I've been walking with God long enough to know that you have to meet people where they're at. The more you talk things up, the harder it is for God to work."

Summer paused for a moment. "I guess you're right. I just want her to understand how much I love and care about her."

"I understand, but you can't control her life *and* yours. Misa's going to have to live her own life. You can't resolve everything for her. She'll connect with God in her own way. You have to be careful not to try to make things happen with your own hands."

"Yeah. *Whoa*—look at all these people," Summer remarked as she surveyed the checkout lines. "Well, I guess I better get comfortable."

"What else would you expect? I'll run and put gas in the car. Then I'll pull around the front after I finish so we can load up."

"That'll work. See ya soon."

Paige pulled into the gas station and grabbed the only vacant pump after waiting several minutes. She was determined to take advantage of the one-day gas special. She knew they'd hike the price back up several cents per gallon the next day. Then she recognized Misa's car parked on the side of the store, with her personalized "Misa" tags.

She figured the man sitting in the driver's seat must be Van.

However, the woman who climbed into the passenger's side was *not* Misa. She leaned over and kissed the man.

Well, I guess that isn't his sister. Why do I have to be the witness? Why am I always in the middle, God?

"Dad! Come in!" Summer shouted as she ran to the door. "Was your flight alright?" she asked as she grabbed his arm.

"Yeah, it was fine. It smells good in here. I heard you've been working hard tryin' to get this dinner together. The Hens would be proud. Are you sure you still don't want any help?" her father asked.

Thank God they decided not to come, she thought. "I might need a little help, Dad; we'll talk about that in a minute. Evan . . . Martin called. He said that he, Rodney, and Sam were coming over at about seven. You didn't inform me about this little gathering," she said as she pulled away from her father.

"I know, baby. I thought while you and Paige were cooking for tomorrow's dinner, me and the fellas would hang out, watch television and play some dominoes." Their lips smacked.

"Would they happen to be bringing any guests?" she asked, looking him directly in the eye.

"I don't know. I told them they were welcome to bring somebody. Babe, you know how I am. We always have an open door." He moved past her and placed his father-in-law's baggage on the floor.

"Since when?" Summer wiped flour off her hands with a dish towel. "I look a mess."

"No, you don't. You look beautiful."

"Yeah, uh-huh. Go ahead and smooth it over. I know before this night is done we're gonna have a house full of people." She snapped the dish towel on his behind.

"Baby, I promise we won't get in your way." He motioned her father toward the living room.

"Famous last words. I'll be in there to talk later. Paige should be over any minute. Make sure after you rest a minute you take Daddy's stuff upstairs and show him around."

"I guess I will do a little male bonding with my son-in-law. Make sure you call me if you need me. Oh, by the way, how's my girlfriend doing?"

"Daddy, if I didn't know any better I would think you and Paige had a thing for each other."

"Now, you know better than that." He winked. "That's my 'other daughter.' "

"Right. I'm going to keep my eye on you two."

Several hours later, the cooking festivities continued. The immediate area around the kitchen was warm from the heat of the oven and stove. Summer thought the aroma made her new house feel cozy and lived in. The "new home" aura was being transformed into a comfort zone. She now felt a family presence she'd remembered from childhood.

The inviting atmosphere made people feel welcome and relaxed. The living room was softly warmed with a pale yellow, sage, and gold–tone decor. A neutral sectional with generous soft cushions invited their guests to recline. Plants, photographs, and strategically placed candles accented the airy and slightly minimalist living room.

At Evan's invitation, his friends arrived early in the evening with their wives or dates. Paige played host as Summer took sporadic breaks to join the group. By this time, most of the cooking had been done to full effect. Summer was happy to be in the kitchen, slicing, stirring, and mixing on her marble countertops, surrounded by her stainless-steel appliances. The kitchen was generous and the island was perfect for preparing a large dinner. She was relieved Paige was there to help. The dinner was a much bigger project than Summer had expected. She was worn out already.

When she went back to prepare her last pie, she was close to her breaking point. She turned on the beater and it failed to start. She checked the plug, then stared at the mixture and wiggled the plug again. "Paige! Paige!" she yelled.

Paige bolted into the kitchen only to find Summer slumped over the island, sobbing.

"Summer, what's the matter, girl, are you okay?"

"You were right, girl. I can't do it. I'm a horrible wife. What was I thinking? I'm not Hannah or the Hens. I just can't do it anymore." Then when she stood up she spun around and knocked the flour bag on the floor. "Oh no . . ." she said and started crying harder.

"Summer." Paige tried to conceal her laugh.

"What?" Summer said with flour across her forehead.

"Girl, I think you need to rest. You've done a great job for your first Thanksgiving. Nobody is expecting it to be perfect. It's okay. Forget about the pie. I'll clean up. You go out there and relax with your husband."

Summer took a paper towel and dabbed her eyes. She saw her reflection in the kitchen window and started laughing.

Paige turned around and started laughing too. "You're gonna be alright. I promise, I won't tell anybody if you won't."

With slight aches in her body and a need to get a full night's sleep, Summer heard the CD player go to full blast. She knew what was coming.

"Summer, babe, c'mon. We're about to have karaoke," Evan said.

"Evan, this isn't Dave and Buster's. Our neighbors are going to put us out," she said as she walked into the living room.

Ignoring her, he pulled a folding chair to the middle of the floor, then pulled her waist until he sat her on his lap.

"I know you want to leave me . . . Ain't too proud to beg . . ." Evan sang with animation, serenading her. Everyone in the room's cheers coaxed them on. Summer just shook her head at her husband as he was engrossed in his Motown moment.

"Okay, I'm next," Paige said as she cleared her throat with all seriousness. "*Mi-mi-mi* . . ."

"Oh, brother," Summer said as she rolled her eyes. "I know you just did not pull out that old raggedy tape from your purse."

"Your tender smile gives me happy thoughts of you . . ." Paige sang with intense facial expressions as she moved her hips from side to side. She moved over to Summer's father and pointed as she gave him a sultry look and posed as she belted out "Hooked on Your Love" from the sound track to the movie *Sparkle*.

No one wanted to hurt Paige's feelings, but Summer finally had to snatch the microphone away from her before she launched into a fourth song for her miniconcert.

Summer's father ended with the finale, or what they thought was the finale. "You gotta be a special lady . . . and a very exciting girl . . ." The men got up, jumped behind him and added finger snaps as they stood in a line. The moved from side to side and raised their arms and spun around.

Summer shook her head. She hadn't even realized the doorbell was ringing. It was her Uncle Groovy. He didn't even say anything, but handed his bag to Paige and ran straight to the line of singing men.

Oh, Jesus, we will never get to bed tonight.

". . . Get down, Billy Brown!" Uncle Groovy said aloud. They had already bypassed that part of the song.

When the song was over, Summer started to pull the plug out of the machine.

"No, one more. You know I just got here and I've got to sing my song," Uncle Groovy insisted.

Although everyone was ready for *Showtime at the Apollo* to be over, they appeased him. "Okay, I want all the 'funky-delics' in the house." Unashamed of his protruding gut, he snapped his fingers and said, "One, two, three . . . Ain't gonna bump no more with no big fat woman. Ain't gonna bump no more with no big fat woman . . . C'mon, sing it wit me . . . no big fat woman, bump no more . . ."

"Okay, Uncle Groovy, we don't want to wear you out," Summer said as she patted his arm. "Anyway, I love y'all, but I'm tired. Whatever happens better be cleaned up or fixed before the morning," Summer warned as she walked up the stairs then collapsed on her bed.

Fried Turkey

Summer awoke, rolled over, and looked at the clock. "I slept too long. I still have so much to do!" She jumped up, put on her robe, and headed down the stairs. The aroma of her father's homemade biscuits and eggs quickly soothed her frustration.

Summer relished the moment. She enjoyed having her dad all to herself for a little while. She knew Misa would be over soon, and, well, who knew what would happen. Their dad hadn't met Van yet, and she couldn't figure how the whole scene would play out. Her eyes looked up at the stairs as she heard footsteps. She watched a sleepy-eyed Paige slowly creeping down the stairs. Part of her head scarf hung in her face, obstructing one eye. Her flowery grandma-like duster left something to be desired.

"*Ooh, girl*, you look rough. You could've at least taken your scarf off. I'm definitely gonna throw that duster away if I can get my hands on it."

"Forget you, Summer—I still look good . . . with or without a scarf. The duster is comfortable and it's not going anywhere. Besides, I smelled food. I didn't have time to worry about lookin' cute."

"I'm just playing. By the way, thanks for all your help last night."

"No problem. You did most of the work anyway. The table looks beautiful. Everything's going to taste great. It's your first Thanksgiving in your new house!" Paige said with excitement. They grabbed hands and chuckled like school-aged girls.

"Yeah, thanks to you and Dad, we were able to pull it together. This dinner *was* a bit much."

"I knew it was time to take over when the beater broke and—well, I'm not gonna go there."

Summer chuckled as they both followed their noses to the kitchen.

"Hey, Dad," Paige said to Summer's father as he turned away from the stove.

"Hey, how are my girls? Biscuits are in the oven, coffee is on, and fried apples are in the skillet . . . Yeah, I know, *I'm the man*," he said as he patted his chest.

Summer walked over and planted a kiss on his cheek. "Dad, you always spoil us! I can't believe you're up and dressed already." She noticed his starched khakis, red sweater, and loafers.

"You know only people from your generation like to stay in the bed all day. I've been up, read a little scripture, and even went for a little walk around the block. I had to check out the neighborhood. I bet I got more energy than the both of you put together."

She sat at the table, waiting for her father and anticipating her plate. "I'm not even gonna go there with you, Dad."

Hours later, Paige grabbed a piece of cornbread off the table and started to nibble. "What time's Misa coming over?"

"That's probably her now, and I *know* you're not eating my cornbread," Summer said, sneering at Paige on her way to answer the door.

"Hey, everybody. Happy Thanksgiving." Misa strolled in with Van on one arm and a brown bag in the other hand. Van held Diva's leash in his hand as the little dog pranced in behind them. "We brought the party favors since everybody is saved and sanctified in this house."

Here we go, Summer thought while her eyes inspected the couple. From the outside, Misa and Van looked like the couple of the year. They had on color coordinated outfits. Summer was trying to figure out how Misa was going to breathe in those leather pants after she ate all that Thanksgiving food. *She does look good, though*, Summer thought. She noticed how Misa's ankle-length sweater trimmed with a shawl collar accented her shapely frame. She figured Van's leather pants had to be custom made, with his big butt and very thick and muscular legs.

Summer discreetly held her nose. "Can you take that dog to the garage or the den? I really don't want it around the food."

"You just don't like my baby. *She's* not bothering anyone. I'd planned to take her there anyway. Don't worry, you know she's potty trained."

"Yeah, whatever."

Paige turned her head and whispered in Summer's ear, "Be nice."

Misa eyed Paige from head to toe before she spoke. "Look at

our Paige—what a cute outfit. They sure are making some cute clothes in plus sizes now."

Plus sizes!!? I wear a size twelve—okay, maybe fourteen, at the most . . . The only plus-size item on me is my foot, which I may have to put up her . . . Restraint, restraint. Be the bigger person. Be nice, be nice.

Paige turned away from Misa. "I'm sorry, we haven't had a chance to meet," Paige said and extended her hand to Van.

Misa tossed her thick hair and forced out an introduction. "Oh, Van, this is Paige, Summer's friend. Remember? I mentioned her. Yes, the sun *rises* and *sets* over Paige."

His baritone voice emerged from his bouncer-like body. "Nice to meet you."

That was him at the gas station. Too bad he's a buster. He's definitely fine. Paige's hand almost evaporated in his large grip. She noticed the diamond-encrusted watch on his left wrist and the diamond and platinum necklace around his neck. Fine, but too gaudy for her taste.

"Hey, hey. I thought that was my other beautiful daughter. Now I have all three of my girls here!" Their father emerged from the living room.

Paige and Summer both cringed, knowing his comment would stir up Misa's jealousy. "Hello, Father. You're looking well," she said with a loose embrace. "This is Van. Van, this is my father, Alfred Ledoux."

The two men shook hands. "Oh, nice to meet you. Well, Van, is it? I haven't heard much about you."

"Daddy, I never tell you about *any* of my relationships. You have me confused with Summer. You know she tells you everything."

Her father cleared his throat. He quickly shifted gears. "Well, Misa, I'll have to come visit your new place before I leave. I heard it was beautiful."

"You can come over tomorrow after Van and I clean up. We ran out so fast, I'm not sure what condition we left the place in."

Everyone paused, looked at one another, and tried to act as if they didn't know what that comment meant. Van appeared uneasy as he shifted his body slightly.

"Y'all go ahead and head into the living room. I have to, umm, check on the cornbread," Summer said as she glanced sideways at Paige.

"I'll help," Paige offered quickly, and followed her.

"Did she say when she and Van cleaned up? Am I hearing things?" Summer asked as she lifted the lid on her pot of greens. "I know she isn't living with him already. She barely knows him." She slammed the lid down.

"That's what it sounds like to me," Paige confirmed. She decided now really wasn't a good time to mention what she had seen at the gas station. *No need to add fuel to a raging fire.*

"What are we waiting on? I'm ready to eat," Evan whined from the living room couch.

Summer was circling her dining room table, making sure everything was in place. She was thankful for the china Misa had given her. "Uncle Groovy and Aunt Gerty haven't got back yet with the rest of the fried Cajun turkeys," she yelled back at Evan.

"Well, we have one turkey. We can start on that."

"No, that would be rude; they're on their way. You know they never answer their cell phone because they don't know how to use it. We can wait a few more minutes."

Paige came in and placed the butter dish on the table. She decided to pull out a chair and rest for a minute. "Girl, your Uncle Groovy is a trip."

"That he is, as long as he doesn't take off his shoes," Summer added.

"Why?"

"Girl, his feet smell like funky corn chips. I don't know how Aunt Gerty stands it."

"Don't talk about Uncle Groovy like that," Evan said as he passed through the dining room on the way to the kitchen.

"His feet do smell like corn chips," her father yelled from the living room.

"There's the doorbell. Y'all, please be quiet. That's probably him," Summer said.

"I don't believe it," Paige said as she looked through the peephole. "It's Quinton." *This should be interesting. Who needs* The Young and the Restless *when you have this?*

Everyone looked at Evan.

"Well, he didn't have anywhere to go, and . . ." Evan said as he shrugged his shoulders. "I didn't think it would hurt," he said in his most innocent voice. Summer just rolled her eyes at him.

"Hey, stranger," Paige said as he walked in.

"Hey, Happy Thanksgiving." Quinton replied as he eased through the doorway. He was caught slightly off-guard when he saw Misa with a date. He thought she might be there, but alone. He tried to play it off but instantly knew this was a bad idea.

"Happy Thanksgiving." Summer gave him a quick hug and kiss on the cheek.

"Here, I brought some napkins." Quinton handed her the plastic bag.

"Wow, you really went all out. Ha! I'm just kidding. At least you aren't like *some* people who brought their own plastic containers to take home leftovers," Summer said as she looked at Paige.

"Excuse me, but I don't plan on cookin' for the next few days. Unlike other people, I'm not going to use up your good dinnerware, trying to take a plate home. Just call me *extra* prepared."

"Just call her extra *greedy*," Misa mumbled under her breath.

"Hey, Misa. What's up, man," Quinton said, and shook Van's hand.

"Van, Quinton . . . Quinton, this is Van," Misa said, not looking at either of them.

"Well, we need to go on and eat," Summer's father said.

"Finally," Evan said after a deep breath. The doorbell rang again, and everyone collectively sighed.

"Fried turkey in the how-ow-ow-ow-ouse . . . fried turkey in the hiz-ouse," Uncle Groovy said as he walked in.

"Look, fool, put the turkey down before you drop it," his wife barked. "Hey, everybody. Sorry we're late, but your uncle got lost again."

"Uncle, you just came here last night. That's the third time you got lost. What's the problem?" Summer asked.

"The night is the night and the day is the day. I'm still the captain of my ship. I navigate through rough seas, calm seas . . . I don't need them Internet directions you gave me. I use instinct, see," he said, pointing to the corner of his eye.

"*What?*" Paige said.

"The sad part is, he doesn't even drink," Summer whispered to Paige. "Everybody, let's eat."

So far, so good—only the sound of forks scraping plates and an occasional belch. But then again, it's only fifteen minutes into the meal, Summer thought. Everyone was gathered around the table. There wasn't room for another plate with the spread of golden Cajun fried turkey, candied yams, biscuits, corn pudding, ham, mashed potatoes, collard greens, string beans, macaroni and cheese, corn, stuffing, and cranberry sauce.

"So, Misa, what brought you to Houston? We thought we'd never see you in this part of the country," Aunt Gerty said, reaching for the gravy.

"Well, I just decided I was tired of New York. It was time for a change."

"Oh, really? I could've sworn Summer told me you moved here because of some man," her Aunt Gerty said without looking up from her plate.

Lights, camera, action—the holiday drama has begun. Summer inhaled. Quinton shifted in his chair. Paige cleared her throat and grabbed another roll, and Van's eyes peered sideways at Misa.

"Oh, did she *really*?" Misa looked at Summer and sneered. "Well, for everyone's information, that was *not* the case. I moved to Houston because *I* wanted to. I have men falling at my feet all over the world. Do you think I would let some man I barely knew talk me into moving across the country? I think not. Misa runs Misa's life. This is exactly why I wanted to stay on the East Coast. Too much family *all up in my damn business.*" She glared at her sister.

Summer just sat there without comment. The trigger had been pulled. Just about anything she said would catapult them into a full-scale confrontation. Normally, it would have been a private war of words. But there were other potential casualties sitting around the table. So she decided to withdraw from retaliation.

Silence.

Summer tried to figure out what everyone was thinking as she scanned the faces around the room. She looked directly across the table. *Poor Quinton. How uncomfortable this must be for him.*

Quinton poured gravy over his turkey. *I can't believe Evan didn't tell me that this dude was going to be here. She knows good and dang well I was the one who got her to move to Houston. If you mess with fire, you get burnt.*

Paige slowly savored her macaroni and cheese. *Quinton should have hooked up with me, and he wouldn't be going through this. He needs some meat with his potatoes. What could he possibly do with that skinny thing?*

Evan inhaled his favorite sweet potatoes. *I wonder what time the game comes on tomorrow?*

Her Aunt Gerty had just shoved a spoonful of greens into her mouth. *I wonder what these collards are seasoned with, ham hocks or fatback?*

Her Uncle Groovy stared at the ceiling. *How could I have gotten lost again? Was it right on Mason or left at Barker Cypress?*

Her father spooned more mashed potatoes on his plate. *Why did my wife leave me here all by myself? Did Misa say she was living with Stan, Van . . . oh, whatever his name is?*

"Well, Stan, what type of work do you do?" Summer's father said, interrupting the silence.

"It's Van. I'm an agent," he said as he cleared his throat and sat up in his chair.

"Oh, really. So what kind of agent?" Summer asked.

"He's a sports and entertainment agent," Misa said.

Quinton jumped in. "So who are some of your clients, man?"

"Well, you wouldn't know them. I start looking at athletes in high school. I have more rap artists right now. A couple of them were at Misa's birthday party."

"Oh yeah, I remember. Those had to be the ones at the party with the triple platinum teeth," Paige said.

"Well, you know, that's just their style. They have their own image," Van added.

"So what did you do before that?" Summer waved her fork in front of her face, awaiting a response.

"Oh, a little real estate. Then I was part owner of a nightclub."

"*Interesting*."

"Summer, please—not everyone can have a boring job like Evan."

"Hey, I love my job," Evan said as he paused from spooning stuffing into his mouth. "Keep me out of this, Misa."

"I think it's time to move to the living room," Aunt Gerty said.

"No, it's not. Summer, what's with the inquisition?" Misa asked.

"You really don't want to ask that question." Summer picked up her plate and walked toward the kitchen.

Everyone else started to move toward the living room, ignoring the familiar tension that constantly brewed between the two sisters.

Paige remained in the dining room and started clearing the dishes. Summer expected Misa to follow her into the kitchen to continue their "discussion," but instead Misa opted to grab the package containing her liquid party favors. Summer watched out of the corner of her eye as she mixed two drinks of cognac and Coke. She tried her best not to comment. Normally she'd ask her to refrain from drinking in her house. But in the interest of a peaceful evening, she made an exception.

"I really don't want to hear it," Misa warned. "There's nothing wrong with a little beverage to celebrate the holidays. Y'all are so dry." She turned and headed toward the living room, not giving her sister the opportunity to respond. Misa then handed Van one of the glasses and sat on his lap.

Meanwhile, Paige continued clearing the table, ignoring all the other activities in the house. She was thinking about her family and what they might be doing. Her immediate family was in North Carolina. She spent most holidays there or in Houston with other relatives. This year she'd decided to do something different. She felt just as welcome around Summer's family, despite Misa. She realized that every family had holiday drama, and she was enjoying herself, for the most part.

When she bent forward to reach for the basket of rolls, she sensed eyes watching her movements. She turned her body slightly, catching Quinton peeking at her. *I knew he liked some meat with his potatoes.* She pretended not to notice. *But I would never entertain anyone's leftovers.*

Quinton had been checking her out during dinner. He discreetly noticed the glow of her face across the table. Paige had really made an effort to look nice. Her outfit was a departure from her teacher attire. She normally took advantage of her profession's casual dress code, but today she was a little more festive, with a black skirt trimmed with leather paired with stylish black boots that hugged her thick calves. Her rarely exposed legs caught his attention. The red satin wraparound blouse added color to Paige's natural-looking face. Quinton also took notice of the wispy layered haircut that softly framed her facial features. Her makeup had been applied to perfection, drawing attention to her full, glossy lips.

In the past, he hadn't been totally oblivious to Paige. But he was hesitant to mess with her. He knew that a man had to come correct with a strong woman like her. She was intimidating. She was a *serious* Christian. Not just any kind of Christian, but a sold-out, tongue-talking, scripture-quoting woman of God. Quinton attended church, but he wasn't on that level. Besides, he knew Paige was a member of the huge nondenominational church that came on television. It was different from the other gospel churches he attended in that it was missing the "hellfire and brimstone" message of churches he grew up in. The music was also different. It wasn't that soulful. He'd never seen a church with so much diversity.

I'm trippin', Quinton thought, acknowledging his possible vulnerable state. He needed to stay away from the "woman bandwagon" for a little while. Although Misa had taken him for a ride, he knew her presence still made him weak. It was the thrill of the chase for him. He hadn't intended to fall for her so strong, and she had chewed him up and spit him out quick. He was growing tired of that type of foolishness and could only blame himself for making wrong choices based on wrong things.

Quinton had to get Misa out of his system. He was definitely going to make it an early evening. He snapped out of his thoughts when he heard Summer calling from the kitchen.

"Anybody ready for some dessert?" she yelled. Summer's peace had been restored as a result of a trip to the bathroom for prayer. Maybe it wasn't her place to say anything about Van, even if it was hard for her to watch Misa get involved with someone she didn't have a good feeling about. That was Misa's choice. She vowed to try to believe the best of Van and stay out of it.

Paige moved to the kitchen and started slicing some of the pies. She knew as well as Summer that these men wanted to be waited on hand and foot. They were planted in front of the television for the remainder of the night.

"Babe, can you get me some sweet potato pie?" Evan said, grabbing Summer's leg as she walked by.

"Umm-huh. Look at you, you lazy thing. I believe you're starting to get a gut."

"Girl, please—you know I have that eight-pack goin' on."

"In your dreams."

Mr. Ledoux stretched and repositioned himself in his recliner. "We can't talk about diet until January first."

"Alright. Daddy, what do you want?" While Summer was waiting on her father's answer, she watched as Misa kissed and licked Van's ear. Summer became irritated. She didn't behave like that around their dad, and she was married. She knew it was Misa's little act.

"I'll have pecan pie," Quinton volunteered. His cell phone rang. He opted to go upstairs for privacy and not to disturb anyone else. When Quinton finished his call he decided to use the restroom before he came back downstairs.

When he opened the door to come out, Misa was standing right at the doorway. He almost ran into her. She stood there for a moment purposely, not letting him by. In a teasing fashion, she stared him straight in the eye and moved closer.

"What are you doing? Let me by, please," he said, trying not to look at her.

She let out a quiet, mischievous laugh. "You really don't want me to move, now do you?"

Before he could answer, she gently nudged him back into the bathroom. It didn't take much. The next thing he knew he was twisted around and his back was against the closed door, with her body pressing against his. She grabbed his hands and placed them around her waist, then moved them down toward the curve of her spine.

"You look good, babe," Misa whispered as she moved in to kiss him softly on his lips. "You want me, don't you? I look good, don't

I? You can't resist this. I know you can't. No matter how hard you try to play it off. You can't," she said, tracing his lips with her finger. She brushed her lips across his face.

Quinton was helpless. He was a strong, almost-two-hundred-pound man, but he was helpless. Before he knew it, he grabbed her face with both hands and firmly pressed his lips against hers. She responded with soft moans as he raked his fingers through the waves of her hair. He had flashbacks, remembering how good it felt to be so close to her. His mind was telling him to stop. It yelled and screamed, *You can't see her for the manipulator she is?* The warmth of her body silenced his protests. His insides surrendered to the sensation and rush of the moment.

Her dewy lips slid across his. Quinton's hands started to wander as the rush of the moment overtook his senses. Minutes later, as if electrocuted, he stopped instantly and arrested her hands. Without saying a word, he pushed her away. He opened the door and eased out. He paused and took several deep breaths outside the door while his eyes rolled up toward the ceiling.

After a few seconds Misa walked out as if nothing had happened. Without looking his way, she whispered, "You're so weak," and continued to walk toward the stairs.

He felt anger, guilt, and heat. He went back into the bathroom and ran cold water to dab his face.

Just as Quinton made it downstairs, Paige greeted him with a piece of pecan pie. Her pleasant expression turned neutral as she noticed a bit of makeup on his shirt. He reached out to grab the plate. "Oh, Paige, thanks, babe. I appreciate it," he said in a real low voice. Despite his lack of eye contact, he felt transparent. He returned to his seat and noticed Misa wasn't in the living room. Neither was Van. He released a low sigh of relief.

"I've heard it all now. I can't believe Misa is wasting a good piece of pie on that dog," Summer said as she came in with a slice of cake and sat on the floor. "She spoils that mutt like she's a child. I read about people and their pets, but this is ridiculous."

Misa suspected she heard Van's heavy footsteps. She didn't turn around to acknowledge he'd entered the den.

"Happy Thanksgiving, my little Diva," she said as she spooned little pieces of pie into the dog's portable dish.

"You seem to be giving that dog more attention than you've given me this whole evening." Van grabbed her from behind.

"Van, *please*. I've been with you all night."

"Well, I need *lots* of attention."

"*Please*."

Before she could stand up straight, he grabbed her arm and yanked her upright. He turned her around and got right in her face. "Look, I am not one of your wimpy, kiss-behind men you're used to dealing with. Don't think you can play with me."

She felt the need to whisper. "What are you doing?"

The next thing she knew, he grabbed her by the neck and shoved her against the nearby wall. "Did I tell you to talk?" His eyes dug a hole in her soul.

She didn't move. She could barely breathe. The back of her head began to hurt from the impact of the wall. She was paralyzed with fear and disbelief.

"I don't play games with women. You took just a little *too* long to powder your nose a few minutes ago. You understand me? You need to get your drunk behind in there and get your purse. We're going home now." His voice had a seriousness and finality she'd never heard before.

Misa didn't utter a word. She walked slowly to untie her dog.

She was in the living room within moments. Again, she managed to pull herself together within a few steps.

"Well, I think it's about that time. We're going to head home," she said, attempting to sound upbeat.

Evan was still focused on the television. "Already? It's not even ten o'clock."

"Is everything alright? I thought I heard some bumping or something," Summer said as she stood up.

"Oh, yeah, the dog. We just got a little carried away playing with her."

"Hmm. Okay," Summer said, looking at Van.

Playing the role of a gentleman, he helped Misa put her sweater on. "Well, it's been a long day. Besides, Misa and I rarely get to spend quiet time together," he quickly added.

"Well, I never get to see my daughter," her father remarked as he looked at Misa.

Her hands were slightly shaking. "Oh, Daddy, I'll be over tomorrow."

"You promise?"

"I promise." She walked over and hugged him.

Her reluctant hugs with him rarely lingered for more than a moment. This time was different. Summer noticed how Misa held on to their dad longer than usual.

"I'm so tired. We really need to get some rest. Aunt Gerty, Uncle Groovy, be safe. I had a good time. Summer, I'll talk to you," Misa said softly, and grabbed her purse off the floor.

"Always a pleasure, dahlin'. Now, Van, you take *good* care of her. That's our princess. She's the only famous one in the family," Aunt Gerty said.

"I'll take good care of her," Van said.

Thanksgiving Past

Elizabeth beat the potatoes and heard the timer go off for the oven. She held the phone to her ear as her sister, Joy, instructed her on how to make the stuffing.

"Um-huh, got it," she said as she poured the mashed potatoes into a bowl.

"And Elizabeth . . ."

"Yes, Joy?"

"Just enjoy having a nice meal in your new home."

She stopped and smiled, acknowledging the comfort her sister's words always brought.

"Daddy's here!" She heard Misa, almost five, jumping down the stairs two steps at a time.

"Misa, don't you run down those steps!" she said as she pulled the curtain away. There she is . . . *She thought she saw Hannah get out of the car*

from the kitchen window. She pulled off her apron, smoothed her ponytail back, and took a deep breath. "It is going to be fine. It is going to be fine," she said, her hands shaking as she smoothed the fabric on her skirt and tugged at her cashmere sweater slightly. She ran to the bathroom to check her makeup quickly and heard their voices. She stepped into the living room.

"Grandmere!" Misa said as she ran to Hannah.

"Hey, sweetie." She picked her up. "Give Hannah a kiss!" Misa grabbed Hannah's neck and their lips smacked.

"Be careful," Alfred said as he kissed his wife. "Mmmm, how are you doing, sweetheart?"

"Oh, fine." She waited for Hannah to finish hugging Misa. "Hannah," she said as she walked over and kissed the older woman on the cheek.

Hannah hugged her. "Alfred, git my bags. I know it's a mess up in that kitchen," she said as she walked past Elizabeth. Elizabeth's heart sank.

He looked at his wife and winked at her. "It's going to be okay," he mouthed.

She followed Hannah to the kitchen. "Alfred, you have to go back to the store and get some yams. Child, you have to make the candied yams. You can't have Thanksgiving without the sweet potatoes. Have a seat, darling."

Elizabeth sat down. "I—but . . ."

"It's okay. You've done fine so far. Alfred, go on. Didn't you hear me?"

Misa stood in the chair. "Can I help?"

"Sure you can, sugar."

After dinner, Hannah and Elizabeth stood side by side doing the dishes. Alfred had long dozed off in front of the television.

Minutes had passed before the two women spoke. When they finished drying the last plate, Hannah put on a pot of coffee. They sat at the table.

"Well, Elizabeth, I have to admit, I didn't think you and Alfred would last this long."

Here it goes, *Elizabeth thought.* Some backhanded comment. Some way of telling me I'm lucky to be with Alfred.

Elizabeth got up to get coffee mugs and poured coffee, hoping to ward off any discomfort. Her hands were visibly shaking.

"Sit down," Hannah said.

Elizabeth sat and placed the coffee on the table.

Hannah looked her directly in the eye. "Now, I know we have had our differences. It's true. I wanted Alfred to marry Antoinette Michon. She blew it. She got spoiled."

"What?"

"She got pregnant by some local trash. She lost the baby, but it must have been God's will."

Elizabeth's face wrinkled.

"Oh, you didn't know? Thought Alfred told you. Doesn't matter. This was at least a year or so before you two met. Anyway, it's been five years, and you've given me a beautiful granddaughter, although I'm still not sure where the name Misa came from. Nobody can tell me what it means either. Names should mean something. Anyway, Elizabeth, all I'm saying is, I've had my doubts, but you make him happy. I had reservations because I want this family to stay strong. We have to be careful about things." She paused briefly. "I know about your past, Elizabeth."

"My past?"

"Yes, your past," Hannah said in a low voice.

"I grew up in a foster home with Joy. I'm not certain to this day who my real parents are. All I know is my mother was really young."

Hannah stared at her. "I've done some checking. There's pretty much nothing I can't find out. Elizabeth, you're related to the LaCroix family."

Elizabeth got up and grabbed one of the pies and started slicing it. "I know a LaCroix family. Heard things about them, but I can't be related to them."

"Elizabeth, you are. It's not a pleasant thing, but we are who we are. We can't change where we came from. But the Good Lord can wash us clean. Alfred didn't know it. Neither did I. I don't think anyone else in the parish is sure about it. But you are related to Madame LaCroix. She's your grandmother."

Elizabeth dropped the plate and it shattered on the floor. She ran to the front of the kitchen. Thankfully her husband was still sound asleep.

"A madame, a prostitute? That's where I came from?"

"I know it's hard to take. But I had to know what kind of spirits you were bringing into this family. It took years of research, but I finally found out a month ago. I was just waiting for the time to tell you. Now I know how to pray. We can't be passin' down that type of spirit to the next generation. So now that we know your grandmother was a who—"

"Don't say it." Her eyes got smaller. "You don't know that."

"Elizabeth, your secret is safe with me. If you want to know the whole story, she put your mother out for not wanting to be a prostitute. She ran away and met a man, your father, and got pregnant with you and your sister. Her mother didn't want to have anything to do with her and he left her. Your mother didn't have a pot to piss in and had to put you both in foster care."

Elizabeth was stunned. She couldn't be this cruel. She couldn't make this up, could she? *she thought.*

"Whoa, I am so tired," Alfred said as he walked in the kitchen.

"Oh, somebody had a little accident. Honey, do you want me to clean this up?"

"Uh, no—I'll get it, don't worry." She rushed to get the broom and dustpan and started cleaning the glass up as she tried with all her power not to let the tears forming in her eyes drop.

"Alfred, I'll get you a nice slice of sweet potato pie and some coffee," Hannah said as she stood up.

Hidden Agenda

Misa purred softly, feeling the smooth layers of her satin sheets pour over her naked body. Her skin tingled as ringlets of tousled hair lightly grazed her bare back. She rolled over, grabbing a silk pillow to run her fingers through its beaded fringes. Frustrated by Van's absence, she shoved it to the floor.

He'd dropped her off immediately after leaving Summer's house and kept going. He returned about three a.m., reeking of cigar smoke and alcohol, offering no explanation. As soon as he had entered the room, he came straight to her side of the bed. He yanked away the covers, whispering in a husky, sexy voice that he wanted her. Remnants of Van's foul mood had appeared to subside as his large hand maneuvered from the top of her back to the inside of her thigh. His serious tone and the strength of his touch hinted that the word "no" wasn't an option.

Soon his imposing figure was pressed against her. She couldn't resist the strength of his chiseled arms, his authoritative voice. She found her legs wrapped around his generous muscles. Her slender frame was enveloped in the cavity of his massive body. Van's charisma and overpowering presence placed her under a spell. He'd managed to escape again before she awoke that morning.

She'd been angry, but her intense emotion was suppressed by intimate satisfaction. Misa dismissed the notion that she was growing increasingly weak under Van's strength. She was convinced that she was still in control.

Suddenly Misa recalled her father's invitation, realizing she'd have to get up soon. She sat up and slid her back against the supple leather headboard.

Her hands tiptoed lightly across her stomach while she savored thoughts of last night's Thanksgiving dinner. She hadn't had a homemade meal like that in quite some time. She was surprised it had turned out so well. She was proud of the great job Summer had done with the meal. *Why didn't I tell her?*

The warm, satisfied feeling from food and lovemaking was disrupted by the image of Van slamming her against the wall in her sister's den. She slid two fingers through her hair to feel her scalp. The back of her head was slightly tender from the impact with the wall. Van had never acted like that before.

In the past three months Misa had spent with him, he never showed any signs of force. She hoped it was an isolated occurrence. She hated to think Summer's suspicious attitude had any merit. Misa's forehead crinkled as she grunted in disgust over her sister's attempt to second-guess her judgment.

Misa suddenly pictured her brother-in-law's face. She tried to imagine what Summer saw in Evan. He wasn't bad-looking, but he wasn't what she would call fine or even sexy. He was safely attractive. He did absolutely nothing for Misa. *Maybe sometimes boring could be good.*

She made a sweeping motion across the smooth fabric of the comforter with both her hands. Then she stretched her arms toward the ceiling. Her eyes circled the room. Misa was already growing tired of her bedroom decor. The inspiration for the room had come from a modeling assignment in India. She'd purchased several yards of sari fabric to show her interior decorator the design concept. The space was drenched in burgundy, fuchsia, cranberry, red, yellow, and gold tones. Beaded and fringed pillows made of the finest satin and textured silks were everywhere. Moroccan–inspired lamps hovered over uniquely shaped boxes that stored her personal items. But the heavy fabric draped from the ceiling and the darkness it created had begun to aggravate her. Misa thought the room was too shadowy and confining. She now wanted a fresh, clean beach look for her bedroom. She would get with Winston, her designer, soon. He was already working on a new feng shui concept for the living room.

Misa grabbed the remote, and then reached over in her nightstand drawer for a cigarette. She was an occasional closet smoker, which was simply an "occupational hazard." *At least I'm not a chain-smoker like she was.* Much to her dismay, she had some of her mother's habits, which she generally claimed to despise. She clicked the remote and instantly recognized the face of Joan Crawford peering at her in black-and-white.

She always got a big kick out of the old Bette Davis and Joan Crawford flicks. They brought back a collage of memories. Weird memories, like the Sundays when she and her mother would watch all the classic movies.

Misa thought of her mother as both the "strong" mother and the "weak" mother. The "strong" mother was the one she remembered from elementary school, the mother who made her favorite homemade snacks and fussed over her. The mother who tied crisp white ribbons around her long ponytails and dressed her in her favorite blue cape. *I was fashionable even back then*, she thought, and smiled in between slow puffs.

Her smile then faded, recalling the "weak" mother. The mother who would abandon her with hospital visits. The mother who slipped in and out of normality as if it were a dress. The mother who had pain that no pill seemed to cure. Misa had asked God for so long to heal her. She prayed for a healthy mother, not one who appeared to unravel slowly over time. God had failed her. He never made her well.

Anger rose in her again. She extinguished the cigarette on the nearby ashtray, then pulled her knees to her chest. Misa wrapped her arms around her shins and rocked her naked body slightly for comfort. She needed her mother's hands, her kisses and her hugs.

Her longing grew to resentment. She remembered the many unexplained disappearances. Deep in her heart, Misa knew she was being selfish. She ashamedly blamed her mother for things she'd had little control over. *But wasn't I the victim in all of this too? Besides, what Black woman actually has a nervous breakdown? What in her life was that jacked up that she couldn't hold on? What did she have to do besides being a housewife and a mother that was so hard? Millions of women have done it over the history of time.*

She felt her heart racing as anxiety circulated through her body. Her chest got tight. She couldn't breathe. She searched the drawer again until her hands found the orange plastic bottle. It'd been months since she'd taken them, but she had to give in. Misa paused to watch Joan Crawford's helpless face stare at her. The tortured woman screamed from her wheelchair, yet no one could hear her. She saw her mother's face, then her sister's.

She was reminded of their constant struggle to connect. She knew Summer thought she was cold and unfeeling. Contrary to her belief, Misa *did* cry.

There was so much Summer didn't know. Misa wanted to climb into her sister's arms and tell her she had been to a shrink. That she was trying to heal. That she knew the same demons her mother had dealt with—she was fighting to deal with them too. But she couldn't share this with Summer. Misa vowed never to let her sister see her melt down, no matter what. She just couldn't be a hypocrite.

She wrapped her hand tighter around the bottle of pills. Misa stood up, and the chill in the air made her body shiver. Contrary to the previous pleasant day, it was a record low in Houston. Unpredictable, just like she was. "This weather is so crazy, you can't tell the seasons apart anywhere. Yep, we're living in the last days," she said, echoing her grandmother's words.

Remembering her brought a smile to Misa's face. Hannah was quite spiritual, but she had her own way of quoting and interpreting scriptures. The two of them had had a special bond, an unspoken understanding. Hannah was the one person she trusted. Even when she messed up, Misa felt she could talk to her grandmother even if she pissed her off. Hannah would definitely chastise her, but that was it. She still knew how to have a good time.

Misa rolled off the bed and walked toward the bathroom, stepping over clothes strewn on the parquet wood floor. She paused in front of the full-length mirror as she did every morning. She stood to inspect her naked body for any changes. She did a half-turn, admiring the firmness of her bottom half and the fullness of her breasts. She was proud of every inch of her body, although she'd paid for part of it. "Some women would kill for what I have," she remarked.

Still, she couldn't understand why she'd never made the Victoria's Secret Fashion Show. She blamed her agent. It couldn't have been because she was too curvy. She was no more voluptuous than Tyra Banks. She was on her way out, anyway. It would almost be over. She was fortunate to still get work. She easily looked five years younger than she really was, and she never told her real age. But she was getting tired. She honestly didn't care about what secrets Victoria had, or anybody's *Sports Illustrated* swimsuit. For the first time in her life, she was losing her competitiveness.

She grabbed her silk kimono off the closet doorknob and slipped it on. She stepped into the bathroom and filled a glass with water. Misa watched her reflection in the mirror as she swallowed the pill. She had to blink twice. Never before had she looked so much like her mother. Her facial features were gradually changing.

"Whatever," she mumbled after the pill slid down the back of her throat. As much as she hated to admit it, she needed that medicine. Without it, she'd live life in extremes. She'd fly, ruled by impulse, or slide into the pit, that deep, dark hole where the air was thick and heavy. In the pit, nothing seemed to matter. In the pit, she was lifeless. Her thoughts spiraled out of control and tomorrow seemed impossible. She resented the fact that she had to take medicine just to be normal. Just to have a "good damn day." *It's just not fair*.

She walked back into the bedroom, then kicked Van's boxer shorts across the floor with her toe. For the first time she realized that it was easier to let a man into her bedroom than to trust her family. She inhaled deeply as her medicine began to take over. She was starting to feel good now . . . in control.

She sat at her desk, intending to check her e-mail. Her agency was going to send her the itinerary for her trip in three days. She suddenly had mixed feelings about leaving Van behind. She wasn't happy about going out of town. Maybe she could talk him into coming with her to Hawaii. She grabbed a key from under her desk and unlocked the drawer. Misa searched through the loose papers until she found her latest journal. She decided that she was going to express her feelings in the only other safe way she knew how, her writing. Some entries were random thoughts. Others were letters plus lots of poetry.

Only one other person knew about her writing, her former roommate from New York, Bella. One day Misa in a rush forgot to lock her desk drawer. Papers were sticking out. Bella noticed the papers and went to shut the drawer. She saw part of a poem and pulled out the paper. She ended up reading almost all of Misa's poetry.

Misa completely ignored Bella's comment that she was a gifted writer, and she stayed angry with her for weeks. She felt violated and vowed that no one else would ever read her personal thoughts again. No one had access to her world without permission.

Her father sat on the couch and did an inspection of the ultracontemporary living room of Misa's condo. He heard the echo of his foot tapping in the open, industrial-like space. He studied the pictures that reflected her world travel: black-and-white stills of Paris, photos of the Caribbean and other exotic places. An art lover, he could also appreciate the metal sculptures displayed on several podiums. The room felt more like an art gallery than an actual home. However eye-catching all this was, he was disappointed that there wasn't one family photo hung up on the textured walls. It was such a stark contrast from the warm and lived-in atmosphere of Summer's house.

He noticed the Italian *Vogue* cover. He remembered clearly that that was the first magazine that gave Misa a cover. He was very proud of her accomplishments. He must have bought a hundred copies. He sighed and realized Misa had taken good care of herself, but he was sad she had missed the last few years of her mother's life.

Misa's dog sprinted into the living room, jolting him back to reality. She let out a few yips and parked herself in a ladylike manner right at his feet. As much as Diva irritated him, he decided to pick her up and place her on his lap. The dog's visit was brief. As soon as she heard her owner's footsteps coming down the spiral staircase, she jumped out of Alfred's lap and ran over to Misa's feet.

"Dad, I'm sorry to keep you waiting. Wanna go grab a cup of coffee? There's this neat little café in River Oaks. They have the best fresh pastry," Misa said as she climbed down the steps.

"Sounds good, as long as you drive."

"Not a problem."

Misa quickly double-checked her makeup in the metal-framed mirror on the wall. She finger-combed her hair and tucked one side behind her ear, exposing one of her large hoop earrings. She grabbed her Hermès bag, and they were out the door.

"You know, Summer wanted us to go shopping. I hope she isn't angry," Misa said as she eyed the waitress bringing her croissant.

"She'll be okay. She dropped me off and kept going. She's too busy thinking about all the bargains she's going to pick up," her father said as he sipped on his coffee. "It's nice out here." He eyed the quaint shopping strip lined with boutiques and restaurants.

"Yeah, it's nice to sit outside," Misa said, though she would've preferred to be next door shopping instead of talking with her dad. She picked at her food with a fork.

"Misa, you need to eat. You're skin and bones."

"Dad, please don't start with the weight. How do you like our place?"

Our place. "It's nice. Where's Van?"

"He's out running some errands. He thought we needed some father-daughter time."

"Oh. Well, I thought he would join us. He seems like an okay guy," Alfred felt himself struggling to say.

"Yeah, he . . . he is," she said. She took a deep breath. "Go ahead, Dad. I know you want to say something else."

"Umm—just not sure what to make of him. Nothing to compare him with, I guess. You know I haven't met too many of your male friends."

"That's because you were busy chasing them away."

"That was then. I'm talking about more recently."

"Well, there haven't been too many I'd want you to meet. Van, he's cool. We have great chemistry."

"Where are his people from?" Alfred asked as he ran his fingers over his silverware.

"His people? Now you sound like Grandmere. He's originally from Las Vegas."

"Oh. How long have you known him?"

"About three months. Dad, I know where you're going with this."

"It's just that you haven't known this man that long, and

you've moved him in with you. It's bad enough you're shacking up with somebody, but one you barely know?"

Misa paused. Normally she'd be on a tirade by now, but she was out of energy. She inhaled then released the air through her nostrils, as she'd done in her yoga class. "Dad, you didn't want to trust me when I moved to New York, but it turned out fine. I'm grown now, traveled all over the world—" She abruptly stopped herself.

"I'll leave it alone, but I don't like it."

"Dad, you don't like the majority of the things I do."

"That's not true. That's what you've convinced yourself of."

Misa delayed her response to take another sip of her water. She rolled the liquid around on her tongue, then let it glide down the back of her throat. "Well, you didn't say anything when Summer married Evan so quick."

"They're two different situations and you know it. That's marriage. This isn't."

"Well, I'm sorry the Good Lord hasn't dropped somebody out of the sky for me yet."

Misa moved her food around on her plate with her fork. She kept her head down as if she were back in fourth grade. Here it was, that uncomfortable silence they always had.

"Dad, can we just change the subject?" she said, then waved to the waitress to order another water.

Her father rested his elbows on the table and clasped his hands before he spoke. "So, Summer told me you went to the cemetery."

Not that subject. "Yeah . . ."

"You know your mother was so proud of you."

"It didn't seem like it when I left." Her words sliced through his.

His eyes fell down. "Misa, I never said this before, but I'm so sorry about what happened the night you left."

"Dad, that was a long time ago. I just don't want to even talk about it. I closed that door a long time ago. Things just got so heated and out of control." She paused. "It's just that you blamed me for it all. Let's just leave the past in the past," she said, trying to believe her own words.

"If I could take it all back, I would. I was wrong. I was under a lot of pressure. You're right. It wasn't fair to you." He grabbed her hand.

I'm sure you would take that back and a whole lot more.

Misa was tempted to visit her sister when she dropped her father off, but she chose to go home instead. She figured by this time Van should be back. He'd called twice on her cell phone at the restaurant. She ignored the calls and didn't bother to check the messages either. She refused to show anger in front of her father. Misa was confident that she could handle her own affairs, but she wasn't looking forward to seeing Van when she walked in the door.

As she pulled into the garage, a nagging irritability set in at the sight of his car. She got out, opened the door to her loft, and marched up the stairs. She didn't call his name. When she walked into the bedroom, he appeared startled and immediately turned around.

"Hey, babe, I missed you."

"Where have you been since this morning?" She was caught off-guard by his pleasant attitude.

"I know you are not questioning me, are you? The last time I checked we weren't married."

"That's not the point," she said as she found her confidence waning.

"Look," he said as he walked closer to her, "let's not fight. I had to take care of some business." He grabbed her waist and ran his fingers through her hair. "I thought about you all day." He gripped her tightly and put his mouth over hers.

Her body went limp at his touch. He felt so warm and comfortable. He picked her up and laid her across the bed. After he kissed her on the neck and tried to slide his hand under her shirt, she pushed his hand away. "Van, I'm not in the mood. I just want to rest."

He rolled off her and slid close to the headboard. She inched her body backward and slid under his arm to lie across his chest. She raised his ribbed tank top to feel his smooth warm skin against her face. Her slender fingers traced the indention of his stomach muscles. She liked him when he was like this. He was gentle, relaxed, and the only thing she heard was his deep breathing.

He stroked her hair. "Did you get my messages?"

"I was in the restaurant with Dad. We were talking."

"The next time I call you, I don't care if you are talking to *Jesus* . . . you need to answer the phone." His voice grew heavier. She could sense his chest tightening.

"Van, that's ridiculous. That's my phone and *I* pay the bill. I'll answer it when I want . . ." Her last words trailed off.

He paused and his arm started to twitch. "*Like I said*, the next time you see my name on your ID, answer the phone. I'm sure you won't have any problems doing what I ask."

Misa ignored his threat *and* his double standards. She inched farther underneath the weight of his solid build. She wrapped her leg around his thick muscular thigh. His hand reached down to unbutton her pants and pull her zipper down. Misa was still a bit angry with him but sensed her insides getting warm. Before she knew it, his large hands were sliding her pants off. The tension of the day oozed out of her body. His skin poured over her like hot chocolate syrup . . . slowly melting over her until she dissolved.

Misa scrambled to throw a few more items into her garment bag. She always kept a small tote full of toiletries packed since she was on the go so much. She wrote out a note to remind Van to give Diva her medicine. She'd decided not to take her this time. She'd tried her best to get Van to come with her. *Who would turn down a free trip to Hawaii?* She couldn't figure out why he couldn't give himself the week off. Van was his own boss, after all. Nevertheless, a small part of her was actually looking forward to it. Maybe the break from him would be good. Perhaps he'd miss her so much, the reunion would be worth it.

"Babe, are you ready?" she heard his voice yell from downstairs.

"I'm coming." Misa quickly checked her face in the mirror. She wheeled the firmly packed luggage to the hallway and called for Van to come and get it. She heard his strong footsteps pounding the metal stairs.

"I told you to pack last night. I hate all this rushing."

"Well, it's not my fault you monopolized all my time. You acted like a deprived child. You would think you hadn't had any attention in weeks. You've really been crazy lately." She grabbed her newsboy cap and pulled it down over her forehead.

"That's no excuse. It's still your responsibility to handle your business. Besides, you should be thankful. Most women would do anything to get this type of lovin'," he said as he grabbed her and pulled her toward him.

"Alright, you're gonna start something again," she said as she moved closer to him. She wrapped her arms around his neck and maneuvered her lips around the edge of his ear.

He winced and pulled her hands down. "Okay, we need to go. If we don't move now, it's going to be on. Misa . . . you are just fine." He shook his head and lifted her garment bag from the bed.

"Yep, that's what I get paid for." She walked toward the bedroom door. "Wait, I'll be right behind you. I need to get my shades."

"Alright, but for the last time, you *know* what time it is."

Without responding, Misa went back to her desk and several other places to make sure things were locked up. Perhaps she was trippin', but experience taught her she could never be too careful.

A New Season

Summer tried to time her arrival perfectly. She hated being the first person to show up at the department meetings. If she got there too early, she'd have to make small talk with her coworkers and the management.

Slowly, the group filed in. First her supervisor, a short, portly man who perspired regardless of the room temperature. His nerves were always on edge, and he appeared startled whenever someone spoke to him. Summer put on her best politically correct smile. "Mornin', Ed," she said as she reached for her coffee. She figured sipping on a cup of coffee would excuse her from having to talk so much. Soon after, Mary Jane, Bill, Sarah, Greg, and the rest of the department filed in. Betty, the administrative assistant, followed, but her big starched hairdo arrived before she did.

Summer's supervisor sat at the head of the long table, shuffling and rearranging a stack of papers. He looked a little more frazzled and fatigued than usual. She could see the puffiness and dark circles around his eyes, even through his thick horn-rimmed glasses. She wasn't crazy about Ed, but she'd had worse supervisors. He was fair but would do anything to please the powers that be. If upper management sneezed, he was there to wipe their nose, snot and all.

"Ah, good morning and thank you all for coming. Everyone, please, please take a seat," Ed said as he wiped his forehead with a handkerchief. He started spreading out his papers and passing around handouts. He stumbled around numbers, financial information, company policy, the "bottom line," and the only word that got Summer's attention—"layoff."

She was surprised but not shocked. She'd heard talk of more layoffs but didn't realize it would be this soon. She didn't think that a company with such a reputation would lay people off so close to Christmas. But that thought was proven wrong when she was handed her packet. She looked inside. Instead of a golden parachute, hers was more like bronze or pewter. Nevertheless, she was thankful.

Summer saw Betty's tears and Bill turn as red as a beet with rage, but her response was different. Although concerned, she wasn't worried, even despite her recent house purchase. She simply touched the cross dangling from the chain around her neck. She was reminded that God was her true supplier, not her job. *To everything there is a season . . .*

Summer and Paige trounced through the mall and completely forgot about eating dinner. She had wanted to avoid the traffic on I-10 at all costs, but the freeway was still heavy with cars around seven o'clock. They decided to make a pit stop at Summer's house to eat before she took Paige home. Finally they reached her driveway and she pressed her garage door opener. As she pulled in, she was almost relieved to see that Evan hadn't made it in yet. Then she remembered the meeting he'd mentioned. Summer popped the back door of her Explorer and jumped out.

"Girl, we really got some good deals," Paige said as she lifted a bright pink shopping tote from the back of the car.

"I got everybody on my Christmas list except a few people," Summer said as she unlocked the door to her house. She immediately removed her shoes and dropped her packages.

Paige was right behind her and headed straight into the living room. "Hey, it's almost eight o'clock. Where's Evan?"

"Girl, he had an investment club meeting. You know him, always planning our money. His client load is down and this layoff doesn't help. I'm still not worried, though."

"Doesn't he get a salary?"

"Yeah, but you know he does financial consulting on the side. That's where he makes most of our money for savings. He plans to do his consulting business full-time in a couple of years. Lord, if I don't fix that man something to eat, I'm gonna hear his mouth. Never mind; I'll just order something." She reached into the broom closet to get a phone book. Before she could pull it out, she heard her husband's car pull into the garage.

"There he is. Girl, move some of these bags into the bedroom closet."

"Uh-uh. My name is Bess and I'm not in this mess," Paige said as she crossed her legs and put her hands behind her head.

"Thanks for having my back," Summer said as she grabbed several bags and took them to the guest bedroom.

Evan walked in and set his briefcase on the kitchen floor.

"Hey, baby," Summer said as she sprinted from the back room. She wrapped her arms around him and kissed him quickly on his lips. "I was just getting ready to order something for us to eat."

"Who's us?"

"You, me, Paige."

"Oh, don't bother. I ate at the meeting," he said as he flipped through the mail.

"You couldn't have had a full meal. I know they just had snack food."

"It was at Johnny's house. His wife cooked *real* food."

"Well, what do you mean by that?"

"Nothing, honey, nothing at all." He loosened his tie and walked through the living room.

"Hey, Evan," Paige said.

"Hey." He didn't bother looking at her.

Summer came out of the kitchen and placed her hand on her hip. She stared at his back as he headed upstairs. The next thing she heard was the bedroom door close.

"Was that a slam? Well, what in the world is his problem?" she asked.

"Who knows. Whatever it is, I'm sure my presence won't make it any better. I sensed a little attitude."

"Please, Paige. It has nothing to do with you. I'll give him a little while to relax. Meanwhile, we can still have girl time."

"You know, I was gonna hang around for the Chinese food, but I think I need to get back home. I have some papers to grade, and you have a husband obviously in need of attention. Don't sweat it. We've had our share of girl time."

"Paige, don't be silly. You don't have to leave. I invited you back here so we could eat."

"Yeah, but right now you need to see what's up with Mr. Evan. Something is *definitely* wrong."

"I can't imagine what it is, but if you insist I'll take you home now. Honey, I'll be right back. I'm going to drop Paige off," she yelled. Evan didn't respond.

When Summer returned, it was close to eight-forty-five. She walked into the kitchen and the smell of peppers, onions, and mozzarella cheese quickly encircled her nostrils. The cardboard box from the local pizza place sat atop the island. *That Negro said he wasn't hungry. Okay, that's it. I'm gonna get to the bottom of his foolishness.*

She marched to their bedroom. She walked in to find Evan sitting up in bed, reading an issue of *Black Enterprise*. Parts of the *Wall Street Journal* were at the foot of the bed. He looked quite comfortable in his cotton pajama bottoms and T-shirt. She noticed the paper plate on the nightstand with several pieces of pizza crust on it. He didn't even acknowledge her entrance.

Two can play this game. Summer reached into her dresser drawer and pulled out her sweats and a tank top. She refused to utter a word as she walked toward the bathroom. She changed her clothes and pulled her hair away from her face with a hair clip.

She was about to walk out of the bathroom, then paused before her exit. She bowed her head slightly and closed her eyes. *Okay, Jesus, You sent me this man, so I have no choice but to seek Your guidance. You said, if any of us lacks wisdom that You would give it to us freely. Please tell me what's wrong with my husband before I say something crazy. I thank you in advance for your wisdom. Amen.*

Her stomach growled, so she detoured to the kitchen to get a few slices of pizza. She returned to their room and walked around to her side of the bed. She grabbed a magazine and began flipping through its pages. Unable to concentrate, she finally tossed the magazine on the floor.

"Evan," she said slowly and sweetly.

"Yep." His eyes remained fixed on the magazine.

"Let's have a little *chit-chat*," she said as she patted him on the leg.

" 'Bout what?"

"Oh, nothing in particular. How was your day?"

"It was fine."

Finally she sat up on her knees and then straddled his legs.

"Summer, what do you think you're doing?"

"I'm just trying to figure out what's wrong with you." She placed her hands on the sides of his reading glasses to remove them.

He grabbed her hands and his forehead wrinkled. "Summer, don't do that."

"Why are you so irritable?" She drew back and folded her arms.

"What? Summer, I'm just not in the mood to play right now. I just want to read my magazine in peace. You played all day with Paige. You should be out of energy by now."

"Played all day"? What does he mean by that tacky comment? "Well, I'm not going to move until you tell me what's wrong."

"Okay, alright. I'll tell you what's wrong." He gently pushed her off his legs and got up from the bed. He returned with two large shopping bags. "This. This is what's wrong."

"Evan, is that what all this drama is about? A little shopping?"

"Summer, we set our budget for the holidays. You've come in with packages for the last three days. You just got laid off and my business is slow. Not to mention how our investments suffered because of September eleven."

"Evan, how do you know I spent over my budget? If I did, it wasn't that much. You're being hypersensitive. You know how much I love Christmas. In our family we buy everyone gifts. Besides, I bought some things for you too."

"*And* for yourself. Baby, we've worked hard to avoid a lot of debt. If we stay on our plan, we'll be okay. We can still save. You have to stay focused."

"It's the holidays. Evan, you know this little bit extra will not throw our savings off. We still have money in the bank. I deserve to spend some of my severance the way *I* want too."

He dropped the bags and sat on the bed. He touched her face gently. "Baby, I'm not saying you have to check with me about everything. I just want you to understand, this isn't the time to be frivolous. The economy is crazy. You don't know how long it's going to take for you to find another job."

"I guess you're partially right, but I'm not sure if I even *want* another job. I might want to go back to school or something."

"That wasn't a part of *our* plan. Remember, *we* decided that I was going to go full-time with my consulting business in exactly three years. We're still on schedule, but one of us needs a steady income. Where are all these impromptu plans coming from? We have to be responsible."

"Now I'm irresponsible?" she said, throwing her hands in the air. "But, hold on, I see what this is *really* about. It's about you and *your* plans. Evan, things happen. Yes, planning is important, but you need to loosen up a little. Everything doesn't always happen according to our schedule. We certainly can't trust jobs or even put our faith in money."

"Yeah, but God will honor responsibility and discipline."

"I understand all of that," she said as she looked in his eyes, "but I also know we have to be flexible. You created the timetable for your business. We don't know what God's timetable is. Besides, *His* timing is the best. I still support your dreams. I just wish you wouldn't be so stringent."

His face softened. "Summer, I certainly don't want you to feel like you're imprisoned or anything. I don't want you to start resenting me. I want us to enjoy our money just as much as you do. If we work hard and don't overspend, we'll prepare for our future, for our kids. I just wish you would come to our investment group. There's so much you could learn."

"Whoa, whoa—kids? We're not even there yet. That's a ways down the road. As far as the investment meeting, I don't have the desire to go. I trust you to handle all that." By this time she had slid behind her husband's back and begun massaging his temples.

"You find time to hang out with Paige but can't make time in your schedule to better handle our money," he said as he closed his eyes.

"Hanging with Paige is different. It's relaxing. She makes me laugh. She just doesn't take herself so seriously. I like being around people like that."

"Well, she really knows how to make herself at home here, that's for sure. She needs to get a life."

"Evan, I'm really disappointed in you. How can you be so selfish? Besides, she *has* a life. Are you saying my friend is no longer welcome here?" She stopped rubbing his temples.

"How did you get that out of what I just said?"

"All I'm saying is, Paige respects you a lot. She's a true friend to us both. Besides, you have some nerve. I don't say anything when you and your sweaty frat brothers come trouncing through my living room after your basketball games. I don't say a word. I cook for your funky behinds and everything. It may not be *real* food, but I don't hear any of them complaining."

"Okay, Summer, I'm sorry. You do cook real food. I know I was a little rude earlier."

"A little? You were acting childish. You embarrassed me." She stopped rubbing his temples and wrapped her arms around him.

"Summer, okay, I was a little stressed today. You have a point." He paused. "I think we come from different backgrounds. You know I was very poor up until I was a teenager. I don't want to see those days *ever* again. That fear drives me, but I also get anxious."

"Well, I understand a little better where you're coming from. We can't be so concerned about money that we can't even relax. That isn't trusting God. He'll let us know how to invest, what to save, and anything else. All we have to do is ask for wisdom. I know you know this already, Evan. It's *His* money anyway."

"I hear you." He paused again. "You're right."

"Of course I am . . . Okay, just kidding," she said with a laugh.

"M*mm*, this feels good, babe." He grabbed the palm of her hand and pressed his lips against it.

"Now, isn't this better?" she said as she kissed him on the neck.

"Yeah, it is."

"You're a big baby, you know that?" She moved her hands to his ears and started to playfully caress them. She waited for the desired response.

"That tickles!" He tried to contain his laughter.

Her hands moved to the sides of his stomach. "You're so cute when you're ticklish. You know you turn into a big goofball." She watched as her husband transformed into an eight-year-old little boy.

"Okay, Summer, that's *enough*," he said as he grabbed her

hands. Her round face burst into a smile, revealing the one dimple on her cheek. She retreated from her antics with the satisfaction that they'd reached a truce.

"Evan!" she said in a voice of alarm.

"What? What's wrong?"

"I think we had our first *real* argument!"

"Oh, brother," he said as he rolled his eyes.

Calm Before the Storm

Misa was relieved that the fashion shoot was over. She'd been looking forward to a free day to have some time to herself. As she walked across the beach, the warm moist sand felt soothing to her feet. She finally reached her lounger and dropped her straw tote bag in the sand. Misa loosened her yellow and white floral sarong, exposing her entire bikini ensemble. She loved the way its yellow color looked against her molasses-colored skin. She paused to make sure the ties on each side of her string bikini bottom were secure. She sat on the chaise and started to twist the length of her hair up.

She grabbed her sunscreen and slathered the lotion over her body. She enjoyed the oily sensation as the liquid slid between her palms and the rest of her skin. Misa was no stranger to the sun. She could appreciate the dark effect it had already produced, but she didn't want to skimp on protecting herself. She placed her shades atop her head, leaned back, and gazed out at the sea. She admired the contrast between the black sandy beach and the aqua blue ocean. She watched the white foam of the waves crash against the rocks. She noticed how the sand glistened when the tide rolled back into the sea. She slid her shades over her face then adjusted her chair to a comfortable incline.

Misa'd always had a fascination with water. It was often her poetic inspiration. The tropical waterfalls of Hawaii roused her curiosity just as much as the murky bayous of Louisiana. *Perhaps I would've studied marine biology in college. If I had went.* She laughed as if the mere suggestion were ridiculous.

Misa became hypnotized while gazing at the waves. She watched them cascade in and out in a rhythmic fashion. She closed her eyes, inhaling the aroma of lush tropical greenery and listening to the voice of the sea. She enjoyed the solitude, with no cameras, makeup, or demands. Her naked face felt light and refreshed. Her skin could breathe. Misa felt the ocean mist tingle her pores.

She figured she'd make the most of this time. Soon Bella would come bouncing over to disturb her peace. Misa loved her friend, but Bella could talk her head off. Still, they'd had little girl time, so she was looking forward to seeing her.

Misa didn't think she'd miss Bella so much. With their hectic schedules, it had been hard for the two of them to keep up since Misa left New York. In a strange way, seeing Bella would somehow compensate for Van's absence.

She reached into her straw purse to grab her cell phone. She hit speed dial to call Van, but after six rings she hung up. She dialed her home number and the answering machine picked up. She decided not to leave any messages. Misa figured he wasn't answering just to aggravate her. She dropped her phone back into her tote bag and stretched her hands behind her head. Misa decided she'd forget about Van and make the most of the two days left.

She soon succumbed to the weight of her eyelids and finally dozed off.

"Aloha!" Bella said as she approached Misa.

Misa jumped up, startled at the sound of her friend's voice. "Bella, please calm down."

Bella reached for her face and gave her a kiss on each cheek. "You look gorgeous, my friend."

"You do too," Misa said, inspecting Bella's curves and her platinum-colored bikini. The sun had already turned Bella's olive complexion almost as dark as Misa's. Her features were very stunning. Her chestnut brown hair had a slight wave to it and made her blue-green eyes very prominent. Faint freckles decorated her high cheekbones and peeked through her deep tan. Her lips were pouty and her nose very narrow. Bella was beautiful by model industry standards, and she had the wicked ability to work the catwalk like no other.

Bella sat on the chaise on the other side of her friend. There were times when Misa had to remind herself that she was living her dream. It seemed like just yesterday that she was a new model arriving in New York. She and Bella got there around the same time, and the agency had found them an apartment together. Bella was born in Venezuela and spoke fluent Spanish. Her father was a furniture designer and they traveled back and forth to the States. The girls hit it off instantly and both made their mark in the fashion and social circles of the city. Although Misa had a constant flow of work, Bella had shot past Misa to supermodel status. She had the title and the finances that went with it.

Bella embraced everything about American culture, *especially* Black men. The two of them traded cultures. Bella taught Misa an appreciation for Latin dance and music. Misa schooled her on hip-hop culture, Black art, and Sylvia's Southern cuisine. Although they were only a few years apart, Misa felt like a protective older sister to Bella. Bella was really naive at first, but it wasn't long before they were both partying and slipping beyond the velvet rope of all the trendy nightclubs together. Just thinking of all their "ventures" made Misa tired; Bella's antics eventually far surpassed Misa's uninhibited ways.

"So, tell me, what's up with you? How's Houston treating you? Any sexy cowboys?"

"I'm really just settling in. Trying to get used to being so close to family. Personally, my life isn't really that exciting anymore. What about you? Who's this new man in your life?"

"You won't believe it."

"Yes, I will. Nothing you do surprises me anymore. I'm surprised I haven't heard about it in the tabloids yet. You have a new man every month."

"Not true, Misa. Not true." She playfully slapped her friend's arm. "Okay, he's a musician."

"Oh, so you're tired of athletes?"

"Mi-sa, don't tease. This one's very different. Wild. Every day with him is like an adventure. And girl, the sex—crazy ridiculous. We do it everywhere, even in public . . ."

"Okay, that is TMI."

"TMI?"

"Yes, *waaaay* too much information. I don't need to hear all that."

"Since when did you become a prude? I remember when a certain someone was dating a certain rapper in town. I didn't say anything when you gave me a play-by-play account of your events."

"Okay, that was then, this is *now*. So who's this guy?"

"He's a rock star, the lead singer of the band Suicide."

"Never heard of them. What kind of name is that? In the words of my sister, 'I'm gonna have to pray for you.' "

"Ooh, I'm gonna really have to get you out of Houston now. Misa, you are gettin' way too serious on me. Where is my friend? What happened to the good old days?"

"If you haven't noticed, I'm getting a little older. I started slowing down long before I left New York. Boy, did I have some good times. We *were* really out there. The first few years in our place, we turned it out," Misa said as she stared into space.

"No, girl, New York turned *us* out."

"Yeah, I guess you're right."

"Well, you only go around once," Bella said as she sipped her bottled water.

"I know I pushed the limit on several occasions. I'm glad I gave my body a rest. At the rate I was going, who knows what would've happened."

"I still use a little cocaine, but nothing like before. It was just a phase," Bella remarked.

"It's a trip when you wake up in the morning and have no idea what happened or who you were with the night before," Misa added.

"You remember that time your sister came to visit us? She was so excited. Poor thing—she was just a little overwhelmed."

"Yeah, I was trying to show her a good time. She was really quiet the night we left the club. I asked what was wrong when we got back, but she kept saying, 'Nothing,' in a really quiet voice."

"Wow, I remember that night. Poor baby. She wasn't even legal yet."

"Yeah, she begged my parents to come, and she wanted to have the New York experience, so I let her have it!"

"How is she, anyway? I bet she's all grown up now."

"She's fine, living that white picket fence dream and all that other BS."

"Is she happy?"

"Seems like it."

"What you gonna do for Christmas?"

"Girl, go back home and chill out with my *new* man."

Bella sat up and looked at her friend. "I knew it; you were holding out on me. What's his name? What does he do?"

"Calm down, calm down. Well, he's built like the Rock and just thinking about him makes me want to scream. He's sweet. He's an agent."

"So, how did you meet?"

"This is the tripped-out part. He came to my birthday party and I was seeing somebody else at the time. Well, we had hooked up by the morning . . . if you know what I mean. You know how our parties always turn into a slumber event."

"Gosh, girl, you didn't waste any time. What did you do with the other guy?"

"Oh, he didn't even realize he had been ousted until a few days later."

"You are vicious," Bella said as she reached over and smacked Misa's hand. "So what are the plans for tonight?"

"I'm not really trying to hang all night long, but I will stop through the magazine function. I'll show up, have a drink or two, then I'm heading back to my room."

"*Jeez*. Bor-ing."

"Excuse me?"

"I don't know. I think it's time for me to come to Texas. I want my old Misa back."

Misa watched as the last piece of luggage was retrieved from the carousel. Her eyes searched once more in the dwindling pool of people for Van's face. She'd been standing there for about fifteen minutes. She distinctly remembered telling Van exactly what time her flight was going to arrive and exactly where to meet her. She was getting angrier by the minute. She had been in such a good mood when she got off the plane. Misa was even more excited because on her last day in Hawaii she actually went Christmas shopping. She was anxious to get back to wrap her gifts. For the first time in years, she was feeling the holiday spirit.

Although she'd had several items shipped, there were still a few extra bags to carry. Misa finally walked over to get a luggage cart, fussing all the way there at Van for being late. She piled her luggage on top of the cart and pulled out her cell phone. She speed-dialed his cell once more, and still no answer. Then she called home, and still no answer. She left an angry message both times. She finally decided to take a cab. Before she could even get halfway to the curb, two young girls approached her for an autograph. She certainly wasn't in the mood, but she obliged. She quickly rushed into the cab once she saw several people moving toward the car.

During the ride home, her anger was briefly stifled with a momentary fear that something bad actually had happened. She did her best to suppress the negative thoughts creeping into her head. She exited the car and rushed to the door so the driver could unload her bags. Once inside the doorway, she noticed everything appeared to be in its place. On her way back out to pay the driver, she saw a note taped to the large mirror over the couch.

Baby,

I apologize. I had to go out of town on an emergency. Please don't be angry. I'll explain later. Diva is at the Dynasty Kennel. I will call you soon. Please don't be mad at me. I promise I'll make it up to you.

Van

After she paid the limo driver, she sat on the couch in disbelief. *He could have called. What in the hell is wrong with him?* She sat there for about a half hour, staring into space, before she decided to go upstairs. Because it was late, she knew the kennel had already closed. She decided to pick up Diva early in the morning.

Her legs went a little limp as she stood up from the couch. She grabbed the lightest piece of luggage and moved toward the staircase. Each footfall felt heavier as she climbed the steps. Her anxiety increased as she reached the last stair. She slowly crept down the hallway. Everything upstairs appeared normal. Yet for some reason her stomach was churning. Her right hand was slightly shaking as she turned the knob to her bedroom. She cracked the door and slid through the opening. Immediately she flipped on her light. *Everything is in place. I'm just tired.* She quickly stripped to her bare body. At that point she chalked up her anxiety to the traveling. She decided the only thing she needed at that moment was a glass of Merlot and a milk bath in her sunken tub.

Summer thought she was dreaming when she heard the phone ring. She finally reached over and knocked the receiver off the nightstand. She felt around on the floor until she had a grip on it. She put the phone to her ear and tried to speak with her eyes still closed. Her first words wouldn't come out because her voice was so hoarse.

The word "Hel-lo" escaped from her throat at last.

"Summer . . . ?"

She looked at the glaring digits on the alarm clock. A big orange "3:14" stared back at her. Then she looked over at Evan, who was still dead to the world. "Paige, is that you? What's wrong? It's three o'clock in the morning. Is somebody hurt?"

"*Umm*, I don't know. I mean, I'm not sure. I just know I had to call you."

"Paige, please don't tell me you called about something that could wait a few more hours till the morning?"

"Summer, maybe it could have, but I didn't want to take any chances."

"Wait a minute," she whispered as she sat up, "I'm going to go in the other room so Evan won't wake up." She pulled her covers back and slid into her slippers. She headed into the other bedroom.

"Paige, what is it that couldn't wait? This *better* be good." Summer heard the rain splatter against the window. It had been pouring when they went to bed, but the storm had slowed down to a sporadic patter.

"I know you're going to think I'm crazy."

"Just say it."

"Okay, alright. Have you heard from your sister?"

"Well, she called me this past Sunday evening. She was at the airport and let me know she got back from Hawaii."

"So, did she say anything about Van? Did she mention anything was wrong?"

"No, nothing. She was on him to pick her up from the airport and said she was just checking in to say hello. She didn't mention anything was wrong at all."

"Have you heard from her since then?"

"No, I just assumed if Van hadn't shown up she would have called back. I had no reason to be concerned. You know Misa and I can go several days or even weeks without talking, especially if a man is in her life. Sometimes she's locked up in her place and simply won't answer the phone. She sleeps all the time. Anyway, Paige, if something is wrong, you need to tell me."

"Well, Summer, it's just a dream I had."

"What? You woke me up in the middle of the night about some freakin' dream! Are you crazy? Let me answer that . . . Yes, you are crazy."

"Please just listen. I would never be able to forgive myself if I didn't do what the Holy Spirit was telling me to. It's not the first time I've had this dream, but this time it was so clear. I saw the whole thing. Before, the dream would stop at a certain point. But you need to go check on your sister now. *Right now!*" she said with urgency.

Summer jumped at a sudden crash of thunder that came from out of nowhere. "You're trippin' big-time." She eyed the water pouring down the window like a river.

"Okay, remember when I told you about the dream I had before? There was rain and glass?"

"Yeah, I remember."

"Well, this time the dream started out the same, but then I saw your sister in her bedroom. It was raining outside. She had been crying all night. Her face was stained with mascara. She had an empty plastic bottle in her hand. She tried to kill herself, then started to crawl to the bathroom. She was calling for you, Summer. You have to take me seriously. You need to go over there now!"

"Okay, okay. Paige, I'm gonna go over there now. I won't wake Evan. In case you're wrong, I don't want him to think we're two crackpots."

"Do you want me to meet you there?"

"No, I'll be fine. I'm gonna throw on my coat and tennis shoes and just go. Evan's such a hard sleeper. He probably won't even hear me leave. In the meantime, just pray," Summer advised as she moved toward the door.

"I'm sorry. I know this sounds crazy, but I don't want to take any chances. I've had dreams that have really come true. Summer, it's late. I'm going to meet you there anyway. I'll just stay outside. Do you have a key to her house?"

"Yeah, she gave me a key when she first moved in. I used to feed the dog and check on her place when she had a couple impromptu trips. The worst that can happen is she'll curse me out if we're wrong."

In a matter of seconds Summer eased down the stairs, grabbed her trench coat from the hall closet, slid on the tennis shoes by the door, and jumped into her Explorer. She tried to drive carefully, but she knew she was going a little too fast for the wet roads. Fortunately she made it to Misa's neighborhood without any problems. She blasted her Ce Ce Winans tape all the way to keep her spirits up, quoting scriptures almost the entire way. "The Lord will perfect that which concerns me . . . No weapon fashioned against me (or my family) shall prosper . . . If this is nothing, I'm going to kill Paige, literally kill her."

When she turned down Misa's street, she instantly recognized Paige's Jetta. Summer walked up as Paige rolled down the window.

"I'll sit right out here," Paige said through the cracked window. She watched as her friend walked toward the door, and the rain began to pour down.

"This is just great," Summer said as she held her trench coat together with one hand and rang the bell with the other. She knew her sister wouldn't appreciate her just marching in. She rang it again. Still no answer. Finally she used the key and quickly unlocked the door. The downstairs was pitch black. She called out to her sister as she removed her wet coat and placed it on the entryway floor. The CD player was still going. She instantly recognized Sade's lyrics. "I'm crying everyone's tears . . . I feel like I am the king of sorrow . . ." Her silky voice was serenading an empty, dark room.

"Misa? Are you here? Misa?" Summer called as she peeked in each room downstairs. They were all empty. She did hear Diva scratching at the office door. Summer walked over and cracked it slightly. She shut it, then moved toward the staircase. She was just satisfied to hear the dog's scratching and a few yips.

She climbed the stairs and headed toward her sister's room. She thought she heard a little noise coming from Misa's bedroom. She cracked the door and saw that there were candles still burning. But no one was in the bed. From what she could see, the room was in disarray. Papers were strewn everywhere. Plates of half-eaten food and clothes were on the bed. *Where in the heck are they this time of the morning?*

She walked around to the other side of the bed, and there her sister was passed out on the floor, face-down.

Summer bolted to her and called her name. She shook her and slapped her face. She was relieved at least to feel that her sister's body was still warm.

"What, Summer, what? Get off me!" Misa yelled while trying to push Summer away.

"Misa? Oh my God, are you all right? What's going on?" Summer noticed her hand clutched tightly around a bottle of pills. The bottle was about half full. She tried to grab it but Misa resisted and finally shoved the bottle under the bed.

"Will you get a grip? I'm fine. I just had too much to drink. What are you doing here?" she said, looking up through her squinted eyes. She tried to brush her wild hair away from her face with the palm of her hand. "Damn, it's cold in here." Her forehead creased in the middle as she frowned. She grabbed her T-shirt and pulled it down over her thong underwear.

"I—I don't know. I thought something was wrong. Where's Van? What happened to this room?" Summer said as she surveyed the mess.

"I don't want to talk about it. It's none of your business. Just help me get up," Misa barked, while failing at her attempt to stand on her own.

Summer grabbed her arm and helped her struggle to her feet.

Misa placed her hand over her eyes, then massaged the bridge of her nose. "Wow, I was really out of it. Look, um, Summer," she said as she tried to focus, "I'm taking a trip. I have to leave right away. Umm, could you hand me my tote bag over there? I need to pack a few items."

"Are you crazy? You aren't in any condition to go anywhere!" Summer objected. She'd never seen her sister look so terrible, ever. Her hair was tangled and she had a horrible case of raccoon eyes. Her breath smelled awful.

Misa stopped moving and looked at her sister. Her eyes started to blur. She pointed and started grinning. "*Whoa*, look at you, girl. Why do you still have your pajamas on? I know Evan didn't let you out of the house like that." It was obvious the alcohol and whatever else she'd had were still lingering in her system.

Despite her good intentions, Summer's mouth suddenly took over. She'd lost her patience. "You've got some nerve. Obviously you haven't looked at your *damn* self. You look like a super-mess instead of a supermodel." When the last syllables rolled out of her mouth, Summer knew she'd made a mistake. *I should have just ignored her.*

"Please, honey, even on my worst day I've looked better than you," Misa said, trying to place her hand on her hip and balance herself.

Summer looked right into her sister's eyes. She paused before she spoke, weighing each choice of words carefully. "You'd better be glad you're not in the right state of mind, or else I would—" Summer hesitated.

"Do *what*? Remember, you're a Christian, and good Christians don't get mad," Misa said with a sneer as she turned her back to her sister.

Summer stopped. It was as if Jesus Himself came down and grabbed her. She had to reason with herself. *I know this is not her talking. Holy Spirit, whatever is going on, please take control right now. Lord, please keep me from saying or doing anything I may regret.* Her prayer was enough to keep her own mouth closed. She had no idea what to do. Finally, she sat on the bed in silence.

Her eyes followed Misa and her attempt to pack. She dropped clothes and objects into her luggage at random. To Summer this was all starting to look like a scene from a bad movie. "Misa, where are you going? I can't let you go anywhere like this."

Misa kept on packing without a verbal response. *I can't. I just can't tell her. I couldn't stand hearing her self-righteous gloating . . . I just don't feel like hearing "I told you so." I'm going to work this out on my own. I've been through worse.* "I'm fine, dammit. Leave me alone. If you hadn't broken into my house, I'd be gone already. Summer, just go home. What could have possibly made you come over at this time of the night? Anyway, you see I'm fine . . . You've done your Christian deed for the week, so please go home," Misa barked as she pointed toward the door. "Excuse me, did I stutter? I said, take your tired, sanctified behind home!" she commanded.

Summer didn't say a word. She stood, feeling like someone was drawing her hand way back. Summer swung her hand with all the effort she could draw up from ten years of frustration. Quickly, it was over. Just like that. The Ledoux slap.

Misa's eyes grew wide and she let out a gasp as she felt the side of her face. Summer knew she was about to get slapped back. Misa walked up to Summer, got so close she could kiss her. Instead of feeling Misa's hand on her face, she felt hot breath as words were forced out of her mouth. "You know what? I know you have lost your mind. I'm gonna show some mercy." Misa released a half laugh as she lifted a finger to Summer's face. "Please, get the *hell* out of my house."

Her eyes burned with heat as she waited for Summer to obey her command. Summer slowly walked to the door with her head hanging down. She was numb, but with each step, hurt flooded her heart. She felt no peace leaving her, but anger, fatigue, and her own shameful behavior silenced all protests. It was time to give up. Misa would never have understood why Summer had shown up on her doorstep tonight. She grabbed her coat, walked out the front door in a daze, and didn't look back. When she got to Paige's car, she could barely get a word out.

"Was she in there? Is everything alright?" Paige asked.

"She was there, alive. She'll be okay, I guess. I'm going home," Summer said with her eyes looking down at the wet grass. Her teardrops mixed with the rain.

Paige started her engine and watched her friend, oblivious to the downpour, walk to her car. After she got in and took off, Paige decided to follow her home to make sure she got in safely. Paige knew she'd be ready to talk in the morning.

After Summer left, Misa collapsed back onto the bed. She slept for a couple of hours. When she awoke, she barely remembered their exchange of words, but she remembered the slap. After pulling herself together as best as possible, she finally got on the road with no particular destination. She just needed to drive to clear her head. Strangely enough, she found herself headed toward New Orleans. At some point she was going to tell someone what had happened. For now, she'd just drive to her freedom. It hurt her to leave Diva behind, but she needed to feel totally free.

She turned on her CD player and sung at the top of her lungs: "Once you dig in . . ." The song awakened the wild child in her, and she shook her head from side to side. She pictured Lenny Kravitz on stage, seducing her with his guitar. She surrendered to his rock-and-roll world as she beat on the steering wheel as if it were a drum. She was totally relaxed in her favorite vintage T-shirt, athletic pants, and faded denim jacket. She was about to reach into her bag of chips when she noticed the raindrops getting heavier. Soon she could barely see through the windshield. She was about to pull over when words interrupted the music. *When the car starts to spin, turn the wheel to the right.*

Immediately, the car went into a tailspin. She turned the steering wheel to the right and felt the car spinning out of control. She couldn't scream. She opened her mouth but nothing came out as the car skidded wildly off the road. Misa felt the weight of the car turning over. Next, she saw broken glass, felt her neck snap forward, then back. Everything went black.

Life, Interrupted

"Mr. Broussard . . ." a voice said on his speakerphone.

"Yes, Nancy?"

"Your wife is on line one."

Evan checked the time on his computer. It was 2:45 p.m. "Okay, I got it, Nance." He picked up the receiver and punched the button. "Hey, baby, you must really miss me. You're lucky you caught me. I have a meeting in fifteen minutes," he said.

"Evan, I'm getting ready to get on the road. I'm driving to New Orleans. It's Misa. She's been in a car accident. She wasn't too far from New Orleans. They had to life-flight her in. Daddy called me from the hospital." She heard the quiver in her own voice.

"Summer, you don't sound like you need to drive anywhere. Baby, just let me put you on the next flight out."

"Evan, I can't. I have to go now." She thought she'd already released all her tears, but she broke down again.

"Summer, listen to me. There's already been one accident. Be rational. You don't need to get on the road. I'm coming with you."

"Just come home right now. I need you here *now*."

"Okay, um, let me think. I had a presentation this afternoon, but I'll get Jim to do it for me. I'll be there in fifteen minutes. Summer, don't walk out that door, *please*."

She didn't respond.

"Summer!" he yelled. "Do not move. Do you hear me?"

"Yes, yes, Evan, I heard you. If you are not here in twenty minutes, I'm going."

Evan had never moved so fast in his life. He grabbed his suit jacket and several files, then shut down his computer. He was thankful that his boss was in his office. He let him know what was going on and left him with the presentation material. His boss told him to take several days if he needed to. Evan had planned to go with or without his permission.

His heart raced as he jumped on the freeway. He took deep breaths to calm himself down. This definitely wasn't the time to get a traffic ticket. He hit speed dial on his cell phone and called the house.

"Hello?"

"Honey, I'm on my way. Do you know the details?"

"Dad said she must have lost control of the car because of the slippery road. She probably was speeding. I'm not sure what was going on. I think Misa was upset. I know she was. She's still in surgery. He didn't say much else. He's called twice, but there hasn't been any new information."

"Okay, uh, I'll be there in a few minutes. In the meantime, pack a few things for me. Can you do that?" he said as he dodged through the traffic.

"I already have."

"That's my girl."

Summer and Evan held hands as they briskly walked down the busy corridor to the nurses' station. Summer blocked out the wheelchairs, stretchers, patients, and rooms she passed along the way.

"Hi, I'm looking for—" She saw her father out of the corner of her eye. She let go of her husband's hand and ran toward him. She grabbed him tight before she said anything.

"How is she?" Summer gave her father the same wide-eyed look of expectation she had when she was a little girl. Back then, she thought he could fix anything. She believed he could always say something to make any situation better. She searched his face for that same assurance.

"She's out of surgery, and it's possible that the worst is over with. She's still in critical condition. The doctor said there was some injury to her spinal cord, and her face has some major lacerations and bruises. She suffered a slight concussion and some internal bleeding. Fortunately they were able to stop the bleeding immediately. We can't see her yet."

Summer examined her father's glassy eyes. She instantly straightened her back and tried to hide any sign of fear. *God, You already have my mother. Please don't take Misa now. This is not her time. Lord, she's Your lamb, Your precious one, please, Jesus . . .* Summer grabbed her father's hand. "Daddy, it's gonna be fine. God's in control. Let's find a more comfortable place to sit."

He wanted to believe his daughter, but all he could remember was his wife. *I thought she was going to be fine too. I prayed, but she didn't make it. How could I have faith that Misa is going to be fine? God, I'm still angry with you. Now my baby might be taken away from me too?* He felt fear pressing in on his heart, choking his faith.

Summer could almost read her father's mind. "Daddy, it could've been worse. She's *still here*. That's the blessing."

Her father was assured instantly. Suddenly he felt ashamed for even questioning the Lord. "Well, let's head down to the waiting room. It's going to be a long night." They walked slowly down the hallway. Once they settled in the waiting area, there was silence. Summer looked over at her father. His head was bent down, and his eyes were closed. Her eyes then met her husband's. He nodded at the floor and they both got up and walked over to her father. They got on their knees, and all three grabbed hands.

"Daddy, we serve a big and powerful God. You always tell me, 'Much prayer . . .' "

" '. . . much power,' " her father said softly.

Evan began to speak, slow and soft. Soon words were pouring out of his spirit:

"Dear Lord, thank You for Your son Jesus, the Holy Spirit and eternal life. Forgive us of our sins. We come boldly to the throne of grace, not of ourselves but in the name of Jesus. You said, 'The effectual prayers of the righteous availeth much' and 'Where two or more are gathered in Your name, You are in their midst.' Thank You for sparing Misa's life. Heal and restore her mentally, physically, and spiritually. Father, we believe that she's already healed by Your stripes. We decree that every organ and tissue in her body will function to perfection. We thank You for giving the doctors wisdom and anointed healing hands. We decree that Misa 'will live a long life and declare the works of the Lord.'

Father God, we walk away from this prayer with great confidence. In Jesus' name, Amen."

When their eyes opened, they realized that several strangers had joined them. As they stood and conversed, it became clear that they weren't strangers at all. They were all family members in the body of Christ.

Summer slowly opened and closed her eyes as she snuggled against the starched white pillowcase. Then she jumped up, realizing where she was. She startled Evan, who had finally dozed off. They'd both fallen asleep on the waiting room couch with her head on his lap. Her father was gone.

"Babe, what's going on?" Evan mumbled, disoriented.

"I'm sorry. I didn't mean to wake you."

He rubbed the back of his neck. "That's okay. I just felt you move and I was already on the edge. I didn't sleep that well."

She yawned and arched her back. "I wonder where Dad went."

Evan grabbed his glasses from the table next to the couch. "Maybe to get something to eat?" He rubbed his eyes, then put his glasses on.

"Hey, sleepyheads. I got some doughnuts and coffee," her father said cheerfully as he walked through the doorway.

"Hey, Daddy, you seem refreshed this morning. You must've heard some good news."

He paused, then smiled softly. "Well, I guess you could say that. The Lord gave me a word of confirmation. Misa's going to be fine. I woke up this morning with such an overwhelming peace."

Summer grabbed one of the cups of coffee from the cardboard carton and stuck her hand in the white paper bag for a glazed doughnut. "Dad, last night, right before I went to sleep, I felt that same peace. I just *know* she's going to be okay."

Silence fell on the room as they each took a minute to sip the coffee. Summer contemplated telling them about what had happened the night before Misa got on the road, but she opted to remain silent. Right now she just wanted to keep the mood positive, though her stomach was in knots and she couldn't block out the memory of the night her sister had left. She replayed the argument and exchange of words and was horrified at her actions. *I have to be able to tell her I love her . . . that I'm sorry. If only I could take it back. It was my fault. Why couldn't I stop her?*

"I spoke with one of the nurses and she said the doctor would be in soon. We may get to see her shortly," her father said.

About fifteen minutes later, a short, older-looking man with dark olive skin walked through the waiting room doorway. What hair he had left was completely white. His skin was clear but slightly wrinkled. He looked down at the clipboard and took a deep breath. Finally, he looked up, adjusted his wire-frame glasses, and started to speak. "The Ledoux family?" he said with a slight Indian accent.

Her father stood up. "Yes. I'm Mr. Ledoux." He quickly walked over to shake the doctor's hand.

"You are Misa's father? You must be other family," he said, nodding at Summer and Evan.

"I'm her sister. This is my husband."

"Okay, let's see here, well. The most critical injury for Ms. Ledoux was some slight damage to her spinal cord. A few more inches and there may have been some irreparable harm. Right now there is some partial paralysis."

Summer's stomach started to churn a bit. Evan placed his arm around her shoulder and pulled her closer to him. *I walk by faith and not by sight.*

"She had a minor concussion, and her face suffered numerous bruises and cuts from the broken glass. There was some internal bleeding initially, but I believe we discovered it in time. The worst injury was to the neck and spine. She's going to have major physical therapy down the road, but there's a great possibility she'll walk almost normally. Her neck is fractured, so she will be immobile for a while. It will be a slow recovery, but she could eventually come out of this okay. It's hard to tell at this point. She has to be dedicated to the healing process. She definitely had some angels watching out for her."

All three of them seemed to stop breathing for a moment while the doctor's words lingered in the air. "So what now? Can we see her?" her father finally said.

"You should be able to sit with her for a little while. She's still unconscious and heavily sedated."

Summer looked down and moved her feet slightly from side to side. She bit her lip and blinked to prevent the water in her eyes from forming into a stream of tears.

"If you like, two of you can come in just for a few minutes."

Summer's father held his hand out and she placed her hand firmly in his grip. Her eyes met Evan's; he gave her a nod and sat back down on the sofa. He removed his glasses and rubbed his eyes. Then he leaned his head back in quiet meditation as the two walked toward the hallway.

They followed the doctor to the doorway of Misa's room. Summer noticed a sheet of paper beside the door with the name Ledoux scribbled on it. She slowly opened the door. First she saw her sister's feet, then she noticed the cast on her right arm. Her eyes moved toward the neck brace and finally to her face, which was almost completely bandaged. The part of Misa's face that she could see was discolored from bruises and cuts.

Summer took a deep breath and tried to pull her heart up from the floor. *This is my sister?* She grabbed and squeezed her father's hand.

He ran his fingers down the rail of the bed, then ever so lightly rubbed the skin on Misa's left arm. He leaned over and gently kissed her bandaged face.

They both sensed Misa's peace, assured she was aware of their presence. For the moment, that was all they needed. Summer's eyes shifted to the window. The Lord whispered gently to her spirit, *Your eyes see facts, but* My Word *is the truth.* My Word *says she's already been healed.*

Damage Control

Summer's mind was racing through her to-do list. *Call Misa's agency, pick up Diva from the dog hotel, stop by her place to pack more clothes and other items.* As her car sat poised to enter the freeway, she clicked on the radio. She sucked her teeth as she recognized the soulful but tacky rendition of a favorite Christmas carol, "Angels We Have Heard on High." The beat was off, the group rapped part of the lyrics, and the notes were dragging out unnecessarily. *Sometimes you just shouldn't mess with a classic.*

Her mood remained less than festive as heavy droplets from the downpour beat against her window. She was sick of rain. Until she heard the Christmas music, Summer had almost forgotten the holiday was just five days away.

Some Christmas this is going to be. There was so much to do during her two days in Houston to prepare for her stay in New Orleans. She was going to hate being away from Evan for several weeks, but she knew she didn't have a choice. Summer had to be there with her father and Misa.

At least Evan will be in New Orleans for Christmas and New Year's Eve. She smiled at the thought. She realized that the timing of the layoff had given her the freedom to stay with her sister as long as she needed.

She drove slowly down the highway and got on the beltway toward Misa's place. A few melodic bars of another song began, "Silent night, holy night . . . all is calm . . ." That's more like it. Her racing thoughts of the day's agenda came to a halt. The soft, angelic version of the old classic was an immediate reminder of what Christmas was *really* about. She found herself in a moment of quiet reverence. Her lips pressed together as a soothing hum rose from her spirit. The comfort of God's presence and holiness filled the confines of her car.

With a renewed holiday spirit, Summer detoured toward the kennel for Diva. She figured the dog had been there long enough. Besides, she was still struggling with guilt over Misa. *I need to tell her I'm sorry. What if she never gets better? Why did I leave her?*

As much as that dog worked her nerves, she was Misa's pride and joy. So at least she could take care of her until Misa got well. But her Christmas spirit was immediately challenged once she arrived at the kennel. "What? Are you sure this is the total cost of the bill? There has to be a mistake." Summer's heart was beating fast. *I can take a quick vacation to the Bahamas for this amount of money*.

There were several people sitting with small and large dogs who looked up to see who the crazy woman was losing it at the counter.

"Miss . . ."

"Broussard."

"This is the correct charge. See, here is the itemization," the girl said as she brushed a strand of hair from her face.

"Food, lodging, pedicure, pet massage, psychiatrist? You gotta be kidding me." She looked down at Diva, prancing from behind the kennel in a canary yellow cashmere sweater. Summer could have sworn the dog put her narrow nose in the air when she passed a collie.

Before Summer could say another word, the kennel employee handed Summer the leash and Diva started jumping up and down. Summer took a deep breath, then pulled out her credit card. *Evan is going to kill me.* She finally picked up Diva, and the dog started licking her frantically all over her face. *What else can I do? I can't just leave the mutt there.*

Once in the car, Diva would barely sit down. She was barking and obviously overexcited. Summer figured the dog must've sensed something was wrong. "Diva! CALM DOWN!" Summer surprised herself at how loud she yelled. The dog stopped instantly, then collapsed on the seat and put her head down.

Before Summer pulled off, she grabbed the dog and brushed her hair with her hand. Diva quietly whimpered. Summer was about to really feel bad until she noticed the diamond-studded color on the dog. "Doggie bling . . . and I can't even get a birthday gift?" She finally got over it and pulled off. Somewhere on her way to Misa's house, she started to enjoy Diva's company. She figured she could put up with her until Misa got well. It was the least she could do.

At last she arrived at Misa's place and knocked on the door. No one had seen or heard from Van, so she wasn't surprised that there was no answer. When she walked in, the living room looked the same. Nothing was out of order. She let go of Diva's leash and the dog started to run around in circles. *Stupid dog. Maybe she'll wear herself out.*

Summer went upstairs to the bedroom. The room was still messy, but Misa had at least cleaned up the dirty plates. *We need one of Hannah's good old-fashioned house blessings*, she thought as she stepped over a pile of dirty clothes.

She walked toward the closet and began gathering some of her sister's things. She figured she'd find the most comfortable items: sweatpants, T-shirts, and sweaters. She knew Misa wouldn't be coming home from the hospital for a while, but she'd be prepared. She noticed that several boxes in the bottom of the closet had been scattered. Papers and bills were all over the floor. In one of the boxes, Summer found several of Misa's credit cards, bank statements, and other financial matters. She decided to gather the papers and put them in a plastic shopping bag for now.

She walked out of the closet and started to head downstairs for a glass of water. Then she stopped in front of Misa's desk. She stared at it, then took a good look around the room. Her eyes focused on the pictures and little figurines on her vanity. She ran her fingers over her perfume bottles. She picked up the makeup brushes made with pretty ivory handles.

She soon found herself searching through her drawers. Her fingers were on a scavenger hunt—for what, she didn't exactly know.

She opened the drawer of Misa's nightstand and found tons of old photographs. She looked at several pictures of her sister in front of the Eiffel Tower. She saw a picture of her kissing a White man. She saw pictures with her and Bella dressed up in their nightclub outfits. She shoved the pictures back in the drawer.

She realized that she was looking for clues. She had no idea who her sister really was. She knew Misa the model, Misa the outgoing, confident young woman, Misa who could have any man fall at her feet. But who was Misa her sister?

She ran her finger across the top of Misa's jewelry box. She smiled faintly as she touched the tattered lid. The old box was painted pink with ballet slippers, ribbons, and roses. They both had gotten one for Christmas when they were kids. Summer remembered being so excited that holiday. She'd gotten her first piece of real jewelry, a gold locket and chain.

Summer lifted the top and a ballerina popped up and almost startled her as the music began to play. She watched the plastic ballerina slowly twirl as the chimes formed a melody. Summer smiled as she recalled her sister asking Christmas morning, "Mom, how come she's not brown like me? There are brown ballerinas. Don't Summer and I take ballet lessons?" Her mother smiled and simply said, "Yes, of course there are, and the two most beautiful ballerinas both belong to me." Their mother grabbed them both and hugged them.

That was one of the best Christmases ever. Their mother had come out of the hospital just in time. They baked cookies in their new toy oven. There was so much laughter and no crying or yelling. There was more laughter and dancing at the Pink Mansion. Summer realized that it would never be exactly like that again. Everything had gotten all disconnected and broken from the time Misa left. *Why couldn't we just pick up where we left off?*

Yet she was determined to see her family put back together. Summer let her fingers search through the tangled jewelry. Most of it was the costume kind. She figured Misa kept her good jewelry somewhere else. She let her fingers wrap around a locket. She pulled the chain apart from the clump of jewelry and pulled it out. She turned it over and read the inscription. "To Misa, My Heart."

She opened the locket and saw the picture of Misa and their mother was still in there. She took a deep breath, closed her eyes, and held the heart to her chest.

Lord, right now I don't have many scriptures. I can only tell You how I feel. I already know You are going to heal my sister's body. I thank You for that, but Lord, there are some unresolved hurts in this family. You know each one of us has hidden pain, bitterness, secrets. My sister and I, we're struggling. There's an invisible wall between us. No matter how hard we try, we end up reliving the past. Lord, I want our family to spend the rest of our lives loving each other unconditionally. Whatever it takes, Lord. Father, as You restore my sister's health, make our family whole again. Lord, I know You'll move in Your way. You always have.

Summer was about to move off the bed when she noticed that the lock on Misa's desk looked damaged. She opened the drawer and looked in it. Nothing seemed particularly interesting, so she closed it.

She remembered the last night that she was in Misa's bedroom and the plastic bottle Misa had gripped in her hand. She suspected it was still under the bed, so she bent down to look. She didn't find the bottle but saw several wrapped gift boxes. She grabbed one and pulled it out.

Summer looked at the tag, which read, "To Summer, from Misa—Merry Christmas." She realized her sister had bought Christmas gifts and wrapped them herself. She could tell because they didn't have the perfectly wrapped paper from the stores. Summer had to keep herself from breaking down. She reached under the bed and retrieved all the gifts. There was even one for Paige.

When she reached for the last gift, she noticed there was a small leather book behind it. She grabbed it and pulled it out. *A journal?* She was tempted to read it, then changed her mind. Those were her sister's personal thoughts. She held it in her hand for about five minutes.

Finally she decided she couldn't help but read a little. Perhaps it would explain why her sister was such a mess that night. She opened the pages. There were dates and random thoughts. Sometimes she'd address a letter to Jesus. Summer gasped as something rushed through her spirit. *She does know Christ.* She read several pages until she came to a series of poems. *I never knew she wrote poetry.* Her eyes started to read one poem.

MOTHER'S LOVIN'

Alone as I lay, in the thickness of the night,
I held on to your warmth, with all of my might.
I'm often fooled—as real as it seems,
the vision of you is only a dream.
The pain I've felt since you've been gone
can't even compare to love gone wrong.
I struggle to make something grand of myself,
with money and world souvenirs on my shelf.
Deep in my heart, the struggles you knew
threaten my life, for now I am you.
Now I feel your unconfessed fears
and silent rage often muffled with tears.
Your fight was wrought with wounds so deep,
pulling you down to a heavenly sleep.
Love wasn't enough—you needed his touch.
The hurt inside you had become too much.
The lamb you are, you paid the price,
to me an unjust sacrifice.

The life you lived was filled with love.
God sought to heal you up above.
I'm keeping you close, right here in my heart.
As mother and daughter, we're never apart.
No need to worry—we've both been set free.
The Christ that saved you…
now forever keeps me.

M. L.

Summer could not believe the words she'd just read. The poem expressed thoughts she'd never heard from her sister's mouth. She was overwhelmed with emotion. Then she searched for more poems as she flipped the pages. She didn't see any others but found her sister's most recent entry toward the last few pages:

Dear God:

It feels good, like I'm floating. Part of me wants to be selfish and end this pain, but even a fool knows suicide is a sin. So, I'm floating, compliments of an exquisite Merlot and sleeping pills. It's just about to kick full-force, so I better write quick. I'm not stupid enough to think that this concoction will wash away my problems, but it's giving me some serious relief. Right now, I got some major issues. None of this is going to fix itself. I considered myself somewhat intelligent. I don't have a degree, but I've never let anybody get over on me.

Until now. I've been robbed. I mean literally robbed. I thought Van cared about me. I know he couldn't have been acting. He had to move fast, 'cause I know he was falling in love with me. I mean, the things he said while we were together… How could he? He's a criminal.

I can't believe I was actually missing him, while he was robbing me blind. My credit cards, my bank account . . . God, I don't know what I'm going to do.

God, tell me what to do. I have to get up . . . I can't move. Can't call the cops. He was supposed to be my boyfriend. Stupid, stupid, stupid! Can't call my sister.

I'm going to sleep. I'm so tired. If I could just get to sleep. God, don't you be mad at me too. Just fix it. Isn't that what you do? Fix everything?

M. L.

New Revelation

Paige sat drumming her fingers on the wooden table while waiting for Summer. She took a quick peek at her watch. *She said she wasn't that far away.* Normally she wouldn't mind waiting. The male scenery at the Breakfast Klub was usually quite pleasing to the eye. But on this particular day the weather had discouraged the normal flow of patrons. Instead, she studied the black-and-white artwork by the local Houston talent lining the walls.

The cozy restaurant was the latest buzz among urban professionals. It was ideally situated in midtown among newly constructed lofts, clubs, and cafés. Like Harlem in New York, this area was becoming the cultural melting pot of Houston. Paige was amazed it took so long for a

Black-owned eating establishment to show up in one of the nation's largest cities.

She decided to flip through the glossy pages of the *Onyx* magazine she'd scooped up on the way to her seat. Paige was puzzled at the urgency of Summer's phone call. Still, it was the ideal time to break the news about her change of holiday plans. She wouldn't be able to take the trip with Summer to New Orleans for Christmas. Paige had too many things going on in her own world to deal with. For one, the young pregnant girl she'd been counseling at church had run away and had been missing for several days. She had called Paige and threatened to hurt herself if she wouldn't help her. *That isn't what I signed up for. I am not a foster mother.* She just needed a departure from reality, something different. Just then, she noticed Summer bolting through the restaurant door. She quickly rushed to the table, bringing a trail of rainwater with her.

"Hey, girl . . . I got soaked," Summer said as she slid the umbrella under the table. Then she removed her jacket and dropped into the chair.

"You got caught in the downpour. It wasn't raining when I came in."

"Yeah . . . hold on, I need to get a cup of coffee. Did you order anything?"

"I was just gonna get coffee too. I wasn't that hungry."

"Omigosh, are you not feeling well?"

"I'm gonna ignore that one, missy. I don't need to eat *all* the time, thank you very much. Like I said, coffee was doing me just fine, but then one of the owners flashed a smile at me. It was over. He's so cute and friendly. Before I knew it, I'd ordered the chicken and waffles entree."

"See, that's how they get you, girl. Do you think all these

women come here just to eat? It's all that charm and charisma they slather on top of the food."

"If I'm not mistaken, I think you called it *good customer service*. Besides, he's married," Paige offered. "Anyway, what's—"

Before she could finish her sentence, Summer jumped up to place her own order at the counter and grab some coffee. She returned to the table and began pouring sugar into her mug.

"How about some coffee with your sugar? Girl, what's wrong? You certainly don't need that, 'cause you seem extremely wired already. What's going on?"

"Give me a minute. I just need to settle down." Summer lifted the cup to her lips and took a sip. "I don't know *what* to do. I *really* don't know what to do."

Paige snapped her fingers close to Summer's face. "Hello, is anybody home? What's going on?"

"Okay. I went over to Misa's to get some more of her things, and . . ." She paused in midsentence. She frowned and tilted her head. "*Umm*, something's different. Did you just get your hair done? What's with all the makeup?" She grabbed both of Paige's hands and inspected them. "Do I see a manicure? You never get your nails done. What's going on?"

"I don't know what you're talking about. Can't a sister look good? Aren't you tired of seeing me in sweats and T-shirts? Can't a sister spend sixty-five dollars on her hair without the Spanish Inquisition?"

"*Whoa*. Calm down. Don't be so defensive. I just noticed you looked—I don't know, just different today. I mean good different. Something's going on. You'll 'fess up eventually."

"Summer, hello, Summer . . . we're here for you. Remember? You called this emergency meeting. What was so urgent that you have to drag me out in this rain?"

"Girl, I don't know where to start. I have a dilemma." She snapped back to reality. "Something very serious has happened. I mean besides Misa's accident. I went to her place this morning to pack a few more of her things. I started looking around her room. Then I found one of Misa's journals. I know it was wrong, but I read some parts of it. I guess I was just trying to get inside her head. The night before the accident she wrote some very deep things. Disturbing things. She *was* really thinking of killing herself. She also mentioned Van, and, well, he—I don't know, this seems *so* crazy . . ."

"Summer, please just tell me what's going on. I can't take it!"

"According to what she wrote in her journal, Van has stolen a major amount of her money," she said, lowering her voice to a whisper.

"Summer, you are lying. Oh my God!" Paige shouted, then placed her hand over her mouth.

"Will you please keep your voice down."

"You were right, this is big. I mean *seriously* big . . . like *America's Most Wanted* big! What are you going to do? Wait. This is the dream. It all makes sense now. The money, the broken glass. I wasn't crazy!"

"I know. *I know*."

The waiter came and placed Summer's food on the table. As soon as he finished, they resumed the conversation.

Paige started slicing her waffles. "Has anyone notified the police?"

Summer slid some eggs on her fork with her toast. "I haven't. I don't know what Misa did before she left town. She's still not that coherent, so it wouldn't make sense to ask her now. Even so, I can't tell her that I read her journal. She would be *furious*."

"Please, Summer, use the sense that God gave you! A crime has been committed, and you have to do what you have to do. Who cares about Misa's feelings right now? We can't wait for her to get well to do something. Who knows where that fool might be by that time. He could be out of the country for all we know."

Paige calmed herself and took a breath. "I understand how you feel," she continued. "She'll probably be angry you read her journal, but we have to prioritize here. We're not talking ten or twenty bucks, are we? I assume we're talking thousands, or maybe even millions."

Summer threw down her fork in disgust and brushed the crumbs off her hands. "I can't eat this. My appetite is gone," she mumbled to herself. "Can I actually file the report . . . even though I'm not the victim? I've never had to deal with anything like this. Suppose Misa doesn't want to file charges against him?"

"You have evidence that a crime has been committed. I think that's enough. Besides, it's ridiculous to think she wouldn't file charges, and you can't worry about that right now."

"It would make sense to me, but in her journal she *specifically* said she didn't want me or anyone else to know."

"Forget all that ridiculousness. She wasn't even sober. I say we call Quinton right now and tell him *everything*. He'll know what to do."

"Quinton? After the way she treated him?"

"Summer, you know Quinton is better than that. His nose may have been wide open, but I think he can separate his professional work from his personal life."

"You're right. The boy has a little sense. He takes that cop thing seriously, and he's not vindictive. I guess I don't have a choice."

"Quinton has more than a *little* sense, and no, you don't have a choice."

"Okay, okay. Why are you getting so defensive? I'll call him right now."

Summer dialed his number on her cell phone. As she suspected, he wasn't at home and was probably on duty. She left an urgent message on his machine. She also called the police station and left a message there. She took a deep breath. "I guess I just have to wait to hear from him. Gosh, with all my family drama, I haven't even had a chance to ask how you've been. We'll be leaving for Louisiana on Friday around six o'clock. I hope you'll be ready to go."

"Summer, I'm doing okay. There are some things going on with me. I can't get into it now, especially since you dropped this bomb on me. I do have to say something about Christmas. I, uh, well . . . my plans have changed. Please don't be upset. I can't go to New Orleans with you for the holidays."

"What? You *promised* you were coming."

"I know, I know. Summer, you don't need me. You'll be fine. Your dad and all your aunts will be there. This one time, you can make it by yourself. Summer, I've just had some things happen recently and I just don't have a choice. This is one time I'm gonna have to put myself first. Can't you just accept that?" Her voice got louder.

Summer paused. "I apologize. I'm being selfish. What's going on? You can tell me. We have a few minutes. I'm going to wait a little while to see if Quinton calls back. If I don't hear from him, I'm going to the police station."

"Well, for one, I spoke with my mom a few days ago. Mom is tripping. She wants me to move back. Dad isn't feeling too well; he refuses to take his cholesterol pills. On top of that, Tory, the pregnant girl I was counseling, ran away. Her grandmother called me and told me she'd disappeared. Tory contacted me a week later asking to stay with me. She threatened to hurt herself if she couldn't. I don't know what to—"

A cell phone rang.

Summer held up her index finger. "Wait, Paige. This has to be Quinton." She pushed a key on her phone.

Paige sighed and grabbed one of her chicken wings to nibble on it, but threw it down in frustration.

"Quinton? Thank God." After they had spoken for a few minutes, he agreed to meet her at Misa's house within the hour. He wanted more details, but Summer insisted on telling him everything in person.

"Okay, he's gonna leave in a few minutes. I'm sorry, Paige. What were you saying? Something about another one of your students?"

Paige sighed again. "Summer, the bottom line is, I really need to get away. I went to a travel agent, told her how much I could spend on a trip, and booked a trip to Mexico for Christmas vacation."

"What?" Summer paused to calm down a bit. "It's that serious? Are you going all by yourself? That's way too dangerous!"

"I'll be with a tourist group. It's what I *need* to do right now. I promise when I get back, we'll talk. All I know is, I'm on empty. I can't give anything to you or anyone else right now. I have to make some changes in my own life. I have a lot to think about, and I need to be in a different place to do it. I'm sorry, Summer, but you're just going to have to handle this without me."

"Okay, okay. You've gone above and beyond the call of duty. I can't ask any more of you. I wanted you to come with me, but if it's that bad, then do what you need to. I apologize for not being more sensitive," she said as she grabbed Paige's hand.

"Thanks for not making a big deal about this. Trust me, I'll be praying for you and Misa. I know her situation is serious, and I know prayer will turn this around. Everything's going to work out. I don't know how, but it will . . . for all of us."

Summer just sat there puzzled for a few minutes. She felt torn between her sister's problems and the need to be there for her friend. She stood up, kissed Paige on the cheek, and told her they'd talk soon. She felt bad but knew Quinton would be waiting. Paige sat, watching through the rain-dappled window as Summer sprinted to her car. A vision of crystal blue waters soon replaced the subtle pangs of rejection in her heart.

Summer knocked lightly on the solid wood door. There was no answer. She cracked the door and slowly crept in. She looked over and saw Misa was still sleeping. She tiptoed to the window and opened the blinds. She noticed the gray overcast skies but felt that any light was better than the current darkness.

She paused briefly, her eyes falling on the backyard lawn. She pictured the scenes from her wedding. Summer tried to manufacture the emotions of that special time. For a moment, she could hear the music . . . the laughing. She could smell the gardenias, see the dancing. She released her breath, realizing everything that had happened since then.

Her eyes focused on the hammock hanging from the large tree. For an instant she wished she was ten years old again. She yearned for the times she spent at Magnolia Lane over summer vacation, swinging in that hammock, reading and playing with her cousins, the times she would crawl into Hannah's bed and listen to all her wonderful stories. At this moment she didn't want to take care of anyone else. She wanted to just rest in the arms of her husband.

Yet she didn't have that kind of time. There was too much to be done. She'd settled in the Pink Mansion for Misa's rehabilitation, and she almost had a routine down. The physical therapist was coming to the house at about noon. She had to get Misa up, help her dress, and make her something to eat. Her father had already left for the restaurant. The only thing that kept her excited was that she'd see Evan soon. He was driving up from Houston later that day.

Trying to ignore the threatening fatigue, she quietly whispered, "*I can do all things through Christ who strengthens me.*" She heard Misa clear her throat and snapped back to reality. She walked over and noticed her sister's hair was getting matted and dull. Brushing it would be a battle. Misa let her help with everything but that hair. Summer tried to fight back the tears as she looked at Misa's once thick and lengthy mane, now a short, curly, unstructured mess. They'd had to cut part of her hair at the accident scene because it was caught in the car. She saw Misa's body move under the blanket. Although she was awake, she kept her back to Summer.

They'd made it through the holidays, most of which were spent at the hospital. It had been almost two months since the accident.

Misa had come home after a month and made steady progress. She wasn't completely walking on her own, but she was sitting up, standing with a walker, and taking small steps. Physically she was moving right along. Yet all was definitely not well.

Since the accident, she had not uttered one word to a soul. She appeared to understand what was going on, but she refused to talk. No one knew how long the silence would last.

Summer walked over and brushed the back of her hand across Misa's face. "Hey, sis, we're gonna comb your hair a little today, okay? We can't have a model looking like this." Her voice was upbeat and cheerful.

Misa didn't move.

There was no place for sadness and depression. Summer refused to agree with any negative reports or thoughts. She ignored appearances: her sister's convalescent state, the scarring on her face, and her refusal to speak. Summer was concerned but knew in her heart that Misa would fully recover.

She picked up Hannah's antique gold and pearl hairbrush from the vanity and placed it on the nightstand. Then she pulled the comforter back. She raised Misa's nightgown to her waist and began gently massaging her sister's feet, legs, and hands. She rubbed her arms, then rolled Misa onto her stomach. Summer lifted her gown a little more, then rubbed her back.

As she massaged away the stiffness of her limbs, she quoted scriptures. "*You are healed by His stripes. Every organ, limb, and tissue in your body functions to perfection. Father, You said that we can lay hands on the sick and they shall recover. You are totally and permanently restored in Jesus' name.*"

The Lord had put it on Summer's heart to do this morning ritual. When she had first begun, Misa had glared at her with such anger and intensity. That didn't deter Summer. She just kept going. She hadn't missed a day. Now Misa seemed to calmly anticipate the contact. Summer knew it brought her comfort.

She helped her sister sit up. They moved toward the bathroom to bathe. This was always the longest process. At this point Misa could stand but could not be left alone. Summer helped her to wash up and sometimes gave her a bath at night. She made her baths like a spa treatment, with scented oils, bath gels, and candles.

When they came out of the bathroom, she helped her dress. Then Misa settled on the bed. Summer turned away from her to keep the tears from coming. She was simply worn out. When she faced her again, Misa had picked up the hairbrush. To Summer's surprise, she placed it in her hands. She sat next to her sister and gently brushed her curls, singing, "Amazing grace, how sweet the sound . . ." Her words turned into a soft hum.

Summer jumped off the bed to inspect her work. It wasn't the neatest look, but it was a definite improvement. She heard voices outside the door and then a knock.

"Summer, it's your aunts . . . open up!"

No, please, anybody but the Hens, Summer thought.

They barged into the room as soon as Summer opened the door.

"How are you?" Rose yelled as she took Misa's hand.

"Aunt Rose, why are you yelling? She's not deaf."

"Oh, yeah, that's right."

"Sister, I told you it's not any better," Evelyn whispered loudly as she nudged Rose.

"Aunt Evelyn, if you're not gonna be positive, then you need to leave. Misa is doing better than the doctors thought. She's well on her way to complete recovery."

"I'm not talking about that. I'm talking about her hair. Oooh-wee."

"Jesus," Summer said as she rolled her eyes.

Misa's eyes started tearing up.

"Now, honey, don't you worry about a thing. That's why we're here. Aunt Evelyn's got something for you." She opened the shopping bag she was carrying and started setting a selection of wigs on the bed. "Here's the latest from Beverly Johnson, and, oh, here's the Star Jones. You may like that better because it's more young and fresh . . . Here's a piece you can just slide on . . ."

Misa looked horrified. She fell back on the bed and turned her back to them. She let the tears flow.

"Aunt Evelyn, what on earth are you doing? You know good and darn well Misa is not gonna wear anybody's wig. Her hair is fine the way it is. It's just shorter. What were you thinking?"

"I was just trying to help," her aunt said as she started putting the wigs back in her bag.

Summer took a deep breath. "Okay, I know you didn't mean any harm. But really, Aunt Evelyn, just be a little more thoughtful. This is hard enough as it is."

"Well, I thought I was. Come on, sister, I can see nothing I do is appreciated. Your father told us we could only stay a few minutes anyway. I can see we made a mistake. I spent all this money on these wigs, and, well, some people are just ungrateful."

"I told you, Evelyn, this wasn't a good idea," Summer heard her Aunt Rose say on the way out. "We should have just brought fruit and magazines."

They both walked out the door without saying another word. After the door slammed, Summer just shook her head.

Summer picked up a pile of laundry and dropped it down the stairs ahead of her. When she reached the bottom stair, she headed toward the kitchen to get detergent. On her way back toward the washing machine, the phone rang. She dropped everything and ran back to the kitchen to grab it.

"Hey, girl."

"Paige?"

"Who else?"

"You're not the only person who's ever called this phone. Besides, you know Evan's supposed to get here today. I thought this was him calling from the road."

"Sorry to disappoint you. I just wanted to catch up to you before the love fest began."

Summer cradled the cordless phone between her neck and shoulder. She grabbed the bleach and walked back toward the washroom. "Please, I'm so tired, I don't know what to do with myself. I've had to do a lot more because Dad's been spending extra time at Queen Hannah's. One of his chefs quit. On top of that, I haven't been sleeping that well. So Mr. Evan may be out of luck in the *whoopee* department tonight."

"Don't deprive him too long. I know this is hard on you, but it's hard on him too."

She slid the folding doors away from the washer and dryer and began to load towels into the machine. "Okay, I think you're worrying just a little *too* much about my sex life. It'll all work out. What's going on in your world? I finally got your pictures from Mexico the other day."

"Girl, did I have the fabulous tan or what? It was such a blessing to get away. The trip didn't help my problems disappear, but it was much easier to face everything when I got back."

"How's work?" Summer asked as she began sorting the rest of the clothes.

"Work is work. The students are still driving me crazy. You know what the major problem is." Her voice got lower.

"Yeah, your *new* houseguest."

"Girl, she's about to give birth any second. I don't know what to do. I'm not a foster mother or *any* kind of mother for that matter. I'm a single woman who is used to having my own space. I know I'm a Christian, but I didn't see this as part of the plan."

"Well, you know what they say. If you ever want to make God laugh, make some plans. You can count on God getting us to the destination, but it's rarely in the way we choose!"

"*Very funny*. I still can't relate to this situation. When I was fifteen, my mother put the fear of life in me. Sex was the farthest thing from my mind. My mom would have killed me if I came home pregnant, or with anything less than a B for that matter. Don't get me wrong. I'm not judging her. I just don't know how *I* got caught up in all this. This is my prime. What's gonna happen when this baby gets here? I don't know anything about babies."

"Girl, times have changed. I'm simply amazed at all the crap on television. You don't even need cable for borderline porno these days. I don't know how you protect our youth now. I guess the best weapon is prayer. Anyway, it's *her* baby, not yours. You're not expected to raise her *and* the baby. She needs to go home to her parents." Summer made her way to the living room and dropped into the soft recliner. She tilted the chair back and propped her feet up.

"I know that and you know that, but she *refuses* to go home. Tory feels like nobody wants her. She said she'd rather die than go back home. She's severely depressed. I'm going to try to work things out between her and her parents. It has to be pretty deep for her to feel that way."

"You never know what could be going on. They may seem like decent people to you, but they threw her out. You just never know. I swear, there's going to be a lesson in all of this. It's one of those tests, girl."

"Yeah, but I'm gonna have to figure out something soon. I want my life back. I've been trying to make it comfortable for her. I never make her feel like she's not wanted, but maybe that's the problem. I've made things *too* comfortable for her. She's latched on to me and won't let go."

"Just give it time. You'll know exactly what to do."

"I know. So, what else is going on? Any changes with Misa? Has she said anything yet?"

Summer lowered her voice since her sister was in the downstairs bedroom. "No, she's still not talking. The physical therapy's going well, though. We're just taking it one day at a time. No progress on the investigation. Quinton is working hard on it."

"It's just a shame. People are just so crazy. You just *never* know."

"Yeah, but you know what? I *know* that God's in control. He promises *for our former shame we will receive a twofold recompense.* This is grandmother's good rain."

"Yeah, but I swear, it's been raining for quite a while now, Summer."

"Okay, I know this isn't Ms. Prophetess Intercessor Faith Walker speaking negative."

"Alright, alright."

"*Umm,* Paige, I don't mean to change the subject, but don't we have something to talk about? You're still holding out on me. You never told me exactly what your mother said. You've avoided the topic long enough. It must've been something serious for you to take off to another country."

"If I remember correctly, that wasn't the only reason I went away. When you come home in a couple of weeks, I promise, I'll tell you."

Summer sighed. "I'm letting you off the hook this time. You know it's killing me. Usually my begging works. I can't promise you I won't ask again, but I'll try my best to wait."

"This is one of those sit-down moments. It's like, you think you know yourself, everything about your world, and boom! Life surprises you."

"*What?* Is it really that deep?"

"Never mind. Anyway, try to enjoy your husband's visit. I'm praying for Misa. Remember, he's a man and has needs. Handle your business."

"Paige, please, *get* some business."

"I have some."

"Wait, what? You are holding out. I *knew* it."

"Goodbye, friend . . ."

"Don't hang up. Please, girl, tell me—" She heard a click.

She looked at the phone, then placed it on the coffee table. *I can't believe her*. Summer then heard a car pull up in the driveway and quickly forgot about Paige. She ran to the window and pulled away the curtain. She bolted out the door and down the steps of the porch. Evan parked the car and stepped out.

"Hey, baby, I thought you weren't going to get here for a couple of hours."

"I wanted to surprise you and get here early. I missed you."

She felt her heart leaping out of her chest as her husband wrapped his arms around her. She kissed him, then unzipped his jacket and eased her hands around his waist, pressing her body against his. He closed the coat around her, then held her and rocked her from side to side. He planted several quick, soft kisses on her neck, then grabbed her hand.

"*Mmm*, my baby. It's chilly out here. You need to go inside. I'll grab my bag and meet you in a minute."

"I don't care about the cold; I don't want to let you go. I'll wait."

Summer meant what she said. She wasn't letting go. She wanted to feel his arms around her. She missed his touch. He looked good. His hair had been freshly cut. His cologne awakened her senses, slightly invigorating her tired body. Her spirits were already lifted and her enthusiasm renewed.

"Okay, baby. I can see I'm not going to win this one." After a few minutes, she finally let go. He reached into the car and grabbed his overnight bag. He then bumped the car door shut with his hip. They held hands as they walked up the steps, then hurried inside.

Evan dropped his bag down on the living room rug. He glanced at the large face of the grandfather clock. "Is Misa up? Where's your dad?"

"Dad's at the restaurant. One of the chefs quit. Misa's resting. I know she's asleep. The physical therapist worked with her for a long time today. She's always worn out afterward."

"Uh-huh," he said as they walked into the kitchen. He slid his hand into the pocket of her jeans.

"Oh, I see what you're up to." She pulled away from him and walked over to the cabinet. She reached up and pulled down a coffee mug.

Evan stared intensely at her bottom curves.

"I'm going to make us some hot chocolate," she said with her back to him.

"The only hot chocolate I want is standing right in front of me." He walked over to Summer and slid his hand up the back of her sweater to rub her back. Then he wrapped his other arm around her waist and snuggled under her neck.

"What are you doing? Daddy can walk in here any minute."

"Girl, what are you talking about? This is *mine*," he said, still reaching for the button on her sweater. "If I wanted to, I could get some right here in the kitchen, on the table. If I *wanted* to."

"*Shhh* . . . would you quiet down? Stop talkin' crazy. Misa is sleeping in the room right across the hall."

"*Please*, I love my sister-in-law, but I need to take care of some business."

"Evan, *stop*." She found herself laughing, breaking her serious mode. He turned her to face him and moved her hands around his waist.

"*I* . . ." He kissed her. ". . . *missed* . . ." He kissed her again, full on the lips. ". . . *you*." He brushed his hand over her hair, then grabbed her face with both hands. "Baby, we're going to do something about this hairdo."

"Shut up!" She playfully tapped his face.

He grabbed her hands again, then whispered in her ear, "M*mm*, I want you so much . . . right *now*."

"Evan," she said, slightly pulling away. She couldn't deny that her own desire was kicking in. She couldn't take it. He grabbed her hand and led her into the walk-in food pantry. They embraced and he swept his lips across hers, down her neck and back to her mouth. Soon they were both wrapped around each other and felt each other's desire. Twenty minutes of uninterrupted passion passed.

"What was that?" Summer asked.

"Nothing," Evan said while putting a finger to her mouth.

"I heard a car. That's Dad."

"How can you hear anything?"

"I'm telling you, I heard a car. We're right next to a window."

They quickly scrambled to fix their clothes. Summer looked all around for her underwear. After several seconds she abandoned her search and pulled her pants up, resolving to come back and search for them among the canned goods later. They managed to exit the pantry and sit at the kitchen table moments before the front door opened.

"Hello. Where's my son-in-law?"

"Hey, hey, Dad. We're back here in the kitchen."

"There he is. Y'all know I'm smellin' like hot grease and Cajun spices." He held his hand out and Evan stood up to shake it. He paused a minute and stared at the both of them.

Summer looked her father in the eye. "*What?*"

"Nothing. I'm just happy to see you both. Happy to have people to come home to, is that *okay?*" He walked over and kissed her on the cheek.

"Oh, yeah. We're happy to see you too, Dad," Summer said with a too-wide smile.

"I'm going upstairs to take a shower. I'll check on Misa on my way. I'll let you two get back to, uh, whatever it was you were doing," he said, looking at Evan's jeans.

Evan looked down and realized his zipper was open and his undershirt was peeking out. He looked at Summer and burst out laughing, and she couldn't do anything but blush.

Summer decided to do one of her favorite things: hop on the St. Charles Avenue streetcar and just ride. Evan had left yesterday, and she was feeling a little melancholy. She loved New Orlean's history and architecture and took countless tours of the city.

She often imagined herself as a guide, letting her voice rise and fall in animation, pointing out the Vierre Carre, the Hotel Monteleone, which hosted writers such as William Faulkner and Tennesee Williams, the Absinthe House, one of the few Entresol buildings, and the Lalaurie House, better known as the haunted mansion. She'd show tourists the intricate designs on the ironwork of the LaBranche buildings and take them past the Saenger, a movie house built prior to the '60s that wouldn't permit African Americans to even sit in the balcony at one point.

She soon refocused on her current journey as she passed the century-old buildings on Canal Street. She eyed the Fairmont and the Ritz Carlton, which was housed in the former Maison Blanche department store. Even her appreciation for their regality couldn't soothe her. She sighed, longing to be back in Houston with her husband. She reminded herself that this was temporary and was thankful he understood. He'd driven to New Orleans at least every other weekend, but she could tell he was getting tired.

She soon entered the French Market, and she watched artists sitting on the banquettes, trying to sell their work. She still marveled at the St. Louis Cathedral in the background and could see the river in the distance. She made a stop at the vendor area where they sold fresh fruit, vegetables, and an eclectic array of items. Soon she was en route back. Her dad was at the house with Misa, so she had a break, but she thought she'd been gone long enough.

Once at home, she headed toward the kitchen. She passed Misa's room and doubled back. She thought she was hearing things. She believed she heard a voice singing Kirk Franklin's "Brighter Day." Yet she was certain she heard a live voice. She stood outside the door for several minutes and confirmed her suspicion. She burst through the door.

"Misa! You're singing!" She ran over and grabbed Misa's shoulders. She hugged her. "You're singing!" Her voice was faint, but Summer could make out the words.

Misa looked up and smiled. Still she wouldn't speak, but she smiled.

Summer ran to the staircase. She climbed two stairs at a time, shouting for her father. He was in his study, on the computer. "Dad! Dad!"

"Summer, what's wrong?" He jumped straight up.

"Misa, she's singing! How long have you been up here? You didn't hear anything?"

"I've been up here about an hour or so. I'd just checked on her and she seemed to be resting comfortably. Did she say anything? Did she talk?"

"No, but she was singing, and she *smiled.* This is a breakthrough, Dad. It's a *big* breakthrough. She's going to talk soon." Summer felt like shouting. The tide of the battle was turning.

Speak the Truth and Start the Healing

Summer walked in and placed her bag of groceries on the kitchen island. She needed to start dinner right away because her husband would be coming home soon. She was going to make his favorite, lasagna.

The phone rang. She peeked at the Caller ID. It was her father.

"Hey, baby, how are you?"

"I'm fine. Just makin' dinner."

"Got some good news, sweetheart. Misa talked today. She asked for you. She wouldn't say anything else, just your name."

"Oh my God! Put her on the phone," she said as she jumped up.

"Can't now. She's asleep."

She let out a sigh of slight disappointment. "I *have* to come back this weekend."

"No, Summer, you need to spend time with Evan. That's your first priority. You have spent enough time here. Misa will be fine. Don't try to do God's job. You've been faithful. Let it go for a while."

"But Dad, I—"

"But Dad *nothing*. You can come back in a week or so."

She hung up the phone, feeling butterflies in her stomach. She was excited that Misa had spoken but sad that she wasn't there with her. She took down a jar of tomato sauce and opened it. She turned up the volume on her CD player. She began dancing around the room, raising her hands as the words "Our God is an awesome God" blared. She was so into it that she backed right into Evan. She hadn't even realized he'd come in.

"*Whoa*, what's going on? I haven't seen you this happy in a while. What's the occasion?"

She grabbed his shoulders and shook him. "Evan, Misa talked. She asked for me! She didn't say anything else, but a word came out of her mouth."

He set his briefcase down. "That's great, baby. When are we going to eat?"

She put her hand on her hip and frowned. "I don't think you heard me. Misa talked!"

"I know. That's good news, honey. I'm just glad to have my wife back. I guess you won't have to go back to Louisiana now. By the way, when are you going to change those sweats? Didn't you just have that on the other day?" He kissed her on the cheek and started flipping through the mail.

She overlooked his comment about her clothes. She slammed the knife against the wooden cutting board as she kept slicing the Muenster cheese. "What would make you say that? Of course I'm gonna go back, just for a little while longer."

"She's out of the woods. Your dad can handle it from here. You need to spend time at your *own* house."

Summer was slicing with a vengeance.

"Summer, I've been more than patient. You've done a lot for your sister already. This has been a major sacrifice."

She placed her knife on the counter and quickly turned around. "You've been *more* than patient? This wasn't about *you*, Evan. My sister needed me. I'm going to be there for as long as I have to. I'm not working because God arranged it so I could be with her. Besides, I owe it to her. I should have been the one to keep her from leaving in the first place. I could have stopped her from getting hurt."

"Summer, that's ridiculous. You're blaming yourself, just like you did with your mother. This isn't your fault. You need to stop obsessing about this. Now that you mention it . . . have you thought about going back to work at all? I understand how you feel, but you've spent enough time cleaning up Misa's mess. She's eventually going to have to take responsibility for all this. I know you love her, but we're gonna have to get our lives back to normal. I want my wife here. I don't want to come home to an empty house anymore."

"Oh, so this is about your physical needs."

"You know that's not what I meant. Although that does have something to do with it."

"That's not what this marriage is based on. You haven't been *that* deprived, anyway. Don't you think this is a sacrifice for me too? I don't like being away from you either."

"That's not the *only* thing I miss. I miss you, *my* wife. I miss walking in the door and seeing you standing there. I miss holding on to you at night. I'm tired of explaining to everyone where you are. I've ridden up and down that highway for weeks, and *enough* is *enough*."

She moved closer and looked him in the eye. "I don't have anything else to say about it. I'm sorry you feel that way. You just don't understand. I have to see this thing through."

"I *do* understand. You need to have faith in God. You are not doing the healing, *He* is. You're the one who doesn't get it."

Summer pressed her lips together and turned her back to him. She knew if she kept talking, they'd end up in a full-blown argument. She decided to pray about it later that night.

Evan didn't wait for a response. He loosened his tie, walked over to the refrigerator, and grabbed a bottle of juice. He paused before walking out of the kitchen. "Did anybody call for me?"

"Yeah, some man from the church. Somebody named Calvin. He left his phone number."

"*Oh*, Brother Calvin . . . I joined the usher ministry."

"When? You didn't mention it to me? We don't even know if we're staying at that church."

"We never talked about leaving. Besides, if you'd been here, you would've known I joined the ministry."

"*Whatever, Evan*. I'll call you when dinner is ready."

Summer twisted her body, struggling to get comfortable. She rolled onto her stomach, then onto her back. She stared at the ceiling, then looked over and saw Evan curled up in a ball. She resented his deep slumber since they hadn't exactly made up. No matter what she did, sleep wasn't her friend tonight. She arched her back and finally gave in. She decided to get up and go downstairs. During times like these, she knew God usually had something to say. He was nudging her to pray . . . or do something.

She slid from under the blanket and slipped on her terrycloth robe. She put on her furry footies and crept out of the room and down the stairs. She wasn't ready to pray just yet. She clicked on the television and turned to a *Cosby Show* marathon. She laughed as Cliff Huxtable strutted around in his usual antics. Watching the show put her in a good mood. She missed that type of program. It was in a class by itself. *Those were the good old days*. She used to rush home Thursday nights to see what Denise would wear, Clair would say, or Rudy would do. She started laughing aloud, then lowered her voice. She didn't want to wake Evan, although she was still angry with him.

After the episode ended, she went into the kitchen. She filled her teakettle and turned on the stove for a cup of herbal tea. *God, what do you want me to pray about at this hour?* She didn't get an immediate reaction in her spirit. She started thinking about Misa.

Before she knew it, she was in the chilly garage, looking through a box she'd hidden. She held her robe closed with one hand and searched the box with the other. Her curiosity overcame any guilt she was beginning to feel creeping in. She pulled out two more of Misa's journals and came back inside. She fixed herself some apple cinnamon tea and went into the office. She sat in the big black leather chair, allowing the sweet, hot liquid to warm her insides. She opened the journal and started to read. She'd read about twenty pages and was about to stop, but persuaded herself to read one last entry.

Dear Jesus:

You're not going to believe this. Well, I guess You can, 'cause You're God. I'm gettin' out of here... going to New York! I always knew I was different, always knew I was going to be famous. Me, a model? Please don't let this be a dream, God. That model scout walked right up to me in a crowded restaurant. I'm ready to go too! My prayers have been answered. Don't know why You chose me, God, but I'm happy You did.

It's all for the best. I'm suffocating here. I'm fighting with everybody. It's a bad feeling. How can anybody in this family judge me? As much as Hannah tries to hide it, I know our secrets. I don't want to hurt Mom either. She says if I leave it will break her heart, but I can't live for her anymore.

All I know is I'm gonna come back here a big success. Failure is not an option. I'll miss everyone, especially my baby sister. Please watch over her. As much as she gets on my nerves, I love her... I'd do anything for her. Anyway, God, that's all. I'm starting a new life. I won't come back to this place again unless You bring me back. Thanks again for another chance.

M. L.

Summer read the entry several times. *What secrets? Those were just rumors . . . Have I been that naive?* She scanned the rest of the journal but there were no more details. She heard Evan's footsteps coming down the carpeted stairs. *My sister said she would do anything for me. He's not going to like it, but I have to go back to New Orleans now . . . for more than one reason.*

Something to Say

"This is the best catfish in the world." Summer's father stood over the stove, turning over the crackling seafood in the cast-iron frying pan. The smell of cornmeal and Old Bay seasoning danced under her nose. "Your uncle caught this catfish when he went fishing in Alaska."

Summer watched her father brag about his culinary skills as he always did. It put a smile on her face. She was sitting across from Misa at the kitchen table. She noticed most of the scars on her face were healing, but the doctor said she'd have a few permanent scars on her forehead. She watched as her father carefully maneuvered the hot fish out of the pan with his spatula and placed in on a dish near the stove. Summer noticed that familiar sway in his hips. He always danced to the music in his head whenever he cooked.

"I don't know if Misa should eat this fried stuff. It's been a while since she's had some fried food." He took a fork, picked a small piece of fish, and cooled it with his breath.

"I don't know, Dad. Maybe she shouldn't. You need to bake a piece for her. As a matter of fact, I don't think *you* really need all that cholesterol." Summer kept her eyes on her father.

Misa was looking down at her empty plate and running her finger over her silverware. "Why are you all talking as if I'm not here?" she said softly.

Her father turned around, knocking the spatula on the floor. Summer jumped out of her chair and ran to the other side of the table.

"*What did you say?*" Summer asked, looking in Misa's face.

"I *said*, why are you all talking as if I wasn't in the room. I want some of Dad's catfish." She looked directly into Summer's eyes when she spoke.

"Misa, you are . . . talking. You said a sentence. I knew it was going to happen soon." Their father still stood there in disbelief. Summer grabbed her hands, kissed them, and gave her sister a hug. Misa smiled, and said, "Dad, I'm starving. You can cut up later."

"I don't know about anyone else, but I'm a little tired. I want to go in my room and watch some television. Dad, dinner was great," Misa said. Summer walked over to help Misa out of her chair. She almost didn't need the walker, but to be on the safe side she still used it. Her steps were still slow, but steady.

"Okay, sweetie. We don't want to wear you out." He looked at

Summer, and they each wore a questioning look. Both were wondering how much she actually remembered, and if she really knew what was going on.

Misa paused before she walked into the hallway. Without turning around, she said, "By the way, I know exactly what's happened. Right now I don't want to talk about any of it. Just give me some time, but thank you both for . . . everything."

They watched her shuffle down the hallway to her room, then listened for the door to close. Summer walked over to her father and fell into his arms. She held her eyes closed with her fingers, but the tears managed to escape. Her father allowed his own stream of tears to flow without shame.

Summer felt this moment was surreal. She sat on the porch in the metal swing and rocked gently back and forth. The swing was a little rusted and squealed at every movement, but she loved it. It had been there for years. She and Misa were wrapped up in a quilt, sipping on hazelnut coffee. There was just enough chill in the air to justify the blanket. It was a quiet morning on Magnolia Lane. She looked out on the perfectly manicured lawn. The sun was making its debut, and they both sat in silent contentment. A sudden ruffle in the elephant plants aligning the porch interrupted the stillness. Summer was relieved to see that it was only the tail end of a squirrel scurrying up the nearby oak tree.

Misa finally broke the silence. "How's Evan?"

"Oh, fine I guess."

"What do you mean by 'I guess'?"

"Umm, I don't know."

"Yes, you do." Misa kept her eyes forward.

"Well, I tried to call him yesterday evening. Left him a message on his cell phone and at home. He hasn't called me back yet."

"He will."

"I don't know—he always calls me back right away. We've been having a few arguments here and there."

"He'll call. That man really loves you. He's a good man."

"Yeah, he is. I'm sure there's an explanation."

A few moments passed. "I love it out here," Summer said. She inhaled deeply, lifting her shoulders and letting them fall as she exhaled.

"Me too."

"I thought you hated this place . . . couldn't wait to get away."

Misa looked down in her cup. "I don't really, not now, anyway. I've had time to appreciate it."

More silence.

Summer looked across the road at the grand white Victorian mansion. Her eyes were fixed on the real estate sign on the front lawn.

Misa looked up and stared across the lawn too. "You know, they're finally selling the Covington house across the street."

"Yeah, it's been on the market for a while. Since Randy's parents both passed away, I guess the family no longer wants to hold on to the property." Summer sighed.

"It's a beautiful house. I always loved the balconies off the bedrooms and the marble steps."

"Yeah, it is beautiful, isn't it. Remember the Covingtons and all their splendid grandeur? The garden parties and summer socials. Remember how Mrs. Covington used to take us to those lavish garden parties?"

Summer slid over to the side of the swing, then took another sip of her coffee. She waited for the coffee to slide down her throat, perhaps to build up her courage. The words slowly fell out of her mouth. "Wa-nn-a talk about it?"

"Not now." Misa said softly and abruptly. "I will, but not now." She continued to stare out onto the driveway. She paused for a few moments. "Do you remember all those stories Hannah used to make up? There were so many. She had quite an imagination. I bet they'd make some great children's books."

"Yeah, she sure did." Summer laughed in fond memory. "I don't know where she got that stuff from. I wouldn't want to go to sleep when she tucked me in."

"I know what you mean." Misa smiled. She studied the opulent oak trees that formed an arch over the long driveway. "Did you check the mail?" she asked with some urgency.

Summer snapped out of her daze. "Huh?"

"Somebody needs to check the mail. I don't think you checked it yesterday, did you?"

"Are you expecting something?" Recognizing the quick change of subject, Summer quickly added, "You know, I think you're right . . . we didn't check it yesterday *or* the day before. I'm going to walk down and get it. Be right back." Summer removed the quilt from around her arm and wrapped it around Misa's uncovered shoulder. She slid off the swing and started down the driveway. She remembered when the driveway was nothing but red dirt and rocks. Now it was paved with cobblestone. She missed the crackle of gravel under her tennis shoes. She finally reached the mailbox and flipped open the door. She retrieved several envelopes.

"Summer Ledoux . . ." The voice was familiar, but it couldn't be.

She looked up and saw a very tall man in the driveway across the street. "Phillip? Phillip Souchon?"

"Yeah, it's me." He said, dropping the garden hose in his hand.

She ran over. He wiped his hands on his sweats and gave her a hug. She stepped back and looked up at him. "What are you doing here? I thought you moved to D.C. to go to medical school at Howard?" Summer couldn't believe that this was the stick-thin, nerdy guy from their childhood. He'd grown into a tall, handsome man.

"I quit med school in the first year. It wasn't for me. I was just doing it to please Mother. I'm doing real estate. Have a huge development company. I bought this property from the Covingtons and I'm trying to sell it. It's a beautiful piece of land. I still own our house on our old steet; family rotates it for vacations. Enough about me—what are *you* doing here? I thought you lived in Houston."

"I do. I got married. I'm here because, well, to visit my dad."

"Let me look at you. You're all grown up!" He stepped away from her and twirled her around. Then he pinched her right cheek. "Still got that hole in your cheek!"

"Yeah, but I's a woman now!" She chuckled at her *Color Purple* imitation. "Look at *you*, all handsome and everything." She noticed his solid frame, five-o'clock shadow, and that same wavy hair. And she couldn't overlook those beautiful teeth.

"Please, woman, I look terrible. I need to shave and I threw on these sweats to work in the yard." He looked down as his pants. "I'll plan to come by and speak to your dad."

"He'd love that. Do you have any pictures of your family? You have kids, right?"

He reached for his wallet in his jacket. "Two girls . . . they're my pride and joy." He pulled out the picture of two children who were his spitting image. "You have any?"

"No, I *just* got married. They look just like you. Your poor wife went through all that labor and they didn't give her any play," she said, staring at the photograph. "Is she here with you?"

He got quiet. "No. Summer, my wife passed away two years ago . . . It was pretty sudden—um, I really don't want to get into it."

She handed back the picture. "Oh, I'm so sorry."

"Yeah, it's been tough, but we're doing great. Hey, I'm going to be here for at least a week. Maybe we can grab dinner, sit, talk, and really catch up." He rubbed his stomach. "I sure miss that shrimp etoufee and gumbo from Queen Hannah's."

"Yeah, that'd be great, but I'm sort of burned out on Queen Hannah's, if you know what I mean. Maybe we can do soul food at Two Sister's!" she said. He was the breath of fresh air she needed.

"Hey, *whatever* . . . sooo . . . how's Misa? Where's she living now? I saw her in that *Essence* feature. She's still as beautiful as I remembered. She really made it, huh?"

"She . . . umm . . ." Summer hesitated, knowing she couldn't lie. She turned around and noticed that Misa had crept inside the house. It was a good thing the driveway was quite a distance from the house and partially covered by the trees. "She's here, but—"

His eyes grew wide. "She's here? In Louisiana? I have to see her. Please tell her I'm here and I want us to all go out. Okay?" He placed his hand on her shoulders and shook her a little.

"Yeah, okay."

"What's wrong?"

"Well, I just have to check with her. I know she'll want to see you, but, well, there's just some things going on."

He paused and bent down to read the expression on Summer's face. He knew something was up but couldn't figure it out. "Okay, I understand. You have to check her calendar. She is a big-time model now. Anyway, I have some people coming by in a few hours to look at this place."

"Well, I'm sure she'll want to see you, but not just today. Um, well, don't let me keep you. It was really great seeing you. I gotta go," Summer said as she raised her hand and waved the mail in her hand. She started walking backward toward the road. "We'll get together. I *promise*."

"I'm going to hold you to it." He winked, then picked up the hose on the ground.

Lord, he's fine . . . If I'd known he would have turned out like that . . . She turned and walked back across the street. When she finally reached the porch, she skipped up the steps and pushed in the door. Her dad was waiting for her in the living room.

"Dad, guess who I just saw? Phillip, Phillip Souchon. He wants us all to have dinner. He's doing real estate now. Can you believe it? He's trying to sell the Covington property. He looked so good, but did you know his wife passed away?"

Her father didn't say anything. He put his hand in his pockets and looked directly into his daughter's eyes.

Her forehead wrinkled into a frown. "Dad, what's wrong?"

"I'm trying not to raise my voice. Summer, I'm extremely upset. You just got a phone call a few minutes ago."

"Really? Was it Evan? I've been waiting for him to call me back."

"No. *It wasn't*. It was Quinton. He said to call him about the *investigation*. I couldn't get any details out of him. He just said it had to do with Misa and Van. Summer, what investigation? I want to know what's going on right now."

"Dad, I'm sorry. I didn't mean to keep anything from you, but I thought you were going through enough. I also knew that if I told you the truth, well, you'd lose it."

"What in the world do you mean? If it's something to do with one of my daughters, I have a right to know. Of course I'm gonna lose it!" His voice grew in volume.

"Okay, alright, calm down." Summer turned her head around. "Where's Misa?"

"She went to her room."

"I'll tell you. Dad, I swear, there's a reason I didn't tell you anything. Let's go upstairs, in your study."

They both walked up the steps, and she told her father about Van, the investigation, and how she had found out about Van's scam.

"I don't care about any freakin' journal. Don't you know I could have done something!" he shouted. "You mean to tell me, all this time, this man has been gone with Misa's money? They haven't found him yet? This is crazy." He flew out of the study and was headed downstairs. He was halfway down the steps when he saw Misa standing at the bottom.

"Misa . . . why didn't you tell me? I knew he was no good. Baby, why didn't you tell us . . . ?" He reached the bottom stair. He grabbed her arms and pulled her to his chest. Summer ran down behind him and stopped a few steps from the bottom.

Misa pushed her father away, then looked up at her sister. Anger was burning in her eyes. She tilted her head, then squinted her eyes at Summer. "You read my journal, didn't you?"

Summer grabbed the railings on the stair. "I, I didn't mean to." She took a deep breath. "I'm sorry, I just . . ."

"Just what? How could you possibly justify that? That's my personal business. You had no right to invade my privacy! Then you got Quinton involved? How dare you?"

Summer could see Misa's chest rising and falling with every breath. She felt her sister's eyes burning a hole through her body.

"Misa, please. Your sister didn't mean it. She was only trying to help. Honestly, I'm angry she's kept this from me all this time. We don't keep secrets in this family when someone's in danger or needs help."

Misa's head snapped in the direction of her father, with an incredulous stare. "I didn't want to tell you all what really happened because I knew you'd just say 'I told you so,' " she said. "You never liked Van, neither one of you." Her eyes shifted between her father and Summer. "I just didn't want to have to live with that. I wanted to work this out *myself*. No one in this family can say a word. This entire family is built upon secrets. So why is it so surprising that I would keep them? You, Hannah, Mom, you're all such hypocrites. Why don't we all clean out our closets, because I can't take it anymore."

He looked bewildered. "What in the world are you talking about, Misa?"

"Let me help you. What about the affair, Dad?"

Summer gasped and searched her father's eyes. "Dad, say something. Say something. Tell her that's not true. I know it isn't."

Alfred Ledoux froze.

Summer's heart felt like it was going to drop out of her chest. Her father, for the first time that she could remember, looked absolutely petrified.

"You walk around here like you're Mr. Perfect, but you're not. What about the family name, huh? Hannah working overtime to have the right friends, put us in the right schools, join the right clubs. For what? Tell Summer where our money came from. Tell her that it's dirty. Oh, and how about telling her what happened the night I left?"

Her father's eyes got big. He took in a deep breath. On impulse he raised his hand back, but before it reached Misa's face, Summer grabbed it.

"No," she shrilled.

He didn't say anything but walked past Misa and grabbed his car keys off the hook on the wall. He headed toward the front door. He paused on his way out for a glimpse at the picture of his wife hanging on the wall, then left.

Summer looked at Misa. "You shouldn't have done that" were the only words that escaped from her mouth.

"You shouldn't have read my journal. Anyway, you wanted me to talk, to let it all out, and I did." She turned around and began to walk slowly toward the living room chair.

Summer stared at her sister as she walked away. The anger and hurt in the pit of her stomach smothered the words trying to come out. Seconds later, she approached her sister. She was about to speak when Misa cut her off.

"Summer, you amaze me. Always seeing things through rose-colored glasses, wanting to believe the best in everyone. You just don't know anything about *real* life. I'm not the one that's always wrong. Ugly things happen. Even to your father."

Summer pointed her finger toward Misa's face. "You know what? I know about real life. Just because I haven't traveled all over the world doesn't mean I haven't been through something. I don't have to read your journal to know about what you're going through, because I've been through it myself." Summer felt her voice and her blood pressure rising. She imagined vessels protruding alongside her temple.

"What are you talking about?"

Summer walked around the living room. "Okay, let's get it *all* out. I know you've been taking medication for years, because I've been there too. I've fought the same battle. So despite all the makeup, the clothes, and the cars, you aren't any different. But I wanted to help you deal with it. You want to know something else?" She laughed bitterly. "Since you know so freakin' much, let me tell you something else. And for the record, I kept this to myself for *your* protection, because as tough as you seem, I know you couldn't handle it."

"Here we go . . ." Misa crossed her hands and leaned back in her chair.

Summer just shook her head, then held up her hand. "Do you remember the time I came to visit you in New York for my eighteenth birthday?"

"Yes." Her voice was quick and sharp.

"Do you remember the night we went to the club?"

"Yes," she said, her arms folded.

"Do you remember when you disappeared with Bella in the other room and left me there with that guy? The one who was supposed to be *so* cool? The one who was *supposed* to look out for me?"

"Yes . . ." She was staring into Summer's eyes for clues as to what she was about to say.

"You want real? Well, he took me in another room and raped me. He. Raped. Me." *There, I said it. The ugly word. That dirty, sick word.* "Is that real enough for you? Wait, need more? Reality was going back and waiting six months to take an HIV test. Reality is holding it inside because you're ashamed that you'll be tainted for the rest of your life. That, *sweetheart*"—she poked Misa in the chest—"is reality." Before Misa had a chance to say anything, Summer jumped off the sofa, refusing to let one tear drop before she got to the top of the stairs.

Goodbye

"Mother, why can't you let me go? I was going to have to leave at some point." Misa finally spoke after they'd stood alongside each other, gazing out the sliding-glass door.

"I'm not so sure you're mature enough to go to such a big city right now. Didn't the lady say it would be okay if you waited a year or two? I know you're anxious to do this, but it won't hurt to wait," Elizabeth said as she faced Misa.

"Mother, you're being unreasonable. I have to live a life of my own. I could wait, but it's a once-in-a-lifetime opportunity." Her voice rose higher as she threw up her hands. "Just tell me what you're really afraid of. Why are you holding on so tight?"

Her mother didn't say anything as she focused on the swing in the yard. She remembered pushing

Misa in that swing when she was eight, in her yellow and white jumper. She smiled, then frowned at the sound of Misa's voice.

"Do you think I'm going to mess up in some way? Do you think I'm gonna go to New York and lose my mind?"

"What?" Her mother snapped back to the present.

"In the back of your mind, I know you think I'm gonna shame this family. You, Hannah, all of you, think I just run the streets. Just because it's in our genes doesn't mean I'm going to turn out like some common whore."

Her mother turned toward Misa and squinted. "Where on earth did you get that from?" She felt her heart racing, bracing herself for the answer.

"Come on, Mom, I'm not ten anymore . . . people in this family do talk. If you want to still convince yourself we're royalty, be my guest." She paused. "The bottom line is, I'm not gonna screw this up. I have a goal, contrary to what you may think. I'm determined to succeed at this. Let Summer be the one to go to college. It's just not for everybody."

Her mother sighed. She focused on the matter at hand. "When you have children one day, you'll understand. It's not that easy to let go. And what about Summer? She needs you too. I need you," her mother said in a softer voice as she reached for Misa's face.

Misa turned away, her anger brewing. "You're just being selfish. I can't be mother, sister, and whatever else around here," she said as she folded her arms.

"What are you trying to say—that I haven't even been a decent mother to you? I'm doing the best I can under the circumstances. Do you think I like the way I am? Misa, I'm battling. Don't you dare try to make me feel guilty for being sick."

"All this—the sickness, medicine—it's a crutch. You pay all these doctors tons of money and you haven't gotten any better. It's just a

racket. Regardless, though, you're too dependent on me, Mom. Besides, I don't want to end up like Reese or like the rest of Hannah's projects, or even worse . . . the screwed-up Hens. They're grown women just now trying to figure out who they are. I love Hannah, but I can't sit here and watch her run you and everybody else."

Her mother gasped and paused before she spoke. "Hannah doesn't run anyone's house but her own, and you need to watch your mouth. I'm still the mother and you're the daughter," she said, pointing with emphasis. "Dammit, I'm still the woman of this house." The words flew out of her mouth and bounced around the room with authority.

Misa put her hand on her hip, testing the moment. "Well, you need to act like it, then," she said under her breath. "When's the last time you and Dad even slept together, huh?" Her confidence was building as her voice grew louder. "Mother, you just need to get yourself together and be the wife and mother you're supposed to be. I'm tired of cleaning up vomit, giving you medication like vitamins . . . Mom, maybe you can't help it, but you've missed so much. Just because you're not the woman you want to be, don't ruin it for me. I still have a chance."

Her mother could feel the piercing in her heart. She felt a rush of anger flow through her body. "How dare you!" she said, feeling the sting from Misa's words. Her suppressed rage was building and about to explode like water from a fire hydrant. "Shut up, just shut up. I've had enough!" she yelled. Her reflex reaction caused her to grab and shake Misa. "Just shut up!" she repeated as she shook her. Soon they were entangled as Misa tried to grab her mother's wrists to stop her movement.

Her father heard rumbling from his office and ran toward the noise. All he saw was the two of them, hands flying everywhere. "Misa, what are you doing?" he yelled. He ran over and got in between them. He exerted most of his energy pushing Misa away. Before he knew it, he shoved her with a force that caused her to smash into the sliding-glass door. It shattered into a million pieces, halting all motion in the room.

Misa screamed when she looked down at the blood gushing from her arm. She felt tiny pieces of glass all over the open areas of her skin.

"Misa, I'm so sorry . . . I'm sorry, baby," her father said as he reached out for her. Her mother just stood there, breathing hard, then fell to the ground.

"You stay the hell away from me," Misa said slowly. She looked at her mother with a gaze that dared her to speak. Misa turned away and took off running, and her father went after her. Her mother finally stood as her eyes watered. In her heart, she knew on that night she'd lost her daughter . . . perhaps forever.

Shattered and Silent

Misa walked along the bayou as she caught the sun darting in between the evergreen live oaks. She finally rested on a large branch that bowed to the ground due to the passing years. She wrapped her shawl around her and took a deep breath. In the distance she saw the guesthouse and wanted desperately to run over and talk to Summer. But the anger, guilt, and hurt in her spirit held her hostage. *This was so ugly. It was all so ugly. Why did I let my emotions take over me?* It was like a silent trigger that set her off. The explosive conflict left her with the same feelings as the night she left New Orleans for good, after the incident with her mother and father.

Misa rubbed her arm, still feeling the pain

from the glass particles although it was many years later. The ache in her heart cut deeper as she recalled the last night she truly spoke to her mother. She recalled the careless words she'd hurled at her father and sister. *I accused him and attacked Summer. All this time Summer was in so much pain. I didn't even know. She was trying to help me with Van.* The longer she sat, the more she was willing to admit that she needed help. *I need Him.*

Lord, it's such a mess . . . all of it. It's been so long since I've even felt loved. I can't even recognize it. Please, Father, show me how to let my family love me. Please, Father, I want to be different. I just don't know how . . . the wounds are so deep. How can I get rid of this anger?

Finally she looked up to the sky and quietly whispered, "I need Your help. Please, just tell me what to do. I'm listening, Father . . . please just tell me what to do."

Nothing happened. No major signs. No words dropped in her spirit. Just dead silence.

Weeping May Endure for a Night . . .

Summer's eyes followed her canvas mules as she circled the braided rug. Finally she stopped and detoured to the bay window. She slid several brown-faced rag dolls to one side and sat on the worn seat cushion. She ran her fingers along the glass. The air in the other house was so thick with strife that Summer could barely breathe. She sought refuge in the guesthouse, remaining in seclusion for hours. Initially, her eyes were dry with pain, but after replaying the scene from the morning, she eventually broke down. Her chest caved in as she wept for hours. Holding and rocking herself for comfort, she released all the agony. After an avalanche of tears, she felt a thousand pounds had been lifted. However painful it all was, the Walls of Jericho were *finally* coming down.

She sighed, grabbed one of the rag dolls, and twirled her finger around its locks of black yarn. She allowed herself to feel the room's comfort. She stared at the faces of her grandmother's dolls, remembering their names, vaguely recalling the year each had been added to the collection. Most of the grandchildren stayed in the guesthouse when they came to the Pink Mansion for holidays and vacations. It was one big sleepover. She heard the laughter, giggles, squeals, and the games she and her cousins would play. *Can't live in the past* were the words that invaded her imagination.

Time to come out of seclusion. She walked over to the old beige piano against the wall and ran her fingers across the stained ivories. She stopped when she heard a tap at the door. Before she could get there, it started to crack open. She heard the footsteps of her father's hiking boots.

He poked his head in the door first. "Hey, can I come in?"

"Dad, it's your house. Of course you can."

She met him halfway and they briefly embraced. He kissed her on her forehead, but she avoided his eyes and pulled away. She went and sat on the sofa. He grabbed her chin with his hand to get her to look into his eyes. "Can we talk?"

She put her head back down. "Yeah, sure." She forced an upbeat tone with the last word.

He took a deep breath, grabbed her hand, and placed it inside his. "I guess I need to explain some things. Summer, you know I would never do anything to hurt your mom."

"Dad, just tell me. What was Misa talking about? Was what she was saying true?" She searched his eyes for clues.

He rubbed his forehead with two fingers. "No . . . no. I need to explain." He took a deep breath. He paused, then rubbed his hands together. "Baby, I'm human. We all are: me, Hannah, Evan, your mother. Like in any family, things happen, but it's not an excuse. Your mother struggled, but I loved her."

"Dad, please, just say it." Her voice was steady and calm.

"There was a time when I was tempted. I needed comfort. I was hurt, lonely, and just needed someone to understand. It was a long time ago, one . . ."

"Christmas." Summer's eyes lifted to meet his. She wanted to see his mouth and his facial expression as he spoke.

"What?"

"Dad, I saw you. I didn't see anything happen. But maybe later it did. So, you tell me."

He wrung his hands. "Nothing happened. I had these feelings, and I told your mother. I sort of crossed the line, but baby, I was faithful to your mother. I stood before God and took those vows. It was so hard, baby. It doesn't mean I was perfect. Because I was so angry and frustrated, I took it out on Misa at times. I let Hannah run our house because sometimes I was so tired. I just wish I could take Misa in my arms and hug the pain away. She just won't let me."

"How did Misa know what happened that night?"

"She overheard me when I talked to your mother about it, but she got only half the story. When I discovered she'd been listening, I asked her not to say anything to you. Baby, I'm not perfect, and I have some regrets. I should have never put my hands on Misa."

"What are you talking about?"

"The night she left, there was a fight. She and your mother. I was just trying to break it up." He put his head in his hands and began to cry.

After several minutes, she finally placed her hand on his back. "Dad, I just need to be by myself right now. I'm tired, I miss my husband, and I just need to go home. You and Misa really need to talk. I'm gonna drive back tomorrow."

"Summer, we did, this afternoon. We had a very long talk. She wants to talk to you but figured you needed time alone." He looked up and realized she was exhausted. "You know what, I'll give you your space. I'll let myself out." Before he reached the door, he heard a soft voice.

"Dad, I still love you."

He turned and faintly smiled. "I love you too."

"By any chance, has Evan called? I've been trying to call him all day and he hasn't called me back."

"No, not yet. I'm sure there's an explanation. For now, you need to get some rest."

"Okay," she said, looking puzzled.

"Before I go . . ."

"Uh-huh?"

"You might want to take a look in the kitchen pantry. I think there's something behind the soup cans that belongs to you." He winked, then closed the door behind him.

Summer fell back on the couch and began to laugh. It was the first time she'd smiled in hours.

On a Mission

Summer heard Paige pick up the phone.

"Hey, girl. What are you doing?"

"Summer?"

"Yeah. I'm leaving this morning to come back to Houston. You have company? I thought I heard somebody in the background." She folded a sweater, then neatly placed it in a large duffel bag.

Paige paused for an instant. "No, girl. That was the television. Let me turn it down."

Summer was tempted to tell all the details of what had happened, but she didn't feel like rehashing all that negativity. She went from neatly folding to stuffing the remaining clothes in her bag. "Have you seen Evan?"

"No, why? What's up?"

"I don't know. I've been calling him for the last day and a half and he hasn't called me back. It's not like him. He *always* calls me right back. I'm a little worried."

"I'm sure it's nothing. Don't start jumping to conclusions. If you want, I can ride by the house."

She dropped on the bed. "Well, no, that's okay. I think he's fine. I called his office and he made it to work this morning, according to his assistant. I think he's just being spiteful. It's so out of character for him to act like this. I'll be home by this evening. I'll give you a call then."

"Alright. Are you sure? You know I can do the 'drive by' like back in the day."

She laughed, then fell back on the bed and closed her eyes. "No, girl, you don't have to do that. I'm fine. I'm gonna try to reach him again on the way home."

"Okay, be safe."

"Bye, girl. See you soon."

Summer was about ten minutes away from her house. By now, all kinds of scenarios had popped into her head. She called Evan repeatedly from her cell phone, and still no return phone call. She left several messages blasting him out like never before. "If he's alive, his behind is *mine*," she said, nearing her exit.

She soon rounded the corner to the entrance of her subdivision. She finally reached her block and flew down the street. The neighbor's kids were waving from the sidewalk. She threw up her hand and kept going. When she got to her driveway, she saw Evan's car and a black Honda Accord she didn't recognize. Her mind started running away from her before she placed one foot out of the car. She left her bags in the car and stormed toward the door. She turned the key, fussing because the door wasn't unlocking quick enough. *Hmpf, not gonna return my phone calls*. Her curiosity was eating her alive. Finally, she pushed the door open. Before she knew it, words began to fly out of her mouth as she made her way inside.

"Evan! Evan, I've been calling you for a day and a half. I see your car. You tell *whoever* is up in here, your wife is home. What in the hell is your problem? When *I* call, you *better* answer that phone or call me back *immediately*. Do you hear me? I know you're here." She walked through the kitchen to the bottom of the stairs. She was headed to the office when Evan sprinted into the hallway to meet the deranged woman who *sounded* like his wife.

He grabbed her by the shoulders. "Summer, baby, what are you doing here?"

"What do you mean, what am I doing here? I live here, remember?" She pushed past him into the office and stopped instantly.

Evan ran in and stood next to her. "*Umm*, Brother Calvin Davis, this is my wife—Summer."

The stocky, older bald man stood up hesitantly and reached out to shake Summer's hand. "Yes, um—we were just talking about you." He cleared his throat.

Instead of shaking his hand, she put her hand over her mouth. She finally shrieked, "*Oh, my God!* I'm *so* embarrassed. Evan, why didn't you tell me someone from the church was here? I promise you, I'm not usually like this," she said with her hand placed across her chest. "It's just that, well, I've been calling this knucklehead, I mean my husband, for almost two days and he always calls me back right away. And um, yes, oh, gosh, I've been under a lot, I mean, lots of *real big* stress." She spread her hands out for emphasis, then thumped Evan upside his head. "Why didn't you call me back?"

"Baby, I'm so sorry," he said, half amusedly.

"I'm *really* a good wife." She gently shoved her elbow in his side. "Tell him, Evan." She moved closer, partially hiding her face in her husband's sweater.

"Yeah, she is—I mean, a good wife. She's not really crazy." He started to laugh. He pulled her away and looked into her eyes. "Honey, I was really busy at work. Remember that deadline that I mentioned? You've probably been so preoccupied you didn't remember. Then after work we had Bible study last night. By the time I got home, it was late. When you left all these crazy messages on my machine, I just got angry with you. I decided I was gonna call you back when I got ready. It was childish, and I was being stubborn."

Summer wanted to disappear, literally dissolve, as she looked at the puzzled expression on their guest's face.

Brother Calvin cleared his throat again and finally felt he had clearance to speak. "Brother Evan, I understand. I've been married for over thirty years. You don't need to say a word." He reached for a folder on the desk. He leaned over and whispered in Evan's ear, "Now that everything's all cleared up, I think your wife might need a hug."

Evan looked at Summer, then reluctantly placed his arms around her. He leaned down, gave her a quick peck, and rubbed the top of her hair. "Silly," he whispered in her ear as he hugged her.

"Don't push it," she mumbled under her breath with a forced smile.

"Okay, Brother Evan. Summer, it was really a pleasure to meet you." He placed his cap on his head and tugged at his suspenders. "Now I'm going to head home to *my* wife before *I* get in trouble. And Summer . . . don't worry." He winked at her. "Compared to my wife back in the day, you're a lightweight." He reached for his trench coat and put it on. "Evan," he said as he smacked him on the back, "don't make things harder on yourself than necessary. You got a long way to go, son."

"Yes, sir," he said after a deep breath. "I'll walk you out."

After they got outside, Evan talked to him for several minutes on the porch, trying to stall. He knew Summer wasn't finished with him yet. Something told him it was going to be a long night. It was unlike him to make his wife worry on purpose. Despite his wrongdoing, he felt his anger at Summer's absence was justified. The ten messages she had left laying him out had pushed him over the edge. She'd gone straight ghetto on him, and he'd never seen that side of her before. They'd both acted out of character. He felt it was time for him to take authority over the strife that had crept into his house.

He walked back inside and didn't see her in the living room. What he did find was a trail of her clothes . . . leading upstairs to the bedroom. He grinned to himself. *Yes, it really is going to be a long night.* Both his smile and anticipation grew as he climbed each stair and heard the shower running.

Reunion

Before Misa sat down, she rushed to the restroom to double-check her hair and makeup. It'd been a while since she'd been around a crowd of people. She was extremely self-conscious. The unattractiveness she felt inside had nothing to do with her physical appearance. For the most part, her skin had healed. A few scars on her face and body and the limp in her walk were the only remnants of her accident. Her body was on the mend, but her mind was still in battle. She was determined to win.

Misa turned her head from side to side and ran her fingers through her closely cropped hair. She examined her shimmering lips, lined and painted with lip gloss. Her complexion was perked up with a subtle stroke of blush and bronzer. She played up her eyes with shadow and mascara. She still wasn't sure that this was a good idea. *Well, gotta get out eventually.* It was time to face the world as well as her responsibilities.

This was a good start. Church hadn't been so bad. She noticed more people smiled than stared. She enjoyed the sermon and the music. She was glad she and her father didn't stay around afterward for long, though. Her father insisted they go to the House of Blues for the Gospel Sunday Brunch. She was beginning to feel they should've gone straight home. *Perhaps this was a bit too much,* she thought, lightly dusting a layer of pressed powder on her face. *Well, we're here now.* She shoved the compact into her purse.

She jumped when she heard the door to the bathroom open and noticed a young Black woman walk in. As soon as the door opened, she heard the blended voices of a choir starting up. The woman paused at the other mirror and pulled out her lipstick. She looked at Misa, then smiled and continued tracing her lips. Misa's heart started racing. She felt the woman either recognized her or noticed the few scars on her face.

She sprinted out of the bathroom after a few seconds. She walked briskly toward her table. On the way, her steps slowed to the pace of the worship music. Her father could barely pull out her chair before she sat in it.

"Misa, do you want something to drink besides coffee?"

"Yes, I'll have orange juice." She placed her cloth napkin over her lap and smoothed it with her fingers. She looked around twice, then down at her plate.

"Misa, will you please relax? You needed to get out. You can't hibernate forever. It's been close to five months since the accident. It's time. If you're paranoid, then other people will respond to you that way. Your dress is perfect. Your hair is as beautiful as ever . . . and your face looks fine."

She reached for her father's hand across the table, then took a deep breath. Her heart stopped racing. "Thanks, Dad. I'm fine. You're right. This *was* a good idea." She forced a smile on her face as she quickly looked around. "I noticed Summer called last night. She still isn't talking to me, huh?"

"Yeah, she called. It was so late. She said to tell you hello. Everything's gonna work out fine." He paused and looked around. "Anyway, there's a reason I made you get dressed up and come to this place. I have a surprise," he said as he straightened his tie.

"Dad, you are really sneaky. You know I'm not crazy about surprises, but I guess I can go along with it." The music in the background grew to a marvelous praise. They could barely hear each other.

"It's not time yet. I'll let you know. In the meantime, have you thought about what you're going to do next? I mean, are you going back to Houston? Gonna try to get back into modeling?"

"Dad, I've been thinking about how hard it would be to get back into it. I knew my career was winding down anyway. At least if I walk away now, I'll still have a little dignity. This gives me options. I have the courage to take another path. I think I already have a couple of ideas, but I'd need your permission."

"Why would you need my permission?"

"Well, all that time I was lying in the bed, going through rehabilitation, I kept thinking about Hannah's stories. She had such an imagination. I want to do something with her stories. Those are our legacy."

He lifted his glass of juice. "Like what?"

She sat up straight and leaned forward. "Well, I was thinking about maybe doing some children's books. What do you think?" she said, waiting for an answer.

He finished swallowing his juice. "Well, those *are* family stories.

I'd have to talk to some other relatives, but I don't see it being a problem. I think it's a *wonderful* idea."

"I also thought maybe I could stay here for a little while and help out at Queen Hannah's."

He raised his eyebrows and opened his eyes a little wider. "Are you sure that's what you want to do?"

"Yeah. I'm pretty sure," she said as she nodded slowly.

"Okay. It sounds like a wonderful new start to me. Besides, I could use the company. Misa, I am sorry for everything I have done. I should have been more supportive. I never should have hit you, ever."

"Dad, we've talked about this. Yes, it hurt. I'm just glad we got everything in the open. I'm not gonna lie—it was hard. I just felt lost, like no one understood. I hated the fighting. I just thought you should have been there for me more. Hannah made too many decisions that affected my life."

"I know, Misa, I know. I can't take it back, but I'm sorry. My prayer is that God will heal all this. We were proud of you, Misa. I know it was unfair. You needed your mother. She fought so hard, because in her heart she knew if you left she wouldn't have the chance to make up for all the times she wasn't there."

"I just resented her sickness. Now that I'm older, I understand better what she was going through. Believe me, I'd give anything to tell her that." She took a deep breath. "I think I am going to go to counseling at some point. For now I have to focus on one thing at a time."

"That's great honey. I'm proud of you."

"I just need to talk to Summer. She's not only my sister; she's the only real friend I have. I want a chance to give her as much as she's given me." She paused. "It feels good to admit that. I mean, that I need her."

"If that's a desire of your heart, it *will* happen." Her father stretched his neck and looked toward the entrance behind her.

"What are you up to?"

Before he could answer, she felt two large hands on her shoulders. She was almost hypnotized by the light cologne dancing under her nose. The man stepped alongside her, then looked down into her eyes. "Is this seat taken?" he said, placing his hand on the empty chair beside her.

"Phillip? What are you doing here?" She was elated, yet slightly embarrassed, recalling her fading but still noticeable scars. She got nervous all over again.

"Hey. I'm glad I finally had a chance to see you." He gave her an obvious stare, sending unspoken signals of approval. "You look so good. I like the hair . . . almost didn't recognize you." He pulled out the chair and sat down.

Misa stared at her father, unable to speak. After fidgeting in her chair, she finally had the confidence to make eye contact with Phillip. He was incredibly handsome in his black three-button suit, starched blue shirt, and matching silk tie. The color was such a contrast to his yellow skin. His wavy black hair glistened under the chandelier, and she couldn't help but stare as he licked his lips.

Whoever said light-skinned men were out clearly didn't know what they were talking about.

"Misa? Did you hear Phillip ask you a question?" her father asked.

"Oh, I'm sorry. Well, Phillip, what are you doing here?"

"I've been going back and forth from California, trying to sell the Covington house."

"Yeah, that's right. Summer mentioned you're doing real estate. Never thought you'd be anything other than a doctor. How's that going?"

"Yeah, I finally realized that sometimes you have to break tradition. Mother nearly had a heart attack, God rest her soul. Anyway, the house has been on the market for some time. It's a beautiful property . . . no buyers yet."

"Hmmm. Well, I'm sure a buyer will jump on it soon. Summer told me you have two kids," she said, then looked down at her cup of coffee.

"Yeah, two girls. It's crazy, being a parent."

"Well, I can tell you, you are definitely not the shy, goofy Phillip I used to know," she said.

Her father smiled.

"You gotta grow up sometime," he replied.

"Yeah . . ."

Her father cleared his throat, then raised his glass of orange juice, breaking an awkward pause. "Well, I think when old friends get together you should celebrate with a toast."

"I agree," Phillip added.

"Let's toast to . . ."

"Old friends and new beginnings," Misa said, and raised her glass.

"Hear, hear," the men said as they raised their glasses.

The Debutante

"I said, I'm not going," Misa said, her arms folded.

"You don't have a choice," her mother said as she inspected the dresses the shop had sent over.

"I hate this. I don't like the people. I really don't care about any of it. They're all so boring," she said.

"Misa, it's tradition. This is something your grandmother has worked hard on. We sold all those ads, and, well . . . it wouldn't kill you for one night."

"Mother, it'd be different if I could pick my own escort . . . but Philip Souchon? You know how I feel about that family. They're so fake. And Alma . . ."

"Mrs. Souchon," her mother said as she pulled the plastic off the dress. "I didn't raise you to be disrespectful."

"Mrs. Souchon," Misa echoed. "I just can't stand her, and you know in your heart neither can you! Besides, this isn't even about me. It's about Grandmere."

"Misa, sometimes you just overlook the way people behave. Now we know Mrs. Souchon is a mess, but sometimes you have to deal with all kinds of folks. It's more important for you and Summer to get the kind of experience these organizations can give you," she said as she held one of the dresses up to Misa's frame.

Misa stood still. "I wanted to go to this thing with Joe Johnson. He's fun and handsome and we can have a good time."

"Misa, it's not necessarily about having a good time. It is your coming out as a lady, a young woman."

"Whatever. Shouldn't I have some say-so in some part of this event? It's bad enough y'all are forcing me to do this."

"I'm not the one forcing you . . . Hannah has her heart set on it. Don't disappoint her."

"So let me get this straight. You don't really care if I go or who I go with? It's Grandmere? Why am I not surprised?"

"I didn't say that. I do care. I think it's a very special event. Participating in the Girlfriends' Debutante Ball is an honor. It's something special you'll look back on. It's every young woman's rite of passage."

"Whatever."

"Misa, keep still," she said as she tried to measure the gown's length against her.

"I can't pick my dress, my date . . . What can I do? Why can't you tell Hannah I want to go with someone else?"

"Misa, sometimes we know what's best for you. I don't even know this Joseph person."

"You mean you don't know his family, or what they do." Misa pushed the dress away. "I don't want to go with Phillip Souchon. He's *boring, he never says more than two words when he's around, he's skinny and goofy, and I can't stand his mother."*

"Misa, stop! He's a sweet boy. Don't hurt his feelings. It's one night. It's not like you're going to marry the boy. Please, just to keep the peace. Please . . . just for me? My nerves can't take all this," she said as she looked in Misa's eyes.

Misa took a deep breath. "Fine. But I'm not saying one word to him. He's weird, Mother, just weird. All he does is stare at me. He'll probably grow up to be a serial killer. But if this'll make you all happy . . ." Misa grabbed the first dress and went to the parlor to try it on. When she walked out, she inspected the lace and tulle strapless tiered dress in the full-length mirror as she held her hair off her neck.

Summer walked in the room. "Wow, that's beautiful," she said as she jumped on the bed. "You look like an ice cream cake."

Misa looked at Summer, then her mother, and broke out in tears and ran to the bathroom.

"What'd I say?" Summer said as she shrugged.

"Don't worry about it, baby. Your sister's having a moment. It has nothing to do with you." Her mother sighed and rubbed her forehead.

"She's always having a moment," Summer said as she rolled off the bed and skipped out the door.

Family Business

Misa dried her hands on a paper towel. She took another one, ran it under the faucet, and dabbed her face. She dug in her pocket for her clear lip gloss and moistened her lips. She shoved it back into the mini-apron tied around her hips.

She did one last inspection of herself before exiting the bathroom. *Not too bad.* She was satisfied with her reflection, considering she hadn't looked in anybody's mirror for hours. She pulled on the sleeves of her black fitted cotton shirt and smoothed the fabric of her black slacks. Black top and black slacks had been the practice for years at Queen Hannah's—inexpensive, neat, and understated.

She grabbed her pad and pencil. She

would've been out the door, but she paused as she grabbed the door handle. She wiggled her toes around in the black leather flats she wore. Not only were they the least attractive shoes she had ever owned, but they were also the most uncomfortable. The shoe salesperson had told a big fat lie. It had been several days and they still weren't broken in yet. She stopped wiggling her feet and rushed out the door.

The waitstaff was shorthanded again, so she was on duty. *I asked for this*. She was becoming quite the jill-of-all-trades at Queen Hannah's. Host, waitress, cook—wherever she was needed, she made herself available. She'd gained a much better appreciation for her family's business. Despite the hard work, she was actually starting to enjoy it. It felt good to help. Although some people recognized her, she felt neither embarrassed nor compelled to explain her circumstances.

She walked over to the coffee station to put another pot on. She reached down for some filters. When she stood up, Misa felt two hands lightly touching her waist. She thought it was one of the newer cooks who often flirted with her.

Misa put on her best "I don't think you know who you're messin' with" expression. She grabbed the intruder's hand and whipped around. "I *thought* I told you—Phillip?"

"Hey, hey, I come in peace," he said as he held up his hands.

"You, you . . ." She smacked him on his hand with the plastic bag of filters.

"How ya doin'?" he paused, then moved in slowly to give her a light kiss on the cheek.

She stood there smiling, trying not to blush. Despite her best efforts, her eyes wandered from his head to his toes. She couldn't resist inspecting him. She admired the camel-colored lightweight sweater and black slacks that gave him a casual elegance. A simple gold chain with a small cross hung around his thick neck. A bright smile, able to sell any toothpaste, instantly lit up her heart. She'd seen handsome men before, but Phillip's confidence and positive spirit made him extra appealing.

She placed her hand on her hip. "What are you doing back here?"

"Now, you know I couldn't stay away from you." He playfully tapped her chin with his fist, then paused for a few seconds. "I think I may have a buyer for the house."

"Oh," she said, trying to sound nonchalant.

"Yeah, it took a couple months, but it looks promising."

After a few seconds, Misa spoke up: "Hey, I need to keep working." Her voice became more upbeat. "Umm, maybe we can get together tomorrow or something?" she said as she pulled out her notepad.

"Oh, *yeah*. It *is* kinda crazy in here . . . didn't mean to sneak up on you unannounced. I'm gonna be here for at least a week." He looked around the crowded restaurant. "I figured it was okay to just swing by since this used to be my old stomping grounds. This place paid for lots of books at Morehouse. Mother thought it never hurt to have some good old-fashioned work ethic."

"Yeah, but you spent more time dropping plates and cleaning up broken dishes than serving people," Misa said with a chuckle. "You weren't the most coordinated person. Well, I'd love to travel down memory lane. However, as you can see, we have a full house and we're short-staffed tonight. I can't leave my dad hangin'. College kids will be coming out for summer soon. We'll get some help in a couple of weeks." She fumbled with the pencil behind her ear.

"Oh, I understand, but I have to say, this isn't the Misa *I* knew. You were too cute to wait tables back in the day. Well, I need to get back to the house . . . finalize some paperwork, get settled in," he said, and pointed toward the door.

"I guess you can say I've changed, but it's for the better. Anyway, Mr. Souchon, thanks for gracing us with your presence." She walked with him and stopped right outside the front door. They hugged briefly. She watched him from behind as he headed toward the parking lot. *Mmm, mmphf, mmm.* She felt her insides warming up and decided to run back inside.

She rushed to the nearest table toward a couple who looked to be in their seventies. She knew they'd been seated for a while and expected a cranky reception from them. She noticed they wore understated but very expensive jewelry. He wore a cap embroidered with Sag Harbor on the top. She wore a white and navy blue striped sweater and navy blue slacks. Both had very vibrant maple-colored complexions and heads full of silver hair. She didn't recognize their faces and guessed they were tourists.

"Welcome to Queen Hannah's," Misa said, still under the spell of Phillip's cologne. She breathed a sigh of relief when the couple barely acknowledged her. They were still trying to decide what to order, discussing back and forth what was best for each other's diet. Normally this would have frustrated her, but it gave her more time to think about Phillip. "Would you like a few more minutes?" she said politely.

"Yes, baby. We need just a little more time. Big Daddy can't decide what he wants."

Big Daddy? Misa smiled to herself and recognized that the couple obviously had lots of love and life still in them. *How do you stay committed to a person that long?* She was tempted to pose the question to them when she realized she didn't really have the time. She figured their response would have been a twenty-minute lecture starting with how they had met. Before she could spin around to head to another table, she noticed Phillip coming back through the door.

He walked over to her, out of breath.

"Hey, what's wrong? Is everything okay?"

He paused. "Yeah. I was wondering, if . . ."

"What?"

"If you could dust off one of those aprons for me?"

Misa smiled and bobbed her head up and down. "*Yeah* . . ." She said slowly, "I think we can arrange that." On the way to the kitchen, she took the dishcloth draped over her arm and popped him on the butt.

Joy Cometh in the Morning

The couple strolled through City Park, passing the grand peristyle that stood on the edge of the bayou. Misa eyed the massive structure, guarded by huge lion statues and surrounded by commanding columns. She remembered as children she and her cousins had danced and laughed as if they were at the grand balls held in that same place almost a century ago. She recalled the annual Christmas Celebration in the Oaks. She took in the generosity of nature, with its lush greenery, singing birds, and peaceful air. Her thoughts were interrupted by Phillip's voice.

"After you, madam," Phillip had stopped and placed the blanket on the grass. He waited until Misa found a comfortable position on the blanket. He placed the picnic basket down beside the tree and sat next to her. After his last visit more than three weeks ago, he couldn't wait to return. Although he was there on business, he was glad to have an excuse to see Misa again.

She'd found a comfort zone in him. He was familiar. Misa was surprised to find herself more open with him than with any man she'd ever spent time with. She told him about Van and what she could remember from the accident. She talked about all that had happened with Summer and their strained relationship. She needed the release, and he listened intently. And his response was always the same: "God is in control." She wanted him to say more. She wanted him to hug her, but he kept his distance. Although she didn't get the desired response, just talking brought her great relief.

Misa reached down and slipped off her sandals. She inspected her feet, admiring the red polish and pedicure she'd given herself that morning. She stretched her legs out and allowed the sun rays peeking through the tree branches to dance over them. Phillip inched his body over and placed his head on her lap. Misa jumped slightly, surprised by the romantic nature of his gesture. They hadn't kissed or touched in any intimate way so far. She relaxed and started to run her fingers through his baby-soft curls. Phillip closed his eyes and wrapped his arm around her legs, adjusting his body for comfort. For several minutes, they surrendered to the peace and serenity of the beautiful day.

Soon she gently shook her thighs. Misa tilted her head downward, peeking at his eyes. "Hey, you, I know you're not falling asleep."

Her voice was soothing to him. "*Mmm*—no, just relaxing. I apologize. It just feels so good out here, and you make me feel so relaxed," he said, his eyes still closed.

"Okay, I'm starting to feel neglected," she said as she rubbed the back of his T-shirt.

"Oh, I'm sorry." He moved from her lap and rolled over on his side. He propped his head up with his left hand. "So, Ms. Ledoux, have you been thinking about me?"

Resting on the back of her elbows, she let her head drop back. "I guess," she said nonchalantly.

"Uh-huh. I know you missed me. I could feel it all the way across the country."

"If you say so." She reached over and plucked a clover from the grass. She twirled it around, staring at the leaves.

Again they honored the sights and sounds of nature with their silence. They escaped into their individual worlds, ignoring the voices of several children playing nearby.

"They found Van," she said.

"What?" Phillip said as he sat up.

"Yeah, he was in Chicago."

"He's in custody?"

"Yeah."

"Are you okay? You're going to press charges, aren't you?"

"I'm not sure how I feel. Pretty numb, I guess. As bad as this whole thing was, I actually feel sorry for him. I think he admitted to everything. Maybe part of some deal. There were other people involved . . . some kind of ring. He's gonna serve time."

"Wow." He paused for a moment. "Do you still have any feelings for him?"

"No, not like that. I forgave him a long time ago. I just need closure at this point."

"Was this the closure you needed?"

"I think so. Although I have this unexplainable need to see him—look him in the face. I have to ask him some questions that have been burning in my heart. I believe I'm strong enough to face him. I don't think he's a bad person. He made some bad choices. I'm not excusing him; God's put it on my heart to pray for him."

"Misa, I know you've been through a lot. It takes a certain maturity to look at things that way."

"I don't know about all that. I brought a lot of this mess on myself."

"Don't be so hard on yourself . . . thank God it's over. Any money left?"

"What do you think?" she said, and turned away. A few moments passed. "Okay, enough about that. Let's talk about something a little more pleasant. How are your girls?"

"They're doing wonderful. Kennedy cried when I left. I had to miss Nadia's piano recital, but she understood. They're with my mother-in-law. By the time I get back, they should be good and spoiled. The word 'no' is not in her vocabulary."

"Oh," she said softly. "You could have brought them with you."

"I could have, but I wanted to spend some time with you alone."

"Well, I'm honored."

He moved closer and kissed her softly on her lips. He pulled back quickly and reclined on the blanket. Her insides did somersaults in response. It had been a while since she'd kissed a man, and she hoped it didn't show.

Misa rolled onto her stomach and playfully kicked her feet back and forth. "Well, since you'll be leaving tomorrow, what's on the agenda for the night? I know you have something planned." She shot him a shy grin, surprised with her own coyness, then quickly looked back down.

"Well, I just thought we'd spend a quiet evening at my old house. It's been a while since anyone's been there. We kept it in the family and take turns using it as a vacation house. You can keep me company while I pack up. I figured I'd sneak in a little more time with you. Maybe turn this into a candlelight picnic."

"Oh, yeah, that sounds fine. Maybe we can just chill out in the gazebo. It's supposed to be a pretty night. I always loved that backyard. Ours was big, but you all had the best yard on the street. I love that little bridge and the fountains. Your mom had a beautiful garden."

"Yeah, it was a great place to grow up. But you have to move on. Life is about change. If you try to stay in the past, you may miss your future blessings," he said as he reached out to touch her cheek. He paused. "Life is something else. You plan, you dream, and, well, it rarely turns out like you expect. Just when you think you have it all figured out—"

"God changes the script. Yep, life can be painful, but there's good in between. We have to just pay attention, you know? You have two beautiful children, a great career, and now you have me," she said quietly.

"Oh, really? I remember when you wouldn't give me the time of day."

"I know. I'm sorry, Phillip. I was young, silly."

"Let's not talk about it. I understand. And, as much as I loved my mother, she didn't always treat your mother right. I know it hurt you. My mother, well, she was just different. I won't make excuses for her. I love her. She just thought she was doing the best for us. She just had a hard time. I mean, my dad made sure we didn't want for anything, but all he did was work."

"I guess none of us really had the perfect childhood, despite appearances," Misa said.

"Yeah, but we don't have to dwell on it. I'm blessed, Misa. People give what they can. You're blessed too. Your family wanted what was best for you. Some of them may have gone about it the wrong way, but they tried. You have to be proud of yourself. You went after your dreams and you made it. God's not finished with you yet. He's just starting. I can see it," he said as he looked in her eyes.

"I guess I am blessed, huh? It's funny; God brought me right back to the life I was running from. This time, though, I see it so differently. I'm thankful God *hasn't* given up on me yet. I think I have a few more things to do on this earth. This time it's not going to be about my plan, but *His* plan."

He smiled, then winked at her. "Well, sweetheart, that's probably exactly the way He wants it. He's just been waiting on you to figure that out."

Misa held the photo album on her lap, studying the pictures stuck to the black construction paper. She smiled, then laughed aloud.

"What's going on?" Phillip shouted from the kitchen.

"It's a picture of you, me, Summer, all the kids in your backyard." She held her hand up to her mouth. "I can't believe these flowery bell-bottoms I had on. Those were my favorite pants . . . and you with that little curly 'fro!"

"Hey, I had it going on. Thought I was the man," he said as he sliced the cheesecake.

"Yeah, 'thought' is the right word. I think *someone*—I'm not mentioning any names—had a little crush on me then," Misa said as she turned the pages of the album.

"Naw, I don't think so. Anyway, would you like a little coffee or tea with your dessert?" he said as he stood at the doorway of the kitchen.

"Umm, do you have any wine?"

"Wine? Well, we may be out of luck there." Phillip was about to head out of the kitchen. He stopped and placed the tray down on the counter. Everything in his mind and body was telling him not to do it, but he ignored the voices. After hesitating, he marched past Misa down to the wine cellar.

"Where are you going?" she said as her eyes followed him.

He didn't answer, but returned with a bottle of wine covered in a thin layer of dust. He blew the dust off the bottle of wine and looked at her with a smile. "For old times' sake . . ." he said as he handed her the bottle. He walked back into the kitchen and searched a drawer for a corkscrew. He grabbed some paper cups, placed them on the dessert tray, and walked to the living room. "As promised, the rest of the evening is ours. Let's head outside." He led her toward the back door. They walked quietly through the stone-lined pathway until they reached the gazebo.

"It still looks good out here," she said as she sat down.

"I hired someone to paint and keep up the landscaping."

She focused on the stars and listened to the familiar call of crickets. She could hear the running water of fountains and the little manmade brook that ran through the yard. She jumped at the slight pop of the wine bottle cork and held her cup as Phillip filled it.

"Fancy glasses," she said as she inspected the clear plastic cup.

"I couldn't find any wineglasses."

"Just kidding." She sipped slowly and watched him settle next to her. She let the golden liquid roll around on her tongue and savored the taste. "Mmm, I just wish I could stay here forever."

"You better be careful what you ask for . . ." he said as he pulled her toward his side. He wrapped his right arm around her and sat quietly.

"You're not going to have a glass with me?"

"Maybe, in a minute. I'm not really too much of a drinker." He paused for a couple of seconds. "Well, I guess a little wouldn't hurt." He poured a little in a cup for himself.

"So, Phillip, what's going to happen now?" Despite her apprehension, the words fell off her lips.

"Misa, I'm not really sure. I never thought I would be sitting here with you like this. I've really enjoyed the time we've spent together, but I can't really say what's going to happen. My life is in California . . . kids, work . . . everything. Seeing you again, well, it has thrown me for a loop. Don't get me wrong—it's a good thing, but unexpected. The only thing I can say right now"—he took a deep breath—"is that I don't want *this* to end tonight. I do want to see you in my future."

"So what is this?" she asked as she faced him.

"I'm not really sure. We've been brought back together for a reason. I'm sure I want to see you again, but . . ."

"But *what?* Tell me, is it someone else?"

"No, nothing like that. Misa, let's make the most of *this* evening. Everything else will fall into place. I do care for you, very much. I always have. Let's take it a day at a time. I'm sure it will be clear how all this is supposed to fit together. However, I'm not letting you go."

"That makes me smile," she said as she sipped on her wine. "I can handle that. I've been through so much myself. I'm not sure *what* I'm ready for . . ." She settled more underneath his arm and hesitated before she spoke again. "Phillip, I have to make one thing clear. I respect the fact that you don't want to rush into anything, but I'm not going to just hang out here in limbo. I feel safe with you, really connected. This just feels different, but I do expect you to be honest."

"I hear you loud and clear. Misa, I'm not here to make you some unrealistic commitments. I respect you too much for that. That's why I said we have to take it a day at a time. Hey, no more talking—let's make the most of tonight and figure out the rest as we go along, okay?" He grabbed her hand and kissed it.

"We can do that," she said, though she felt a little unsettled.

"I'll be right back," Phillip said as he jumped up. Misa took another sip of wine as she watched him walk out of the gazebo and toward the porch. She heard him fidgeting with something, then finally heard music playing. He walked back over to her and stood at the bottom of the gazebo steps.

"And now, presenting Miss Misa Ledoux and her escort, Mr. Phillip Souchon!" He took a bow and stretched his hand toward her.

She slowly and gracefully walked down the steps toward her escort. She curtsied, and then stood up to look in his eyes. They clasped their hands and aligned their bodies, preparing to waltz. They moved slowly, then allowed the music to speak to their feet. Soon the ballad urged their bodies to move closer, igniting an undeniable chemistry. She welcomed his complete embrace and leaned against his large chest. She felt his warmth against her face as she brushed against his soft cotton shirt.

They both released suppressed energy as she pressed harder against his solid frame. After circling the yard, their movements slowed to a subtle sway. Eventually they stood still as he cupped her face in his hands. He kissed her the way he'd wanted to the day he saw her again after so many years. The kiss was slow, warm, intense. She broke free, grabbed his hand and led him back to the gazebo.

He sat down and she stood in front of him placing his hands around her lower back. He moved them lower, as the front of her tank top remained invitingly close to his face. His hands then moved up to her shoulders, then slid down her arms, feeling the delicate softness of her exposed skin. She was a bit self-conscious about several scars left from the accident, but he didn't seem to care.

She sat on his lap and placed his hand on her leg. She grabbed his face with her right hand and kissed him. He let all his mental and physical defenses down. She brushed his hair from the crown of his head to the nape of his neck. She placed his hand across her tank top. "Please," she softly pleaded. "I want you to." He was fighting the temptation with everything he had. When he realized what was happening, he jumped up. He stood for a moment, his heart racing, breathing a little deeper.

"What? What's wrong?" she said as she sat back.

"Uh, nothing. I, umm, it's me. It's not you. I can't do this. This isn't what I'm looking for, Misa. I'm sorry, that didn't come out right."

"What do you mean? I thought—didn't you feel it?"

"*Yeah*, I did. I mean I really *felt* it—that's the problem," he said as he brushed his hair back with both his hands.

"Huh?"

"Misa, I have something to tell you."

"Okay, here it comes, the big letdown," she said as she started fixing her clothes. "What is it? You're gay . . . married again? Let me have it. I've been through worse. I can take it."

"No, baby, none of that." He placed his hand across his forehead. He looked down at the wine, then poured it out onto the grass.

"What? Tell me. Okay, it's been a long time for me and—I, I got carried away, I guess," she blurted out.

He looked her in the eye. He placed both his hands on her shoulders for assurance. "It's been a long time for me too. It's not you. Please don't think that. You didn't know."

"Know what? Just say it!"

"Misa, I enrolled part-time in seminary school. I don't really drink . . . I shouldn't have been doing any of this."

"I, I don't know what to say—I'm sorry, I guess. Whoa—I mean, what, are you going to become a minister or something?"

"I'm gonna be in some form of ministry. I haven't figured it all out yet. When my wife passed away, it just hit home . . . it brought me a lot closer to God," he said as he paced the wood floor.

"Wow, I'm really embarrassed," Misa said as she covered her face with her hands. And she was surprised at herself again, that she was letting someone see her be so vulnerable.

He walked over to her and bent down on his knees. He pulled her hands away from her face. "Please, don't be. This was my fault. I should've told you. I definitely shouldn't have got myself in such a compromising position. This is an area I really struggle with—I mean, temptation. You have no idea how much I wanted you, but I can't do this . . . not this way," he said.

"Oh, now I *really* feel good. You're making me feel like some Jezebel."

"I'm sorry. I would never want you to feel that way." He stood up and stared out on the lawn. Finally he reached for her hand. "Hey, I need to get up early . . ." She slid her hand into his and he helped her up.

"Yeah. I know."

"Misa, I made a commitment—to be more disciplined. I'm not trying to do the casual sex thing. Maybe I'm looking for a wife. I don't know. I'm not sure what I want right now. It's been two years since Candace passed away, and . . . it can be confusing."

"Candace. That's the first time you said her name. Look, Phillip, don't say anything else, okay? We don't have to figure this out right now. I think I understand."

"Well, I just feel weird, you know? Misa, spending this time with you *has* changed some things. You've stirred up some things in me I'd forgotten existed. I just want to make sure our feelings are based on the right things. I promise I'll write you and we'll plan to see each other again soon, even if I have to send you a plane ticket to California."

"Yeah, sounds good." She turned away from him. She tried to sound enthusiastic despite the stabbing sensation in the pit of her stomach.

He grabbed her hand and they walked to the car to drive her home. When she arrived, the light in the living room was still on, just like years ago. The light had always stayed on until everyone had made it home. When they reached the doorstep, Phillip hugged her and took a small step back. He kissed two fingers and placed them on her forehead. "Until, next time. *I promise*."

"Yeah, until next time." She smiled faintly, then walked inside.

Misa went to the kitchen and reached into the freezer for some Blue Bell ice cream. But then she put the container back, realizing her tastebuds weren't up for that. Although it was past midnight, she didn't quite feel like going to bed. She knew her father was already asleep or he would've walked downstairs, wanting to talk or watch TV. She grabbed the teakettle and decided to make some herbal tea.

She sat down and put her head on the kitchen table. She refused to try to process everything that had happened with Phillip. She couldn't figure out if it was good or bad. She knew he had feelings for her and meant well, but he clearly had some issues. She lifted her head at the whistle of the kettle and jumped up to quickly move it from the burner.

Misa sat in a daze, soaking her teabag a little longer than usual. Sitting in the quiet kitchen in the middle of the night, she felt pangs of rejection, loneliness, and isolation. *I just need a hug, someone to tell me I'm going to be fine.* She traced the rim on the antique china cup. She heard a small still voice. *I understand, I'm here; I want to hold you, let me.* She knew the Holy Spirit was speaking to her. She looked up with an inquisitive expression, her eyes crying out. *I know, God, but sometimes I need a God with some hands.*

She sat still, drumming her fingers on the table. *Lord, You said if any of us lacks wisdom, that all we need to do is ask. I'm asking, Father: how can I fill this void in my life?*

She felt a response.

Daughter, how often do you get up each morning and talk to Me? How often do you sing My praises? You see, I'll love you anyway, but I want to be intimate with you. I'm pleased to hear your quiet praise. I want to speak to you through My Word. When you search for Me with all your heart, you will find Me. The words were not audible but stirred in her spirit. She knew God was speaking to her.

She sat back in her chair. Misa used to laugh when Hannah would say she'd heard from the Lord. But tonight she'd gotten a personal Word. He'd spoken to her spirit with such clarity.

Suddenly her mind rushed to the morning of the accident. She remembered how God had also spoken to her right before the car skidded off the road. She shuddered, realizing His hand of protection had been on her then. Before she got up from the table, a few more words came to her . . . *Write a love letter.*

A love letter . . . to who? She headed toward the study to get on the computer, but the Holy Spirit led her to her own room. She picked out a beautiful piece of stationery and an ink pen and sat at her rolltop desk. The pen took over.

Dear Summer,

The Lord told me to write you. Isn't that something? I never thought I'd hear from Him like that. Since our argument, we've barely spoken. I've tried to apologize, but I don't get the impression you want to even talk to me.

It's the middle of the night, and I'm not exactly sure why I'm writing, but the words are coming quickly. You probably heard, they caught Van. As much as I hate to admit it, you were right. It was just my stubborn pride. I'm glad it's over.

I've been trying to stay busy. Dad probably told you that I've been working a lot at Queen Hannah's. I don't think I've ever worked so hard in my life. I don't even bother with the mani-pedi routine.

I've started writing. I'm taking some of Hannah's stories and turning them into children's books. Maybe you could help me with the illustrations or something. Anyway, I'd just like you to be a part of it. Yes, it's true; I'm hanging up my stilettos.

My life is so different now; I have such a better appreciation for everything... our home, family, and the restaurant. I took a lot for granted. You can't truly enjoy anything if you aren't right with God. I guess you figured that out long before I did.

I can't begin to tell you how sorry I am for what you went through in New York. You are so strong. Despite everything, you had the power to still love, to forgive. I had to ask myself over and over again, "Why her and not me, God?"

I have many regrets. Although I can't change what's happened, I can try to be a better person from this day forward. I didn't mean to get so deep. Just wanted to say what was on my heart.

Summer, I need you... your friendship, your love. I may

never be as close to you as Paige is. I've always envied your relationship. I couldn't give you any love, because I didn't love myself. I realize now, life is so short; we only have but a little time on this earth.

I've had a lot of time to think. A lot has happened. Believe it or not, I've been seeing Phillip Souchon the few times he's come back to town. We've had some great talks, lots of laughter, and I think I'm starting to develop feelings for him. (I know, slow down.) I think he cares for me, but he didn't say exactly where this is headed.

Since I haven't had much relationship luck, your advice is welcome (smile). What should I do next? It's not a simple situation. He's entered seminary school. (Proof that God can use anybody—smile). So, I definitely don't know what to do with this one.

One last thing. I'm thinking about giving Dad a birthday party Labor Day weekend. I'd like your help. I was thinking something not too big, then again I thought about including some of his buddies from Dillard. I'll keep you posted.

I love you, Summer. I only have one sister, and you mean a lot to me. If I haven't told you lately, I am proud of the woman you have become, and when I grow up I want to be just like you!

Sincerely,
Mi (1 Cor 13:5)

House Blessing

"Hannah, I need to talk to you."

"Elizabeth, either you're going to help me with this laundry or not," Hannah said, ignoring the urgency in her daughter-in-law's voice. An eleven-year-old Misa came around the corner just as her mother had picked up a handful of clothespins and walked toward the clothesline.

"I know," Elizabeth said, without looking at Hannah.

"Gotta bleach the sheets white, then put in a little lavender oil," Hannah said as she ignored Elizabeth's words. She looked up long enough to see Misa skipping around the corner.

"I finished the windows in the study," Misa announced as she held the glass cleaner up like a prize.

Her mother shot her eyes in her direction. "That's wonderful, baby. Now go find Reese and help her upstairs."

"Okay, Mommy." Misa turned around and headed behind the house. As she got just past the corner, she hid. She couldn't help but eavesdrop. She always did.

"Did you hear me?" Elizabeth said to Hannah once she thought Misa had gone out of her sight.

"What, Elizabeth? What do you know?"

"I found the papers . . . despite all your cleaning, despite all your perfume, bleach, and whatever else . . . you have the nerve to treat me bad, throw my background in my face as if this family was perfect."

"Shut up," Hannah barked through clenched teeth. "Have you been in my things?"

"No, I haven't. One of the children tripped over a nail in the floor. I reached down to try to fix it. I saw some papers in plastic underneath the floorboard."

"So what? So what? Is it so wrong to want to save the rest of the family from shame? Is it so wrong to want to move on?"

"It wouldn't be so wrong, if you weren't such a hypocrite. Making me feel horrible for my past, when your very own family, Black people, owned slaves!" she yelled.

"Shhh! You hush," Hannah said as she finally looked in her eye. "Don't you think I'm ashamed? Knowing that everything that was handed to us came from the bloody hands of slavery. Why do you think I work so hard at the restaurant? Why do you think I try to protect all these children? I got to make up for it somehow. Why do you think I try to keep the family name clean from now on . . . to make up for the past." Hannah looked away.

For the first time, Elizabeth felt pity for her. She'd never seen Han-

nah shed a tear. She didn't know what to do as she watched Hannah wipe her eyes with the end of her apron.

"Elizabeth, please, please, I beg you, please don't say anything. I promised myself to take it to the grave."

"Hannah, this wasn't your fault. You weren't the one who had slaves. It was people way before you. God doesn't hold us accountable for the sins of others. Don't you read that Bible you've been carrying around? You're in bondage and you don't even know it. He's the one that washes away our sins."

"Elizabeth, I know what you're trying to say. I'm sorry for the way I've treated you. I am, but please, just promise me you'll keep this to yourself. I promised that this family would never see shame . . . they'd never be hungry. I promised they would own something, and I've kept my word. Please, Elizabeth, I'm not gonna be here forever."

Elizabeth took a deep breath. As much as she wanted to make Hannah feel horrible, rub her face in the past as she'd done to her, something in her spirit just couldn't do it. She finally had something on Queen Hannah, the all-powerful woman who'd barely tolerated her.

She took a deep breath. "Okay, okay, Hannah. I won't say anything. But I'm gonna pray that you make your heart right with God before you leave this earth . . . whatever that means to you."

Misa stayed huddled nearby. She didn't hear everything, but she heard enough to know the family she thought she knew was nothing but a masquerade.

Get Up!

"Yes, can you be here at six a.m. this Saturday?" Misa said, bracing herself for the answer.

"Six a.m.?" her Aunt Evelyn echoed. "What on God's earth do you need me to do that early? I've haven't been up that early since, since one of Hannah's . . ."

"House blessings!"

"Lord, child, how did you possibly come up with such an idea?"

"It's been at least six or seven years since we've had one. You remember, Hannah used to say it kept the dark out and ushered in the light. We've had our share of trauma over the past few years; maybe this is the reason why!"

"Well, do you really need me there? Stanley and I have our couple's massage scheduled for that day."

"Aunt Evelyn—"

"Okay, alright."

"Will you call Aunt Joy?"

"You call her. You're the one that's organizing this event."

"Aunt Evelyn, it's for all of us. As much as you hate to admit it, Grandmere wasn't always right, but she at least tried to keep the family together."

"Well, I'll get Rose if you call Joy. We'll get the grandchildren together too."

"Okay. Sounds good. I'm excited!"

"Since when did you ever get excited over a house blessin'? We always had to come look for you."

"I want to get the house ready for Dad's birthday. Besides, times have changed, Aunt Evelyn! Times have changed!"

"Okay, pay attention!" Misa sat the grandchildren around the dining room table. "You may be too young to understand this now, but you need to learn the value of hard work," she said as she eyed each grandchild from five years up to the teens. Her Aunt Evelyn had done a good job of rounding up every child in the extended family for the house blessing. "Things just don't fall into your lap. They come from hard work. Sometimes it's other folks' hard work, but you'll have to work too or you'll lose what you've been given. Everything you see around you: this table, that chandelier, that backyard, was a result of someone's hands. You understand?"

The little ones shouted, "Yes, ma'am." The teens rolled their eyes and murmured.

"I'm watching you," Misa said as she stared at her fourteen-year-old second cousin, Palmer. He rolled his eyes again and sighed with his arms folded.

She smiled to herself as she remembered Hannah giving the same speech, although Hannah always had a switch handy for back talk. "Now go to your assigned stations. I don't want to see any dust, and I want every window to sparkle like a diamond!" Misa watched as the children scattered to their assignments.

The house blessing was a tradition Hannah started. Although she didn't expect the children to work that hard, she at least wanted them to understand the importance of a work ethic. She wanted them to understand that the house, the restaurant, all of it, were products of hard work. Misa laughed as she remembered marching in line with the other children, dust rags, furniture polish, and buckets in tow. They weren't allowed to do much else besides dust and clean the windows when they were little. When they got to be teenagers, they did more strenuous, intense housework like cleaning, mopping, sweeping, beating rugs, and other chores. Their reward was a huge dinner that was prepared at the restaurant. It was also a time of family, prayer, and family fellowship. This tradition Misa wanted to keep, but some of the others could definitely go.

Misa made sure she had plenty of oil, frankincense, and myrrh. She gathered with her aunts, uncles, cousins, and other family, and they prayed. They prayed for an anointing to come upon the house. They prayed for God's protection and God's prosperity. They prayed for forgiveness, healing, and restoration. They prayed for past sins, they prayed for deliverance, then they anointed the house from top to bottom. By the end of the day, they were all exhausted.

"Whoa, we haven't had one of those in a while," Aunt Rose

said as she collapsed onto the couch. "But it was needed. I felt the heaviness lifting from this place."

"Yeah, it did feel good. God is definitely present!"

Everyone got silent as they reflected on the moment.

Misa sat on the porch with Reese. The metal swing let out a recurring screech, as they gently rocked back and forth. Reese had managed to get a moment by herself, since the kids were in bed. *Not a hair out of place*, Misa thought. *Even with four kids in tow, she's still the picture of perfection*.

"Girl, it has been a long day. What possessed you to call a house blessing?" Reese asked as she saw a firefly in the distance.

"Just thought we needed to get together . . . as a family. Besides, I think we needed it. There was just too much negativity in the air."

"I hear you." Reese reached into her pocket and pulled out a cigarette.

"Since when did you start smoking?"

"Girl, I've been smoking for a minute now. I just don't let Efrem know," she said as she took a long drag from the cigarette. "Look who's talking—you've been smoking since we were sixteen." She crossed her long golden legs.

"Yeah, but I quit a month ago . . . for good. Got one body, got to take care of it!"

"Yeah, well, if this is my one vice, I'll take it," Reese said as she inhaled and blew smoke out the side of her mouth. She flicked the ashes off the end of her cigarette.

"Reese, are you happy?" Misa said after a few moments of silence. She felt her body craving a cigarette.

"If you equate happy with numb, I guess so. Don't get me wrong: I love Efrem, I adore my children . . ."

"You have to, with fo' kids." Misa started laughing. "Girl, you needed to close the candy shop after two."

"I know, but I guess I thought if I kept making the babies it would slow Efrem down," she said. "Yeah, right."

"I gotta give it to you, girl, you look good. I guess some people are just made for makin' babies," Misa said as she eyed Reese's stomach.

"I don't know. I guess I haven't done much else. Don't have time for anything else. I just wish I'd had the courage to do what you did."

"I don't know if it was courage or the fact that I was just a fool! I mean, I saw the world, but when I left here, I was such a mess."

"What's better, being a mess and seeing the world, or being a mess and staying back here?" She turned to look at Misa.

Misa didn't say a word.

"Misa, I just wish I had some support. I can't talk to my mother. She is so caught up. I mean, this is not 1965. She means well, but she always taught me that I had to be a good wife, no matter what. She always told me, 'Men will be men. Your job is to keep him happy, keep him fed, and make sure he stays in your bed . . .' "

"Jeez, that's ridiculous. You know where she got that from."

"Hannah," they both said.

"Misa, I gotta change. I'm still young. I can't live like this anymore."

"You thinking about leaving him?"

"No. I don't know. I do think we need counseling, but I would never bring it up."

"Why not? Wouldn't you want to give him a chance to work on your marriage?"

"I guess."

"And you know he's not going anywhere with all those children y'all had. He'd be broke. You aren't slick—that's why you had them," Misa said as she slapped Reese's leg.

"Very funny. Seriously, we have to do something. Our relationship has just grown so cold. When he comes in, he grabs the kids, plays with them, then eats dinner. We don't laugh or talk anymore."

"Yeah, sounds like you all need some help. Then again, Efrem never really was the life of the party. He was always a bit of a bore."

"Gee, thanks."

"Seriously, Reese, you're grown. If you don't take control of your life now, you'll look up and be just like the Hens . . . no offense. They're so confused. They don't know what to do without Hannah."

"You know I hate when you call them that . . . but I know. Misa, I do realize how crazy this family is. We have to be the ones to break the cycles. But me personally, I don't even know where to start."

"How about opening your mouth! I don't know—it's hard to change. I guess you have to take one step at a time. Let's start tonight."

"What do you mean?"

"Let's do something crazy. Remember when we used to go skinny-dipping in the lake?"

"No, Misa, we can't."

Misa was already standing and yanking on Reese's arm. "C'mon. You need a little adventure!"

"Misa . . . I'm gonna kill you. You always get me in trouble!"

"We gotta do something to get you out of this rut. Might as well start now!"

"You know what? What the hell! I gotta start somewhere!"

"That's the Reese I know and love!"

Jazz Funeral

"When I die, I don't want you to cry for me. I've lived a good life. More than good. If I'm not right with God by then, I will be soon after." Summer's grandmother's words echoed as she felt the concrete under her sandals. The sound of her heels marching in the street was drowned out by the brass horns and pounding of the snare and bass drums. This was the only way anyone in the Ledoux family "went home": with a jazz funeral. There were no words, just music.

Initially, Summer held her head down as the band played "Nearer My God to Thee." Soon the cymbals clanged and the band with their white hats and adorned sashes started to jam with "My Bucket's Got a Hole in It." When they began a few notes of "When the Saints Come Marchin' In,"

Summer marched with her head up. The music got in her spirit as she watched the band members swinging their shiny instruments.

As they passed some of the houses, people were waving from the porch and clapping their hands. But more than half the parish was marching with them in honor of Hannah.

Her nieces and nephews laughed and raised their hands, mocking the marching entourage. In New Orleans, it was a privilege to have a jazz funeral. So it was the only way Hannah's life could be celebrated. As they marched past Jackson Square, Summer thought again about the words Hannah had uttered. What did she really mean when she said, "I'll be right with God . . . soon after"? *Summer didn't try to figure it out. She dismissed the thought as she was pushed toward the banquette, or sidewalk. More and more people joined in as the music got louder. She finally made her way back up to the horse-drawn carriage with her grandmother's body. Someone handed her a yellow umbrella, and she grabbed it as she twirled, danced, and sang openly and out of key, loud and unashamed.*

The Ledoux family gathered in the lawyer's office. By request, the only people in attendance were Hannah's five children. Alfred Ledoux was the executor of the estate. The lawyer started reading the will: "To my beloved son, Alfred Ledoux, I bequeath my home, restaurant, and the balance of my assets after my charitable contributions, notwithstanding the other provisions of this will. To my beloved daughters and sons, I bequeath each a sum of $50,000."

The Hens both looked at each other. Rose crinkled her forehead, and Evelyn pulled out a handkerchief to wipe her forehead. Evelyn jumped up. "That can't be right. Read that again! Did she go mad? We have to contest."

Alfred shot his eyes at her and she got quiet. "Evelyn, please, let the man finish."

The lawyer kept reading through formalities and paragraphs of legalese. Then he stated, "I know this is a shock. I made sure our business, our land, and our home will forever remain a part of the Ledoux family. I made sure my immediate family will be comfortable. That in consideration, it is at this time that I must make myself right with God. I need to be a blessing to someone else. Despite all my prayers that God would wash it and make it clean, I still feel the need to do something else. There's blood on our hands, and you know it. We were owners of ourselves, Black slave owners. For that I am ashamed. We must repent for our sins. This is the only way I know how. I hereby bequeath $3 million to the following five charities . . . Now I am right with God."

The children let out a collective gasp. Down went one Hen, then another, and family members burst into yelling, fighting, and demands to contest the will. It was not a pretty sight.

Good Things Come in All Kinds of Packages

Misa had grown increasingly nervous over the past ten minutes. She paced up and down the wooden pier, biting her lip. She smiled as a chatty group of senior citizens passed by to board the ship. She was beginning to think this wasn't the best idea, considering her family's habitual lateness. She thought she'd outsmarted them, putting the wrong time on the invitations. From the looks of things, they'd obviously figured that out. She thought a dinner cruise with a small group of family and friends was a great way to celebrate her father's birthday. But the timing issue was dampening her spirit.

Misa finally stood still and faced the water. Leaning against a wooden pole, she regained her composure. *Okay, breathe, stay calm.* The sun was melting into the horizon, with an occasional wind whipping her dress ruffle against her leg. She clung to her straw hat with one hand and prayed to herself. *Okay, have a little faith. Please, Lord, don't let them miss this boat.*

Most of the other family and friends had arrived and boarded the boat. She stared at the rectangular face of her watch. *They have about twenty minutes.* There was no sight of her father or the rest of the family. Misa was certain that Summer had received her last letter and was coming, but they hadn't communicated since Summer had sent her written *RSVP*. She had included a note mentioning that three extra people were coming—another couple and Evan's coworker. *They better not be trying to fix me up.* She wasn't crazy about being dateless for the evening, but she certainly wasn't desperate. That's why she had made an *extra* effort to look good. She didn't want pity from anyone, especially from the messy-behind Hens.

She nervously peeked at her watch again. Soon her prayers turned into pleas and a few tears. *All this planning—when I see them, I'm gonna . . .* Her ears perked up. She thought she heard her aunt's cackling. She spun around and saw a pack of loud Black people coming up the pier. As soon as she recognized one face, she let out a sigh of relief. She rushed down to meet them and the heel of her sandal caught in between the wood on the pier. She tripped and almost fell down. Her hat flew out of her hands and the wind carried it down the way. *That's just what I need.* Despite the price she had paid for it, she was too disgusted to think about chasing it. She caught her balance and stood still. When the group came closer, she recognized her father, aunts, and uncles. She thought she saw Summer running behind them in the distance.

Misa placed her hand over her heart in relief. She walked closer toward her father, then reached out to hug him. She was busy fussing when she felt a tap on her shoulder. She turned around and Phillip stood there with her hat in his hand. "I think this belongs to you."

She was speechless. He looked so handsome in his cream linen slacks and polo shirt. Her heart was doing cartwheels, but she contained herself. She took a deep swallow for composure. *Be cool. Don't look desperate or too happy*. "Okay, who invited *you* here?"

"Guess?" he said, looking in Summer's direction.

Misa walked past him over to her sister. She grabbed and hugged her. Everyone watched as they held each other. With watering eyes, Misa stepped back.

"We were late because we had to pick up Phillip from the airport. His flight was running a little late. If we had called, it would have spoiled the surprise," Summer said. "Sorry, we didn't mean to make you nervous." She grabbed Misa's hands. "I know we need to talk. After the boat ride, okay?" she said, then whispered, "I did get the letter . . . First Corinthians thirteen."

Misa nodded and smiled. "Oh, I thought you had a few more people coming with you?" Then she looked down the pier and saw Paige and Quinton rushing toward them. Paige looked stunning in a red sleeveless wrap dress with a silver choker adorning her neck. Her layered haircut grazed her shoulders, and Paige's face was literally glowing. Quinton looked refined in cream slacks and a navy vest. He added a white shirt and blue and red striped necktie. *He never looked that good before*, Misa thought.

"Hey," Paige said quietly, and braced herself for Misa's to-be-expected nasty response. Quinton grabbed her hand and didn't let go.

Misa couldn't help but say, "*Whoa*, you two a couple now?"

The Hens peered at the trio intensely.

Quinton raised Paige's hand and kissed it. "*Yeah.*" He cleared his throat. "Yes, we are."

Paige began to speak quickly, rambling. "It was such bad timing. We started seeing each other right before your accident," Paige added. "It just happened. One day we were talking on the phone, the next day we were on a plane to Mexico." She took a deep breath.

Misa stood there with a blank expression. All eyes were on her, waiting for a reaction. She smiled quietly and grabbed Paige's other hand. "When I met Quinton, I wasn't ready for a man like him, but you were. I guess you were 'his good thing.' I wish nothing but the best for you. Besides, see that fine thing over there? That's gonna be *mine*," she said, pointing to Phillip.

"Okay, can we finish this episode of *The Young and the Restless* on the boat?" Evelyn said. "I'm gettin' hungry. Y'all were rushing me so bad, I'm not even sure my new wig is on right."

Misa noticed the wig *was* a little lopsided.

"This is a Star Jones. I'm not gonna embarrass Star *or* myself with a crooked wig. We *both* have an image to uphold. I'm gonna fix this as soon as I get to a restroom," she said, marching ahead and tugging on the wig. "C'mon, Stanley," she commanded as she yanked his hand.

"Okay. We've got about seven minutes to get on this boat. I still haven't let y'all off the hook, but if we don't hurry up the party is gonna be on this pier," Misa said. She rushed to catch up with her father. As they moved toward the boat, she leaned over and kissed him on the cheek. "Dad . . . Happy Birthday."

Misa enjoyed the larger cruise ships but liked the feel of the smaller boat better. She felt closer to the water. She gazed out on the river, wishing she had something to write with. She was experiencing emotional highs she'd never felt before, wanting to capture the essence of the evening with words. She looked up at the infinite darkness framing a perfect moon. *Perhaps this time I'm to simply bask in the moment.* She sat on the bench, searching the heavens for signs as the boat rocked slightly. She pictured her mother, grandmother, and other ancestors dancing and singing amid the stars. She closed her eyes, lost in the moment. She inhaled, and then exhaled. *This is what real freedom feels like.*

"Hey, you," Phillip spoke quietly. "You look so peaceful. I hated to disturb you. Your sister said they're getting ready to cut your father's cake and open his gifts. She says she won't start without you."

She turned toward Phillip and reached out her hands. He pulled her up with a force that threw her body into his. He kissed her slowly, just like she'd remembered. They started to walk off toward the dining area.

"Wait," she said. "I'm really happy to see you, but can you please tell me what happened? After you left, you didn't call, write, or anything, like you'd promised. That was painful, Phillip, really painful." She searched his eyes for an explanation.

"I know, I'm *very* sorry. That wasn't the best way to handle things. I was going to apologize. How can I say this?" He hesitated. "Misa, when you give your life to the Lord, you don't do anything without His permission. I needed to go back and pray about us. I was moving a little too fast for my own good, or so I thought. I didn't mean to hurt you, and I know I could have handled it better. I got scared. I spent some time in fasting and prayer. I needed God to show me if you were someone I should invest time in or if it was just my flesh talking. I don't want to scare you or anything, but I don't want to date just for the sake of dating. Does any of this make sense?"

"Well"—Misa hesitated—"what *did* God have to say about all this?"

"Sometimes when God has someone in mind for you, he needs to clean house. Misa, God had a little more work to do on me. I have a much better idea of what I want. I can give you my best now. If I'd made a commitment to you then, I may not have been able to keep it. I'm glad I took the time to pray."

Misa stood there. She wasn't quite sure how to respond.

He put two fingers to her lips to keep her from speaking. "I have to say one more thing. During the last week of fasting, I still wasn't clear what God was telling me. At that point, I rested. That Monday, your sister called me and invited me to celebrate your dad's party—right after I'd just prayed. *Father, Your will be done*."

"Oh," she said softly.

"Misa, I know in my spirit, the Lord has brought us back together. I can't say I'm ready to get married today, but I definitely see a strong potential." He pulled out a plane ticket from his pocket and placed it in her hands. "This is a ticket to California. I know it's short notice, but I want you to come back with me at the end of this week to visit. You can meet the kids and everything."

Misa examined the ticket as if it were a foreign object. Then she looked at Phillip with a puzzled expression on her face. Finally she spoke. "Phillip, I knew the first time you came back to New Orleans that God had sent you to my life." Her words were fading into a chorus of "Happy Birthday." "I'm willing to take a chance. I would love to come and visit."

He grabbed her face and kissed her. He barely had the opportunity to kiss her again before he felt Misa's lips jerk away from his.

"Please, you two are holding up the program," Summer said as she pulled her sister away and led her to the dining room. The room was filled with laughter, and soon the crowd was chanting, "Go Groovy, Go Groovy . . ." Uncle Groovy and Aunt Rose were on the floor. To everyone's surprise, Rose stopped to drop it like it's hot.

"Whoa, I enjoyed that," she said as she fanned herself.

"Who's that woman sitting near Daddy?" Misa whispered to Summer.

"I don't know. Some floozy that latched on to him earlier. She attached herself to his side and won't let go. She abandoned her own group a long time ago."

Misa inspected the woman's long flowery skirt and sleeveless silk V-neck blouse. She looked to be about fifty, at least ten years younger than her father. Her professionally coifed shoulder-length hair was free from any strands of gray. *An obvious dye job.* It bounced with the smallest move, and she played it to the max with exaggerated gestures. Her makeup was natural-looking, all except the fire engine red lipstick. Misa had to admit they looked good together.

Whenever the woman laughed she threw her head back and grabbed Alfred's hand. *Oh, brother—my dad is a true honey magnet.* Reading Summer's overprotective thoughts and trying to let go of her own, she quickly uttered, "Let him have a little fun. It's his birthday. Besides, she's attractive and seems nice."

Summer looked around at her family's faces. Everyone was smiling, happy. Despite the challenging past years, she was grateful. Many of her prayers had been answered, although she couldn't help but wonder why the process had been so long and hard. She sighed and refocused on the party.

New Orleans is still a good place, she thought. "And my family is still crazy," she said to herself as she watched the Hens doing "Da Butt."

The Pink Mansion was full, just as it had been the weekend of Summer's wedding. After the cruise, everyone came back to the house and crashed. Summer was glad to wake up next to her husband with no rush to get up. But she knew if she wanted to eat she'd better get in the kitchen soon, with so many mouths in the house.

Getting out of bed was a struggle. She was entangled with Evan, who was clearly still knocked out. She smacked his hand, "Boy, let me get up." When she finally got up, he made some weird snorting noise and rolled over. *I used to think that was cute.*

She showered and grabbed her overnight bag in search of some comfortable gear. She grabbed her sweatsuit but changed her mind. She opted for a pair of floral capri pants and a bright yellow tank top. She stuck her toe out, admiring her fresh pedicure, then slid her feet in her wedge sandals. She looked back at Evan, still snoring. *Oh well, every man for himself. I'll save you some bacon, honey.*

As soon as she got outside, the aroma of buttery homemade biscuits danced under her nose. As she picked up her pace through the grass she could smell fried potatoes seasoned with onion. *Ahh.* She walked through the back door of the main house. As suspected, the Hens were sitting around the table.

"Alfred, I bet that hot mama shoved her number down the pocket of your blazer. She may have looked innocent, but I've seen her type before. Sittin' in the front pews of the church every Sunday and standing in the back of the juke joints every Saturday night."

"You would know, Rose."

"What do you mean by that? Well, I did have it going on back in the day, but I didn't have to chase after any man."

"Mornin'," Summer said as she bounced in.

"What's all this sashaying about?"

"Probably got some last night," Evelyn said.

"I'm going to ignore that," Summer said. She walked over to the stove and kissed her father on the cheek. "Hey, Daddy. Misa up?"

"No, the beauty queen has not graced us with her presence yet. You know that child was never an early riser," Evelyn said.

"She is *now*," her father said. "Since she's been helping in the restaurant, she's become more disciplined."

"Oh, yeah, she's an official member of the working class. Miracles do happen," Rose mumbled.

"I was happy to see that Souchon boy," Joy interjected.

"Yeah, that *long, tall* glass of water. He sure did turn out handsome. Now, that's what you call bootylicious! And he's got money too!" Evelyn added.

"Auntie, you are *really* trippin'. That homemade stocking cap on your head must be too tight."

"Shoot, ain't no use in throwing away a good pair of stockings. Y'all paying for stuff we invented years ago. Humph, a do-rag. That came from the cut-off stocking cap, and folks paying five dollars for it. I should have come up with that," she said as she felt the top of her head. "Speakin' of money, have you found a job yet, honey? Or do you plan on moving back to the Pink Mansion like your sister?"

Summer reached into the refrigerator for some orange juice. "*No* and *no*. Why do y'all let her show out like this?" she said, looking at her other two aunts.

"We gave up a *long* time ago. Let it go."

"You know, it's a shame about his wife, though. Misa may have lucked up with that one . . . *if* she plays her cards right. You know that Misa can mess up a good thing," Rose said, lifting her coffee cup.

Summer grabbed a biscuit from the basket near the stove. She started to break off a few pieces and let them melt in her mouth. "Auntie, quiet down. He's asleep on the living room couch," she said in a lower voice. "I'm not going to let you talk about Misa like that. She's in a good place now, and I know she's more than capable of a good relationship. Besides, he's lucky too. It's not like Misa is chopped meat. She's a beautiful, intelligent girl, just like her sister," Summer quipped, then smiled wide. She walked over to give each aunt a kiss.

"Well, I didn't mean to offend anyone."

"Yes, you did," Joy said as she buttered a muffin.

"Well all *I* know is, if Stanley kicks the bucket, I'll be back on the market. You think I'm gonna wait around too long before I start dating again?" She pointed to her husband, and on cue he grunted.

"Never mind," Summer said as she rolled her eyes.

"Don't get smart with me, *missy*. I heard about the thong underwear in the pantry."

"Dad!" Summer squealed. Her eyes grew wide as she looked at her father.

He turned around with his spatula. "Sorry, baby. I couldn't resist."

"Whatever you heard, it's *not* true," Summer insisted.

"Um-hmm," Aunt Rose said as she twirled her fork in the air. "You take after your mother's side of the family with that freaky stuff."

"It's nothing wrong with being a little freaky," Evelyn said.

"Let's say I did lose my drawers in the pantry? I'm married; I can be as freaky as I want to," Summer said, reaching for a piece of bacon off the table. "Yeah, how you like that? Ah-ha, I'm grown."

"Not around the Campbell's soup, you can't," Rose replied, then sipped her coffee.

"*Anyway*, I'm going to Misa's room." Before Summer walked into the living room, she heard lips smacking. Phillip was covered up in his blanket and Misa was sitting next to him on the couch, kissing him good morning.

"Hey, hey, that's disgusting . . . ill, morning breath!"

They both jumped up at the sound of her voice. Phillip's face turned red.

"No need to play it off for me. It could have been worse. One of the Hens could've busted you. What do you two have on the agenda?"

"We were just gonna play it by ear," Misa said as she grabbed the remote off the coffee table. "Thinkin' about setting up the horseshoes or croquet outside."

Summer dropped in the recliner. "Whoa, don't get *too* wild now. Talk about changes. I think Dad said something about everyone going bowling or playing miniature golf."

Misa sat up on the edge of the couch. "I don't know how much more of the Hens I can take."

Summer reclined her La-Z-Boy chair. "Well, we don't get together like this often. Besides, it'll be fun. You gotta love the Hens," Summer said just before leaving the room.

Alfred sat in his study and picked up the picture of his wife. He sighed deeply. With his door slightly ajar, he heard soft footsteps coming up the hallway. He stood still, wanting to embrace the moment. Inside he had a peace that he wanted to hold on to. He smiled and his eyes watered a bit. He heard a soft knock on the door. Joy came in. He looked up and did not say a word.

"Hey, you," she said as she eased in. "Mind if I come in for a minute?"

"No, not at all," he said as he placed the picture on the shelf.

He walked around and sat on the edge of his desk. She walked past him toward the window and stood for a moment. "So, I guess things have settled down?" she said without turning around.

"It's getting there. I'm a little worried about the Hens and the money situation."

"They'll be okay," she said in a monotone voice.

He walked over to her and placed his arms on her shoulders and turned her toward him. He looked into her eyes. "I could never hurt my girls. Joy, we almost blew it. It still bothers me years later."

"But we didn't. Not really."

He took a deep breath, then hugged her. She freed herself from his arms, then touched his face with her hand. She kissed his cheek, then walked away. Alfred took another deep breath, stared at Elizabeth's picture, then walked out of the study.

Extreme Makeover

"Keep still, Aunt Rose, we will be done in a minute."

"I just don't like all this mess on my face," she said as she sat in the chair.

"Mother, you look beautiful," Reese said as she bounced her two-year-old on her lap.

"I don't know—you all won't let me see it. I feel like I have a ton of makeup on," Rose said.

"Just trust me," Misa said as she finished lining her lips. "Okay, a little lip gloss for the finish. Are you ready?"

"Okay already." Rose wiggled away from Misa and stood up. She slowly turned around and walked toward the full-length mirror. She put her hand over her mouth and inspected herself from top to bottom. "Misa, I—I didn't even know I could look like this." She touched her hair, which had gone from tight curls to a flatironed shoulder-length bob that framed her soft features. Her face was glowing with shades of nutmeg, bronze, and peach. Misa had traded Rose's usual frumpy dress for a colorful wrap dress.

"I'm sexy," she said.

"She's sexy. She's a dime and the top of the line . . ." one of her granddaughters said. Rose put her hand up to her mouth.

"It's the new me, I guess." She hugged Misa, and tears starting running down her face.

"Okay, Mother, you can't mess up your makeup," Reese said.

"I know, it's just that you don't even realize . . . I've locked myself away for so many years." She looked at Reese and grabbed her for a hug. "I'm sorry, baby, I'm sorry."

"Mom, sorry for what?"

"If I've done anything to make your life miserable, please forgive me. I want you to be happy, but I want you to be free to make your own choices." She extracted herself from the hug and looked in her daughter's eyes.

"Mother, I'm okay. I am making my own choices now. I'm going to take time out for myself and do what I've been wanting to do for a while. I don't know—I'm not sure what it is, but there is more to me than being Mrs. LaSalle. Maybe I'll go to school or start a business. I don't know, but Mother, I am going to make some changes too." They held hands, then hugged again. Everyone in the room fought the tears.

Summer could not believe how much fun the last two days had been. She was sad that they had to drive back to Houston in a few hours. She couldn't leave before visiting the cemetery. She was happy that Misa had offered to drive so they could have a chance to spend a little time together. They laughed most of the way about the Hens and talked about Phillip. Before they knew it, they reached the site and jumped out of the car. They walked slowly through the cemetery, but there was no sadness. They both felt an overwhelming peace as they approached the grave. Summer smiled on the inside when she noticed how the tomb had been kept up. She could tell by the flowers that her mother had had a recent visitor. She turned to Misa and gave her a look.

"As soon as I was able, I came once a week," Misa said, not looking in Summer's direction.

Summer closed her eyes and swallowed. Her sister's words touched her deeply. "Thank you," she whispered quietly as she stared at the flowers.

"For what? You don't have to thank me for something I was *supposed* to be doing anyway."

"Well, thanks *anyway* for honoring our mother."

"It's the least I can do. I'm still fighting the guilt, but each day is getting better."

Summer grabbed Misa's hand and walked her to a bench. "Misa, don't let guilt destroy you. Don't let it take the joy out of what God's done and still is doing in your life. We *all* make mistakes."

"I never thought Summer Ledoux made mistakes. *No*, not you," Misa teased.

"Very funny—yes, *even* me. I made a mistake by shutting you out. I made a mistake by not trusting my husband."

"Yeah, I heard about Brother Calvin." Misa laughed.

"Is anything a secret anymore in this family? *Jeez*—we're going from one extreme to the other."

"Calm down. I thought it was hilarious. Boy would I have paid to see that one," Misa said with a smile.

"Anyway, what I wanted to say—and this is serious—is that you don't have to repay me, God, or anyone else for what you think you did wrong. Once you've asked for His forgiveness and committed to change, that's enough. He'll work out the rest. Guilt only blocks your blessings."

"Well, it can start to weigh me down if I let it. I had no idea how deep it was," Misa said as she stared at the ground.

"I won't let you beat yourself up like this. It's over, Misa. You're a different person."

"Yeah, I know. I'm trying hard to accept the good coming into my life."

"It's hard when you've had so much pain. It's hard to even feel worth. That's where Jesus comes in."

Misa looked up and their eyes locked. "I just wanna know . . . when did you become so wise?"

"I don't know. You know what, Misa? I think I went through my trials a little bit sooner than you did. I let God in my heart just a little sooner than you did. That's all. You're just seeing the finished product. When I look at you, I see a strong, confident woman of God. We are both blessed, and God loves us the same."

"I hear the words, but sometimes I don't feel it. I pray for His favor, but I still feel disconnected. I want to have deeper conversations with Him."

"Misa, that doesn't happen overnight. It's a process, and don't let anyone tell you different. Look at how much He's done in your life already!"

"I know that, but every now and then it hits me. When I start thinking about how difficult this year has been, I get overwhelmed when I realize how much I've been through. I'm not sad about it anymore. It's like God won't let me cry anymore. The hardest part is over. I'm not depressed, but a little numb. I have to fight to keep my joy."

"Let me let you in on a little secret," Summer said as she moved closer to her sister. "Most of us don't automatically feel joy. It's not like joy just meets us in the morning. I have to motivate myself all the time, stir myself up on the inside with praise music, thinking good thoughts, whatever works for the moment."

"Okay, now I don't feel so bad. I thought I was just supposed to feel happy all the time," Misa said, her smile wider.

"Who told you that? Anyway, if you don't know you're blessed, let me help you out. Because of everything that's happened, you have a deeper relationship with God. You've faced and conquered some, if not all, of your fears. You've discovered your purpose. I've discovered *my* purpose. Our family was healed in so many ways, and if you don't know by now, you have people who love you . . . even the Hens."

Misa sat there humbled, realizing how much she was in fact blessed. She had been tested, but made it. She hadn't given up *or* given in and was a better person for it. She grabbed on to Summer's hand with new energy.

"Hey, Phillip says he knows some publishers that might be able to look at my books. So, will you help me with the illustrations? You're good with graphics and you paint so well," she said, her voice more upbeat.

Summer folded her hands and raised her eyebrows. "Of course I will . . . on one condition?" she said with a laugh.

"What's that?"

"Will you please take your dog back? I've done my auntie duties."

"Yeah, but you have to admit, Diva grew on you, didn't she? Tell the truth."

"I guess so," Summer admitted slowly.

Misa playfully slapped her thigh. "*Anyway*, back to what you said earlier . . . tell me what your purpose is."

"It's one of my gifts. Well, it's weird, because it has nothing to do with what I went to school for. I know it's my spiritual gift."

"Tell me!"

"I think I have the gift of healing. I mean, when I massaged you all those times, it's like God told me what to do. He told me how much pressure to use; I felt my hands get really warm."

"Summer, I get chills when I think back to that time. I thought it was my imagination, but I felt the warmth in your hands. I just thought it was some ointment you were using."

"No, I didn't use anything that would bring that type of effect. It's really deep, Misa."

She turned to Summer and said the words she'd heard her grandmother utter often: "God is good."

"Yeah," Summer said as her eyes fixed on the many rows of tombs. "But he sure has a funny way of answering prayer."

Misa peeked at her watch and snapped her fingers in front of Summer's eyes. "Hey, we probably need to get back."

"Okay, you go ahead; I promise I'll catch up in a second."

"Oh, yeah, sure. I think I understand," Misa said as she nodded knowingly.

Summer watched Misa head toward the car, then stood up.

She walked slowly and paused at the family tomb. She couldn't contain the smile that lit up her face. "Well, Mom, your daughters are restored." Although it was eighty degrees and she hadn't felt the wind all day, a light breeze encircled her. Then she heard it. The chimes. This time she didn't question it. Before she took off she stopped and whispered, "Oh, yeah, Mom, I started to block Dad's action with the old girl from the cruise, but I guess it's about time for him to have a friend." She laughed a hearty, purposeful laugh, walking, then dancing toward the car. She heard words singing in her heart. She reached to open the car door and paused to let out an audible "Amen."

"What? Did you say something?" Misa said as she noticed Summer staring at the powder blue sky.

"No, not really."

Misa waited for Summer to get in the car and shut the door. She looked at her sister curiously and smiled. "I think I understand." Then she started the engine. "Wait, we need some traveling home music . . . you're gonna like this!"

Summer waited as Misa pressed the button to get to her favorite song on the CD. She heard a few bars and a huge smile crept across her face. She'd been listening to the same Kirk Franklin CD all the way from Houston. Misa rolled down the windows.

"*Ho-san-na . . .*" Misa sang.

"*For-ev-er.*" Summer clapped.

They joined in together: "*Ho-san-na, for-ev-er and ever . . . Hosanna forever.*"

Reading Group Companion

Sweet Magnolia deals with issues of forgiveness and family communication while keeping matters of the spirit close at heart. Here are some questions meant to provoke discussion and gentle debate about the impact the novel has made on your life.

1. How do you feel about Misa's decision to accept her modeling opportunity? Do you think her decision to leave affected her mother's health? Was her mother being fair by asking her to stay?

2. Do you think the relationship that Alfred and Joy shared was inappropriate? Explain. If yes, at what point do you think they may have crossed the line?

3. What do you like and dislike about the character Hannah? How do you feel about her decision regarding her will?

4. How do you think Summer and Misa could have avoided their big confrontation? Why do you think they had such a hard time communicating with one another?

5. Some readers might perceive Summer as having a martyr mentality. Why does she feel so committed to solving her family issues and protecting the family name?

6. Why do you think it took so long for "the Hens" to find themselves?

7. Why do you think Hannah had such a big influence on her family in terms of money, religion, and career choices?

8. Do you think the mental illness that threatened Elizabeth and her daughters was a generational or a spiritual issue? Or both? What types of things could be done to break such a negative cycle in a family?

9. What are some things that cause siblings who grow up in the same household to take completely different spiritual, personal, or familial paths?

10. How important is preserving and creating family traditions today compared to previous generations?

11. What are some of your past and present family traditions?

12. Why do you think some people are healed through prayer alone and others may need a combination of prayer, counseling, and medication?

13. Why do you think Misa was able to see Phillip Souchon differently as an adult? What are some of the spiritual factors that contributed to her new vision of him?

14. What do you think of Phillip's decision to stop his communication with Misa to get spiritual clarity?

15. What do you think of Quinton and Paige coming together? Why was he able to see her differently after his breakup with Misa?

16. Do you think Summer's husband, Evan, was being unreasonable about wanting her to come home after Misa got better? Why or why not?

17. Misa entered into a relationship with Van relatively quickly. Why was she able to trust men she didn't know more easily than her own family members?

18. Could you relate to Summer and Misa's relationship? Why or why not?

Sweet Magnolia Experience

Sweet Magnolia is about family healing, preservation, and restoration. There is also a strong element of family tradition in the novel. Here are a few suggestions to encourage healing and forgiveness in any family relationship. I've also provided a few suggestions to encourage establishing new and positive traditions in your own family!

1. Be honest. It is important to spend time with yourself to truly understand your past. The worst thing you can do is pretend that everything is okay. It takes courage to realize that perhaps your family is not perfect. Take time to journal your feelings. Write down people and circumstances that have had a negative impact on your life so you may start your healing process. This is not a time to dwell in the pit, but simply acknowledge true hurt and pain so you can move on to a new life.

2. Avoid judgment. People are simply people, even family. We are all at different stages of our lives and do things based upon our

individual maturity, spirituality, and life experiences. Try to be empathetic. People who are hurting hurt others until God intervenes. Even then we are all a work in process.

3. Seek help. Sometimes we need someone else who is equipped to help us through the process. That aid may be on a basic level, like getting support from a trusted friend or Christian counselor, while for more serious issues, you may need to seek professional help. You must decide how you want to be healed. God honors our boldness and can work through people.

4. Remove yourself from the hurtful situation. In order to heal, sometimes you have to move away from the source. If you feel continuous hurt whenever you encounter a situation or family member, walk away until you are strong enough and can explore the issue on your own. Surround yourself with positive loving people who can build you up while you walk through healing.

5. Write a letter. And you can choose not to send it. Pouring out your uncensored feelings is cleansing. Use specific examples, like "It hurt when you . . ." These allow you to get to the root of your true pain and begin to liberate you.

6. If possible, talk with people about how you're feeling. Sometimes talking and listening are all you need to heal a broken relationship. However, make sure you don't rehash the same old issues. Truly have the goal of beginning a new relationship.

7. Choose to forgive. The only way to truly forgive is through God. Ask him to give you a new heart for this person. Ask God to

show you if you have gone wrong in any way and ask Him to help you to forgive this person. Let Him work on you and your heart first, and watch things start to change. Study scriptures on forgiveness and journal.

Now for the fun stuff! Here are some tips to start some new traditions in your family (partial list from *Ways to Start Traditions in Your African-American Family,* by Norma L. Jarrett).

A QUILT

Have a quilt made especially for your family. Better yet, have several family members make one. Take a quilting class together. Use special fabrics and symbols that make it personal to your family. Plan to hang it in a special area and pass it down to the next generation.

A FAMILY RECIPE BOOK

Start a family cookbook. Include various recipes from family members, like your child's favorite cookies and your grandmother's famous cakes. Name each dish after a family member. Have it bound and copied for family reunions or to give as a wedding gift for family members.

MEMORY LETTERS

Record the memories of your child in a letter. Write a letter to your child each year. Begin with the year they were born. Record observations, thoughts, feelings, current events, etc. On a particular birthday or before they leave for college, present the letters to your child in a special box or wrap them like a scroll.

AN ANNUAL FAMILY RETREAT

With your church or on your own, have a family retreat. Have good food, fellowship, prayer and fun. Invite another family. Bring friends of the family. Plan events and play games. Have each family member pick a favorite scripture or lead a prayer. Try a park or resort. The whole family will return renewed and refreshed.

A BRIDAL KEEPSAKE BOX

Have a bridal keepsake box made for your daughter if she's getting married. Have it made of white satin or in her wedding colors. Decorate it with sequin, ribbon, or lace trim. Fill it with various items such as satin slippers, a family photo, a sachet, lingerie, "something old, new, blue." Also include in it a decorated envelope that has personal notes written by each family member for a special surprise.

TREE TRIMMING

Have a tree trimming ceremony. Present each child with his or her own ornament at Christmas time. Make the ornament personal for that year. They can have their favorite sport, age, or cartoon character on them. You can find them at any gift and card store in your local mall.

SCRIPTURE OF THE WEEK

Have a scripture of the week. Place it in a conspicuous place where everyone will see it (like the refrigerator). This will encourage Bible study. Have a different family member responsible for choosing a scripture every week.

A SPRING CLEANING FESTIVAL

Set aside a day (or two) for a spring cleaning festival. Have a lottery to determine who will do what chores. Reward your family with dinner or a special night out.

CAR DEDICATION

If you decide to buy your child a car when they reach driving age, have a car dedication ceremony. Thank God for the car and pray for the safety and protection of the driver. Have the family member officially name the car. Give gifts such as air freshener, mats, and car wash coupons.

START A LIBRARY

Encourage reading. Start a library of books signed by authors. It could be as simple as a large shelf. Have each family member make a contribution. Visit bookstores and attend book signings to build your collection. You can also have an annual book reading contest. Have your children compete and give a prize to the child who has read the greatest number of books.

FAMILY BABY BLANKET

Purchase baby blankets in a neutral color. Have the last name of your family monogrammed on the blankets. Present them to the new mothers in your family for their newborns.

FATHER'S DAY

Have a Father's Day family roast. Cook Dad's favorite dinner. Ask each family member to "roast" the family patriarch. Don't forget to have each person tell what he or she loves about the honored guest.

"GIVE ME A BREAK"

Set aside one week a year where the children give their parents a break. The children will wait on the parents hand and foot and will make them feel extra special. Let the parents be on the receiving instead of the giving end for a little while. They will greatly appreciate it.

EXPLORE THE ARTS WITH THE FAMILY

Take the family to several cultural events a year. Try the symphony or the opera. Expose them to something new. You will all be more well-rounded individuals.

HAVE A FAMILY AWARDS CEREMONY

Present awards for "most improved" or "best grades," "cleanest room," etc. Give out ribbons or gift certificates. Watch your children's self-esteem soar.

HAVE AN ANNUAL SLUMBER PARTY

Slumber parties are not just for little kids anymore. Have an annual slumber party for all the women in your family. Have food, videos, music, and good old-fashioned family fellowship. Have awards for the best and worst pajamas. Cook a big breakfast in the morning.

HAVE A "GREEK" NIGHT

If any of your family belongs to a Greek fraternity or sorority, have a Greek Night or a picnic. Have everyone wear paraphernalia. Draw names prior to the event to exchange gifts that day. (Non-Greek family members can join in the fun too.)

TALENT SHOW

Have a family talent show. Give out small trophies or ribbons. Make it a night of fun and a showcase of talent. Take plenty of pictures and put them in a special family album.

MAKE ME OVER

Have a mother/daughter makeover day. Get your hair and nails done. Have lunch at your favorite place. Take a picture together.

HISTORY LESSON

Learn about your city's local history. Find out the specific African American culture of your city. You may have treasures right underneath your nose.

VALENTINE'S DAY

Have every family member celebrate Valentine's Day (married and single). Draw names a few days before the holiday, and show family members how much they are loved.

SCHOLARSHIP

Start a scholarship fund at your local high school or university. Establish it in the name of a deceased family member.

STARTING A NEW JOB

Boost the confidence of a family member. When they start a new job give them a token to take with them. It could be a nice pen, a notepad, or a calendar.

FAMILY CREST

Have someone design a family crest. Use it on all your stationery. Have it attached to a shirt.

NEW YEAR'S CELEBRATION

Have a family gathering to celebrate New Year's. Let each person write on a piece of paper what blessings were a part of the past year and what their resolution is for the New Year. Have each person read the paper out loud and have the group guess who wrote it. Have a New Year's Eve toast with sparkling cider so the kids can join in the toast.

ABOUT THE AUTHOR

Norma L. Jarrett is originally from New Jersey and currently resides in Houston, Texas. She is a graduate of North Carolina Agricultural and Technical State University and Thurgood Marshall School of Law. She's a member of Alpha Kappa Alpha Sorority, Inc. (AKA), and Christian Women in Media and Arts (CWMA).

Norma is the author of the novel *Sunday Brunch*, published by Harlem Moon. In addition, Ms. Jarrett has written and produced a play, *Sunday Brunch—The Book Skit*, based on the novel. Her work has received attention in *Essence*, *Upscale*, *Gospel Truth*, *QBR*, *Black Expressions*, *Rolling Out*, and other publications. Ms. Jarrett has also received the "Outstanding Young African-American Leader of Houston" award from Interfaith Ministries, and the Sister Circle "Best Christian Fiction" award for *Sunday Brunch*. She also earned a Certificate of Congressional Recognition from Congresswoman Sheila Jackson Lee on behalf of the U.S. House of Representatives in honor of her literary work.

Ms. Jarrett continues to make national appearances to promote her literary vision. Her third novel is scheduled to be released by Harlem Moon in 2007. She currently attends Pastor Joel Osteen's Lakewood Church. Please visit her Web site at www.normajarrett.com